THE MAD HATTER MYSTERY

JOHN DICKSON CARR (1906-1977) was one of the greatest writers of the American Golden Age mystery, and the only American author to be included in England's legendary Detection Club during his lifetime. Though he was born and died in the United States, Carr began his writing career while living in England, where he remained for nearly twenty years. Under his own name and various pseudonyms, he wrote more than seventy novels and numerous short stories, and is best known today for his locked-room mysteries. His beloved series character, Dr. Gideon Fell, was based on author G. K. Chesterton and appeared in twenty-four novels.

OTTO PENZLER, the creator of American Mystery Classics, is also the founder of the Mysterious Press (1975), a literary crime imprint now associated with Grove/Atlantic; MysteriousPress.com (2011), an electronic-book publishing company; and New York City's Mysterious Bookshop (1979). He has won a Raven, the Ellery Queen Award, two Edgars (for the *Encyclopedia of Mystery and Detection*, 1977, and *The Lineup*, 2010), and lifetime achievement awards from NoirCon and *The Strand Magazine*. He has edited more than 70 anthologies and written extensively about mystery fiction.

THE MAD HATTER MYSTERY

JOHN DICKSON CARR

Introduction by
OTTO PENZLER

**AMERICAN
MYSTERY
CLASSICS**

Penzler Publishers
New York

Published in 2019 by Penzler Publishers
58 Warren Street, New York, NY 10007
penzlerpublishers.com

Distributed by W. W. Norton

Cover image: Andy Ross
Cover design: Mauricio Diaz

Paperback ISBN 9781613161333
Hardcover ISBN 9781613161326
eBook ISBN 9781613161340

Library of Congress Control Number: 2019901469

Printed in the United States of America

9 8 7 6 5 4 3 2 1

THE MAD HATTER
MYSTERY

INTRODUCTION

THE MYSTERY story has undergone incalculable developments since its creation. What had for many years been assumed to be a mystery—the detective story—was, in fact, merely one slice of the very large pie that also includes wedges of crime fiction, thrillers, police procedurals, espionage novels and tales of suspense.

Of these sub-genres of the mystery, it is my contention that the most difficult to produce, or rather to produce well, is the novel of pure detection. There can be no slovenliness of plot here, or else there will be an element, however innocuous it may seem, upon which the astute reader will pounce and, when it remains unexplained or unremarked upon at the end of the book, the novel will be dismissed as being unfair, no matter how brilliantly executed all else may have been accomplished.

The greatest of the great names continue to be read today, coming on a hundred years, because they understood the rules, adhered to them, and had the talent, if not the outright genius, to produce works within the precise strictures of what was permitted. Who are the immortals who wrote these towering monuments of detection fiction? You know their names already: Agatha Christie, Dorothy L. Sayers, Ellery Queen, S.S. Van Dine,

Philip MacDonald, R. Austin Freeman, Anthony Berkeley, Freeman Wills Crofts, A.E.W. Mason and, of course, John Dickson Carr. These were the first gods in the pantheon of detective fiction authors. Some are undoubtedly more readable than others. Try as I might, I could never make it from beginning to end of a Crofts novel without losing the battle against Morpheus. There are other greats who fail to make the list because the purity of their detective puzzles suffered by comparison, even though they created charming and often baffling plots which were often transparent or left unexplained gaps.

Carr once provided his definition of a detective story, and it is a good one, however simple it may seem. "The detective story," he wrote in an introduction to *The Ten Best Detective Novels*, an anthology he prepared but which was never published, "is a conflict between criminal and detective in which the criminal, by means of some ingenious device—alibi, novel murder-method, or what you like—remains unconvicted or even unsuspected until the detective reveals his identity by means of evidence which has also been conveyed to the reader.

"This is the skeleton," he continues, "the framework, the Christmas tree on which all the ornaments are hung. If the skeleton has been badly hung, or the tree clumsily set in its base, no amount of glittering ornament will save it. It will fall over with a flop. Its fall may create a momentary sensation, especially among children; but adults are only depressed when they see the same sort of thing happen in fiction."

Although the majority of his books were set in England, Carr was born in the United States, in Pennsylvania, in 1906. His first detective novel, *It Walks by Night*, was published in 1930 when he was 24 years old. During an Atlantic crossing, he met an English woman, Clarice Cleaves, who he married in the United States but, deciding that England was the ideal place in which to write detective stories, settled there in 1932.

He was immediately successful and prolific, publishing 30 books by the end of 1939. Writing books in such enormous quantities forced him to create a second identity, Carr Dickson, quickly changed to Carter Dickson when his original publisher, Harpers, protested that the name was too similar to the original.

After Henri Bencolin solved the crime in the first book, Carr created Dr. Gideon Fell, his best-known and most popular character. A voracious reader of detective stories as a child and young man, Carr greatly admired G.K. Chesterton's Father Brown stories and modeled Fell on the author. They came to know each other in the 1930s, as both were members of London's famous and very prestigious Detection Club, where they vehemently disagreed about the only two things Chesterton felt worthy of discussion, religion and politics; Chesterton was a Catholic and left wing, while Carr was Presbyterian and conservative.

Chesterton's girth was as prodigious as his ego, hence the estimable figure cut by Dr. Fell, who is described in a scene in *The Mad Hatter Mystery* thus: "There was the doctor, bigger and stouter than ever. He wheezed. His red face shone, and his small eyes twinkled over eyeglasses on a broad black ribbon. There was a grin under his bandit's mustache, and chuckling upheavals animated his several chins. On his head was the inevitable black shovel-hat; his paunch projected from a voluminous black cloak. Filling the stairs in grandeur, he leaned on an ash cane with one hand and flourished another cane with the other. It was like meeting Father Christmas or Old King Cole."

Under the Carter Dickson name, he produced a series of novels featuring Sir Henry Merrivale, who was often likened to Winston Churchill. Although not originally patterned after him, the curmudgeonly Merrivale acquired more and more of the future prime minister's characteristics as the series progressed.

When World War II erupted, Carr was summoned by the U.S. military and returned to America, only to have the BBC request his services and be promptly returned to London, where he produced propaganda programs and a popular weekly show titled *Appointment with Fear*.

After the war, he wrote the official biography of Sir Arthur Conan Doyle. When a left-wing government came into power, he took his wife and three daughters, as well as their English nurse, back to America to "escape Socialism," as he stated it. When the Labour Party was voted out in 1951, he and his family returned to England, staying until 1958 when he moved to Greenville, S.C., where he lived until his death in 1977.

The undisputed alcove he holds and will forever hold in the virtual Mystery Hall of Fame is as the creator of the most brilliant "locked-room" mysteries ever written. While many writers tried their hands at producing "impossible" crimes, they were generally able to sustain the endeavor for a only book or two, while the vast majority of Carr/Dickson titles were in this most demanding of all sub-genres. These mysteries, as one would suspect, generally involve murder in a sealed room, often guarded, in which a hapless victim is executed, often at a specific hour, as warned by the unsuspected killer. Secret doors, hidden panels and other obvious devices are not permitted—especially not in Carr's books. His imagination was so fertile in this regard that in one of his most famous novels, *The Hollow Man* (titled *The Three Coffins* in the United States), Fell delivers a lecture regarding impossible crimes in which he offers several dozen methods by which the murders may be accomplished.

The Mad Hatter Mystery is one of Carr's masterpieces, with all the essential elements of his finest work: an impossible crime, a dark atmosphere and the inimitable Dr. Fell. It also is a high spot in the rarified world of bibliomysteries—stories in which rare books and manuscripts play a major role; in this case, the theft of a previously unknown manuscript by Edgar Allan Poe, and not just any manuscript, but one of towering historical significance. What this superb detective story also has is a last word which many readers may find shocking. Do not peek!

If you have an intellectual mind, one that enjoys being challenged by an author who openly dares you to be as clever as he is, all of the early works of Carr and Dickson will give you all the mental gymnastics you can handle. So will the works of other authors who worked in the rarified atmosphere of impossible crimes. In addition to the greatest of the greats mentioned above (though few are impossible crimes), you might want to try any of the four novels about The Great Merlini, the stage magician created by Clayton Rawson; *Too Many Magicians* by Randall Garrett, in which he establishes a parallel universe where the laws of magic apply, yet writes a superb, fair-play locked room mystery; or Gaston Leroux' superb, if slightly slow-moving, *The Mystery of the Yellow Room*, in which the young police reporter Joseph Rouletabille discovers how someone in a hermetically sealed room could have been murdered.

—OTTO PENZLER

THE MAD HATTER MYSTERY

Plan of the Tower of London's South Side, Giving on the Thames Wharf, where the Action of this Story takes Place.

The reader will please observe that the Bloody Tower, to which frequent reference is made, is built above the gate marked 3 in the plan; that the gate of this tower does not lead into the tower itself, but to a roadway going past the Wakefield Tower. The door of the Bloody Tower faces Tower Green, and is reached by a stairway from the roadway mentioned (8).

1. TRAITOR'S GATE.

2. STEPS WHERE THE BODY WAS FOUND.

3. GATEWAY OF BLOODY TOWER.

4. WINDOW FROM WHICH PARKER SAW DRISCOLL AND THE UNKNOWN.

5. SMALL WARDER'S ROOM, NORTHERN SIDE OF BYWARD TOWER, WHERE QUESTIONING TOOK PLACE.

6. WARDERS' HALL, SOUTHERN SIDE OF BLOODY TOWER, WHERE VISITORS WERE DETAINED.

7. WHERE MRS. LARKIN STOOD.

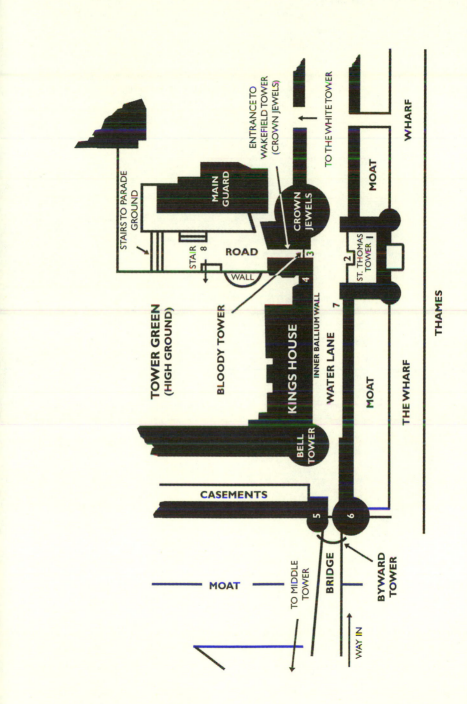

WHARF

THE WHITE TOWER

MOAT

ENTRANCE TO
WAKEFIELD TOWER
(CROWN JEWELS)

STAIRS TO PARADE
GROUND

MAIN
GUARD

CROWN
JEWELS

ROAD

STAIR
8

WALL

3

2

ST. THOMAS
TOWER

4

7

THAMES

TOWER GREEN
(HIGH GROUND)

BLOODY TOWER

KINGS HOUSE

INNER BALLIUM WALL

WATER LANE

MOAT

THE WHARF

BELL
TOWER

CASEMENTS

5

6

MOAT

TO MIDDLE
TOWER

BRIDGE

BYWARD
TOWER

WAY IN

I

A Cab Horse in a Barrister's Wig

IT BEGAN, like most of Dr. Fell's adventures, in a bar. It dealt with the reason why a man was found dead on the steps of Traitors' Gate, at the Tower of London, and with the odd headgear of this man in the golf suit. That was the worst part of it. The whole case threatened for a time to become a nightmare of hats.

Abstractly considered, there is nothing very terrifying about a hat. We may pass a shop window full of them without the slightest qualm. We may even see a policeman's helmet decorating the top of a lamp-post, or a pearl-gray top hat perched on the head of one of the lions in Trafalgar Square, with no more than an impression that some practical joker is exercising a primitive sense of humor. Young Rampole, when he saw the newspaper, was inclined to grin at the matter as just that.

Chief Inspector Hadley was not so sure.

They were waiting for Dr. Fell at Scott's, which is in the heart of Piccadilly Circus. You descend a flight of stairs from Great Windmill Street to a lounge like a club, brown panels and easy-chairs in red leather, with the brass-bound kegs behind the bar and the model of a ship on the ledge of the stone mantelpiece. Sitting in an alcove with a glass of beer, Rampole studied the chief inspector. He was wondering. He had only arrived from America that morning, and the press of events seemed rather sudden.

He said, "I've often wondered, sir, about Dr. Fell. I mean—his position. He seems to be all sorts of things."

The other nodded, smiling faintly. You could not, Rampole felt, help liking the chief inspector of the C.I.D. He was the sort of man who might be described as compact; not tall or heavy, yet giving the impression of being so; very neatly dressed, with a military mustache and smooth hair the color of dull steel. If there was a quality about him you noticed at once, it was a quality of repose, of quiet watchfulness. His movements were deliberate. Even his eyes, which seemed to go from gray to black, had that deliberate faculty, and he rarely raised his voice.

"Have you known him long?" Hadley asked, examining his glass.

"As a matter of fact, only since last July." The American found himself rather startled to remember that. "Good Lord! It seems years! He—well, in a manner of speaking, he introduced me to my wife."

Hadley nodded. "I know. That would be the Starberth case. He wired me from Lincolnshire, and I sent the men he wanted."

A little more than eight months ago. Rampole looked back on those terrifying scenes in the Hag's Nook, and the twilight by the railway station where Dr. Fell had put his hand on the shoulder of Martin Starberth's murderer. Now there were only happiness and Dorothy. Now there was London in the cool, misty days of March, revisited for the first time since then.

Again the chief inspector smiled faintly. "And you, I believe," he continued in his deliberate voice, "carried off the young lady. I hear glowing reports of you from Fell. He did rather a brilliant piece of work in that affair," Hadley added abruptly. "I wonder—"

"Whether he can do it again?"

The other's expression grew quizzical. He turned his head. "Not so fast, please. You seem to be scenting crime again."

"Well, sir, he wrote me a note to meet you here."

"And," said Hadley, "you may be right. I have a feeling," he touched a folded newspaper in his pocket, hesitated and frowned. "Still, I thought that this thing might be rather more in his line than mine. Bitton appealed to me personally, as a friend, and it's hardly a job for the Yard. I don't want to turn him down."

Rampole wondered whether he was supposed to know what his companion was talking about. The chief inspector seemed to be musing, in a hesitant fashion, and his hand kept straying to the newspaper in his pocket.

He added, "I suppose you've heard of Sir William Bitton?"

"The collector?"

"Ah," said Hadley; "I fancied you would. Fell said it would be in your line, too. The book-collector, yes. Though I knew him better before he retired from politics." He glanced at his watch. "He should be here by two o'clock, and so should Fell. There's a train from Lincoln which gets into King's Cross at one-thirty."

A thunderous voice boomed, "*Aha!*" They were conscious of somebody flourishing a cane at them from across the room, and of a great bulk filling the stairway to the street. The bar had been very quiet; this entrance caused one white-jacketed bartender to start violently. The only other occupants of the room were two business men conversing in low tones in one corner, and they jerked round to stare at the beaming appearance of Gideon Fell.

All the old genial days, all the beer-drinking and fiery moods and table-pounding conversations, beamed back at Rampole in the person of Dr. Fell. The American felt like calling for another drink and striking up a song for sheer joyousness. There was the doctor, bigger and stouter than ever. He wheezed. His red face shone, and his small eyes twinkled over eyeglasses on a broad black ribbon. There was a grin under his bandit's mustache, and chuckling upheavals animated his several chins. On his head was the inevitable black shovel hat; his paunch projected from a voluminous black cloak. Filling the stairs in grandeur, he leaned on an ash cane with one hand and flourished another cane with the other. It was like meeting Father Christmas or Old King Cole. Indeed, Dr. Fell had frequently impersonated Old King Cole at garden pageants, and enjoyed the role immensely.

"Heh," he said. "Heh-heh-heh." He came rolling over to the alcove and wrung Rampole's hand. "My boy, I'm delighted. Delighted! Heh. I say, you're looking fine. And Dorothy? . . . Excellent; I'm glad to hear it. My wife sends her warmest regards. We're going to take you back to Chatterham as soon as Hadley tells me what he wants with me. Eh, Hadley? Here, let's all have a drink."

There are people before whom you instantly unbend. Dr. Fell was one of them. No constraint could exist before him; he blew it away with a superb puff; and, if you had any affectations, you forgot them immediately. Hadley looked indulgent, and beckoned a waiter.

"This might interest you," the chief inspector suggested, handing Dr. Fell a wine-card. He assumed a placid, innocent air. "The cocktails are recommended. There is one called an 'Angel's Kiss'—"

"Hah?" said Dr. Fell, starting in his seat.

"—or a 'Love's Delight'—"

"Gurk!" said Dr. Fell. He stared at the card. "Young man, do you serve these?"

"Yes, sir," said the waiter, jumping involuntarily.

"You serve an 'Angel's Kiss,' a 'Love's Delight,' and—ah—if my eyes do not deceive me, a 'Happy Virgin'?

"Young man," continued the doctor, rumbling and polishing his glasses, "have you never reflected on what American influence has done to stalwart England? Where are your finer instincts? This is enough to make decent tipplers shudder. Instead of saying, 'A bitter,' or 'A Scotch and splash, please,' like scholars and gentlemen, we are now expected to coo for— Hah!" He broke off and scowled ferociously. "Can you imagine Buffalo Bill striding into a Western saloon and roaring for an 'Angel's Kiss'? Can you fancy what Tony Weller would have said if he called for hot rum punch and received a 'Love's Delight'?"

"No, sir," said the waiter.

"I think you'd better order something," suggested Hadley.

"A large glass of beer," said the doctor. "Lager."

Snorting, he produced his cigar case and offered it round as the waiter took away the glasses. But with the first healing puffs of smoke he settled himself back benignly against the alcove.

"I hadn't meant to draw a crowd, gentlemen," he rumbled, making an immense gesture with the cigar. Heads, which had been poked through the doorway to the restaurant adjoining, were discreetly withdrawn. One of the business men, who had almost swallowed the stick skewering the cherry in his drink, had settled down again to conversation. "But my young friend here will tell you, Hadley, that I have been working for seven years on the materials of my book, *The Drinking Customs of England from the Earliest Days*, and I blush to have to include such manifestations as these, even in the appendix. They sound almost bad enough to be soft drinks. I—"

He paused, small eyes blinking over his glasses. A quiet, impeccably-dressed man, who seemed like a manager of some sort, was hesitating near their alcove. He appeared to be ill-at-ease, and feeling slightly ridiculous. But he was contemplating Dr. Fell's very picturesque shovel hat, which lay across the cloak on a chair. As the waiter brought three rounds of beer, this man entered the alcove.

"Excuse me, sir," he said, "but may I make a suggestion? If I were you, I should be very careful of this hat."

The doctor stared at him for a moment, his glass halfway to his lips. Then a bright and pleased expression animated his red face.

"Permit me, sir," he requested earnestly, "to shake your hand. You are, I perceive, a person of sound taste and judgment. I wish you could talk to my wife on this matter. It is, I agree, an excellent hat. But why should I exercise more than my usual care in guarding it?"

The man's face was growing pink. He said, stiffly, "I had no wish to intrude, sir. I thought you knew. That is to say, there have been several such outrages in this vicinity, and I did not wish to have our patrons incommoded. That hat—well, hang it!" the manager exploded, volplaning down into honest speech, "that thing would be too much. He couldn't miss. The Hatter would be bound to steal it."

"Who?"

"The Hatter, sir. The Mad Hatter."

Hadley's mouth was twitching back, and he seemed about to burst out laughing or leave the table in haste. But Dr. Fell did not notice. He took out a large handkerchief and wiped his forehead.

"My dear sir," he said, "this is most refreshing. Let me see if I follow you. Am I to understand that there is in this neighborhood a hatter of such notoriously unbalanced mind that, as I walk innocently past his shop, he would be apt to dash into the street and steal my hat? That is carrying the aesthetic sense too far. I must courteously but firmly refuse," continued Dr. Fell, raising his voice warmly, "to run up Piccadilly pursued by impassioned hatters. I am too old, my dear sir; and I am too fat; and, if you want still a third reason, I am convinced that among your friends you are known by the playful nickname of The March Hare."

In contrast to the manager's low, nervous tones, he had been trumpeting across the room. The business man with the cocktail gave a slight moan, put on his coat, and moved hastily towards the door. The other business man stayed grimly at his table.

Even the chief inspector, in his own quiet way, was flustered. He said, sharply, "Thank you very much. This gentleman has just arrived in London; he knows nothing about it. I can explain."

As the red-faced manager hurried towards the restaurant, Dr. Fell sighed.

"Now you've driven him away," he protested, querulously, "and I was just beginning to enjoy it. I perceive among London hatters a bustling, up-to-the-minute, go-get-'em spirit. Still, I hope you don't have mad tailors who rush out of their shops and remove the trousers of casual passers-by. That would be a trifle alarming." He took a deep drink of beer, and shook his great head of hair like a mane. Then he beamed on his companions.

"Blast you," said the chief inspector. He struggled with dignity, and lost. "Oh well. Confound it, I hate scenes, and you seem to revel in them. All the same, he was talking perfect sense."

"Eh?"

"He was talking perfect sense," Hadley repeated, with some irritation. He fingered his close gray mustache. "It's a kid's prank, of course. But it keeps on and on. If he'd stopped at stealing one or two hats, and this infernal newspaper ragging hadn't begun, no harm would have been done. But it's making us look foolish. And it's got to stop."

The doctor adjusted his glasses.

"Do you mean to say," he demanded, "that a real hatter is going about London stealing—"

"'Mad Hatter' is what the newspapers call him. It was started by this young cub Driscoll, the free-lance. Driscoll is Bitton's nephew; it would be difficult to muzzle him, and if we did try to muzzle him we should look foolish. *He's* doing the damage. Laugh, by all means!" Hadley invited, frigidly.

Dr. Fell lowered his chins into his collar. The twinkle in his eye had become more pronounced.

"And Scotland Yard," he asked, with suspicious politeness, "is unable to apprehend this villainous—"

Hadley retained his repose with an effort. Hadley said, in a quiet voice, "I don't give a damn, personally, if he steals the Archbishop of Canterbury's miter. But the effect of a police force's being laughed at is not at all humorous. Besides, suppose we catch him? To the newspapers the trial would be much funnier than the offence. Can you imagine two solemn wigged counsels battling as to whether the defendant did, or did not, on the evening of March 5th, 1932, abstract the helmet of Police Constable Thomas Sparkle from the head of the said constable, in or about the premises of Euston Road, and did thereafter elevate the said helmet to the top of a lamp-standard before the premises of New Scotland Yard, S.W.—or whatever it is they say?"

"Did he do that?" Dr. Fell queried, with interest.

"Read it," said Hadley, and drew the newspaper from his pocket. "That's young Driscoll's column. It's the worst, but the others are almost as facetious."

Dr. Fell grunted. "I say, Hadley, this isn't the case you wanted to talk to me about, is it? Because if it is, I'm damned if I help you. Why, man, it's glorious! It's like Robin Hood. It's like—"

Hadley was not amused. "That," he answered, coldly, "is not the case. But out of what I have on hand, I hope to put a brake on Driscoll. Unless—" He hesitated, turning something over in his mind. "Read it. It will probably delight you."

Rampole glanced over the doctor's shoulder as the latter read:

HAT FIEND STRIKES AGAIN!

IS THERE A POLITICAL SIGNIFICANCE IN
THE MOVEMENTS OF THE SINISTER
MASTER MIND?

By Philip C. Driscoll, our special correspondent in charge of the latest Mad Hatter atrocities.

London, March 12. *Not since the days of Jack the Ripper has this city been so terrorized by a mysterious fiend who strikes and vanishes without a clue, as in the exploits of the diabolical criminal genius known as the Mad Hatter. On Sunday morning fresh exploits of the Mad Hatter challenged the best brains of Scotland Yard.*

Passing the cab-rank on the east side of Leicester Square about 5 a.m., P. C. James McGuire was struck by a somewhat unusual circumstance. A hansom cab was drawn up at the curb, from which certain not untuneful noises indicated that the driver was asleep inside. The horse (whose name has subsequently been ascertained to be Jennifer) was chewing a large stick of peppermint and looking benevolently upon P. C. McGuire. What especially struck the quick-witted policeman, however, was the fact that on her head Jennifer wore a large white wig with flowing sides—in fact, a barrister's wig.

Though some caution was manifested in taking steps when Mr.

McGuire reported to Vine Street Police Station the presence of a horse in a barrister's wig eating peppermint in Leicester Square, ultimate investigation proved it true. It became obvious that the Hat Fiend was again at large.

Readers of the Daily Herald *are already aware how, on the preceding day, a beautiful pearl-gray top hat was discovered on the head of one of the lions on the Nelson Monument in Trafalgar Square, looking towards Whitehall. By its inscription it was found to belong to Sir Isaac Simonides Levy, of Curzon Street, the well-known member of the Stock Exchange. Under cover of a light mist, that cloak of evil-doers, it had been twitched from Sir Isaac's head as he was leaving his home the preceding evening to address a meeting of the Better Orphans' League. It will be obvious that Sir Isaac, in a pearl-gray top hat for evening wear, was (to say the least) conspicuous.*

The origin of the wig on Jennifer's head was, therefore, clear to the authorities. At the present moment its owner has not been ascertained, nor has he come forward. This modesty has led to all sorts of speculations, but clues are few. Mr. Aylmer Valence, the driver of the hansom cab, could shed no light on the matter. Detectives believe that the Mad Hatter must have been near the cab-rank only a few moments before the arrival of P. C. McGuire, inasmuch as the stick of peppermint was scarcely a third gone when the policeman first saw her. It is further inferred that the criminal was well acquainted with Leicester Square, and probably with the horse Jennifer, since he took advantage of her liking for peppermints to place the wig upon her head. Beyond this, the police have little to work on.

This is the seventh reported outrage in the last week. It would not be too far-fetched to wonder whether any sinister political scheme underlies this.

"There's more of it," Hadley said, when he saw Dr. Fell fold over the paper at this point, "but it doesn't matter. I hate this damned ragging, that's all."

"Undoubtedly," said Dr. Fell, sadly, "you police are a persecuted lot. And no clue, I suppose. I'm sorry I can't take the case. Perhaps, though, if you sent your best men to all the sweet-shops near Leicester Square, and inquire who bought—"

"I didn't bring you down from Chatterham," Hadley retorted, with asperity, "to talk about an undergraduate prank. But I may stop this young pup Driscoll from writing such tosh, and that will stop the rest of them. I wired you that it had something to do with Bitton; Bitton is this boy's uncle, and holds the purse strings. One of the most valuable manuscripts in Bitton's collection, he tells me, has been stolen."

"Ah," said Dr. Fell. He put aside the paper, and sat back with his arms folded.

"The devil about these thefts of manuscripts or rare books," Hadley continued, "is that you can't trace them like an ordinary theft. In the case of precious stones, or plates, or even pictures, it's fairly simple. We know our pawnshops and our receivers of stolen goods too well. But you can't do it with books or manuscripts. When a thief takes something like that, he has a definite person in mind to whom he intends to dispose of it; or else he's acting under the buyer's orders, to begin with. In any case, you can be sure the buyer won't tell."

The chief inspector paused.

"And the Yard's intervention in the matter is further complicated by the fact that the manuscript stolen from Bitton was one to which he had—well, a rather dubious right himself."

"I see," murmured the doctor. "And what was it?"

Hadley picked up his glass slowly, and set it down hastily. Nobody, least of all the business man who remained drinking in one corner, was prepared for another stormy entrance to the bar that afternoon. Feet clattered on the brass stair-rods. A tall man in a flapping greatcoat strode down into the room; the bartender drew a deep breath, resignedly, and tried not to notice the wild look in the stranger's eye. The bartender murmured, "Good afternoon, Sir William," and returned to polishing glasses.

"It's not a good afternoon," Sir William Bitton announced, violently. He passed the end of his white scarf across his face, moist from the thickening mist outside, and glared. His white pompadour stood up like the foam on a beer glass. "It's a hell of an afternoon, that's what it is. Ah, Hallo, Hadley! Now, look here, something's got to be done. I tell you I won't—" He strode into the alcove, and his eye fell on the paper Dr. Fell had discarded. "So you're reading about him, are you? You're reading about that swine who steals hats?"

"Quite, quite," said Hadley, looking about nervously. "Sit down, man! What's he done to you?"

"What's he done?" inquired Sir William, with deadly politeness. He raised the forelock of his white hair. "You can see for yourself what he's done. It was an hour and a half ago, and I'm still boiling. I boil every time I think of it. Right in front of my house—car standing there—chauffeur down buying cigarettes. *I* went out to it. Misty in the square. Saw what I thought was a sneak-thief putting his hand into the side pocket of the car door through the window in the tonneau. I said, 'Hi!' and jumped on the running-board. *Then* the swine shot out his hand and—"

Sir William gulped.

"I had three appointments this afternoon before I came here; two of 'em in the City. Even going to make monthly calls. Call on Lord Tarlotts. Call on my nephew. Call— Never mind. But

I couldn't and wouldn't go *anywhere,* because I hadn't got one. And I was damned if I'd pay three guineas for a third one that swine might— What's he done?" bellowed Sir William, breaking off again. "He's stolen my hat, that's what he's done! And it's the second hat he's stolen from me in three days!"

The business man in the corner uttered a faint noise, shook his head despondently, and hurried out of the bar.

II

Manuscripts and Murder

HADLEY RAPPED on the table. "A double whiskey here," he said to the waiter. "Now sit down and calm yourself. People think this is a madhouse already. And let me introduce you to some friends of mine."

"D'ye do?" said the other, grudgingly, and bobbed his head at the introductions. He resumed in his high, argumentative voice as he sat down. "It's infuriating. It's maddening. All those visits; make 'em regular as clockwork, every month. The only reason I came here was because I'd *got* to see you if I'd had to come without my boots. Ha. No other hat in the house. Think of that! My daughter'd made me give the others to my valet; wouldn't wear them in a pigsty; just bought two new hats last week—top hat and Homburg. And Saturday night this maniac pinched the top hat, and this afternoon he got the Homburg. By God! I won't have it! I tell you—" He glared round as the waiter appeared. "Eh? Oh, whisky. Just a splash, thanks. That'll do. My daughter said, 'Why not chase him?' *Me?* Chase my hat? Ha. Sheila has no brains. Never had."

Spluttering, he sat back to take a drink, and Rampole studied him. Everybody knew, by hearsay, of this man's fiery humors.

14

Jingo newspapers frequently dwelt on his career: how he had begun in a draper's shop at the age of eighteen, become a whip in Parliament at forty-two, managed the armament policy of one Government, and had gone down still battling for a bigger navy in the peace reaction after the war. He had been the prince of jingoes; his speeches were full of reference to Drake, the longbow, and hurrah for old England; and he still wrote letters vilifying the present Prime Minister. But his best-known activities were before the war, and he had retired completely from public life at little more than forty-five. Now Rampole saw a man hardly past his prime at seventy; wiry, vigorous, with a long neck thrust out of his wing collar, and uncannily shrewd blue eyes. His fingers were restless and tapping. The face was bony, with a high, frail forehead, the eyebrows like white mustaches, and the mouth at once thin and mobile—an orator's mouth.

Suddenly he put down his glass and stared at Dr. Fell with narrowed eyes. "Excuse me," he said, in his jerky but wonderfully clear fashion, "I didn't catch your name at first. Dr. Fell? Dr. Gideon Fell?—Ah, I thought so. I have been wanting to meet you. I have your work on the history of the supernatural in English fiction. But this damned business about hats—"

Hadley said, brusquely, "I think we've heard quite enough about hats, for the moment. You understand that according to the story you told me we can't take official cognizance of it at the Yard. That's why I've summoned Dr. Fell. There's no time to go into it now, but he has—helped us before. I am not one of those fools who distrust amateurs. And it is particularly in his line. All the same—"

The chief inspector was troubled. Suddenly he drew a long breath. His slow gray eyes were almost black now. Evenly he continued.

"Gentlemen, neither am I one of those fools who call themselves thoroughly practical men. A moment ago I said we had heard quite enough about hats; and before I saw Sir William I thought so. But this second theft of his hat—has it occurred to you that in some fashion—I do not pretend to understand it—this may relate to the theft of the manuscript?"

Sir William seemed about to utter a snort of protest, but the lines tightened round his eyes, and he kept silent.

"It had occurred to me, of course," Dr. Fell rumbled, beckoning the waiter and pointing to his empty glass, "that the theft of the hats was more than an undergraduate prank. It's quite possible that some scatterbrained chap might want to *collect* stolen hats; a policeman's helmet, a barrister's wig, any sort of picturesque headgear he could proudly display to his friends. I noticed the same habit when I was teaching in America, among the students. There it ran to signs and signboards of all kinds to decorate the walls of their rooms. Is that right, my boy?"

Rampole nodded. "Yes. And it went to fantastic lengths sometimes. I knew one chap who made a bet that he would steal the street sign from the corner of Broadway and Forty-Second Street in broad daylight. And he did it. He put on overalls, slung a bucket of paint over his arm, and carried a short ladder. Then he propped the ladder against the post, climbed up, unscrewed the sign, and walked away. There were thousands of people passing at the time, and nobody even glanced at him."

"For a collection, yes," said the doctor. "But this is a different thing, you see. This chap isn't a lunatic collector. He steals the hat and props it up somewhere else, like a symbol, for everybody to see. There's one other explanation."

Sir William's thin lips wore a wintry smile as he glanced from

Rampole to the absorbed face of the doctor; but shrewd calcula-tion moved in his eyes.

"You're a quaint parcel of detectives," he said. "Are you seri-ously suggesting that a thief begins pinching hats all over London so that he can pinch a manuscript from me? Do you think I'm in the habit of carrying valuable manuscripts around in my hat? Besides, if I must become slightly crazy myself, I might point out that it was stolen several days before either one of my hats."

Dr. Fell ruffled his big dark mane with a thoughtful hand. "The repetition of that word 'hat,'" he observed, "has rather a confusing effect. I'm afraid I shall say 'hat' when I mean almost anything else. Suppose you tell us about the manuscript first—what was it, and how did you get it, and when was it stolen? It wasn't the one of Coleridge's *Kubla Khan*, was it?"

The other shook his head. He finished his whisky and leaned back. For a moment he studied Dr. Fell sharply, with heavy-lid-ded eyes. Then a sort of dry, eager pride edged his look.

"I'll tell you what it was," he answered, in a low voice, "be-cause Hadley vouches for you. Only one collector in the world—no, say two—know that I found it. One of them had to know; I had to show it to him to make sure it was genuine. The other I'll speak of presently. But I found it."

His dry bones seemed to stiffen. Rampole, who could never understand this ghoulish eagerness to finger and possess original manuscripts or first editions, regarded him curiously.

"I found it," Sir William repeated. "It is the manuscript of a completely unknown story by Edgar Allan Poe. Myself and one other person excepted, nobody except Poe has ever seen it or heard of it. Find that hard to believe, do you?" There was a frosty pleasure in his look, and he chuckled without opening his mouth.

"Listen. It's happened before with Poe's work, you know. You've heard how the very rare first edition of *The Murders in the Rue Morgue* was found in a trash basket, haven't you? Well, this is better. Much better. I found it—by chance, yes. But it's real. Robertson said so. Ha. *Listen.*"

He sat back, his hand moving along the polished table as though he were smoothing down sheets of paper. He resembled less the traditional figure of a collector than a pawnbroker explaining a particularly shrewd stroke of business.

"I've never collected Poe manuscripts. The American societies have a corner on those. But I have a first edition of the *Al Araaf* collection, published by subscription while he was at West Point, and a few copies of the *Southern Literary Messenger* he edited in Baltimore. Well! I was poking about for odds and ends in the States last September, and I happened to be visiting Dr. Masters, the Philadelphia collector. He suggested that I have a look at the house where Poe lived there, at the corner of Seventh and Spring Garden Streets. I did. I went alone. And a jolly good thing I did.

"It was a mean neighborhood, dull brick fronts and washing hung in gritty backyards. The house was at the corner of an alley, and I could hear a man in a garage swearing at a back-firing motor. Very little about the house had been changed, except that a door had been knocked through the one next to it and turned the two houses into one. It was unoccupied, too—they were altering it just *then*.

"From the alley I went through a gate in a high board fence, and into a paved yard with a crooked tree growing through the bricks. In the little brick kitchen a glum-looking workman was making some notations on an envelope; there was a noise of hammering from the front room. I excused myself; I said that the house used to be occupied by a writer I had heard of, and

I was looking round. He growled to go ahead, and went on ciphering. So I went to the other room. You know the type; small and low-ceilinged; cupboards set flush with the wall, and papered over, on either side of a low black mantelpiece with an arched grate. But—Poe had scribbled there by candlelight, and Virginia plucked at her harp, and Mrs. Clemm placidly peeled potatoes."

Sir William Bitton obviously saw that he had caught his audience, and it was clear from his mannerisms and pauses that he enjoyed telling a story. The scholar, the business man, the mountebank—all these peered out of his bony face and showed in a rather theatrical gesture.

"They were altering the cupboards. The *cupboards*, mind you." He bent forward suddenly. "And again—a jolly good thing they took out the inner framework instead of just putting up plaster-board and papering them out. There was a cloud of dust and mortar in the place. Two workmen were just bumping down the framework, and I saw—

"Gentlemen, I went cold and shaky all over. It had been shoved down between the edges of the framework—thin sheets of paper, spotted with damp, and folded twice lengthwise. It was like a revelation, for when I had pushed open the gate, and first saw those workmen altering the house, I thought, 'Suppose I were to find—' Well, I confess I almost lunged past those men. One of them said, 'What the hell!' and almost dropped the frame. One glance at the handwriting, what I could make out of it, was enough; you know that distinctive curly line beneath the title in Poe's MSS., and the fashioning of the 'E. A. Poe'?

"But I had to be careful. I didn't know the owner of the house; and he might know the value of this. If I offered the workmen money to let me have it, I must be careful not to offer too much, or they would grow suspicious and insist on more."

Sir William smiled tightly. "I explained it was something of sentimental interest to a man who had lived here before. And I said, 'Look here, I'll give you ten dollars for this.' Even at that, they were suspicious; I think they had some idea of buried treasure, or directions for finding it, or something. The ghost of Poe would have enjoyed that." Again that chuckle behind closed teeth. Sir William swept out his arm.

"But they looked over it, and saw that it was only—'a kind of a story, or some silly damn thing, with long words at the beginning.' I was in agony for fear they would tear the sheets; folded in that fashion, they were very apt to tear without their age and flimsiness. Finally they compromised at twenty dollars, and I took the manuscript away.

"As you may know, the leading authorities on Poe are Professor Hervey Allen of New York and Dr. Robertson of Baltimore. I knew Robertson, and took my find to him. First I made him promise that, no matter what I showed him, he would never mention it to anybody."

Rampole was watching the chief inspector. During the recital Hadley had become—not precisely bored, but restive and impatient, with a frown between his brows.

"But why keep it a secret?" he demanded. "If there were any trouble about your right, you were at least first claimant; you could have bought it. And you'd made what you say is a great discovery. Why not announce it and get the credit?"

Sir William stared at him, and then shook his head. "You don't understand," he replied at length. "And I can't explain. I wanted *no* trouble. I wanted this great thing, a secret between Poe and myself, for *myself*. For nobody else to see unless I chose. *Mine*, can you understand? It would be almost like knowing Poe."

A sort of pale fierceness was in his face; the orator was at a loss for words to explain something powerful and intangible, and his hand moved vaguely in the air.

"At any rate—Robertson is a man of honor. He promised, and he will keep his promise, even though he urged me to do as you say, Hadley. But, naturally, I refused. Gentlemen, the manuscript was what I thought; it was even better."

"And what was it?" Dr. Fell asked, rather sharply.

Sir William opened his lips, and then hesitated. When he spoke again, it was in a thin, wiry voice from deep down in his throat.

"One moment, gentlemen. It is not that I do not—ah—trust you. Of course not. Ha! But so much I have told openly, to strangers. Excuse me. I prefer to keep my secret a bit longer. Well enough to tell you what it was when you have heard my story of the theft, and decide whether you can help me. Besides, we have taken a great deal of time already."

"*You* have taken it," the chief inspector corrected, placidly. "Well, Doctor?"

There was a curious expression on Dr. Fell's face; not contemptuous, not humorous, not bored, but a mixture of the three. He rolled in his seat, adjusted his eyeglasses, and peered thoughtfully at the knight.

"Suppose you tell us," he suggested, "the facts of the theft, and whom you suspect. You do suspect somebody, don't you?"

Sir William had started to say yes, and closed his mouth. He responded, "It was taken from my house in Berkeley Square—let me see. This is Monday afternoon. It was taken at some time between Saturday afternoon and Sunday morning. Let me explain.

"Adjoining my bedroom upstairs I have a dressing room which I use a good deal as a study. The greater part of my collection is, of course, downstairs in the library and my study there.

I had been examining the manuscript in my upstairs study on Saturday afternoon."

"Was it locked up?" Hadley inquired. He was interested now.

"No. Nobody—at least, so I thought—knew of it, and I saw no reason for unusual precautions. It was merely in a drawer of my desk, wrapped in tissue paper to preserve it."

"What about the members of your household? Did they know of it?"

Sir William jerked his head down in a sort of bow. "I'm glad you asked that, Hadley. Don't think I shall take umbrage at the suggestion; but I couldn't make it myself. At least—not immediately. Naturally I don't suspect them; ha!"

"Naturally," said the inspector, placidly. "Well?"

"At the present, my household consists of my daughter Sheila—"

A faint frown was on Hadley's face. He stared at the table. "As a matter of fact," he said, "I was referring to servants. But proceed."

He looked up, and the calm eyes met the knight's shrewd ones.

"—of my daughter Sheila," the latter continued, "my brother Lester, and his wife. My nephew by marriage, Philip, has a flat of his own, but he generally eats Sunday dinner with us. That is all—with the exception of one guest. Mr. Julius Arbor, the American collector."

Sir William examined his finger nails. There was a pause.

"As to who knew about it," he resumed, waving a careless hand; "my family knew that I had brought back a valuable manuscript with me, of course. But none of them is in the least interested in such matters, and the mere words, 'another manuscript,' was sufficient explanation. I dare say I may have occasionally let fall hints, as one does in enthusiasm when he is sure nobody will understand. But—"

"And Mr. Arbor?"

Sir William said, evenly, "I had intended to show it to him. He has a very fine collection of Poe first editions. But I had not even mentioned it."

"Go on," said Hadley, stolidly.

"As I have said, I was examining the manuscript on Saturday afternoon; fairly early. Later I went to the Tower of London—"

"To the Tower of London?"

"A very old friend of mine, General Mason, is deputy governor there. He and his secretary have done some very fine research into the Tower records. They wanted me to see a recently discovered record dealing with Robert Devereux, Earl of Essex, who—"

"Quite," said Hadley. "And then?"

"I returned home, dined alone, and afterwards went to the theatre. I did not go into my study then, and after the theatre it was rather late; so I turned in immediately. I discovered the theft on Sunday morning. There was no attempt at burglarious entry at any time; all the windows were locked, and nothing else in the house had been touched. The manuscript was simply missing from the desk drawer."

Hadley pinched at the lobe of his ear. He glanced at Dr. Fell, but the latter was sitting with his chin on his chest, and did not speak.

"Was the drawer locked?" Hadley went on.

"No."

"Your rooms?"

"No."

"I see. What did you do then?"

"I summoned my valet." Sir William's bony fingers rapped flatly on the table; he twisted his long neck, and several times started to speak before he resumed. "And I must confess, Hadley, that I was at first suspicious of him. He was a new man; he had been in my employ only a few months. He had the closest access to my rooms and could prowl as he liked without suspicion. But—well, he seemed too earnest, too dog-like, too thoroughly stupid at anything beyond his immediate duties; and I flatter myself on my ability to judge men."

"Everybody does," Hadley agreed, wearily. "That's why we have so much trouble. Well?"

"As it happens, my judgment was correct," snapped Sir William. "My daughter Sheila engaged him. He had been fifteen years in the service of the late Marquess of Sandival; I spoke to Lady Sandival myself, yesterday, and she scoffed at the idea of Marks being a thief. As I told you, I was suspicious of him at first. He was obviously upset and tongue-tied, but that was a product of his natural stupidity."

"And his story?"

"He had no story," Sir William said, irritably. "He had noticed nothing suspicious, seen nothing whatever. I had difficulty getting it through his head how important the thing was; even what I was looking for. It was the same thing with the rest of the servants. They had noticed nothing. But I was not unduly suspicious, because they are all old retainers; I know the history of every one."

"What about the members of the—household?"

"My daughter Sheila had been out all Saturday afternoon. When she returned, she was in the house only a short time, and then she went out to dinner with the chap she's engaged to. General Mason's secretary, by the way. But," he added, with suspicious haste, "ah—very well connected, I am told, young Dalrye is.

"What was I saying? Ah, yes. My brother Lester and his wife were visiting friends in the west of England; they only returned on Sunday evening. Philip—Philip Driscoll, my nephew—comes to see us only on Sundays. Consequently, nobody noticed anything suspicious at the time the manuscript could have been stolen."

"And this—Mr. Arbor?"

The other reflected, rubbing his dry hands together meditatively.

"A very fine—ah—specimen of the best Hebrew type," he answered, as though he were examining something for a catalogue. "Reserved, scholarly, a trifle sardonic at times. Quite a young man, I should say; scarcely more than forty— Ah, what were you asking? Mr. Arbor, yes. Unfortunately, *he* was not in a position to observe. An American friend of his had invited him to the country for the week-end. He left on Saturday, and did not return until this morning. That's true, by the way," he added, dropping into normal speech and almost leering across the table; "I phoned up about it."

Rampole thought, *Damn you!* And then he thought, *After all, the man has been robbed of his most valued possession; he has a right to suspect outsiders, even grave-faced book-collectors like himself.* The thought of these solemn gentlemen scrabbling about like children after a manuscript brought a grin to his face. He suppressed it instantly as he caught Sir William's cold eye.

"And I definitely don't want scandal," the knight concluded. "That's why I came to you, Hadley. So there it is. Plain, simple, and not a single damned clue."

Hadley nodded. He seemed to be debating something.

"I've brought you in a consulting expert," he said, slowly, nodding towards the doctor. "Dr. Fell has come some little distance as a favor to me. Hence I shall wash my hands of the business, unless you should find the thief and want to prosecute. As I—ah—hardly think you will. But I should like to ask a favor in return."

"A favor?" Sir William repeated, opening his eyes. "Good God! Yes, of course! Anything in reason, I mean."

"You spoke of your nephew, Mr. Driscoll—"

"Philip? Yes. What about him?"

"—who writes for the newspapers."

"Oh, ah. Yes. At least, he tries to. I've exerted considerable influence to get him a real position on a newspaper. Bah! Between ourselves, the editors tell me he can turn out a good story, but he hasn't any news sense. Harbottle says he would walk through rice an inch deep in front of St. Margaret's and never guess there'd been a wedding. So he's free-lancing. He won't believe what I say. Now if I were writing—"

Hadley turned an expressionless face and picked up the newspaper on the table. He was just about to speak when a waiter hurried to his side, glanced at him nervously, and whispered.

"Eh?" said the chief inspector. "Speak louder, man! . . . Yes, that's my name. . . . Right. Thanks." He drained his glass and looked sharply at his companions. "That's damned funny. I told them not to get in touch with me unless— Excuse me a moment, gentlemen."

"What's the matter?" inquired Dr. Fell, rousing himself from some obscure meditation and blinking over his spectacles.

"Phone. Back in a moment."

They were silent as Hadley followed the waiter. In Hadley's

look there had been a startled uneasiness which gave Rampole a shock. The American looked at Sir William, who was also staring curiously.

He returned in less than two minutes, and Rampole felt something tighten in his throat. The chief inspector did not hurry; he was as quiet and deliberate as ever; but his footfalls sounded louder on the tiled floor, and under the bright lights his face was pale.

Stopping a moment at the bar, he spoke a few words and then returned to the table.

"I've ordered you all a drink," he said, slowly. "A whisky. It's just three minutes until closing time, and then we shall have to go. I should appreciate it if you would accompany me."

"Go?" repeated Sir William. "Go where?"

Hadley did not speak until the waiter had brought the drinks and left the table. Then he said, "Good luck!" hastily drank a little whisky, and set the glass down with care. Again Rampole was conscious of that tightening sense of terror.

"Sir William," Hadley went on, looking at the other levelly, "I hope you will prepare yourself for a shock."

"Yes?" said the knight. But he did not pick up his glass.

"We were speaking a moment ago of your nephew, Philip."

"Yes? Well, good God! Get on with it! What about him?"

"I am afraid I must tell you that he is dead. He has just been found at the Tower of London. There is reason to believe that he was murdered."

The foot of Sir William's glass rattled on the polished table-top. He did not move; his eyes were fixed steadily and rather glassily on Hadley, and he seemed to have stopped breathing. In the long silence they could hear motor horns hooting in the street outside.

A nerve in Sir William's arm kept twitching. He had to take his hand from the glass to keep it from rattling on the table. He said, with an effort, "I—I have my car here."

"There is also reason to believe," Hadley went on, "that what we thought a practical joke has turned into murder. Sir William, your nephew is wearing a golf suit. And on the head of his dead body somebody has put your stolen top hat."

III

The Body at Traitors' Gate

THE TOWER of London.

Over the White Tower flew the banner of the three Norman lions, when William the Conqueror reigned, and above the Thames its ramparts gleamed white with stone quarried at Caen. And on this spot, a thousand years before the Domesday Book, Roman sentinels cried the hours of the night from Divine Julius's Tower.

Richard of the Lion's Heart widened the moat about a squat gray fortress, fourteen acres ringed with the strength of inner and outer ballium walls. Here rode the kings, stiff-kneed in iron and scarlet; amiable Henry, and Edward, Hammer of the Scots; and the cross went before them to Westminster, and the third Edward bent to pick up a lady's garter, and Becket's lonely ghost prowled through St. Thomas's Tower. There were tournaments on Tower Green. There were torches for the feasts in William's hall. Up Water Lane moves now that shadowy company of eight hundred years, in the echo of whose names you can hear arrows sing, and the thud of weighted horses.

A palace, a fortress, a prison. Until Charles Stuart came back from exile it was the home of the kings, and it remains a royal palace today. Bugles sound before Waterloo Barracks, where once the tournaments were held, and you will hear the wheel and stamp of the Guards. In the green places under the trees, a raven comes to sit on a drinking fountain, and looks across at the spot where men and women with bandaged eyes mounted a few steps to put their heads upon a block.

On certain dull and chilly days there creeps from the Thames a smoky vapor which is not light enough to be called mist nor thick enough to be called fog. The rumble of traffic is muffled on Tower Hill. In the uncertain light, battlements stand up ghostly above the brutish curve of the round-towers; boat whistles hoot and echo mournfully from the river; and the rails of the iron fence round the dry moat become the teeth of a prison. Low-lying under the shoulder of Tower Hill, the few white stones almost startling against dingy gray, these walls show thin slits for windows, and you think upon the unholy things which have gone on inside them. Of the two children smothered by lantern-light, and pale Raleigh walking the ramparts in ruff and feathered hat, and Sir Thomas Overbury racked with poison in the lower room of the Bloody Tower.

Rampole had visited the Tower before. He had seen it in the grace of summer, when grass and trees mellow the aisles between the walls. But he could visualize what it would be like now. The imaginings grew on him during that interminable ride in Sir William's car between Piccadilly Circus and the Tower.

When he thought about it afterwards, he knew that those last words Hadley spoke were the most horrible he had ever heard. It was not so much that a man had been found dead at the Tower of London. He had eaten horrors with a wide spoon during those days of the Starberth case in Lincolnshire. But a corpse in a golfing suit, on which some satanic hand had placed the top hat stolen from Sir William, was a final touch in the hideous. After placing his stolen hats on cab horses, lamp-posts, and stone lions, this madman seemed to have created a corpse so that he could have at last a fitting place to hang his hat. The evil grotesquerie of the situation was enhanced because Rampole had already smiled at the antics of the thief as an undergraduate jest. With his memories of the Tower of London, it seemed an admirable choice of a place wherein to decorate a dead man thus.

The ride was endless. In the West End there had been a fairly light mist, but it thickened as they neared the river, and in Cannon Street it was almost dark. Sir William's chauffeur had to proceed with the utmost care. Hatless, his scarf wound crazily about his throat, strained forward with his hands gripping his knees, Sir William was jammed into the tonneau between Hadley and Dr. Fell. Rampole sat on one of the small seats, watching the dull light fall on the knight's face through the blurred panes of the limousine.

Sir William was breathing heavily.

"We'd better talk," Dr. Fell said in a gruff voice. "My dear sir, you will feel better. It's murder now, Hadley. Do you still want me?"

"More than ever," said the chief inspector.

Dr. Fell puffed out his cheeks meditatively. He was sitting forward, his hands clasping one cane so that his chin was almost upon them, and the shovel hat shadowed his face.

"Then if you don't mind, I should like to ask—"

"Eh?" said Sir William, blankly. "Oh. No, no. Not at all. Carry on." He kept peering ahead into the mist.

The car bumped. Sir William turned and said, "I was very fond of the boy, you see," and then continued to crane his neck ahead.

There was a silence, while the horn honked savagely, and the three figures in the rear seat wove about before Rampole's eyes.

"Quite," said Dr. Fell, gruffly. "What did they tell you over the phone, Hadley?"

"Just that. That the boy was dead; stabbed in some way. And that he wore a golf suit and Sir William's top hat. It was a relay call from the Yard. Ordinarily, I shouldn't have got the call at all. The matter would have been handled by the local police station, unless they asked the Yard for help or we intervened of our own accord. But in this case—"

"Well?"

"I had a feeling. I had a feeling that this damned hat business wasn't sheer sport. I left orders—and got smiled at behind my back for it—that if any further hat antics were discovered, they should be reported to the Yard by the local station, and sent through Sergeant Anders directly to me. There. *That's* what a fool I thought I was." Hadley jerked his head, and stared across at Dr. Fell with vindictive eyes. "But, by God! I told you I wasn't one of those fools who boasted about being a thoroughly practical man. And I'll take charge of this case myself."

"That's sensible. But I say, how did the people at the Tower know it was Sir William's hat?"

"I can tell you that," snapped Sir William, rousing himself. "I'm tired of picking up the wrong hat when I go out in the evenings. All top hats look alike in a row, and initials only confuse you. I have Bitton stamped in gold inside the crown of the formal ones, opera hats and silk ones; yes, and bowlers too, for that matter." He was speaking rapidly and confusedly, and his mind was on other things. He seemed to utter what thoughts went through his head without thinking about them at all. "Yes, and come to think of it, *that* was a new hat, too. I bought it when I bought the

Homburg, because my other opera hat got its spring broken. I'd only worn it once before; it was—"

He paused, and brushed a hand over blank eyes.

"Ha," he went on, dully. "Odd. That's odd. You said my 'stolen' hat, Hadley. Yes, the top hat was stolen. That's quite right; how did you know it was the stolen hat they found on Philip?"

Hadley was irritable. "I don't know. They told me over the phone. But they said General Mason discovered the body, and so—"

"Ah," muttered Sir William, nodding and pinching the bridge of his nose. He seemed dazed by trifles. "Yes. Mason was at the house on Sunday, and I dare say I told him. I—"

Dr. Fell leaned forward. In a subdued way he seemed excited.

"So," he said, "it was a new hat, Sir William? A new hat?"

"Yes. I told you."

"An opera hat," Dr. Fell mused, "which you were wearing for the first time. When was it stolen?"

"Eh? Oh. Saturday night. When I was coming home from the theatre. We'd turned off Piccadilly into Berkeley Street. It was a muggy night, rather warm, and all the windows of the car were down. Besides, it's rather dark along there. What was I saying? Oh, yes. Well, just opposite Lansdowne Passage Simpson slowed down to let some sort of blind man with a tray of pencils, or something, get across the street. Then somebody jumped out of the shadows near the entrance to the passage, thrust his arm into the rear of the car, twitched off my hat, and ran."

"What did you do?"

"Nothing. I was too startled. Just—just spluttered, I suppose. What the devil *can* one do when a person—"

"Did you chase the man?"

"And look a fool? Good God! No. Rather let him get away."

"So naturally," said Dr. Fell, "you didn't report it. Did you catch a glimpse of the man?"

"No. It was too sudden, I tell you. *Flick*, and it was gone. Ha. Damn him. And now— You see," Sir William muttered, hesitantly, turning his head from side to side—"you see— Never mind the hat; I'm thinking about Philip. I never treated him as I should. I was as fond of him as a son. But I always acted the Dutch uncle. Kept him on a starvation allowance, always threatened to cut him off, and always told him how worthless he was. I don't know why I did it, but every time I saw that boy I wanted to preach. He had no idea of the value of money. He—" Sir William struck his knee with his fist. He added, in a dull voice, "Never mind now. He's dead."

The limousine slid among gigantic red houses, and street lamps made pale gleams through its windows in a canopy of mist. Emerging from Mark Lane, it swerved round the Monument and descended Tower Hill.

Rampole could see nothing more than a few feet ahead. Lamps winked in smoky twilight, and the immensity which should have been the river was full of short, sharp whistle blasts answered by deeper hootings from a distance. Cart wheels rattled somewhere. When the limousine passed through the gate in the rails surrounding the whole enclosure, Rampole tried to rub the blur from the window to peer out. Vaguely he saw a dry moat paved in white concrete, with a forlorn hockey-net near the middle. The drive swung to the left, past a frame building he remembered as the ticket office and refreshment room, and under an arch flanked by low, squat round towers. Just under this arch they were brought up short. A sentry, in the high black shako and gray uniform of the Spur Guard, moved out smartly and crossed his rifle on his breast. The limousine slithered to a halt and Hadley sprang out.

In the dim, ghostly half-light another figure emerged at the sentry's side. It was one of the Yeoman Warders, buttoned up in a short blue cloak and wearing the red-and-blue Beefeater hat. He said, "Chief Inspector Hadley? Thank you. If you'll follow me, sir?"

There was a quick, military precision about the whole proceeding which made Rampole shiver. But that, he reflected, was literally what it was. The Yeomen Warders were selected from sergeants of the Army of long and distinguished service, and rank as sergeant-majors with warrant rank. There would be no waste motion.

Hadley asked, shortly, "Who is in charge?"

"The chief warder, sir, under the orders of the deputy governor. These gentlemen?"

"My associates. This is Sir William Bitton. What has been done?"

The warder looked impassively at Sir William, and back to Hadley.

"The chief warder will explain, sir. The young gentleman's body was discovered by General Mason."

"Where?"

"I believe it was on the steps leading down to Traitors' Gate, sir. You know, of course, that the warders are sworn in as special constables. General Mason suggested that, as you were a friend of the young gentleman's uncle, we communicate directly with you instead of with the district police station, and deal with the matter ourselves until you arrived."

"Precautions?"

"An order has been issued that no one is to enter or leave the Tower until permission has been given, sir."

"Good! Good! You had better leave instructions to admit the police surgeon and his associates when they arrive."

"Yes, sir." He spoke briefly to the sentry, and led them under the arch of the tower.

A stone bridge led across the moat from this (called the Middle Tower) to another and larger tower, with circular bastions, whose arch formed the entrance to the outer walls. Gray-black, picked out with whitish stones, these heavy defenses ran left and right; but the damp mist was so thick that the entrance was entirely invisible. As he crossed the bridge with Dr. Fell, Hadley and Sir William striding ahead behind the warder, Rampole felt himself shivering once more. It was all at once ancient and modern, with the swift deadliness of both times.

Just under the arch of this next tower, another figure appeared with the same eerie suddenness as the others: a thick, rather short man with a straight back, his hands thrust into the pockets of a dripping water-proof. A soft hat was drawn down on his brows. He came forward, peering, as he heard their muffled footfalls on the road. He peered again in the mist and started slightly.

He said, "Good God, Bitton! How did *you* get here?" Then he hurried up to grasp Sir William's hand.

"Never mind," Sir William answered, stolidly. "Thanks, Mason. Where have you got him?"

The other man looked into his face. He wore a gingery mustache and imperial, drooping with the damp; there were furrows in his dull-colored face and lines round his hard, bright unwinking eyes. For some moments he regarded Sir William with those unwinking eyes, his head slightly on one side. There were no echoes in this vast place. Only a querulous tug whistled on the Thames.

"Good man!" said the other, releasing his hand. "This is—"

"Chief Inspector Hadley. Dr. Fell. Mr. Rampole—General Mason," explained Sir William, jerking his head. "Where is he, Mason? I want to see him."

General Mason took his arm. "You understand, of course, that we couldn't disturb the body until the police arrived. He's where we found him. That's correct, isn't it, Mr. Hadley?"

"Quite correct, General. If you will show us the place? Thank you. I'm afraid we shall have to leave him there, though, until the police surgeon examines him."

"For God's sake, Mason," Sir William said, in a low voice, "*who*—I mean, how did it happen? *Who did it?* It's the insanest—"

"I don't know. I only know what we saw. Steady, now! Would you like a drink first?"

"No. No, thanks. I'm all right. How was he killed?"

General Mason drew a hand down hard over his mustache and imperial. It was his only sign of nervousness. He said, "It appears to be a crossbow bolt, from what I can judge. There's about four inches projecting from his chest, and the point barely came out the other— Excuse me. A crossbow bolt. We have some in the armory. Straight through the heart. Instantaneous death, Bitton. No pain whatever."

"You mean," said the chief inspector, "he was shot—"

"Or stabbed with it like a dagger. More likely the latter. Come and look at him, Mr. Hadley; and then take charge of my court"— he nodded towards the tower behind him—"in there. I'm using the Warders' Hall as a—what d'ye call it—third-degree room."

"What about visitors? They tell me you've given orders no-body is to leave."

"Yes. Fortunately, it's a bad day and there aren't many visitors. Also, fortunately, the fog is very thick down in the well around the steps of Traitors' Gate; I don't think a passer-by would no-tice him there. So far as I'm aware, nobody knows about it yet. When the visitors try to leave, they are stopped at the gate and told that an accident has happened; we're trying to make them comfortable until you can talk to them." He turned to the warder. "Tell the chief warder to carry on until I return. Find out if Mr. Dalrye has got the names and addresses of all the visitors. This way, gentlemen."

Ahead of them the hard road ran arrow-straight. Towards the left, a little distance beyond the long arch beneath which they stood, Rampole could see the murky outlines of another round tower. Joining it, a high wall ran parallel with the road. And Ram-pole remembered now. This left-hand wall was the defense of the inner fortress; roughly, a square within a square. On their right ran the outer wall, giving on the wharf. Thus was formed a lane some twenty-five or thirty feet broad, which stretched the whole length of the enclosure on the riverside. At intervals along the road, pale gas-lamps were strangled in the mist, and Rampole could dimly see the spiky silhouettes of tree branches.

Their footfalls rang in the hollow beneath the walls. On the right gleamed the lighted windows of a little room where post cards were sold; the head and hat of a Yeoman Warder were dark-ly outlined as he peered out. For perhaps a hundred yards along this road General Mason led them; then he stopped and pointed towards the right.

"St. Thomas's Tower," he said. "And that's the Traitors' Gate under it."

It was full of evil suggestion. The tower itself went almost unnoticed because of the great gateway over which it was built. Traitors' Gate was a long, flattened arch of stone, like the hood of an unholy fireplace in the thick wall. From the level of the road, sixteen broad stone steps led down to the floor of a large paved area which had once been the bed of the Thames. For originally this had been the gateway to the Tower by water; the river had flowed in at a level with the topmost steps, and barges had moved under the arch to their mooring. There were the ancient barriers, closed as of old: two heavy gates of oaken timbers and vertical iron bars, with an oaken lattice stretching above them to fill in the arch. Thames wharf had been built up beyond, and the vast area below was now dry.

It had made a powerful impression on Rampole when he saw it before. And he needed to reconstruct such details from his imagination, for the great arch was blurred with mist. Faintly he could see the ugly teeth of the spikes on top of the gates, and flickers of white through the lattice. But, beyond the iron fence which guarded the descent, the area below was a smoky well.

General Mason took an electric torch from his pocket, snapped it on, and directed the beam towards the ground. A warder had been standing motionless near the fence; and the General gestured with his light.

"Stand at the gate of the Bloody Tower," he said, "and don't let anybody come near. Now, gentlemen. I don't think we need to climb this fence. I've been down once before."

Just before the beam of his flashlight moved down the steps, Rampole felt almost a physical nausea. He was holding tightly to the wet iron railing, and he wanted to shut his eyes or turn away. His chest felt tight and empty, and a small hammer pounded there. Then he saw it.

The thing lay with its head near the foot of the stairs, on its right side, and sprawled as though it had rolled down the entire flight of steps. Philip Driscoll wore a suit of heavy tweed, with plus fours, golf stockings, and thick shoes. Originally the suit must have been of a conspicuous light-brown color, patterned broadly; now it was almost black with wetness. But the watchers scarcely saw these things. As General Mason's light moved along the body, they saw the dull gleam of several inches of steel projecting from the left breast. Apparently the wound had not bled much.

The face was flung up towards them, just as the chest was slightly arched to show the bolt in the heart. White and waxy, the face was, with eyelids nearly closed; it had a stupid, sponged expression which would not have been terrifying at all but for the hat.

The opera hat had not been crushed in the fall. It was much too large for Philip Driscoll; whether it had been jammed on or merely dropped on his head, it came down nearly to his eyes, and flattened out his ears grotesquely. To see the white face turned up, cheek against the stone step, and hat set at a sort of hideous rakish angle over one eye, drew from Sir William a sound which was less a sob than a snarl of fury.

General Mason switched off his light.

"You see?" he said out of the dimness. "If that hat hadn't looked so weird, I shouldn't have taken it off at all, and seen your name inside it. Mr. Hadley, do you want to make an examination now, or shall you wait for the police surgeon?"

"Give me your torch, please," the chief inspector requested, brusquely. He snapped on the light again and swung it round. "How did you happen to find him, General?"

"There's more of a story connected with that," the deputy governor replied, "than I can tell you. The prelude to it you can hear from the people who saw him here when he arrived, earlier in the afternoon."

"When was that?"

"The time he arrived? Somewhere about twenty minutes past one, I believe; I wasn't here. Dalrye, my secretary, drove me from the middle of town in my car, and we got here at precisely two-thirty. I remember, because I heard the clock at the barracks strike when we were driving under the Byward Tower." He pointed back along the road. "That's the Byward Tower, incidentally; the one where I met you.

"We drove along Water Lane—this road—and Dalrye let me out at the gate of the Bloody Tower, directly opposite us."

They peered into the gloom. The gate of the Bloody Tower was in the inner ballium wall, facing them across the road. They could see the teeth of the raised porticullis over it, and, beyond, a graveled road which led up to higher ground.

"My own quarters are in the King's House, inside that wall. I was just inside the gate, and Dalrye was driving off down Water Lane to put the car away, when I remembered that I had to speak to Sir Leonard Haldyne."

"Sir Leonard Haldyne?"

"The Keeper of the Jewel House. He lives on the other side of St. Thomas's Tower. Turn on your light, please; now move it over to the right, just at the side of Traitor's Gate arch. There." The misty beam showed a heavy ironbound door sunk in the thick wall. "That leads to a staircase going up to the oratory, and Sir Leonard's quarters are on the other side.

"By this time, in addition to the fog, it was raining, and I could barely see. I came across Water Lane, and took hold of the railing here in front of the steps to guide me over to the door. What made me look down I don't know. This talk about a sixth sense is damned nonsense, of course, but when you've seen as much death as I have— Anyhow, I did glance down. I couldn't see anything clearly, but by what I did see I knew something was wrong. I climbed over the railing, went down cautiously, and struck a match. I found him."

The general's voice was precise, gruff, and dry. He lifted his heavy shoulders.

"What did you do then?"

"It was obviously murder," the general continued, without seeming to notice the question. "A man who stabs himself can't drive a steel bolt through his own chest so far that the point comes out under his shoulder blade, certainly not such a small and weak person as young Driscoll. And he had clearly been dead for some time; the body was growing cold.

"As to his odd behavior— No; you'll hear that from others. I'll tell you simply what *I* did. Young Dalrye was coming back from the garage then, and I hailed him. I didn't tell him who the dead man was. He's engaged to Sheila Bitton, and—well, you shall hear. But I told him to send one of the warders for Doctor Benedict."

"Who is that?"

"The chief of staff in charge of the army hospital here. I told Dalrye to go to the White Tower and find Mr. Radburn, the chief warder. He generally finishes his afternoon round at the White Tower at two-thirty. I also told him to leave instructions that nobody was to leave the Tower by any gate. I knew it was a useless precaution, because Driscoll had been dead some time and the murderer had every opportunity for a getaway; but it was the only thing to do."

"Just a moment, General Mason," interposed Hadley. "How many gates are there through the outer walls?"

"Three, not counting the Queen's Gate; nobody could get through *there*. There's the main gate, under the Middle Tower, through which you came. And two more giving on the wharf. They are both in this lane, by the way, some distance farther down."

"Sentries?"

"Naturally. A Spur Guard at every gate, and a warder, also. But if you're looking for a description of somebody who went out, I'm afraid it's useless. Thousands of visitors use those gates every day. Some of the warders have a habit of amusing themselves by watching and cataloguing the people who go in and out, but it's been foggy all day and the raining part of the time. Unless the murderer is some sort of freak, he had a thousand-to-one chance of having escaped unnoticed."

"Damn!" said Hadley, under his breath. "Go on, General."

"That's about all. Doctor Benedict—he's on his rounds now—confirmed my own diagnosis. He said that Driscoll had been dead at least three-quarters of an hour when I found him, and probably longer. The rest you know."

General Mason hesitated.

"There's a strange, an incredible story concerned with Driscoll's activities here this afternoon. Either the boy went mad, or—" Another sharp gesture. "I suggest that you look at him, Mr. Hadley; then we can talk more comfortably in the Warders' Hall."

Hadley nodded. He turned to Dr. Fell. "Can you manage the fence?"

Dr. Fell's big bulk had been towering silently in the background, hunched into his cloak like a bandit. Several times General Mason had looked at him sharply. He was obviously wondering about this stout man with the shovel hat and the wheezy walk; wondering who he was and why he was there; wondering about the small shrewd eyes fixed on him behind eyeglasses on a black ribbon.

"No," said the doctor. "I'm not so spry as all that. But I don't think it's necessary. Carry on; I'll watch from here."

The chief inspector drew on his gloves and climbed the barrier. A luminous circle from his flashlight preceded him down the steps. Again Rampole gripped the rail and watched. Unruffled, sedate in blue overcoat and bowler, Hadley was running his light along the huddled figure.

First he carefully noted the position of the body, and made some sketches and markings in a notebook, with the torch propped under one arm. He flexed the muscles, rolled the body slightly over, and felt at the base of the skull; Philip Driscoll was rolled about like a tailor's dummy. Most meticulously he examined the pavement of the area; then he returned to the few inches of steel projecting from the chest. It had been polished steel, rounded and thin, and it was not notched at the end as in the case of an arrow. Now a film of damp overlay the polish.

Finally Hadley removed the hat. The wet face of the small, dandyish youth was turned full up at them, pitiful and witless. Tight reddish curls were plastered moistly against his forehead. Hadley did not even look at it. But he examined the hat carefully, and brought it up with him as he slowly mounted the stairs.

"Well?" demanded Sir William, in a harsh, thin voice.

Over the fence again, Hadley was silent for a long time. He stood motionless, his light off, slapping the torch with slow beats against his palm. Rampole could not see him well, but he knew that his eyes were roving about the lane.

A fog-horn blew one long blast on the river, and there was a rumbling of chains. Rampole shivered.

Hadley said, "There's one thing your surgeon overlooked, General. There's a contusion at the base of the skull. It could have come either from a blow over the head, or—which is more likely—he got it by being tumbled down those stairs after the murderer stabbed him."

The chief inspector peered about him slowly.

"Suppose he were standing at this rail, or near it, when the murderer struck. The rail is more than waist high, and Driscoll is quite small. It's unlikely that even such a terrific blow with that weapon would have knocked him over the rail. Undoubtedly the murderer pitched him over to put him out of sight."

The chief inspector spoke deliberately, and the torch still slapped in measured beats against his palm.

"Still, we mustn't overlook the possibility that the bolt might have been fired instead of being used as a dagger. That's improbable; it's almost insane, on the face of it. If a crossbow is what I think it is, then it's highly unlikely that the murderer went wandering about the Tower of London carrying any such complicated apparatus. Why should he?"

"Well," said Dr. Fell, musingly, "why should he steal hats, for that matter?"

Rampole saw another jerk of General Mason's shoulders, as though he were trying to shake off a cloud of insane contradictions. But he did not speak, and Hadley went on in his imperturbable voice.

"A knife, or the blow of a blackjack in the fog, would have done just as well. And because of the fog—as you say, General—it's impossible that a marksman could have seen his target very far: certainly not to put a bolt so cleanly through the heart. Finally, there's the hat." He took it from under his arm. "For whatever purpose, the murderer wanted to set his hat on the dead man's head. I think I may take it for granted that Mr. Driscoll wasn't wearing it when he came to the Tower?"

"Naturally not. The Spur Guard and the warder at the Middle Tower, who saw him come in, said he was wearing a cloth cap."

"Which isn't here now," the chief inspector said, thoughtfully. "But tell me, General. You said that so many people are always passing through here. How did they happen to notice Driscoll?"

"Because they knew him. At least, that warder had a nodding acquaintance with him; the guard, of course, is always changing. He's quite a frequent visitor. Dalrye has got him out of so many scrapes in the past that Driscoll came to count on him; that was why he was here today. Besides, the warder will tell you about it. I didn't see him."

"I see. Now, before we go into this matter of the weapon, there's something I want to know. To begin with, we must admit this: whether he was shot or stabbed, he was killed very close to these steps. The murderer couldn't walk about here, with all the warders present, carrying a dead body; these steps were made to order for concealment, and they were used. So let's assume the most improbable course. Let's assume (a) that he was shot with a crossbow; (b) that the force of the shot—and it was a very powerful one—knocked him over this rail, or that the murderer later pushed him over; and (c) that subsequently the killer decorated him with Sir William's hat. You see? *Then from where about here could that bolt have been fired?*"

General Mason massaged his imperial. They were peering at the wall across the way, at the gate of the Bloody

Tower just opposite, and the bulk of a higher round tower just beside it. Farther on, straight along the length of Water Lane, Rampole could discern another archway over the continuation of the lane.

"Well—" said the general. "Damn it all, man, it could have been fired from anywhere. From this lane, east or west, on either side of Traitors' Gate. From under the gate of the Bloody Tower; that's the most likely direction—a straight line. But it's tommyrot. It's out of the question. You can't go marching about here with a crossbow, as though it were a rifle. What's more, just on the other side of that gate is the entrance to the Wakefield Tower. We admit visitors, and there's always a warder on duty there. Good God! Let's be sensible. It couldn't be done."

Hadley nodded placidly.

"I know it couldn't. But, as you say, that's the most likely direction. So what about windows, or the top of a wall?"

"Eh?"

"I said, what about windows or roofs? Where could you stand and shoot a bolt from some such place? I shouldn't have asked, but I can't see anything beyond outlines in this fog."

The general stared at him. Then he nodded curtly. There was a hard, jealous, angry parade-ground ring in his voice when he spoke; it made Rampole jump.

"I see. If you're suggesting, Mr. Hadley, that any member of this garrison—"

"I didn't say that, my dear sir," Hadley answered, mildly. "I asked you a perfectly ordinary question."

The general jammed his hands deeper in the pockets of his water-proof. After a moment he turned sharply and pointed to the opposite wall.

"Up there on your left," he said, "in that block of buildings jutting up above the wall proper, you may be able to make out some windows. They are the windows of the King's House. It is occupied by some of the Yeomen Warders and their families—and by myself, I might add. Then the ramparts of the wall overlooking us run straight along to the Bloody Tower. That space is called Raleigh's Walk, and only a rather tall man can see over the rampart at all. Raleigh's Walk joins the Bloody Tower, in which there are some windows looking down at us. Next to the Bloody Tower on the right, and joined to it, you see that large round tower? That's the Wakefield Tower, where the Crown Jewels are kept. You will find some windows there. You will also—not unnaturally—find two warders on guard. Does that answer your question, sir?"

"Thanks," said the chief inspector; "I'll look into it when the mist clears a bit. If you're ready, gentlemen, I think we can return to the Warders' Hall."

IV

Inquisition

Gently General Mason touched Sir William's arm as they turned away. The latter had not spoken for a long time; he had remained holding to the rail and staring into the dimness of the area; and he did not speak now. He walked quietly at the general's side as they returned.

Still holding the hat under his arm, and propping flashlight against notebook, Hadley made several notations. His heavy, quiet face, with the expressionless dark eyes, was bent close over it in the torch-gleam.

He nodded, and shut up the book.

"To continue, General. About that crossbow bolt. Does it belong here?"

"I have been wondering how long you would take to get to that," the other answered, sharply. "I don't know. I am inquiring. There is a collection of crossbows and a few bolts here; it is in a glass case in the armory on the second floor of the White Tower. But I am perfectly certain nothing has been stolen from there. However, we have a workshop in the Brick Tower, on the other side of the parade-ground, which we use for cleaning and repairing the armor and weapons on display. I've sent for the warder in charge; he should be here now. And he will be able to tell you."

"But *could* one of your display crossbows have been used?"

"Oh yes. They are kept in as careful repair as though we meant to use them as weapons ourselves."

Hadley fell to whistling between his teeth. Then he turned to Dr. Fell.

"For a person who enjoys talking as much as you do, Doctor," he said, "you have been incredibly silent. Have you any ideas?"

A long sniff rumbled in the doctor's nose. "Yes," he returned, "yes, I have. But they don't concern windows or crossbows. They concern hats. Let me have that topper, will you? I shall want to look at it when we get a good light."

Hadley handed it over without a word.

"This," General Mason explained, as they turned to the left at the Byward Tower, "is the smaller Warders' Hall; we have our enforced guests in the other." He pushed open a door under the arch, and motioned to them to pass.

It was not until Rampole entered the warmth of the room that he realized how chilled and stiff he was. A large coal fire crackled under a hooded fireplace. The room was circular and comfortable, with a groined roof from which hung a cluster of electric lights, and cross-slits of windows high up in the wall. There were chairs of hard leather, and bookshelves. Behind a large flat desk, his hands folded upon it, sat a straight-backed elderly man, regarding them from under tufted white eyebrows. He wore the costume of the Yeomen Warders, but his was much more elaborate than those Rampole had seen. Beside him a tall, thin young man with a stoop was making notes on a slip of paper.

"Sit down, gentlemen," said General Mason. "This is Mr. Radburn, the chief warder; and Mr. Dalrye, my secretary."

He waved his guests to chairs after he had performed the introductions, and produced a cigar case. "What have you got now?"

The chief warder shook his head. He pushed out the chair in which he had been sitting for General Mason.

"Not much, I'm afraid, sir. I've just questioned the guards from the White Tower, and the head workman from the repair shop. Mr. Dalrye has the notes in shorthand."

The young man shuffled some papers and blinked at General Mason. He was still rather pale. And instinctively Rampole liked this Robert Dalrye. He had a long, rather doleful face, but a humorous mouth. His sandy hair bristled at all angles, apparently from a tendency to run his hand through it. His good-humored, rather near-sighted gray eyes were bitter; he fumbled with a pair of pince-nez on a chain, and then stared down at his papers.

"Good afternoon, sir," he said to Sir William. "They told me you were here. I—I can't say anything, can I? You know how I feel."

Then, still staring at his papers, he changed the subject with a rush. "I have the notes here, sir," he told General Mason. "Nothing has been stolen from the armory, of course. And the head workman at the shop, as well as both warders from the second floor of the White Tower, are willing to swear that crossbow bolt is not in the collection and never has been in any collection here."

"Why? You can't positively identify a thing like that, can you?"

"John Brownlow got rather technical about it. And he's by way of being an authority, sir. It's here. He says—" Dalrye adjusted his pince-nez and blinked—"he says it's a much earlier type of bolt than any we have here. That is, judging from what he can see of it—in the body. Late fourteenth-century pattern. Ah, here we are. 'The later ones are much shorter and thicker, and with a broader barb at the head. That one's so thin it wouldn't fit smoothly in the groove of any crossbow in the lot.'"

General Mason turned to Hadley, who was carefully removing his overcoat. "You're in charge now. So ask any questions you like. Give that chair to the chief inspector. But I think that proves it wasn't fired, unless you believe the murderer brought his own bow. Then it couldn't have been shot from one of the crossbows here, Dalrye?"

"Brownlow says it could have been, but that there would be a hundred-to-one chance of the bolt going wild."

Mason nodded, and regarded the chief inspector with tight-lipped satisfaction. Rampole saw him for the first time in full light. He had removed his soggy hat and water-proof, and flung them on a bench; evidently there was about him none of that fussiness which is associated with the brass hat. Now he stood warming his hands at the fire, and peering round his shoulder at Hadley: a straight, thick-set figure, rather bald, with ginger mustache and imperial, and a pair of hard, unwinking eyes.

"Well?" he demanded. "What's the first step now?"

Dalrye put down his papers on the table.

"I think you'd better know," he said, speaking between Mason and Sir William. "There are two people here among the visitors who are certain to have an interest in this. They're over with the others in the Warders' Hall. I wish you'd give me instructions, sir. Mrs. Bitton has been raising the devil ever since—"

"*Who?*" demanded Sir William. He had been staring at the fire, and he lifted his head suddenly.

"Mrs. Lester Bitton. As I say, she's been—"

Sir William rumpled his white pompadour and looked blankly at Mason. "My sister-in-law— What on earth would she be doing here?"

Hadley had sat down at the desk, and was arranging note-book, pencil, and flashlight in a line with the utmost precision. He glanced up in mild interest.

"Ah," he said, "I'm glad to hear it. It centers our efforts, so to speak. But don't trouble her for the moment, Mr. Dalrye; we can see her presently." He folded his hands and contemplated Sir William, a wrinkle between his brows. "Why does it surprise you that Mrs. Lester Bitton should be here?"

"Why, *you* know—" Sir William began in some perplexity, and broke off. "No. As a matter of fact, you don't know her, do you? Well, she's of the sporting type; you'll see. I say, did you tell her about—about Philip, Bob?" He spoke hesitantly.

"I had to," Dalrye answered, grimly.

"What did she say?"

"She said I was mad. Among other things."

Hadley had picked up his pencil, and seemed intent on bor-ing a hole in the desk top with its point. He asked, "And the sec-ond person among the visitors, Mr. Dalrye?"

The other frowned. "It's a Mr. Arbor, Inspector. Julius Arbor. He's rather famous as a book-collector, and I believe he's stopping at Sir William's house."

Sir William raised his head. His eyes grew sharp again, for the first time since he had heard the news of the murder; it was curiously as though the color had come back into them, like color into a pale face. His narrow shoulders were a trifle raised, and now they squared.

He said, "Interesting. Damned interesting." And he walked over with a springy step to sit down in a chair near the desk.

"That's better," approved the chief inspector, laying down his pencil. "But for the moment we shan't trouble Mr. Arbor, either. I should like to get the complete story of Mr. Driscoll's movements today. You said something, General, about a rather wild tale connected with it."

General Mason turned from the fire.

"Mr. Radburn," he said to the chief warder, "will you send to the King's House for Parker? Parker," he explained, as the other left the room, "is my orderly and general handy-man. He's been with me since the Boer War, and I know he's absolutely reliable. Meantime, Dalrye, you might tell the chief inspector about the wild-goose chase?"

Dalrye nodded. He looked suddenly older. Putting a hand over his eyes for a moment, he turned uncertainly to Hadley.

"You see, Inspector," he said, "I didn't know what it meant then, and I don't know now. Except that it was a frame-up of some sort against Phil. Do you mind if I sit down and smoke? Thanks."

His long legs were shaking a trifle as he lowered himself into a chair. He got out a cigarette, and Hadley struck a match for him.

"Take your time, Mr. Dalrye," said the chief inspector. "Sir William—excuse me—has told us you are his daughter's fiancé. So I presume you knew young Driscoll well?"

"Very well. I thought a hell of a lot of Phil," Dalrye answered, quietly. He blinked as the smoke got into one eye. "And naturally this business isn't pleasant. Well—you see, he had the idea that I was one of these intensely practical people who can find a way out of any difficulty. He was always getting into scrapes, and always coming to me to help him out of them. Now, I'm not that sort at all. But he was the brooding sort, and any small difficulty seemed like the end of the world; he'd stamp and rave, and swear it was insufferable. You have to understand all this to understand what I'm going to tell you."

"Difficulties?" repeated the chief inspector. He was sitting back in his chair, his eyes half closed, but he was looking at Sir William. "What sort of difficulties?"

Dalrye hesitated. "Financial, as a rule. Nothing important. He'd run up bills, and things like that."

"Women?" asked Hadley, suddenly.

"Oh, Lord! Don't we all?" demanded the other, uncomfortably. "I mean to say—" He flushed. "Sorry. But nothing important there, either; I know that. He was always ringing me up in the middle of the night to say he'd met some girl at a dance who was the absolute One and Only. He would rave. It lasted about a month, generally."

"But nothing serious? Excuse me, Mr. Dalrye," said the chief inspector, as the other waved his hand, "but I am looking for a motive for murder, you know. I have to ask such questions. So there was nothing serious?"

"No."

"Please go on. You said that you helped him."

"I was flattered, I suppose. And I liked to feel I was—well, helping somebody close to Sheila. We all do, hang it. We like playing the all-wise director of destinies; the Olympian angle. Bah! Anyway, as I say, you've got to understand his nature to understand today."

For a moment Dalrye drew deeply on his cigarette.

"He telephoned here early this morning, and Parker answered the telephone in the general's study. I wasn't up yet, as a matter of fact. He began talking rather incoherently, Parker says, and said they were to tell me he would be down here at the Tower at one o'clock sharp; that he was in bad trouble and needed help. In the middle of it I heard my name mentioned, and came out and talked to him myself.

"I thought it was probably nothing at all, but to humor him I said I should be here. Though, I told him, I had to go out early in the afternoon.

"You see, if it hadn't been for that— As it happened, General Mason had asked me to take the touring-car up to a garage in Holborn and have the horn repaired. It's an electric horn, and it got so that if you pressed it you couldn't stop the thing's blowing."

Hadley frowned. "A garage in Holborn? That's rather unnecessarily out of the way, isn't it?"

Again a dull anger was at the back of Mason's eyes. He was standing with his back to the fireplace, legs wide apart; he spoke curtly.

"Quite right, sir. You see it in a moment. But it happens to be run by an old army man; a sergeant, by the way, who did me rather a good turn once. I have all my motor repair work done there."

"Ah," said Hadley. "Well, Mr. Dalrye?"

Rampole, leaning against a row of bookshelves with an unlighted cigarette in his fingers, tried again to imagine that all this was real; that he was really being drawn again into the dodges and terrors of a murder case. Undoubtedly it was true. But there was a difference between this affair and the murder of Martin Starberth. He was not, now, vitally concerned in its outcome. Through chance and courtesy he was allowed to be present merely as a witness, detached and unprejudiced, of the lighted playbox where lay a corpse in an opera hat.

It was as bright as a play in the ancient room. There behind the desk sat the patient, watchful chief inspector, with his steel-wire hair and his clipped mustache, indolently folding his hands. On one side of him sat Sir William, his shrewdness glittering again behind impassive eyes; and on the other was the thin, wry-faced Robert Dalrye, staring at his cigarette. Still bristling, General Mason stood with his back to the fire. And in the largest chair over against the fireplace, Dr. Fell had spread himself out—and he was contemplating with an owlish and naive gaze the opera hat in his hands. He hardly lifted his eyes from the hat; he turned it over and over, wheezing. This taciturnity irritated Rampole. He was used to hearing the doctor roar with a sort of genial wrath, and trample down everybody's opinions before him. No, it was unnatural; it worried the American.

He became aware that Dalrye was speaking, and jerked his thoughts back.

". . . so I didn't think much more about it. That was all, until somewhere about one o'clock, the time Phil said he would be here. The phone rang again, and Parker answered it. It was Phil, asking for me. At least," said Dalrye, squashing out his cigarette suddenly, "it sounded like Phil. I was in the record room at the time, working on the notes for the general's book, and Parker transferred the call. Phil was more chaotic than he had been in the morning. He said that, for a reason he couldn't explain over the phone, he couldn't come to the Tower, but that I had got to come to his flat and see him. He used his old phrase—I'd heard it dozens of times before—that it was a matter of life or death.

"I was annoyed. I said I had work to do, and I damned well wouldn't do it, and that if he wanted to see me he could come down here. Then he swore it really was a matter of life or death. And he said I had to come to Town, anyway; his flat was in Bloomsbury, and I had to take the car to a garage which wasn't very far away; it wouldn't be out of my way if I dropped in. That was perfectly true. I couldn't very well see a way out of it. So I agreed. I even promised to start at once."

Dalrye shifted in his chair. "I'll admit—well, it *did* sound more convincing than the other times. I thought he might really have got himself into a genuine mess this time. So I went."

"Had you any definite reason to believe this?"

"N-no. Yes. Well, make of it what you like." Dalrye's gaze strayed across to the corner, where Dr. Fell was still examining the top hat with absorbed interest. Dalrye shifted uneasily. "You see, Phil had been in rather high spirits recently. That was why I was so surprised at this change of front. He had been making a play with his stories on this hat thief thing—you know?"

"We have good reason to know," the inspector said. His look had suddenly become one of veiled interest. "Go on, please."

"It was the sort of story he could do admirably. He'd been free-lancing, and he hoped the editor might give him a permanent column. So, as I say, I was astonished when I heard him say what he did. And I remember, I said, 'What's the row, anyway? I thought you were following the hat thief.' And he said, 'That's just it,' in a sort of queer, horrible voice. 'I've followed it too far. I've stirred up something, and it's got me.'"

Rampole felt a stab of something like fear. From Dalrye's description it was easy to picture the dapper, volatile Driscoll, white-faced, talking wildly into the telephone. The chief inspector leaned forward.

"Yes?" he prompted. "You gathered that Driscoll thought he was in danger from this hat thief; is that it?"

"Something like that. Naturally, I joked about it. I remember asking, 'What's the matter; are you afraid he'll steal your hat?' And he said—"

"Well?"

"'It's not my hat I'm worried about. It's my head.'"

There was a long silence. Then Hadley spoke almost casually. "So you left the Tower to go to his place. What then?"

"Now comes the odd part of it. I drove up to the garage; it's in Dane Street, High Holborn. The mechanic was busy on a job at the moment. He said he could fix the horn in a few minutes, but I should have to wait until he finished with the car he was working on. So I decided to walk to the flat, and pick up the car later. There was no hurry."

Hadley reached for his notebook. "The address of the flat?"

"Tavistock Chambers, 34, Tavistock Square, W.C. It's number two, on the ground floor. Well, when I got there I rang at his door for a long time, and nobody answered. So I went in."

"The door was open?"

"No. But I have a key. You see, the gates of the Tower of London are closed at ten o'clock sharp every night, and the King himself would have a time getting in after that. So, when I went to a theatre or a dance or something of the sort, I had to have a place to stay the night, and I usually stopped on the couch in Phil's sitting room. Where was I? Oh yes. Well, I sat down to wait for him. I supposed he was at a pub or something. But the fact is—"

Dalrye drew a long breath. He put the palm of his hand suddenly down on the table.

"About fifteen minutes or so after I had left the Tower, Phil Driscoll appeared at the general's quarters here and asked for me. Parker naturally said I had gone out in response to his phone message. Then, Parker says, Phil got as pale as death; he began to rave and call Parker mad. He had phoned that morning asking to see me at one o'clock. But he swore he had not changed the appointment. He swore he had never telephoned a second time at all."

V

The Shadow by the Rail

HADLEY STIFFENED. He laid down the pencil quietly, but there were tight muscles down the line of his jaw. It was silent in the stone room save for the crackle of the fire.

"Just so," he said, quietly, after a pause. "What then?"

"I waited. It was getting foggier, and it had started to rain, and I got impatient. I was cursing Phil and everybody else. Then the phone in the flat rang, and I answered it.

"It was Parker, telling me what I've just told you. He had called once before to get me, but I was at the garage and hadn't arrived. Phil was waiting for me at the Tower, in a hell of a stew. Parker said he wasn't drunk, and I thought somebody had gone mad. But there was nothing to do but return; I had to do that, anyway. I hurried over to get the car, and when I was leaving the garage I met the general."

"You also," inquired Hadley, glancing up, "were in town, General?"

Mason was gloomily regarding his shoes. He looked up with a somewhat satiric expression.

"It would seem so. I had a luncheon engagement, and afterwards I went to the British Museum to pick up some books they had for me. As Dalrye says, it began to rain, so of course there weren't any taxis. And I hate traveling by tube or bus. No privacy. A man's packed in with the herd. Bah! Then I remembered the car would probably be at Stapleman's garage; or, if it weren't, Stapleman would lend me a car to go back in. It's not far away from the Museum, so I started out. And I saw Dalrye in the car, and hailed him. I've told you the rest of it. We got here at two-thirty, and found—him."

There was another long silence. Hadley was sitting forward with his elbows on the desk, rubbing his temples with heavy fingers. Then, from the corner, a curious, rumbling, thoughtful voice spoke.

"Was it a very important luncheon engagement, General Mason?" asked Dr. Fell.

The query was startling in its very naiveté, and they all turned to look at him. His round and ruddy face was sunk into his collar, the great white plumed mop of hair straggling over one ear, and Dr. Fell was staring through his glasses at the top hat in a weirdly cross-eyed fashion. He looked quite vacant.

The general stared. "I don't think I understand, sir."

"Was it by any chance," pursued the doctor, still blankly, "a society of some sort, a board of directors' meeting, a gathering of—"

"As a matter of fact," said Mason, "it was." He seemed puzzled, and his hard eyes grew brighter. "The Antiquarians' Society. We meet for lunch on the first Monday of every month. I don't like the crowd. Gaa-a! Sedentary fossils of the worst type. Hit 'em with a feather pillow, and they'd collapse. I only stay in the organization because you get the benefit of their knowledge on a doubtful question. I have to attend the lunch to stay in, but I leave as soon as I can. Sir Leonard Haldyne—the Keeper of the Jewels here—

drove me up in his car at noon. He's a soldier, and good company, and he feels as I do about it. But wait a bit. Why do you ask?"

"H'mf. Yes." The doctor nodded ponderously. "I suppose your membership in the society is well known?"

"All my friends know of it, if that's what you mean. It seems to amuse them at the Rag."

Hadley nodded slowly, contemplating Dr. Fell. "I begin to see what you're driving at. Tell me, General. You and Mr. Dalrye were the only people at the Tower whom young Driscoll knew at all well?"

"Ye-es, I suppose so. I think he'd met Sir Leonard, and he had a nodding acquaintance with a number of the warders, but—"

"But you were the only ones he'd be apt to call on, weren't you?"

"Probably."

Dalrye's mouth opened a trifle, and he sat up. Then he sank back into his chair. His fist hammered slowly on the arm.

"I see, sir. You mean, then—you mean the murderer had made certain both General Mason and I were out?" The doctor spoke in a testy voice, ringing the ferrule of his cane as he hammered it on the floor.

"Of course he did. If you had been here, he'd certainly have been with you. If the general had been here in your absence, he might have been with the general. And the murderer wouldn't have any chance to lure him to a suitable spot in the fog and put an end to him."

Dalrye looked troubled. "All the same," he said, "I'm willing to swear it was really Phil's voice on the phone that second time. My God! man—excuse me, sir!" He swallowed, and as Dr. Fell only beamed blandly he went on with more assurance, "What I mean is, I knew that voice as well as I knew anybody's. And if what you say is true, it couldn't have been Phil's voice at all. Besides, how did this person, whoever it was, know that Phil had arranged to meet me down here at one o'clock? And why all the rigmarole about being 'afraid of his head'?"

"Those facts," said Dr. Fell composedly, "may provide us with very admirable clues. Think them over. By the way, what sort of voice did young Driscoll have?"

"What sort of—? Well—" Dalrye hesitated. "The only way to describe it is incoherent. He thought so fast that he ran miles ahead of what he was trying to say. And when he was excited his voice tended to grow high."

Dr. Fell, his head on one side and his eyes half closed, was nodding slowly. He peered up as a knock sounded at the door, and the chief warder entered. He had moved through these events as unruffled as he might have moved on this afternoon round of inspection; a precise, mediaeval figure in blue-and-red uniform, with a long mustache carefully brushed.

"The police surgeon is here, sir," he said, "and several other men from Scotland Yard. Are there any instructions?"

Hadley started to rise, and reconsidered. "No. Just tell them the usual routine, if you please; they'll understand. I want about a dozen pictures of the body, from all angles. Is there any place the body can conveniently be taken for examination?"

"The Bloody Tower, Mr. Radburn," said General Mason. "Use the Princes' Room; that's very suitable. Have you got Parker here?"

"Outside, sir. Have you any instructions about those visitors? They're getting impatient, and—"

"In a moment," said Hadley. "Would you mind sending Parker in?" As the chief warder withdrew, he turned to Dalrye. "You have those visitors' names?"

"Yes. And I rather overstepped my rights," said Dalrye. He

drew from his wallet a number of sheets of paper torn from a notebook. "I was very solemn about it. I instructed them to write down names, addresses, occupations, and references. If they were foreigners, their length of stay in the United Kingdom, the boat they landed on, and where they intended to go. Most of them were obvious tourists, and they got alarmed at the red tape; I don't think there's any harm in them, and they didn't show any fight. Except Mrs. Bitton, that is. And one other woman."

He handed the bundle of sheets to Hadley. The chief inspector glanced up sharply. "One other woman? Who was she?"

"I didn't notice what she wrote, but I remembered her name from the way she acted. Hard-faced party. You see, I had it all very official, to scare 'em into writing the truth. And this woman was wary. She said, 'You're not a notary, are you, young man?' and I was so surprised that I looked at her. Then she said, 'You've got no right to do this, young man. We're not under oath. My name is Larkin, and I'm a respectable widow, and that's all you need to know.' I said she could do as she liked, but if she found herself in jug it was no affair of mine. She said, 'Bah!' and glared a bit. But she wrote down something."

Hadley shuffled through the papers.

"Larkin," he repeated. "H'm. We must look into this. When the net goes out, we often get small fish we're not after at all. Larkin, Larkin—here it is. 'Mrs. Amanda Georgette Larkin.' The 'Mrs.' in brackets; she wants that clearly understood. Stiff handwriting. Address— Hallo!"

He put down the sheets and frowned. "Well, well! The address is 'Tavistock Chambers, 34, Tavistock Square.' So she lives in the same building as young Driscoll, eh? This is getting to be quite a convention. We'll see her presently. For the moment—"

Sir William had been rubbing his jaw uneasily. He said, "Look here, Hadley, it isn't quite the thing— I mean, don't you think you'd better bring Mrs. Bitton away from the crowd? She's my sister-in-law, you know, and after all—"

"Most unfortunate," said Hadley, composedly. "Where's that man Parker?"

Parker was a most patient man. He had been standing hatless and coatless in the fog just outside the crack of the door, waiting to be summoned. At Hadley's remark he knocked, came inside, and stood at attention.

He was a square, brownish, grizzled man with a military cut. Like most corporals of his particular day, he ran largely to mustache; nor did he in the least resemble a valet. The high white collar pinioned his head, as though he were having a daguerreotype taken, and gave him a curious expression of seeming to talk over his inquisitor's head.

"Yussir," he said, gruffly and quickly.

"You are General Mason's—" Hadley was going to say "valet," as fitting to a retired commander, but he substituted "orderly." "You are General Mason's orderly?"

Parker looked pleased. "Yussir."

"Mr. Dalrye has already told us of the two phone calls from Mr. Driscoll. You answered the phone both times, I believe?"

Parker was ready. His voice was hoarse, but his aspirates under perfect control, and he tended, if anything, to be a trifle flowery. This was an important occasion.

"Yussir. On both occasions I had reason to go to the telephone, sir."

"So you had some conversation with Mr. Driscoll?"

"I did, sir. Our talks was not lengthy, but full of meat."

"Er—quite so," said the chief inspector. "Now, could you swear it was Mr. Driscoll's voice both times?"

Parker frowned. "Well, sir, when you say, 'Could you swear it?'—that's a long word," he answered, judicially. "To the best of my knowledge and discernment from previous occasions, sir, it were."

"Very well. Now, Mr. Dalrye left here in the car shortly before one o'clock. Do you remember at what time Mr. Driscoll arrived?"

"One-fifteen, sir."

"How are you so positive?"

"Excuse me, sir," Parker said, stolidly. "I can inform you of everything that happens at the time which it happens, exact, sir, by the movements at the barracks. Or by the bugles. One-fifteen it was."

Hadley leaned back and tapped his fingers slowly on the desk.

"Now, take your time, Parker. I want you to remember everything that happened after Mr. Driscoll arrived. Try to remember conversations, if you can. First, what was his manner? Nervous? Upset?"

"Very nervous *and* upset, sir."

"And how was he dressed?"

"Cloth cap, light-brown golf suit, worsted stockings, club tie, sir. No overcoat—" He paused for prompting, but Hadley was silent, and he went on. "He asked for Mr. Dalrye. I said Mr. Dalrye had gone to his rooms in response to his own message. He then demonstrated incredulity. He used strong language, at which I was forced to say, 'Mr. Driscoll, sir,' I said, 'I talked to you myself.' I said, 'When I answered the telephone you thought I was Mr. Dalrye; and you said all in a rush, "Look here, you've got to help me out—I can't come down now, and—" That's what you said.'" Parker cleared his throat. "I explained that to him, sir."

"What did he say?"

"He said, 'How long has Mr. Dalrye been gone?' I told him

about fifteen minutes. And he said, 'Was he in the car?' and I said 'Yes,' and he said—excuse me, sir—'Oh, my God! that's not long enough to drive up there on a foggy day.' But, anyway, he went to the telephone and rang up his own flat. There was no answer. He said to get him a drink, which I did. And while I was getting it I noticed that he kept looking out of the window."

Hadley opened his half-closed eyes. "Window? What window?"

"The window of the little room where Mr. Dalrye works, sir, in the east wing of the King's House."

"What can you see from there?"

Parker, who had become so interested in his story that he forgot to be flowery, blinked and tried to right his thoughts. "See, sir?"

"Yes! The view. Can you see the Traitors' Gate, for instance?"

"Oh. Yussir! I thought you was referring to—well, sir, to something *I* saw, which I didn't think was important, but now I get to thinking—" He shifted from one foot to the other.

"*You* saw something?"

"Yussir. That is, it was after Mr. Driscoll had left me, sir."

Hadley seemed to fight down a desire to probe hard. He had half-risen, but he sat back and said, evenly, "Very well. Now go on with the story, Parker, from the time you saw Mr. Driscoll looking out of the window."

"Very good, sir. He finished his drink, and had another neat. I asked him why he didn't go back to his flat, if he wanted to see Mr. Dalrye; I said he could take the tube at Mark Lane and it wouldn't be a very long ride. And he said, 'Don't be a fool; I don't want to take the chance of missing him again.' Which was sound sense, sir. He said, 'We'll keep ringing my place very five minutes until I know where he is.'"

Parker recounted the conversations in a gruff, sing-song voice, and in such a monotone that Rampole could tell only with difficulty where he was quoting Driscoll and where he spoke himself. The words were thrown steadily over Hadley's head.

"But he could not sit still, sir. He roamed about. Finally he said, 'My-God-I-can't-stand-this; I'm going for a walk in the grounds.' He instructed me to keep ringing his flat after Mr. Dalrye, and that he would keep close within call. So he went out."

"How long was he with you?"

"A matter of ten minutes, say, sir. No; it was less than that. Well, sir, I paid no more attention. I should not have seen anything, except—" Parker hesitated. He saw the veiled gleam in Hadley's eyes; he saw Sir William bent forward, and Dalrye pausing with a match almost to his cigarette. And he seemed to realize he was a person of importance. He gave the hush its full value.

"—except, sir," he suddenly continued in a louder voice, "for the match-in-ashuns of fate. I may remark, sir, that earlier in the day there had been a light mist. But nothing of what might be termed important. It was possible to see some distance, and objects was distinct. But it was a-growing very misty. That was how I come to look out of the window. And that was when I saw Mr. Driscoll."

Hadley's fingers stopped tapping while he scrutinized the other. Then they began to tap again, more rapidly.

"How did you know it was Mr. Driscoll? You said the mist was thickening."

"So it were. Yussir!" agreed Parker, nodding so vigorously that the points of his collar jabbed his neck. "I didn't say I saw his face. Nobody could have recognized him that way: he were just an outline. *But,* sir, wait! There was his size. There was his plus-fours, which he alwis wore lower-down than other gentlemen.

And when he went out he was a-wearing his cap with the top all pulled over to one side. Then I saw him walking back and forth in Water Lane in front of the Traitors' Gate, back and forth, and I knew his walk."

"But you can't swear it was actually he?"

"Yussir. I can. Becos, sir, he went to the rail in front of Traitors' Gate and leaned on it. And whereupon he struck a match to light a cigarette. And—mind you, sir, if you'll excuse me—not another man here has the eyesight *I* have, and just for a second I saw part of the face. It was one of them big sputtering matches, sir, if you know what I mean. Yussir, I'm positive. I know. I saw 'im just before the other person touched 'im on the arm."

"*What?*" demanded Hadley, with such suddenness that Parker took it for a slur on his veracity.

"Sir, so help me God. The other person that was standing over by the side of Traitors' Gate. And that come out and touched Mr. Driscoll on the arm. Mind, sir, I'm not sure of that, becos the match was out. But it looked as though "

"I see," Hadley agreed, mildly. "Did you see this other person, Parker?"

"No sir. It was too dark there; shadowed, sir. I shouldn't even have seen Mr. Driscoll if I hadn't been watching him and saw 'im strike the match. It were what I should call a Shape."

"Could you tell whether this person was a man or a woman?"

"Er—no, sir. No. Besides," explained Parker, drawing in his neck again, "it were not in any manner of speaking as though I was watching, sir. I turned away then. I was not endowed with the opportunity to see no further occurrences."

"Quite. Do you know at what time this was?"

Parker screwed his face up into a grimace which was evidently regret. "Ah!" he said profoundly, "ah, I confess you've got me, sir. You see, it transpired between the quarter-hours of the clock. It were shortly past one-thirty. More I couldn't tell you, not if I wanted to, sir. Except I know it were not so late as a quarter to two. Becos that was when I phoned Mr. Driscoll's flat again and Mr. Dalrye had arrived there, and I told him Mr. Driscoll was here a-waiting."

Hadley brooded, his head in his hands. After a time he looked across at General Mason.

"And the doctor here said, General, that when you discovered the body at two-thirty Driscoll had been dead at least half an hour—probably three-quarters? Yes. Well, that's that. He was murdered within ten minutes or fifteen minutes after this so-called Shape touched his arm at the rail. The police surgeon will be able to tell us exactly. He's rather a wizard at that sort of thing."

He paused, and looked sharply at Parker.

"You didn't notice anything more, did you? That is, you didn't go to look for Mr. Driscoll, to tell him you'd found Mr. Dalrye?"

"No, sir. I knew he would come back and ask me, if he was that impatient, and, anyway, Mr. Dalrye was a-coming down here. Though he swore some. I thought it was funny Mr. Driscoll not coming up to ask, sir. Of course," Parker said, deprecatingly, "I can comprehend at the present juncture why he didn't."

"I think we all can," said the chief inspector, grimly. "Very well, Parker. That's all, and thank you. You've been most helpful."

Parker clicked his heels and went out glowing.

The chief inspector drew a long breath. "Well, gentlemen, there you are. That fixes us. The murderer had considerably over half an hour's time to clear out. And, as the general says, what between rain and fog the sentries at the gates wouldn't have been able to see anything of a person who slipped out. Now we get down to work. Our first hope—"

He picked up the sheets containing the names of the visitors.

"Since we have something to go on," he continued, "we can use our guests. We know the approximate time of the murder. Hallo!" he called towards the door, and a warder opened it. "Will you go down to the Bloody Tower and send up the sergeant in charge of the police officers who have just arrived? Thanks."

"I hope it's Hamper," he added to his companions. "It probably is, too. First, we'll put aside the slips made out by the three people we want to interview ourselves—Mrs. Bitton, Mr. Arbor, and, just as a precaution, the careful Mrs. Larkin. Let's see, Larkin—"

"Mrs. Bitton didn't make out any, sir," Dalrye told him. "She laughed at the idea."

"Right, then. Here's the Arbor one. Let's see. I say, that's a beautiful handwriting; like the lettering on a calling-card. Fastidious, this chap." He examined the paper curiously. "'Julius Arbor. 440 Park Avenue, New York City. No occupation.'"

"Doesn't need one," Sir William growled. "He's got pots."

"'Arrived Southampton, March 4th, S.S. Bremen. Duration of stay indefinite. Destination, Villa Seule, Nice, France.' He adds, very curtly, 'If further information is necessary, suggest communicating with my London solicitors, Messrs. Hillton and Dane, Lincoln's Inn Fields.' H'm."

He smiled to himself, put the sheet aside, and glanced hastily at the others.

"If you've ever heard any of these other names, gentlemen, sing out; otherwise I'll let the sergeant handle them.

"Mr. and Mrs. George G. Bebber, 291 Aylesborough Avenue, Pittsburgh, Pa., U.S.A. Jno. Simms, High Street, Glytton, Hants. He adds, 'Of the well-known plumbers, as above.' Mr. and Mrs. John Smith, Surbiton. Well, well! That's descriptive enough. Lucien Lefèvre, 60 Avenue Foch, Paris. Mlle Clémentine Lefèvre, as above. Miss Dorothea Delevan Mercenay, 23 Elm Avenue, Meadville, Ohio, U.S.A. Miss Mercenay adds M.A. to her name, underscored heavily. That's the lot. They sound harmless enough."

"Sergeant Betts, sir," said a voice at the door. A very serious-faced young man saluted nervously. He had obviously expected an inspector, and the presence of the chief was disturbing.

"Betts," said Hadley. "Betts—oh yes. Did you get a picture of the dead man's face?"

"Yes, sir. They've set up the outfit in that Tower place, and the pictures are drying now. Ready in two seconds, sir."

"Right. Take a copy of that picture and show it to all the people listed here; the warder will show you where they are. Ask them if they saw him today; when and where. Be particular about *anybody* they may have seen in the vicinity of the Traitors' Gate at any time, or anybody acting suspiciously. Mr. Dalrye, I should be obliged if you would go along and make shorthand notes of anything important. Thanks. And—"

Dalrye rose, reaching for pencil and notebook.

"I want particularly to know, Betts, where they were between one-thirty and one-forty-five o'clock. That's vital. Mr. Dalrye, will you kindly ask Mrs. Lester Bitton to step in here?"

VI

The Souvenir Crossbow Bolt

"Now, THEN," Hadley pursued. Again with meticulous attention he straightened the pencil, the notebook, and the flashlight before him. "The police surgeon will bring in the contents of Driscoll's pockets, and we can have a good look at the weapon. I'll leave it up to the chief warder to take charge of questioning the warders about whether they saw anything. How many warders are there altogether, General?"

"Forty."

"H'm. It's unlikely that Driscoll would have strayed far from the vicinity of the King's House; he was waiting for that phone call. Still, we shall have to go through with it."

General Mason bit off the end of a cigar. "If you're going to question the whole personnel of the Tower," he observed, "that's the least of your worries. There is a battalion of the Guards stationed here, you know, to say nothing of workmen and attendants and servants."

"If necessary," Hadley answered, placidly, "we'll do it. Now, gentlemen. Before we see Mrs. Bitton, suppose we try to clarify our ideas. Let's go around the circle here, and see what we all have to say. Sir William, what strikes *you* about the case?"

He addressed the knight, but out of the corner of his eye he was looking at Dr. Fell. The doctor, Rampole noted, again with vague irritation, was otherwise occupied. A large, damp, shaggy Airedale, with affectionate eyes and a manner as naive as the doctor's, had wandered into the room and bounded instantly for Dr. Fell. The Airedale was sitting up, ears cocked expectantly, while the doctor bent over to ruffle his head.

Rampole tried to collect muddled thoughts. He was here purely by chance, and he had somehow to justify his presence. When Hadley again mentioned the weapon a moment ago, it stirred some question which had been at the back of his brain since Dalrye had read out the warder's description of the type of crossbow bolt with which Driscoll was slain. He saw once more the thin, polished steel protruding from the dead man's chest, and the question in his mind grew sharper. He was not sure he could explain it.

Sir William was speaking now. His face was still dull, but the deadness of shock was beginning to pass from it. Before long he would be again his sharp, jerky, impetuous self.

"That's easy," he said, twisting the ends of his white scarf. "You can't miss it. It's the absolute lack of motive. Nobody in the world had the slightest reason for killing Philip. If there was anything you could safely say about him, it was that everybody liked him."

"Yes. But you're forgetting one thing," Hadley pointed out. "We're dealing in some fashion with a madman. It's useless to deny that this hat thief is mixed up in it. Whether he killed Philip Driscoll or not, he seems to have put that hat on his head. Now, from what Dalrye said, it's clear that Driscoll was on the hatman's track pretty closely."

"But, good God, man! You can't seriously suggest that this

fellow killed Philip because Philip found out who he was! That's absurd."

"Quite. But worth looking into. Therefore, what's our obvious move?"

Sir William's hooded eyelids dropped. "I see. Philip was turning in regular copy to his newspaper. One of his articles appeared today, in the morning edition. That means he turned it in last night. And if he went to the office, he may have told his editor something?"

"Precisely. That's our first fine of inquiry. If by any wild chance his agitation today was caused by some sort of threat, it would probably have been sent *to* the office; or at least he might have mentioned it there. It's worth trying."

There was a deep, delighted chuckle. Hadley looked up in some annoyance, to see Dr. Fell stroking the dog's head and beaming at him with one eye closed.

"Rubbish," said Dr. Fell.

"Indeed?" said the chief inspector, with heavy politeness. "Would you mind telling us why?"

The doctor made a capacious gesture. "Hadley, you know your own game, Heaven knows. But you don't know the newspaper business. I, for my sins, do. Did you ever hear the story of the cub reporter whose first assignment was to cover a big Pacifist meeting in the West End? Well, he came back with a doleful face. 'Where's your story?' says the city editor. 'I couldn't get one,' says the cub; 'there wasn't any meeting.' 'No meeting?' says the city editor. 'Why not?' 'Well,' says the cub, 'the first speaker had no sooner got started than somebody threw a brick at him. And then Lord Dinwiddie fell through the bass drum, and a fight started all around the platform, and they began hitting each other over the head with the chairs, and when I saw the Black Maria at the door I knew there wouldn't be any more meeting, so I left.'"

Dr. Fell shook his head sadly. "'That's the sort of picture you're drawing, Hadley. Man, don't you see that if Driscoll had found out anything, or particularly been threatened, it would have been *news?* News in capitals. HAT FIEND THREATENS *DAILY SOMETHING* MAN. Certainly he'd have mentioned it at the office; he was trying desperately to get on the staff, wasn't he? And the stupidest cub in Fleet Street wouldn't have passed up such an opportunity. Rest assured you'd have seen it today on the first page."

"He mightn't," Hadley said, irritably, "if he had been as nervous as he seems to have been. He'd have kept it to himself."

"Wait a bit. You're wrong there," put in Sir William. "Give the boy his due. Whatever he was, he wasn't a coward. His upsets never came because he feared any sort of violence; he was only upset over—well, messes, as you've heard."

"But he said—"

"That isn't the point, you see," Dr. Fell said, patiently. "To publish anything of the sort couldn't have done any harm. They might say they'd found a vital clue, or that there had been a threat. The first would only warn their victim. The second would have been more publicity, which the hat fellow wanted in the first place; look at the way he acts. It would have done no harm, and assuredly it would have helped young Driscoll's job."

"Suppose he'd actually found out who the man was, though?"

"Why, the newspaper would have communicated with the police, and Driscoll would have got the credit and more assignments. Do you seriously think anybody would have been afraid, at the time, of a person who seemed to be a mere genial practical joker? No, no. You're letting the hat on the corpse run away with your own sense of humor. It's unbalanced you. There's another explanation, I think. I'm willing to agree with Sir William's statement that the boy wasn't a coward; but what was it he *did* fear? There's a tip. Think it over."

Grunting, he returned his attention to the dog.

"I have something to say to you in a moment," the chief inspector told him. "But, for the moment, let's continue. Have you any suggestions, General?"

General Mason had been smoking glumly. He took the cigar out of his mouth and shook his head.

"None whatever. Except that it's fairly obvious now he was stabbed and not shot with that bolt. That's what I'd thought all along."

"Mr. Rampole?" Hadley saw that the American was ill at ease, and he raised his eyebrows encouragingly. "You've said nothing at all so far, which is wise. Any ideas?"

Three pairs of eyes were fixed on him, and he tried to be casual under the scrutiny. This might be the test as to whether he heard anything more of the case after today. He couldn't keep shoving his ideas at them like a cocksure schoolboy; and when he was asked for them, he had to talk sense.

"There was something," he said, feeling his voice a trifle unsteady. "Though it's probably not important. It's this. The crossbow bolt didn't come from the collection here, and one of the warders said its pattern was late fourteenth century. Now, it isn't probable, is it, that Driscoll was really killed with a steel bolt made in thirteen hundred and something?" He hesitated. "I used to dabble a bit with arms and armor; one of the finest collections in the world is at the Metropolitan Museum in New York. In a bolt so old as that one, the steel would be far gone in corrosion. Would it be possible to get that bright polish and temper of the one used to kill Driscoll? It looks new, and not thinned at all. If I remember correctly, you have no arms exhibits here previous to the fifteenth century. And even your early-fifteenth-century helmets are worn to a sort of rusty shell."

There was a silence. "I begin to see," nodded the chief inspector. "You mean that the bolt is of recent manufacture. And if it is—?"

"Well, sir, if it is, who made it? Certainly there aren't many smiths turning out crossbow bolts of fourteenth-century pattern. It may be a curio of some kind, or there may be somebody who does it for amusement or for decorative purposes. I don't suppose it was made here?"

"By Gad!" General Mason said, softly, "I believe he's got something. No. No, young man, I'm pretty sure it wasn't made here, or they'd have mentioned it."

Hadley made a note in his black book. "It's a long shot," he remarked, shaking his head, "but undoubtedly there's something in it. Good work! Now we come to my usually garrulous colleague, Dr. Fell. For Lord's sake," he snapped, in exasperation, "let that damned dog alone, will you, and try to pay some attention? What are your erudite comments on the testimony we've heard?"

Dr. Fell cocked his head on one side. He seemed to meditate.

"The testimony," he repeated, as though he were coming upon a new angle of the case. "Ah yes. The testimony. Why, I'm afraid I wasn't paying a great deal of attention to it. However, I do want to ask one question."

"That's gratifying. What is it?"

"This hat." He picked up the topper and flourished it. "I suppose you noticed. When it was put on the boy's head, it slid down over his ears like the bowler on a Hebrew comedian in a comedy. Of course, he's very small, Sir William, and you're tall. But you have rather a long and narrow head. Wasn't it too large even for you?"

"Too—" The other looked bewildered. "Why, no! No, it wasn't too large. Hold on, though. I remember now. When I was trying on hats at the shop, I remember one I tried on, among others, was too large. But the one they sent me was quite all right, a good fit."

"Well, would you mind putting this one on?"

Sir William sat back. For a moment he seemed about to stretch out his hand, as General Mason took the hat from Dr. Fell and passed it across. Then he sat rigid.

"You'll have to excuse me," he said through his teeth. "I—sorry, but I can't do it."

"Well, well, it's of no consequence," Dr. Fell said, genially. He took back the hat, pressed it down so that it collapsed, and fanned his ruddy face with it. "Not for the moment, anyhow. Who are your hatters?"

"Steele's, in Regent Street. Why?"

"Mrs. Lester Bitton," said a voice at the door. The warder on guard pushed it open.

Mrs. Bitton was not backward. She came into the room with an assurance which betokened a free stride, and she radiated energy. Mrs. Bitton was a slim woman in the late twenties, with a sturdy, well-shaped figure like a swimmer's. If on close observation she was not exactly pretty, health and vigor made her seem so. Even in winter she seemed to have a suspicion of tan; she had level, rather shining brown eyes, a straight nose, and a humorous but determined mouth. Her light-brown hair was caught under the tilt of a tight blue hat; beneath a broad fur collar the tight-fitting coat showed off her full breasts and rather voluptuous hips. As she caught sight of Sir William she became less assured. The level eyes grew somber.

"Hallo!" she said. The voice was quick and self-determined. "Bob didn't tell me you were here. I'm sorry you got here so soon." She studied him, and added, with complete seriousness, "You're not built for this sort of thing nowadays. It's bad for you. You ought to take it easy."

Sir William performed the introductions, and sat down again with the air of one who says, "You see? These modern women!" Rampole set out a chair for her beside Hadley's desk. She sat down, subjected them all to an inspection, took a cigarette out of her purse, and lit it before anybody could offer her a match.

"So you're Mr. Hadley," she observed, studying him with her head slightly back. Then she looked at Sir William. "I've heard Will speak of you." Once more she made a cool inspection of everybody in the room, finally craning round the better to see Dr. Fell. "And these are your inspectors or something. I'm afraid I kicked up rather a row across the way. It was stuffy in there, and some impossible woman kept talking to me. But then I didn't know. Even when Bob told me—told me it was Phil, I didn't believe him."

Despite her assurance Rampole got a definite impression that she was nervous and that she had made this strong initial rush to carry her over some sort of barrier. She knocked some ashes on the floor, and kept tapping her cigarette over it afterwards.

Hadley was impassive. "You know the circumstances, Mrs. Bitton?"

"What Bob was able to tell me. Poor Phil! I'd like to—" She paused, seeming to meditate punishments for a murderer, and jerked her hand to dislodge non-existent ashes from the cigarette. "Of course it was absurd asking me to fill out that silly paper. As though I had to explain."

"It was merely a matter of form. However, you understand

that all the people who were here near the time of the tragedy must be questioned. We brought you here first," Hadley smiled, "because we wanted to get the routine business over with as soon as possible."

"Of course I understand that. I've read detective stories." She looked at him sharply. "When was Phil killed?"

"We'll come to that in a moment, Mrs. Bitton." Hadley smiled and made an urbane gesture. "Let's get things in order, if you don't mind. To begin with, I dare say this isn't the first time you've visited the Tower? Naturally, you're interested in the—er—historic treasures of the place?"

A rather humorous look crept into her face. "*That's* a gentleman's way of asking me my business," she approved. The eyes wandered to Sir William. "I imagine Will has already told you about me. He thinks I haven't any interest in musty ruins and things like that."

General Mason was stung. The word "ruins" had shocked him. He took the cigar out of his mouth.

"Madam," he interposed, warmly, "if you will excuse my reminding you—"

"Certainly," she agreed, with a bright smile, and looked back at Hadley. "However, that's not true. I *do* like them. I like to think about those people in armor, and the tournaments and things, and fights; provided nobody tries to give me a lot of dates or tell me what happened in them. I can't tell one king from another, and why should I? That's all out of date, as Lester says. But I was going to tell you why I was here. It wasn't the Tower, exactly. It was the walk."

"The walk?"

"I'm afraid, Mr. Hadley," she observed, critically, and took a cool survey of him, "that you don't walk enough. Good for you.

Keeps you fit. Lester is getting a paunch; that's why I take him on walking tours as often as he'll let me. We just came back yesterday from a walking trip in the West Country. So today I decided to walk from Berkeley Square to the Tower of London."

Now she had succeeded in stinging Hadley, and she seemed unconscious of it. But the chief inspector only nodded.

"Of course I couldn't persuade Lester to come along. Lester is a Conservative. He is always upset over the state of the country. Every morning he looks at the newspaper, says, 'Oh my God,' and broods all day until he has his liver-trouble. I had him on a walking tour in the south of France last summer, and he was grousing about it every minute. So I came down here alone. And then I thought, 'So long as I'm here, I might as well look at the place.'"

She explained this carefully, almost querulously, and straightened her supple body in the chair.

"I see. Do you remember what time you arrived?"

"'M. I'm not sure. Is it important?"

"I should appreciate an answer, Mrs. Bitton."

She stiffened. "One o'clock or some time afterwards, I fancy. I had a sandwich in the refreshment-room up by the gate. That was where I bought the tickets for the towers; three of 'em. A white one, a pink one, and a green one."

Hadley glanced at General Mason. The latter said, "For the White Tower, the Bloody Tower, and the Crown Jewels. There's an admission fee for those."

"'M, yes. Did you use these tickets, Mrs. Bitton?"

She held the cigarette motionless before her lips. For a moment, the movement of her full breast was quicker. Then her lip curled slightly. Hadley had remained impassive, but he had picked up his pencil.

"I had a look at the Crown Jewels," she replied, with an expression of candor. "I didn't think they were so"—she searched her memory—"so hot. They looked like glass to me. And I'll bet they're not real, either."

General Mason's face had assumed a brickish hue, and a strangled noise issued from him. Then he controlled himself and went on smoking in vicious puffs.

"May I ask why you didn't use the other tickets, Mrs. Bitton?"

"Oh Lord, how should I know? I didn't feel like it, I suppose; I changed my mind." She slid her body about in the chair, seeming to have lost interest. But her eyes looked strained. "I did wander about a bit in that inner courtyard up there, where the big stone buildings are, and the ravens. I liked the look of the soldiers. And I talked to one nice old Beefeater."

This time General Mason did speak. He said, with cold courtesy, "Madam, may I request you not to use that word? The guards at the Tower are called Yeomen Warders, not Beefeaters. The term is applied—"

Mrs. Bitton seemed to catch rather eagerly at the correction.

"I'm sorry. Of course I didn't know. You hear people talk, that's all. I pointed to that place where the stone slab is, where it says they used to chop people's heads off, you know, and I asked the Bee—the man, 'Is that where Queen Elizabeth was executed?' And he nearly fainted. He cleared his throat a couple of times, and said, 'Madam—er—Queen Elizabeth had not the honor to be—ah—I mean, Queen Elizabeth died in her bed.' And then he reeled off a list of people who got their heads chopped off there; and I said, 'What did she die of?' and he said, 'Who, ma'am?' and I said, 'Queen Elizabeth,' and he made a sort of funny noise."

"They'll get their reward in heaven," General Mason said gloomily.

Hadley was not impressed. "Please keep to the subject, Mrs. Bitton. When did you leave?"

"My dear man, I don't carry a watch. But I know that I came down from the parade-ground under the arch of that big place called the Bloody Tower. And I saw a group of people standing over by the rail around these steps, and there was a Beefeater who asked me if I would mind going on. So I suppose it was after you found—Phil. Anyway, when I got to the front gate they wouldn't let me out. And that's all *I* know."

"Did you run into Mr. Driscoll at any time?"

"No. Naturally, I didn't know he was there."

Hadley absently tapped his fingers on the desk for some time. He resumed suddenly. "Now, Mrs. Bitton, according to your own statement you arrived here in the vicinity of one o'clock."

"Sorry. I told you I didn't know *what* time it was."

"But it was shortly after one?"

"Perhaps. I may have been mistaken."

"The body was discovered at two-thirty, and of course you started to leave after that time, or you wouldn't be here. So you spent all that time looking at the Crown Jewels and wandering about the parade-ground in the fog? Is that correct?"

She laughed. Her cigarette had burnt down to her fingers, and she jumped a little as she felt the fire. Dropping it on the floor, she regarded Hadley with some defiance. But she was not so cool as before.

"I hope you don't think I'm afraid of a bit of mist or rain? That belongs in the days of Mr. Gladstone, you know. It's comical. Yes, I suppose that's what I must have done. Good Lord! You surely don't think *I* had anything to do with killing Phil, do you?"

"It is my duty to ask these questions, Mrs. Bitton. Since you carried no watch, I suppose you do not know whether you were anywhere near the Traitors' Gate between half past one and a quarter to two?"

She crossed one silk-clad leg over the other and frowned. "The Traitors' Gate," she repeated. "Let's see. Which one is that?"

Hadley nodded towards her handbag. "May I ask what you have there, under the strap on the other side of your bag? Folded over, I mean; a greenish pamphlet of some sort?"

"It's— I say, I'd forgotten all about it! It's a guide to the Tower of London. I bought it for twopence at the ticket window."

"Were you anywhere near the Traitors' Gate between half-past one and a quarter to two, Mrs. Bitton?"

She took out another cigarette, lighted it with a sweep of the match against the table, and regarded him with cold anger.

"Thanks for repeating the question," she returned. "It's most considerate. If by the Traitors' Gate you mean the one where Phil was found, as I assume you do, the answer is no. I was not near it at any time except when I passed it going in and coming out."

Hadley grinned. It was a placid, slow, homely grin, and it made his face almost genial. The woman's face had hardened, and there was a strained look about her eyes; but she caught the grin, and suddenly laughed.

"All right. *Touché*. But I'm hanged if I let you pull my leg again, Mr. Hadley. I thought you meant it."

"You're—ah—impulsive, Laura," Sir William put in, stroking his long chin. Aggressive as he was, he seemed bewildered by this sister-in-law of his. "Excuse me, Inspector. Go on."

"We now come to the inevitable. Mrs. Bitton, do you know anybody who would desire to take Mr. Driscoll's life?"

"I'll never forgive you," she replied in a low, fierce voice, "if you don't find out who killed him. Nobody would want to kill him. It's absurd. It's insane. Phil was wonderful. He was a precious lamb."

General Mason shuddered, and even Hadley winced a trifle.

"Ah," he said. "He may have been—ah—as you say, a—never mind. Though I question whether he, or anybody else, would have relished the description. When did you last see him?"

"H'm. Well, it's been some time. It was before Lester and I went to Cornwall. He only comes to the house on Sundays. And he wasn't there yesterday, now that I come to think of it." She frowned. "Yes. Will was so cut up over losing that manuscript, and turning the house upside down—or did you know about that?"

"We know," Hadley answered, grimly.

"Wait a bit. Wait. I'm wrong," she corrected, putting her hand down on the desk. "He did come in for a short time rather late Sunday night, to pay his respects to us. He was on his way to the newspaper office to turn in his story, I remember: about the barrister's wig on the cab horse. Don't you remember, Will?"

Sir William rubbed his forehead. "I don't know. I didn't see him, but then I was—occupied."

"Sheila told us about this new newspaperline of his, chasing hats." For the first time Laura Bitton shuddered. "And I told him what Sheila told me, about Will's hat being stolen the night before."

"What did he say?"

"Say? Well, he asked a lot of questions, about where it had been stolen, and when, and all about it; and then I remember he started to pace up and down the drawing room, and he said he'd got a 'lead,' and went hurrying away before we could ask what he meant."

At last Hadley was pleased. He glanced over at Dr. Fell, who had taken the dog in his lap now, but Hadley did not speak. A knock at the door preceded the appearance of an oldish, tired man carrying a bundle made out of a handkerchief. He saluted.

"Sergeant Hamper, sir. I have the dead man's belongings here. And the police surgeon would like to speak to you."

A mild-mannered, peering little man with a goatee doddered in at the door and regarded Hadley with a vague stare.

"Howdy!" he said, pushing his derby hat slightly back on his head with the hand containing his black satchel. In the other he held a straight length of steel. "Here's your weapon, Hadley. Hurrumph. No, no fingerprints. I washed it. It was messy. Hurrumph."

He doddered over to the table, examined it as though he were looking for a suitable place, and put down the crossbow bolt. It was rounded, thin, and about eighteen inches long, with a barbed steel head.

"Funny-lookin' things they're usin' nowadays," commented the doctor, rubbing his nose. "Now I can see a use for the things my wife picked up at Margate. Harrumph."

"It's a crossbolt from the late fourteenth century."

"My eye," said the doctor, "and Betty Martin."

"What?"

"I said, 'My eye and Betty Martin.' Look what's engraved down it. 'Souvenir de Carcassonne.' The pirate French sell 'em at little souvenir booths. That's the curse of travelin', that is. Harrumph."

"But, Doctor—" said Sir William.

The other blinked at him. "My name," he observed, with a sudden querulous suspicion, "my name, sir, is Watson. Doctor Watson. And if any alleged humorist—" squeaked the doctor, flourishing his satchel—"if any alleged humorist makes the obvious remark, I'll brain him. For thirty years on this force I've been hearin' nothing else. And I'm tired of it. People hiss at me round corners. They ask me for needles and four-wheelers and Shag tobacco, and have I my revolver handy? Every fool of a plainclothes constable waits patiently for my report so he can say, 'Elementary, my dear—'"

Laura Bitton had paid no attention to this tirade. She had grown a trifle pale, and she was standing motionless, staring down at the crossbow bolt. Even Dr. Watson broke off to look at her.

She said, in a voice she tried to keep matter-of-fact, "I know where this belongs, Mr. Hadley."

"You've seen it before?"

"It comes," said Mrs. Bitton, in a careful voice, "from our house. Lester and I bought it when we were on that walking trip in southern France."

VII

Mrs. Larkin's Cuff

"Sit down, everybody!" Hadley said, sharply. "This place is turning into a madhouse. You're certain of that, Mrs. Bitton?"

She seemed to recover herself from an almost hypnotized stare at the bright steel. She sat down again, drawing jerkily at the cigarette.

"I—I mean—of course I can't say. Things like that are on sale at Carcassonne, and hundreds of people must buy them."

"Quite," Hadley agreed, dryly. "However, you bought one just like it. Where did you keep it at your home?"

"I honestly don't know. I haven't seen it for months. I remember when we returned from the trip I ran across it in the baggage and thought, 'Now, why on earth did I buy *that* stupid thing?' My impression is that I chucked it away somewhere."

Hadley turned the bolt over in his hands, weighing it. Then he felt the point and sides of the head.

"Mrs. Bitton, the point and barb are as sharp as a knife. Was it like that when you bought it?"

"Good Lord, no! It was very blunt. You couldn't possibly have cut yourself with it."

"As a matter of fact," said the chief inspector, holding the head close, "I think it's been filed and whetted. And there's something else. Has anybody got a lens? Ah, thanks, Hamper." He took the small magnifying glass which the sergeant passed over, and tilted up the bolt to scrutinize the engraving along the side. "Somebody has been trying to efface this *Souvenir de Carcassonne* thing with a file. H'm. And it isn't as though the person had given it up as a bad job. The s-o-u part is blurred and filed almost out, systematically. It's as though the person had been interrupted and hadn't finished his job."

He put down the bolt glumly. Dr. Watson, having evidently satisfied himself that nobody was in a joking mood, had grown more amiable. Removing a stick of chewing gum from his pocket, he peeled off its wrapper and popped it into his mouth.

"Well, I'm goin'," he volunteered. "Anything you want to know? No use tellin' you that did for him. I'm not givin' you the technical gubble-gubble. I hate pedants," he explained to the company. "Clean puncture; plenty of strength behind it. Might have lived half a minute. Harrumph. Oh yes. Concussion. Might have got it falling down the steps, or maybe somebody batted him. That's your job."

"What about the time of death, Watson? The doctor here says he died between one-thirty and one-forty-five."

"Oh, he does, does he?" said the police surgeon. He took out an enormous gun-metal watch, peered at it, shook it beside his ear, and put it back with satisfaction. "Harrumph. Later. Yes. Wasn't a bad guess, though. He died about ten minutes to two. Maybe a few minutes this side, that side. I'll take him along in the ambulance for a good look, and let you know. Well—er—goo'-bye. Harrumph."

He doddered out, swinging his black bag.

"But look here!" protested Sir William, when the door had

closed. "He can't possibly know it so exactly, can he? I thought doctors gave a good deal of leeway on a thing like that."

"*He* doesn't," said Hadley. "That's why he's so invaluable. And in twenty years I've never known him more than ten minutes wrong about the time of death. He says he conducts a physical examination after death. Still he was showing off. If we say one-forty-five or slightly less we shall be close to the mark."

He turned to Laura Bitton.

"To proceed, Mrs. Bitton. Let's assume that this bolt came from your house. Who knew it was there?"

"Why, everybody, I imagine. I don't remember, but I suppose I must have shown the junk we accumulated on that trip."

"Had you seen it before, Sir William?"

"I'm not sure," the other answered, slowly. His eyes were hazy. "I may have. But I can't recall ever having seen it. Ah yes. *Ha!* Now I know, Laura. You and Lester made the trip while I was abroad in the States, and I came back after you. That accounts for it."

Hadley drew a long breath. "There's no use speculating," he said. "We shall have to make inquiries at the house. And now, Mrs. Bitton, I don't think we need detain you any longer. One of the warders will escort you to a cab. Or perhaps Sir William will do it. And look here, old man"—he put his hand on the knight's arm—"you've a perfect right to stay, if you like; at least, *I* shan't try to drive you away. But you've had a trying day. Don't you think it would be better if you went home with Mrs. Bitton?"

"No. I'm waiting for something," Sir William answered, wood-enly. "I'm waiting to hear what you have to say to Arbor."

"Which is exactly what you mustn't do, don't you see? It would spoil everything. I don't want to have to give you an order—"

"Tell you what, Bitton," the general suggested, gruffly, "go up to my rooms. Parker will give you a cigar and a brandy, and if there's any news we'll let you know. That Devereux record is in the portfolio in my desk; have a look at it."

Sir William rose to his great and stooping height. As he turned towards the woman, Rampole turned also; and Rampole was startled to see on Laura's face—for a space as brief as a snapping of your fingers—an expression of stark terror. It was not caused by anything she saw; it was the expression of one who remembers something momentarily forgotten; who stops breathless, eyes opening wide. It was gone immediately, and Rampole wondered whether Hadley had noticed it.

"I don't suppose I might be allowed to remain?" she asked, in her cool, clear voice. But two kinks were working at the corners of her nostrils, and she seemed almost to have stopped breathing. "I might be helpful, you know." As Hadley smiled and shook his head, she seemed to weigh something in her mind. Then she shrugged. "Ah, well. Excuse the morbid curiosity. And I *will* go home in a cab. I'm not in the state of mind to enjoy a good walk. Good afternoon, gentlemen."

She nodded curtly. Followed by her brother-in-law, she swung out of the room.

"Hum!" said General Mason, after a long pause. The fire was getting low, and he kicked at it. Then he noticed Sergeant Hamper, who had been standing, patient and forgotten, since Dr. Watson's entrance; and the general did not continue.

"Oh, ah yes," the chief inspector coughed, as though he had just noticed it, too. "Sorry, Hamper, for keeping you waiting. Those are the contents of the pockets you have there, eh? Very well. Put them down here, and see if you can pick up any news from the chief warder."

"Yes, sir."

"But before you do, go across the way and find Mrs. Amanda Larkin. Wait about five minutes, and send her in here."

The sergeant saluted and withdrew. Hadley contemplated the small bundle on the desk before him, but he did not immediately open it. He glanced at Dr. Fell, who was regarding him benevolently, a pipe in his mouth and the front of his cloak full of hair from the demonstrative Airedale. The chief inspector's expression was sour.

"I say, Mr. Hadley," said the general, after scuffling his feet hesitantly. "What did you make of that woman?"

"Mrs. Bitton? I wonder. She's an old hand at evasion, and a very good one. She sees the traps as soon as you set them. And she has rather an ingenious counterattack. She either tries to make somebody angry and jar the proceedings out of line, or else she babbles. But she's not the babbling kind. H'm. What do you know about her?"

"I'd never met her. She seemed to take me for a police officer. But I know her husband slightly, through Bitton."

"What's this Lester Bitton like?"

"I don't like to say," the general answered, doubtfully. "Don't know the man well enough. He's older than she is; considerably, I should think. Can't imagine him enjoying these athletic activities of hers. I believe he made a lot of money in some financial scheme. And he doesn't smoke or drink. Bah!" said General Mason, blowing through his whiskers.

Hadley seemed about to reply, but he thought better of it. Instead he turned his attention to the handkerchief, knotted up like a bundle, which contained the dead man's effects.

"Here we are. Wristwatch; crystal broken, but still running. Bunch of keys. Fountain pen and stylo pencil. Banknotes, silver and coppers—a whole handful of coppers. Only one letter. Oh Lord! Here it is. Pure trash—pale mauve envelope, and scented. Woman's handwriting."

He drew out a single sheet of paper, and Rampole and the general bent over it as he spread it out on the table. There was no date or heading. The message was written in the center of the sheet. *Be careful. Tower of London, one-thirty. Suspect. Vital.— Mary.*

Hadley read it aloud, scowling. "Mary?" he repeated. "Now we've got to find a Mary. Let's see. Postmarked London, W., ten-thirty last night. This thing is beginning to get on my nerves." Pushing the letter out on the desk, he turned to the contents of the handkerchief again. "I must say the sergeant is thorough. He even included the dead man's ring and tie pin. But here's our hope. Loose-leaf notebook, black leather."

Opening the notebook, he let his eye run along the few scrawled lines on the first sheet. Then Hadley struck the desk despairingly.

"Listen to *this!* Notes of some sort, with dashes between. Apparently it's in Driscoll's handwriting.

"'Best Place? . . . Tower? . . . Track down hat . . . Unfortunate Trafalgar . . . can't transfix . . . 10 . . . Wood . . . Hedges or shield . . . Find out.'"

There was a silence.

"But that's gibberish!" General Mason protested, somewhat superfluously. "It doesn't mean anything. At least, it may have meant something, but—"

"But he's left out the connecting words," Hadley supplied. "I've often put things down that way. Still, even with the connectives, it would take a genuine puzzle artist to put that together. It seems to refer to some clue for following our hat man. What clue, I don't know."

"Read that again!" Dr. Fell suddenly boomed from his corner. He had hauled himself up straight, and he was shaking his pipe at them. On his big face was a blank expression which slowly turned to something like amusement as the chief inspector repeated the words.

"Mrs. Larkin is here, sir," said the voice of Sergeant Hamper from the door.

A series of chuckles were running down the bulges of Dr. Fell's waistcoat. His small eyes twinkled, and ashes from his pipe were blown about him. He looked like the Spirit of the Volcano. Then his red and shining face sank down again, and he became decorous as the sergeant ushered in their next visitor. Hadley hastily closed the notebook, and General Mason retired again to the fireside.

Mrs. Amanda Georgette Larkin looked about carefully before she entered, rather as though she expected to find a bucket of water balanced on the top of the door. Then she marched in, saw the empty chair beside Hadley's desk, and sat sown without further ado. She was a tall, rather heavy woman, well dressed in dark clothes of the sort called "sensible"; which word, as in its usual context, means an absence of charm. Mrs. Larkin had a square face and suspicious dark eyes. She adjusted her arms on the chair in the manner of one expecting somebody to adjust straps over them, and waited.

Hadley hitched his own chair round. "Mrs. Larkin, I am Chief Inspector Hadley. Naturally, you understand, I dislike having to inconvenience any of you—"

"Oh, yeah?" said Mrs. Larkin.

"Yes. But you may be able to give us some very important information."

"Maybe," grunted Mrs. Larkin, hitching her shoulders. "I don't know *that*. But, first, before you ask me any questions, either give me the usual warning or else give me your word anything I say will be treated as a confidence."

She had a way of flicking her head from side to side, and half closing her eyes, as she tossed out the words. Hadley considered gravely.

"Are you familiar with the 'usual warning,' Mrs. Larkin?"

"Maybe and maybe not. But I know the law, and what I say stands."

"Then I can only repeat what you already know. I can make no promises. If anything you say has a direct bearing on this investigation, I can't treat it as a confidence. Is that clear? Besides, Mrs. Larkin, I'm almost positive I've seen you somewhere before."

She shrugged. "Maybe you have, and maybe you haven't. That's as it may be. But there's no slop in the business who's got anything on *me*. I'm a respectable widow. I've got a life annuity from my old man, all straight and in order, and I can give you a dozen character witnesses. I don't know anything about your investigation, and I haven't anything to tell you. So that's final."

All this time Mrs. Larkin seemed to be having some difficulty with her cuff. Under her dark coat she seemed to have on some sort of tailored suit, with turned-up white cuffs; whether the left-hand one was sliding down, or her capable fingers had a habit of playing with it, Rampole could not tell. If Hadley noticed it, he gave no sign.

"Do you know what has happened here, Mrs. Larkin?"

"Certainly I know. There was enough talk from the crowd over the way."

"Very well. Then you may know that the dead man is Mr. Philip Driscoll, of Tavistock Chambers, Tavistock Square. On the paper you filled out you say that you lived in this building also."

"I do. What about it?"

"What is the number of your flat?"

A brief hesitation. "Number One."

"Number One. Ground floor, I suppose? Quite so. You must be an old resident, Mrs. Larkin?"

She blazed. "What the hell difference is it to you? It's none of your business whether I'm an old resident or not. I pay my rent. If you've got any complaint to make, make it to the manager of the flats."

Again Hadley gravely considered, his hands folded. "Who would also tell me how long you had been a resident, Mrs. Larkin. After all, it can't harm you to give us a bit of assistance, can it? You never know. Sometime"—he raised his eyes—"sometime it might help you a good deal."

Another hesitation. "I didn't mean to speak so sharp," she told him, moving sullenly in the chair. "Well, if it does you any good, I've been there a few weeks; something like that."

"That's better. How many flats on each floor?"

"Two. Two in each entry of the buildings; it's a big place."

"So," Hadley said, musingly, "you must have lived directly across the way from Mr. Driscoll. Did you know him?"

"No. I've seen him, that's all."

"Inevitable, of course. And passing in and out, you may have noticed whether he had visitors?"

"What's the use my telling you I didn't? Sure I did. I couldn't help it. He had lots of people coming to see him."

"I was thinking particularly of women, Mrs. Larkin."

For a moment she scrutinized him with an ugly eye. "Yes.

There was women. But what about it? *I'm* no moralist. Live and let live, that's what *I* say. It was none of my business. They didn't disturb me, and I didn't disturb them. But if you're going to ask me who the women were, you can save your breath. I don't know."

"For instance," said Hadley. He glanced over at the sheet of mauve notepaper lying spread out under the bright lights. "You never heard the name Mary used did you?"

She stiffened. Her eyes remained fixed on the notepaper, and she stopped fiddling with her cuff. Then she began talking rather volubly in her straight, harsh fashion.

"No. I told you I didn't know him. The only woman's name I ever heard in connection with him was on the up-and-up. It was a little blonde. Pretty little thing. She used to come with a big thin bird with eyeglasses on. One day she stopped me as I was coming in and asked me how she could find the porter to get into his flat. There's no hall porter; it's an automatic lift. She said her name was Sheila and she was his cousin. And that's *all* I ever heard."

Hadley remained silent for a time, regarding the articles on his desk.

"Now, about this afternoon, Mrs. Larkin. How did you happen to come to the Tower of London?"

"I've got a *right* to come here if I want to. I don't need to explain why I go to a public building, do I? I just did." The reply was fired back so quickly that Rampole suspected it had been framed in advance, ready for the proper occasion.

"When did you arrive?"

"Past two o'clock. Mind, I don't swear to that! I'm not under oath. That's what time I think it was."

"Did you make the tour—go all around?"

"I went to two of them—Crown Jewels and Bloody Tower.

Not the other one. Then I got tired and started out. They stopped me."

Hadley went through the routine of questions, and elicited nothing. She had been deaf, dumb, and blind. There were other people about her—she remembered an American cursing the fog—but she had paid no attention to the others. At length he dismissed her, with the warning that he would probably have future questions. Mrs. Larkin sniffed. She adjusted the collar of her coat, gave a last defiant glance about, and stalked out.

The moment she had disappeared Hadley hurried to the door. He said to the warder there, "Find Sergeant Hamper and tell him to put a tail on the woman who's just left here. Hurry! If the fog's any thicker he'll miss her. Then tell Hamper to come back here."

He turned back to the desk, thoughtfully beating his hands together.

"Hang it all, man," General Mason burst out, impatiently, "why the kid-glove tactics? A little third degree wouldn't have hurt her. She knows something, right enough. And she probably is, or has been, a criminal."

"Undoubtedly, General. But I had nothing to hold over her; and, above all, she's much more valuable on the string. We'll play her out a bit. And I think we should discover something interesting. I think we'll find there is nothing against her at present at the Yard. And I'm almost sure we'll find she's a private detective."

"Ha!" muttered the general. He twisted his mustache. "A private detective. But why?"

Hadley sat down again and regarded the articles on his desk.

"Oh, I needn't be mysterious like my friend Dr. Fell. There are any number of indications. Clearly she has nothing to fear from the police; she challenged that with every word. She lives in Tavistock Square. The neighborhood isn't 'flash' enough for her if

she had that much money of her own to spend, and it isn't cheap
enough if she had less. I know the type. She has lived there only a
few weeks—just opposite Driscoll. She obviously had paid a great
deal of attention to his visitors. She told us only one incident, the
visit of his cousin Sheila, because that wouldn't help us; but you
notice she had all the details.

"Then—did you see her fumbling at her cuff? She hasn't been
in the business long; she was afraid it would show out of the arm
of her coat, and she was afraid to take it off over in the Warders'
Hall, for fear of looking suspicious."

"Her cuff?"

Hadley nodded. "These private snoopers who get material for
divorces. They have to make notes of times and places quickly,
and often in the dark. Oh yes. That's what she's up to. She was
following somebody this afternoon."

The general said, "Hum!" He scuffled his feet a moment before asking, "Something to do with Driscoll?"

Hadley put his head down in his hands.

"Yes. You saw the start she couldn't help giving when she saw
that note on my desk. She was close enough to have read it, but
the color of the paper was enough to identify it—if she'd ever
seen any similar notes in connection with Driscoll. H'm, yes.
But that's not the point. I strongly suspect that the person she
was actually shadowing this afternoon was— Whom do *you* say,
Doctor?"

Dr. Fell relighted his pipe. "Mrs. Bitton, of course. I'm afraid
she rather gave herself away, if you listened to what she said."

"But, good God!" muttered the general. He paused and stared
round quickly. "Eh. That's better. I thought for a moment Bitton
was here. You mean to say there's something between Driscoll
and— H'm. Yes. It fits, I suppose. But where's your proof?"

"I haven't any proof. As I say, it's only a suspicion." Hadley rubbed his chin. "Still, let's take it as a hypothesis for the moment, and work back. Let's assume Larkin was shadowing Mrs. Bitton. Now, this White Tower, General. That's the biggest and most important one, isn't it? And it's some distance away from the Bloody Tower, isn't it?"

"Well, yes. It stands alone; it's in the middle of the inner ballium walls just beside the parade-ground."

"And I think you said that the tower where the Crown Jewels are kept is directly beside the Bloody Tower?"

"The Wakefield Tower. Yes. Wait a minute!" said Mason, excitedly. "I've got it. Mrs. Bitton went to see the Crown Jewels. So did Larkin. Mrs. Bitton said she wandered up through the arch of the Bloody Tower, inside the inner wall, and up to the parade-ground. Larkin went to the Bloody Tower. She couldn't keep too close to Mrs. Bitton. And if she went up the stairs of the Bloody Tower to Raleigh's Walk, she could have seen from a height where Mrs. Bitton was going."

"That's what I wanted to ask you," said Hadley, knocking his fists against his temples. "She couldn't have been very far in the mist, of course. It's more probable she did that—*if* she did—to keep up the illusion of being a tourist. Or she might have thought Mrs. Bitton had gone into the Bloody Tower. It's all supposition. But neither of them went to the White Tower, you see. Those may be coincidences, but when you couple them with the presence of those two women here, and the statements of Mrs. Bitton and Larkin, they sound pretty plausible indications."

"You're assuming," said the general, pointing to the table, "that Mrs. Bitton wrote that note?"

"And all the time," Hadley mused, "suspecting she was being watched. See what the note says: 'Be careful. Suspect. Vital.'

She used an obviously crude and ordinary notepaper; but, you remember, Larkin gave a start on seeing it. The letter was posted at ten-thirty last night, in Mrs. Bitton's district, after Driscoll had paid a short visit that evening. Mrs. Bitton had just that day come back from a walking tour in Cornwall—and why, in God's name, a walking trip in Cornwall in the worst part of March, unless somebody wanted to get her away from a dangerous infatuation?"

He got up and began to pace about the room. As he passed General Mason, the latter silently handed him his cigar case. Hadley took a cigar and put it into his mouth, but he did not light it.

"I'm running on, I suppose. Still, if we assume all this, we must assume it was a dangerous infatuation. For here's a private detective who has been planted in a flat opposite Driscoll for some weeks, even during the time she and her husband were away! Does that mean anything? And who planted her there? Offhand, of course, the husband."

"But the name, Mary?" suggested General Mason.

"I've heard many more hilariously funny nicknames—whatd'yecallem—pet names—in my time," Hadley said, grimly. "And the handwriting's undoubtedly disguised. Even if it were stolen it couldn't be used as evidence against her. She's a clever woman, right enough. But look here—"

He struggled with a match to light his cigar.

"Do you see the deep waters we're in *now?* Come along, Mr. Rampole," he prompted, turning so suddenly that the American jumped; "do you see how it mixes everything up?"

Rampole hesitated. "I can see plenty of difficulties," he returned. "That letter would have been delivered fairly early this morning. Now we've been assuming all along that the reason why

Driscoll telephoned Mr. Dalrye had something to do with the hat thief and his pursuit of the hat thief. But Driscoll never actually *said* it did. Dalrye asked him jokingly, if I remember it right, whether he was afraid of his hat being stolen. But all Driscoll actually answered was, 'It's not my hat I'm afraid of; it's my head.' Dalrye thought it referred to the hat affair; but did it?"

He looked bewilderedly at the chief inspector.

"I don't know," snapped Hadley. "But he makes that appointment with Dalrye for one o'clock. The appointment in the letter is for one-thirty. He has received the letter that morning; it's scared him, and he wants Dalrye's help. Then, what? Some *other* person carefully sends Dalrye on a wild-goose chase to Driscoll's flat. Then Driscoll arrives here, in a bad state. He is seen by Parker *looking out of the window*, and later somebody touches him on the arm by Traitors' Gate.

"So what?" Hadley had got his cigar lighted now, after wasting several matches, and he regarded his companions more calmly. "What went on in the merry-go-round composed of Driscoll, Mrs. Bitton, Larkin, and a possible fourth party? Was it some sort of *crime passionel*? And if it was, can anybody on this side of sanity inform me why Driscoll's body should be found wearing Sir William's stolen top hat? It's the hat thief angle that's mad and impossible; but the hat thief is in on this somehow, and I hope you can explain him. I can't."

There was a pause. Dr. Fell took the pipe out of his mouth and spoke rather plaintively.

"I say, Hadley," he remonstrated. "You're working yourself up into a lather. Be calm. Endeavor to cultivate that philosophical outlook of which Marcus Aurelius speaks. So far you've reasoned closely and well; but—to put it pointedly—don't smash your bat over the wicketkeeper's head when you've already made over a century. It'll come out all right. Just keep on in your normal course."

The chief inspector regarded him bitterly.

"Unless our questioning of the other visitors turns up something," he said, "we have only one other person to interview. And thank God. I need a brandy. Several brandies. But for the next few minutes, Doctor, I am going to exercise that philosophical spirit. *You* are going to be the chief inspector. With the next witness it becomes your case. In other words, you are going to examine Julius Arbor."

"With pleasure," said the doctor, "if you'll give me your chair." He hauled himself to his feet as Hadley summoned the warder on guard and gave instructions. "It's what I should have asked to do, in any case, Hadley. Because why? Because a good part of the case depends on it. And that side of the case—shall I tell you what that side of the case hinges on, Hadley?"

"You will, anyhow. Well?"

"It hinges on a stolen manuscript," said Dr. Fell.

VIII

Mr. Arbor's Aura

Dr. Fell hung his cloak over the back of the chair. Then he squeezed himself into the chair and arranged his various ridges of stomach. Folding his hands over this, he twinkled amiably.

"I don't know whether I ought to let you do this," said Hadley. "I don't want the general to think we're both mad. And for the love of God try to control your deplorable sense of humor. This is serious business." He massaged his chin uncomfortably. "You see, General, in his own way Doctor Fell is invaluable. But he gets his ideas of police procedure from the cinema, and he is under the impression that he can act any sort of part. Whenever I let him question anybody in my presence he tries to give an imitation of me. The result sounds like a schoolmaster with homicidal mania trying to find out what fourth-former spread the axle grease on the stairs when the headmaster was coming down to dinner."

Dr. Fell grunted. "Ha," he said. "Your analogy, while classical, supports me rather than you. It seems to me, Hadley, that you are the one who is going about grimly determined to discover who put the barrister's wig on the cab horse. I'm exactly the detective you want. Besides, schoolboys are much more ingenious than that. Now, an outhouse of medium weight, carefully substituted for the statue of the headmaster on the night before the public unveiling of the latter—"

General Mason shook his head. "Personally," he observed, frowning at his cigar, "I remember my own schoolboy holidays in France. And I have always maintained that there is nothing more edifying than the experiment of placing a red lamp over the door of the mayor's house in a district full of sailors. Ahem!"

"Go ahead," Hadley said, bitterly. "Have a good time. I suppose if this case hadn't wound up in a murder you'd be stealing hats yourselves, and thinking up new places to hang them."

Dr. Fell rapped one of his canes sharply across the table. "Man," he said, "I tell you in all seriousness that it's less than a joke. If you were able to think along those lines, along the hat man's lines, you'd see the explanation of at least one thing you regard as gibberish. You might know the whole explanation."

"Do *you* know it?"

"I rather think I do," Dr. Fell replied, modestly.

The general was frowning with an uncertain air. "Excuse me, sir," he said to Dr. Fell, "if I intrude on something that's none of my business. But, since this seems to be a sort of council of war, may I ask who you are? I don't think you're a police official. And yet you seem familiar, somehow; I've been puzzling about it all afternoon. It seems to me that I've met you somewhere, or seen you—"

Dr. Fell contemplated his pipe. For a time he wheezed heavily.

"I'm not sure what I am," he said. "Some people would say a Fossil. But in a manner of speaking you *have* come in contact with me, General. That would be some years ago. Do you remember Allerton, the naturalist?"

The general's hand stopped with the cigar halfway to his lips.

"He was a good man, Allerton was," Dr. Fell said, reflectively. "He'd been sending some beautiful and intricate drawings of butterflies to a friend of his in Switzerland. The patterns of the wings were perfect, in their way. They were plans of the British minefields in the Solent. But he got his Latin a trifle mixed in the notations. His real name was Sturmm, and I believe he was shot here in the Tower. I—er—accounted for him."

A rumbling sound apparently indicated a sigh.

"Then there was good old Professor Rogers, of the University of Chicago. If he'd known just a bit more about American history I don't think I should have been certain. I've forgotten his name, but he played a good game of chess and had a sound liking for drinking bouts; I was sorry to see him go. He used to carry his information written infinitesimally small on the lenses of his spectacles. Or perhaps you recall little Ruth Wilisdale? I was her dear father-confessor. She would have a snapshot of herself taken at Portsmouth, with the newest thing in gun designs just in the background; but I hoped she wouldn't try to use it. If she hadn't shot that poor clerk, for no reason except that he was in love with her, I should have let her go."

Dr. Fell blinked at the steel crossbow bolt.

"But that was in the line of duty. I'm older now. Hadley insisted on that business of Cripps, the Notting Hill poisoner; and that chap Loganray, with the mirror inside his watch; and the Starberth affair was rather forced on me. But I don't like it. Heh. Hmf. No."

There was a knock at the door. Rampole, to whom all this was a revelation, jerked his thoughts back.

"Pardon me," said a calm, slightly edged voice. "I've knocked several times, and there seemed to be no answer. You sent for me, I think. If you don't mind, I'll come in."

Rampole had been wondering what to expect from the enigmatic Mr. Julius Arbor. He remembered Sir William's description earlier that afternoon: "Reserved, scholarly, a trifle sardonic." The American had been vaguely expecting some one tall and thin and swarthy, with a hooked nose. The man who entered now, slowly drawing off his gloves and looking about with cool curiosity, was somewhat swarthy. And in every movement he was austere. But that was all.

Mr. Arbor was not above middle height, and he was inclined towards pudginess. He was perfectly dressed, too well dressed: there was a white piqué edging to the front of his waistcoat, and a small pearl pin in his tie. His face was flattish, with heavy black eyebrows; and the rimless eyeglasses were such delicate shells that they seemed to blend with his eyes. At the moment he had an air of tolerance and false pleasantry. His expression, as he regarded Dr. Fell, conveyed surprise without a muscle moving in his face; conveyed it by a sort of aura.

"Am I addressing Chief Inspector Hadley?" he inquired.

"Good day," said Dr. Fell, waving his hand affably. "I'm in charge of the investigation, if that's what you mean. Sit down. I presume you're Mr. Arbor."

Dr. Fell hardly presented an imposing picture of a dreaded police official. The front of his waistcoat was littered with tobacco ash and dog's hair, and the Airedale itself now wandered over and lay down beside him. Arbor's eyes narrowed slightly. But he shifted his umbrella from the crook of one arm to hang it over the other; he moved across to the chair, inspected it for dust, and sat down. Carefully he removed his soft pearl-gray hat, placed it in his lap, and waited.

"That's better," said the doctor. "Now we can begin." From his pocket he took his battered cigar case and extended it. "Smoke?"

"Thank you, no," the other answered. His manner appeared to

be the utmost in courtesy. He waited until Dr. Fell had replaced the disreputable case. Then he produced an elaborately chased silver cigarette case of his own, containing long and slender cigarettes with a cork tip. Snapping on a silver lighter, he applied it to a cigarette with nicety; then with all deliberation replaced lighter and case. He waited again.

So did Dr. Fell. The doctor studied him sleepily, hands folded over his stomach. He appeared to have endless patience. Arbor seemed to grow a trifle restless. He cleared his throat.

"I do not wish to hurry you, Inspector," he said at length, "but I should like to point out that I have been put to considerable inconvenience this afternoon. So far I have complied without hesitation to all requests. If you will tell me what you wish to know, I shall be happy to assist you in any way I can."

His voice was not precisely condescending. But he tried to convey an effect by concealing it. Dr. Fell nodded.

"Got any Poe manuscripts?" he inquired, rather like a customs officer asking for contraband.

The question was so sudden that Arbor stiffened. Hadley gave a faint groan.

"I beg your pardon?" said Arbor, after a slight hesitation.

"Got any Poe manuscripts?"

"Really, Inspector" said the other. A faint frown ruffled his swarthy forehead. "I don't think I quite understand you. At my home in New York I certainly have a number of first editions of Edgar Allan Poe, and a few of the manuscript originals. But I scarcely think they would be of interest to *you*. I understand you wished to question me concerning a murder."

"Oh, the murder!" grunted Dr. Fell, with a careless wave of his hand. "Never mind that. I don't want to talk about the murder."

"Indeed?" said Arbor. "I had supposed that the police might

have some curiosity concerning it. However, that is none of my affair. I must remark, with Pliny, '*Quot homines, tot sententiæ*'"

"No, it wasn't," said Dr. Fell, sharply.

"I beg your pardon?"

"It wasn't Pliny," explained the doctor, testily. "That's an inexcusable blunder. And if you must use that deplorable platitude, try to pronounce it correctly. The 'o' in *homines* is short, and there's no long nasal sound to the 'en' in *sententiæ*. But never mind that. What do you know about Poe?"

Hadley was making weird noises in the corner. Mr. Arbor's flattish face had stiffened; he said nothing, but the aura about him conveyed anger. He glanced round at the others, touching lightly his shells of eyeglasses. He seemed not quite certain what to say. Under his scrutiny Rampole tried to make a face like a grim inquisitor; Rampole was enjoying this. If Mr. Arbor could not be called a type, he was at least among a certain class of Americans who had always irritated Rampole, and who can only be described as overcultured. They try to see everything and know everything in as correct a fashion as possible. They go to the right places at exactly the right time. Their pale, assured knowledge of the arts is like their well-groomed houses and their well-groomed selves. When a new Atlantic liner is launched, they discover the proper place to sit in the dining salon, and sit there. They avoid errors, and never drink too much. In short, Dr. Fell and General Mason and Rampole were not allies of theirs.

"I am not sure," Arbor said, quietly, "that I know what you are driving at or whether this is an elaborate joke. If so, kindly tell me. You are certainly the most extraordinary sort of policeman I have ever seen."

"I'll put it this way, then. Are you interested in Poe? If you were offered the authentic manuscript of one of his stories, would you buy it?"

This sudden swoop to the practical, Rampole felt, put Arbor right again. There was a trace of a smile on his face. But you knew he had been outraged; he had tried to impress a policeman with a casual retort, and instead he had been flicked across his poise. He would try to get his own back.

"Now I see, Mr. Hadley," he said to Dr. Fell. "This tribunal, then, was called because of Sir William Bitton's stolen manuscript. I was a bit puzzled at first." He smiled again, a mere wrinkle in his pudgy face. Then he considered. "Yes, I should certainly buy a Poe item if it were offered to me."

"H'm, yes. You know there has been a theft at Bitton's house, then?"

"Oh yes. And you, Inspector, know that I am stopping at Bitton's home. I should say," Arbor corrected himself, impassively, "I *was* stopping there. Tomorrow I shall remove myself to the Savoy."

"Why?"

Arbor glanced round for an ash tray, saw none; then he held his cigarette out levelly so that, when the ashes fell, they should not fall on his trousers. "Let's be frank, Mr. Inspector," he suggested. "I am aware of what Bitton thinks. I am not insulted. We must accept these little things. *Amara temperet lento risu*, if I may again risk Scotland Yard's correction of my pronunciation. But I dislike awkwardness. You see; or don't you?"

"Do you know the nature of the manuscript that was stolen?"

"Perfectly. In point of fact, I had some intention of intending to buy it."

"He told you about it, then, did he?"

The flattish face was a polite mask of deprecation. Arbor put up a hand to touch his dark hair, which was brushed straight and flat across the big skull. "You know he didn't, Mr. Inspector. But Bitton is like a child, if I may say so. I have heard him let fall enough dark and mysterious hints at the dinner table for even his family to guess the nature of his find. However, I knew all about the manuscript before I left the States."

He chuckled. It was the first human sound Rampole had heard out of him.

"I dislike commenting on the infantile nature of some of these gentlemen, but I fear Doctor Robertson, who had been Bitton's confidant, was indiscreet."

Dr. Fell thoughtfully took the handle of his stick, which was lying across the desk, and poked at the crossbow bolt. Then he glanced up amiably.

"Mr. Arbor, would you have stolen that manuscript, if you were given the opportunity?"

Across the room Rampole saw the despairing expression on Hadley's face. But Arbor was not in the least perturbed. He appeared to consider the question from all angles, gravely.

"No, Inspector, I don't think I would," he replied. "It would entail so much awkwardness, you see. And I dislike violating hospitality in that fashion. Don't misunderstand me. I have no moral scruples," Mr. Arbor explained, gently, like one who says, "I am not a hard hearted man," "and it might seriously be questioned as to whether Bitton has any right to it at all. Under the law, his possession of it could be questioned. But, as I say, I dislike unpleasantness."

"But suppose somebody offered to sell you that manuscript, Mr. Arbor?"

Arbor took off his delicate eyeglasses and polished them with a white silk handkerchief. To do so he was compelled to drop his cigarette on the floor, which he did with repugnance. He was easy, smug, and half smiling now. The black eyebrows were wrinkled with amusement.

"Let me tell you a story, Inspector. The police should know it, to support my claim in case it is—ah—successful. Before I came to England I went to Philadelphia and looked up Mr. Joseph Mc-Cartney, of Mount Airy Avenue, who owns the property on which the manuscript was found. For the fact that it was found there I had the testimony of three honest laboringmen. I laid my case with a tolerable degree of frankness before Mr. McCartney. *He* was the owner. I informed him that if he would give me a three months' written option on that manuscript, wherever it might be, I would hand him one thousand dollars in cash. There was also another agreement. It specified that, if the manuscript proved to be what I wanted (the decision to rest with me), I should pay him four thousand dollars for a complete sale. In these matters, Inspector, it is never wise to be miserly."

Dr. Fell nodded ponderously, leaning forward with his chins in his fist.

"Actually, Mr. Arbor, what is the manuscript worth?"

"To me? Well, gentlemen, witness my frankness. I should be willing to go as high as, say, ten thousand pounds."

General Mason, who had been scowling and pulling at his imperial, interrupted. "But, my God, man, that's fantastic! No Poe manuscript—"

"I venture to predict," Arbor said, placidly, "that this one would. Has Bitton described it to you? Ah, I thought not. It would be rather revolutionary." His cool eyes traveled slowly about the group. "Since I seem in the presence of an unusually well-informed group of policemen, I may tell you that it is. It is the first analytic detective story in the history of the world. It antedates Poe's own *Murders in the Rue Morgue*. Dr. Robertson informs me that even from an artistic point of view it surpasses Poe's other three Dupin crime tales. I say that I would give ten thousand pounds. I could name you offhand three fellow collectors who would go as high as twelve or fifteen. And I enjoy thinking what it would fetch at auction—where, I need not tell you, I intend to place it."

Hadley had come up hurriedly to the side of the desk. He seemed almost on the point of tapping Dr. Fell on the arm and getting him out of the chair, to take over the interrogation. But he remained staring at Arbor.

Dr. Fell cleared his throat with a rumbling noise.

"This may be a lot of nonsense," he said, glowering. "Or it may not. How do you know this? Have you seen the manuscript?"

"I have the word of Dr. Robertson, the greatest living authority on Poe. I fear that the good doctor has a short eye to business, or he would have adopted my own course. He only told me all this because—well, Inspector, my wine cellar is considered excellent. And even Imperial Tokay is cheap at the price. Of course, he regretted his indiscretion next day; he had promised Bitton, and he begged me to take no action. I was sorry."

Again Arbor drew out the silk handkerchief and lightly mopped his head.

"Then," said Dr. Fell, "it wasn't a mere matter of a find you were interested in? You were after this manuscript to sell it?"

"I was, my dear Inspector. The manuscript—wherever it is— happens to belong to me. I may remind you— Shall I go on?"

"By all means."

"My business with Mr. McCartney was easily settled," Arbor continued comfortably. "He seemed staggered. It was incredible to him that any written document, save perhaps a blackmailing letter or one of 'them treaty things' to which he referred, could be worth five thousand dollars. I found in Mr. McCartney a great reader of sensational fiction. My next move—you follow it, Inspector?"

"You got yourself invited to Bitton's house," grunted Dr. Fell.

"Not exactly. I had a standing invitation there. At one time, I may remark, my friend Bitton thought highly of me. As a rule, of course, I do not stay with friends when I am in London. I own a cottage in the suburbs, at which I often stay in summer; and in winter I go to a hotel. But, you see, I had to be tactful. He was a friend."

Again Arbor drew out his silver cigarette case. But he seemed to remember that there was no ash tray, and he put it back again.

"I could not, of course," he pursued, "say to him, 'Bitton, I think you have a manuscript of mine. Hand it over.' That would have been distasteful, and, I thought, unnecessary. I expected him to show me his find voluntarily. Then I would lead up to my subject by gradual degrees, explain the unfortunate circumstances, and make him a fair offer. Understand me! I was prepared to pay him his price, within reason, even for my own property. I wished no sort of undignified squabble.

"Now, Inspector—and gentlemen—that was difficult. You know Bitton? Ah. I knew him as a headstrong, stubborn, and secretive fellow; rather a monomaniac on cherishing his discoveries. But I had not expected him to be quite so difficult. He did not speak of his find, as I had expected. For some days I hinted. I thought he was merely obtuse, and I fear my hints grew so outrageously broad that they puzzled even his family. But I am aware now that he must have known, and suspected me. He merely kept his mouth more tightly closed. It was distasteful to me—but I was coming to the point where I should have had to claim my rights. Under the law," said Arbor, his leisurely voice growing suddenly harsh, "I was not required to pay him a penny for my property."

"The sale had not been concluded between you and McCartney, had it?" inquired Dr. Fell.

Arbor shrugged. "Virtually. I had my option. Of course, I was not willing to hand over five thousand dollars on a manuscript I had never seen, even on the word of Dr. Robertson; and a manuscript, besides, which might conceivably have been lost or destroyed by the time I came to claim it. However, to all intents and purposes it was mine."

"Did you tell Bitton you were the owner, then?"

Arbor's nostrils tightened with anger. "Obviously not. Or would he have been so mad as to do what he did—seek the aid of the police when it was stolen?

"But before that. Consider the difficulty of my position. I began to see that, if I asked him outright, this—ah—this lunatic might make all sorts of trouble. He would probably refuse, and question my rights. My rights could be proved; but it would mean delay and all sorts of unpleasantness. He might maintain he had lost the manuscript, and that would be worse. I imagine he would have been quite capable of summoning a policeman and having me thrown out of his house."

Mr. Arbor's aura conveyed an acute spasm of anguish at this thought. General Mason coughed, and Dr. Fell contrived to twist his mustache with a hand that hid his mouth.

"And at *this* juncture," continued the other, tapping the end of his umbrella on the floor, "everything blew up. The manuscript was stolen. And I, you notice, *I* was the loser.

"Now, gentlemen." He sat back and gazed about, fixing the eye of each in turn. "Now you will understand why I have gone into such thorough explanations, and why I wish to establish the ownership of that manuscript. Bitton undoubtedly thinks I stole it. I am not particularly concerned with what he thinks; I have not even bothered to undeceive him. But I cannot have the police thinking so.

"I was away over the week-end during which the manuscript was stolen, and I arrived back only this morning. I was visiting Mr. and Mrs. Spengler, some friends of mine who live close to that cottage of my own I mentioned, at Golder's Green. 'Ah,' says the cunning Bitton; 'an alibi.' And he has the colossal impudence to telephone them in order to confirm it. 'Ah,' he says then; 'it was done by somebody in his employ.'

"Now, all this might be at least remotely possible in Bitton's wild imagination. But you know better. Why, in the name of Heaven, should I go to all the trouble of stealing a manuscript which was already mine?"

Arbor folded his hands with the air of an orator sitting down again.

There was a silence. Hadley, who had perched himself on the edge of the desk, nodded.

"I suppose, Mr. Arbor," he said, "you are prepared to prove this claim of yours?"

"Naturally. An agreement between Mr. McCartney and myself was drawn up by my lawyer in New York and duly attested. A copy of this agreement is now filed with my solicitors in London. Should you care to verify what I say, I shall be happy to give you a card to them."

Hadley lifted his shoulders. "In that case, Mr. Arbor, there is nothing more to be said. Sir William simply took a chance that his discovery would go unnoted." Hadley spoke coldly and level-ly. "Even if you had—hum—abstracted the manuscript, to avoid trouble at Sir William's hands, the law could do nothing. I should not call it very ethical. I tell you frankly, sir, I should call it pretty damned sneaking. But it is perfectly legal."

Mr. Arbor's aura radiated a sort of sputter, like a muffled wireless-key. He tried to draw himself up, but the eye of the chief inspector was a trifle too cold. Then Mr. Arbor became placid again.

"We'll let that pass," he observed, with an effort. "The absurdity of your suggestion is as evident as—ah—your somewhat noticeable manners. That a man of my well-known standing—" The aura sputtered again. Then Mr. Arbor recovered himself. "It would amuse some of my associates in New York," he said. "Ha, ha. Ha. Very amusing. But, as I think we agreed to begin with, perfectly legal."

"Not if it concerned a murder," said Dr. Fell.

There was an abrupt and rather terrible silence.

The doctor had spoken in a casual tone, and he was leaning over to stroke the head of the dog curled up beside his chair. In the stillness they could all hear the last rattle of coals falling in the grate, and, very faintly, the thin sudden note of a bugle from the parade-ground. General Mason automatically reached for his watch as he heard the bugle; but he stopped and stared.

Arbor had been gathering his coat about him to rise, and his hand jerked on the lapel. "I—I beg your pardon?" he said.

"I said, 'Not if it concerned a murder,'" Dr. Fell repeated in a louder voice. "Don't get up, Mr. Arbor. We're going to talk about the murder now. That doesn't surprise you, does it? You offered to talk about it a while ago, you know."

His half-closed eyes opened wide.

"Don't you know *who* was murdered, Mr. Arbor?" he pursued.

"I—I heard them talking over there," the other answered, regarding his interrogator fixedly. "I think I heard somebody say his name was Drakell or Driscoll or something of the sort. But I didn't mix with them. What has a man being killed at the Tower of London to do with *me*?"

"The name was Driscoll. Philip Driscoll. He was Sir William Bitton's nephew."

Whatever sort of effect Dr. Fell had hoped to produce, there was no question about an effect. Arbor's swarthy face turned white; literally white, for mottled blotches stood out against his pallor. The thin eyeglasses jerked on his nose, and he covered them with a shaking hand. Undoubtedly Arbor had a weak heart. The effect was as much physical as nervous. Hadley started forward in concern; but Arbor waved him back.

"You must—you must excuse me, gentlemen," he muttered. His voice grew stronger. "I— It was the shock of hearing the name of—somebody—I did know. This—this Driscoll, was he a small young man, with—let me see—with reddish hair?"

"Yes," said Dr. Fell stolidly. "You did know him, then?"

"I— Yes. That is, I met him—ah—Sunday before last, at dinner in Bitton's house. It was the day I arrived. I hadn't caught his last name. They all called him Phil; that's how I remembered. And a nephew of Bitton, by that name—"

General Mason pulled a flask out of his hip pocket and held it out. "Try this," he said, gruffly. "Brandy. Buck you up."

"Thank you, no," the other answered, with some dignity. "I'm quite all right. But I assure you I don't know anything about this ghastly business. How did he die?"

"He was stabbed with this crossbow bolt," said Dr. Fell, picking it up. "It comes from Bitton's house."

The other said, "Most—interesting—" in a way that sounded

like a horrible burlesque. But he was better now. "I don't want you to think, gentlemen," he went on, with a sort of heavy facetiousness, "that *I* know anything of the poor boy's murder because I seemed—ah—upset when you mentioned it. After all, murderers don't do that, do they? It would be too easy if they did. A person with courage enough to use one of those vicious-looking things isn't apt to faint when it's produced afterward. It was—ah—bringing the thing home, so to speak. The doctor warned me against shocks, gentlemen; I'm not as healthy as I look. Bitton—poor devil. Does he know?"

"He knows, Mr. Arbor. But about young Driscoll: you can't think of any reason for his murder?"

"My dear sir, no! No, of course not. I only met him once, at that dinner. I haven't seen him since."

"He was killed at the Traitors' Gate out there," pursued Dr. Fell, nodding, "and his body thrown on the steps. I don't suppose you noticed anything suspicious while you were here? People near the gate; anything of the sort?"

"No. What I—er—wanted to tell you when I first came in was that it was only by chance I was detained here at all. You see, I wanted to examine that copy of Sir Walter Raleigh's *History of the World* which is on display at the Bloody Tower, in the room where he wrote it. I arrived here shortly after one o'clock, and went directly to the Bloody Tower. I—er—I confess I was shocked at the way they allow such a valuable book to lie exposed and open all day in such a damp place. I presented my card to the warder on duty, and asked whether I might make a detailed examination. He said he was sorry, but that it was a part of the Tower exhibits and that I couldn't handle it without a written order from the resident governor or deputy governor." Arbor seemed a trifle surprised at the interest depicted in the faces of the others. Nobody spoke; he went on talking volubly.

"Even then, he said, it was doubtful whether I could get the order. But I asked to be directed to where I might find either one. He sent me across the way—"

"*Inside* the inner ballium wall?" Hadley interrupted.

"Why—er—yes. Yes. To a row of buildings facing up towards the Green and the parade-ground. But it was foggy, and there were several doors, and I was uncertain. While I hesitated, a man came out one of the doors—"

He paused, puzzled and growing nervous under their eyes.

"A man in knickerbockers and cap?" Dr. Fell inquired.

"I don't know. Er—yes, I believe he did wear knickerbockers; I recall it because they seemed a bit absurd on such a day. But it was foggy, and I could not swear to it. I spoke to him to find out which door I should use, but he brushed past me without listening. Then another warder hailed me and told me that visitors were not permitted on the side of the grounds where I was walking. I explained. He then said he was positive neither of the persons I wanted to see were in their quarters at the time."

"Quite correct," said General Mason, dryly.

"But surely, gentlemen—!" Arbor protested, wetting his lips, "Surely you can't be interested—You are? Well, let me see. I returned to the Bloody Tower and tried the judicious use of a bank note. It was not accepted. So I determined to leave. On my way out to Water Lane I collided with a young lady who had just come under the arch of the gate from Water Lane and was walking very rapidly up the incline that goes towards the parade-ground. You said something?"

"No," said Dr. Fell. "Could you describe this young lady?"

Arbor was again entirely at his ease. By his expression, he seemed to regret his late weakness, and to make up for it by clear, judicial telling of his own story. It was obvious that the import of the story puzzled him. But, at Dr. Fell's question, he reflected carefully.

"No. No, I'm afraid not. I scarcely glanced at her. All I remember is that she was in a great hurry, and that she wore some sort of fur collar, and that she seemed—ah—uncommonly solid. It gave me a jar when we bumped. My wristwatch was a bit loose, and I thought it had slipped off. Well, I walked through the arch of the Bloody Tower, into Water Lane—"

"Now, Mr. Arbor, for the Lord's sake, think! Think! Was there anybody near the railing around Traitors' Gate then? Did you see anybody standing there, or did it seem to be deserted?"

Arbor sat back. "I begin to see the drift," he answered, nervously. "I didn't go close to the rail, or look over. But there was nobody standing near it, Inspector. Nobody!"

"And could you remember the time then?"

"I can tell you the time precisely," said the other. "It was just twenty-five minutes to two."

IX

The Three Hints

IT WAS the placid Hadley who was momentarily jarred out of his calm then. "But look here!" he protested, "the police surgeon said he died at a quarter to—"

"Hold on!" bellowed Dr. Fell. He struck the top of the desk such a sharp blow with his cane that the sheet of mauve notepaper fluttered off. "By God and Bacchus! That's what I wanted! That's what I was hoping and waiting for. And to think I never took this man's testimony of the murder before! I nearly passed it up. My friend, I am grateful. I am profoundly grateful. Now, you're absolutely positive of that time, are you?"

Arbor was growing mollified at being a person of such importance.

"Positive. As I told you, my encounter with the young lady had jarred my watch. I stepped back into the door of the Wakefield Tower to see whether it was in danger of slipping off, and I noted the time just before I walked down to Water Lane."

"Get out your watches, gentlemen," rumbled Dr. Fell, "and let's compare notes. *Eheu!* So! It's a quarter past six. That's what I have, anyhow. What about the rest of you?"

"Quarter past six," said General Mason, "and I'm right. I know."

"Thirteen and a half minutes past," said Rampole.

"And I?" concluded Arbor. "Fifteen and one half minutes past, to the second. I never am wrong. This watch was made by—"

"Never mind," interposed Dr. Fell. "We shan't row about half a minute. That settles it. There is, however, one thing I should like to ask. You said you were on your way out at this time, Mr. Arbor. But the murder wasn't discovered until half-past two. How is it you were caught here when the detention order was issued?"

"That was what I wished to explain a moment ago," Arbor answered, "when I said it was chance. I left one of my gloves behind, on the railing round the Raleigh first edition in the Bloody Tower. They're—ah—rather special gloves," he explained, carelessly. "Carter of Fifth Avenue does them for me, and I have no other pair of exactly this sort."

General Mason looked pained, and Arbor lifted the shiny gray hat from his lap and indicated the gloves.

"I was all the way to the Strand in my cab before I remembered, and I returned. It was about twenty minutes to three when I arrived, and then I couldn't get out."

"I hope that cabby isn't still waiting," the general mused. "It would be unfortunate, Mr. Arbor, if such an unfortunate witness got his head bashed in. Ah," he said, somewhat dreamily, "most unfortunate— Hold on! Wait! I remember now. There's something *I* wanted to ask you."

"With pleasure." Arbor frowned. "You are—"

"I'm the man you wanted to see," the general replied, with some asperity. "I'm the deputy governor of the Tower. And what's more, sir, I'm damned if I let you paw over that Raleigh book. General Sir Ian Hamilton presented that to us. What was I saying? Oh yes. About the Raleigh. You said you'd never seen it. Is this your first visit to the Tower?"

"It is."

"The reason I asked is that you have all the names down pat. You speak familiarly of 'Water Lane,' and the Green, and all the rest of it, when you didn't go any farther than the Bloody Tower."

"Perfectly simple," said Arbor, with the air of a detective speaking to his dull-witted assistant. "I dislike asking directions, my dear sir. It savors of gaucherie." From his pocket he produced one of the green pamphlets. "This little guide, with a map, which I studied before entering the Tower at all, gave me a thorough working knowledge."

Dr. Fell pulled at his mustache.

"I've got just one more question, my friend, and then you are free to go. Are you acquainted with Mrs. Lester Bitton, your host's sister-in-law?"

"Unfortunately, no. You see, as I told you, I have never before stopped at Bitton's house. Mr. and Mrs. Bitton were away when I first arrived. They returned last night, I am told, but I only came back from my weekend this morning, and both were out of the house. I know Lester Bitton slightly. And I have heard Bitton himself speak of her, and seen her portrait. But I've never met her."

"You wouldn't recognize her, then, if you saw her?"

"I'm afraid not."

"Before you go, though," Hadley suggested, "isn't there something you want to tell us?"

Arbor had risen with almost a shake of relief. He was buttoning his coat slowly, so as not to seem in a hurry; but he stopped. "Tell you? I don't understand."

"Any—hints, or instructions, Mr. Arbor? A valuable manuscript virtually belonging to you has been stolen, you know. Aren't you interested in recovering it? It would seem that you are very easily diverted from the loss of a ten-thousand-pound possession, considering the trouble you took to acquire it. Today you were down here, deeply interested in something else. Aren't you making any inquiries at all?"

Arbor, Rampole sensed, had been dreading that question. But he did not immediately speak. He adjusted his hat to a nicety, drew on his gloves, and hooked his umbrella over his arm. This sartorial adjustment seemed to lend him his old cool confidence and bearing.

"Just so," he agreed. "But you are forgetting something. I want no unpleasantness in this matter, gentlemen; I have already outlined my reasons. I prefer not to use the assistance of the police. But I assure you I have not been idle. I have contacts and leads which are—excuse me—not open to *you*. As you say, it is not likely that I shall neglect to investigate." A thin smile on the swarthy face, a cool raising of the black brows, a slight bow. "If you wish to speak to me further, you will reach me at the Savoy. I thank you for—ah—a most instructive afternoon. Good day, gentlemen."

After he had gone there was a long silence. It had grown cold in the room, for the fire was almost out. An expression of malignancy was on General Mason's face. He moved his hands in the air after the fashion of a burlesque hypnotist.

"Hocus-pocus," he muttered. "Allagazam. I hope you haven't got any more witnesses, Hadley. That's enough. First hats, and then love affairs, and now manuscripts. It hasn't helped any. It's only mixed us up worse. What did you make of our aesthete?"

"As a witness," said Hadley, "he was either too difficult or too easy, at various times. He started off smoothly enough. Then he went into a complete funk at the mention of the murder. Finally, I'd swear he was telling the truth when he described what he knew of the happenings here."

"Meaning?" prompted the general.

Again Hadley began to stride about the room. He spoke irritably. "Oh, I can see one obvious explanation. But *that* only complicates matters. See here. He obviously didn't know it was Driscoll who had been murdered here. At least, he didn't know it was the young chap he'd met at Sir William's. And it nearly knocked him over when he heard. Why?

"Put it this way. Arbor's clever, and he's tricky. He genuinely dislikes unpleasantness, because it upsets his own self-conscious dignity; but he has no more courage than a rabbit. You could see that in everything he said. Worst of all, he has an unholy horror of publicity. Agreed?"

"Without a struggle," said the general.

"All right. Now, he tried to make a joke out of the suggestion that he himself might have stolen that manuscript. But when you know Arbor's character, and Sir William's, it isn't quite so fantastic as it sounds. He knew the old man would raise thirty-eight different kinds of hell if he demanded his manuscript. There would be all the red tape, delay, wrangling, and probably publicity, to say nothing of what Sir William's temper might do to Arbor's skin. But if the thing were stolen, Sir William could whistle for it. He had no case. Arbor could point all this out to him (by telephone, if necessary) after he'd safely got the manuscript and left the house. And Sir William wouldn't dare act. Aside from having no case, he'd show himself up in a ridiculous light. Respected ex-Cabinet Ministers can't stand that."

"I doubt whether Arbor would actually pinch the manuscript himself," said the general, shaking his head. "He wouldn't dare."

"Wait a minute. Now, he wasn't worried about that theft. He

wasn't exerting himself, you see. Well, who might have stolen it for him?"

The general whistled. "You mean—"

"It can't be!" snapped the chief inspector, striking his fist into his palm. "It would be too much. But the possibility stares us right in the face, and we've got to think about it.

"Why, I mean this. Arbor said he talked Poe in that house until even the family began to wonder; broader and broader hints. He also said that with the dark and mysterious hints Sir William constantly let fall, everybody must have known about the manuscript. Certainly a clever young fellow like Driscoll couldn't have failed to know it. And Driscoll was there to dinner when Arbor did much of his talking."

"Oh, look here!" General Mason protested in a distressed voice. "I mean to say— Well, it isn't done! An infernal counter-jumper like Arbor might have done it, of course. But if you're suggesting that young Driscoll— Purf! Burr! Bah! Out of the question. Absolutely."

"I didn't say it was true," Hadley said, patiently. "But consider. Driscoll was discontented. Driscoll was always short of money. Driscoll was invariably in a row with his uncle. Driscoll was a madcap, lunatic kid who might regard that manuscript as simply a foolish piece of paper. I confess I did myself, until I heard how much it's worth. So suppose Driscoll takes Arbor aside and says, 'Look here, if you happened to find that manuscript under your pillow one morning, what would it be worth to you?'" Hadley raised his eyebrows. "Perhaps Arbor then explained, as he might, that he was really the owner. Perhaps that didn't matter to Driscoll. But, since Arbor would have had to pay some sort of price to the old man if he bought it outright—well? It was a good chance for a stroke of business. The old man knew the full value of the manuscript. Driscoll didn't. And Arbor's an excellent man of business."

"*No!*" boomed a thunderous voice.

Hadley jumped. There had been in that voice not only protest, but a sort of agonized appeal. They all turned to see Dr. Fell lumbering to his feet, his big hands spread out on the table.

"I beg of you," he said, almost imploring—"I beg and plead with you, whatever else you think of anything in this case, not to get that absurd idea. If you do, Hadley, I warn you, you'll never see the truth. Say whatever else you like. Say that the thief was Arbor, if you like. Say that it was General Mason or Father Christmas or Mussolini. But don't, I entreat you, ever for a moment believe it was Driscoll."

The chief inspector was peevish. "Well, why not? I didn't say I definitely thought it was Driscoll, you understand. But, since you seem to have such a violent horror of the idea—why not?"

The doctor sat down again.

"Let me explain. By all means let me get that point straight, or you'll never understand the rest of it. Cast your minds back a couple of hours. Damn it, where's my pipe? Ah. Well, we were speaking of Driscoll. And Sir William said he wasn't a coward. And I tried to give you a hint, if you recall. I said, 'What *was* he afraid of?'

"Let me repeat that. I agree that Driscoll was far from a coward. I agree with your definition, Hadley, that he was a madcap, lunatic kid. But one thing he most definitely did fear."

"And that?"

"He feared his uncle," said Dr. Fell. After a pause, while he spilled a considerable amount of tobacco in filling his pipe, he went on wheezily. "Look here. Driscoll was an improvident sort, with expensive tastes. He lived entirely off his uncle's bounty. You heard Bitton speak of his 'allowance.' He got precious little from what small free-lance newspaper work he did, and Bitton helped him get along even with that.

"But—Bitton wasn't an indulgent uncle. Quite to the contrary. He was always quarreling with his nephew on some point or other. And why? Because he was so fond of him. He had no son of his own. *He* had risen from small beginnings, and he wanted to see the boy exhibit some of his own violent energy. And do you think Driscoll didn't know that? *Ha!*" said the doctor, snorting. "Of course he did. The old man might squeeze the purse strings tighter than a slipknot. But Driscoll knew he was the old man's favorite. And when it came to the last, I rather suspect Driscoll figured conspicuously in the old man's will. Didn't he, General Mason?"

"I happen to know," the general said, rather guardedly, "that he wasn't forgotten."

"So. Hadley, are you really mad enough to think the boy would have endangered all that? Why, that manuscript was literally Bitton's most cherished possession. You saw how he gloated. If Driscoll had stolen it, and he ever had the faintest suspicion Driscoll had stolen it, out the boy would have gone for ever. You know Bitton's temper and, above all, his stubbornness. He wouldn't have forgiven. There wouldn't have been a penny more from him, alive or dead. And what had Driscoll to gain? At most a few pounds from Arbor. Why should Arbor, a good man of business, give money to a thief for his own property? He would simply smile in that mincing way of his. 'A thousand guilders? Come, take fifty! Or I might tell your uncle where you got this manuscript.'—No, Hadley. The last thing in the world Driscoll would have done would have been to dare steal it. The person he feared most, I tell you, was his uncle."

Hadley nodded thoughtfully.

"Yes. Yes," he said, "that's true. And I have no doubt it's a very interesting lecture you're giving. But why are you so aggressive on the point? Why is it so important?"

Dr. Fell sighed. He was very much relieved. "Because, if you understand that, you're halfway along the right track. I—" Wearily he raised his eyes to the door at another of the inevitable knocks. He went on, vigorously. "But I was going to say that I absolutely refuse to listen to another witness this afternoon. It's past six and the pubs are open. Come in!"

A very tired-looking Sergeant Betts entered.

"I've just been talking to the other visitors, sir," he said to Hadley. "And I'm afraid it's been a long job. They all wanted to talk, and I had to listen for fear of missing something. But not one of them knew anything whatever. All of them spent nine-tenths of their time in the White Tower. It takes quite a while to explore it thoroughly; and they weren't anywhere near the Traitors' Gate between one-thirty and two o'clock. They seemed straight, so I let them go. Was that correct, sir?"

"Yes. But keep those names and addresses in case you need them." Wearily Hadley passed a hand over his eyes. He hesitated, and then looked at his watch. "H'm. Well, it's getting late, sergeant, and we'll run along. I'll take charge of these articles on the table. In the meantime, I want you to cooperate with Hamper and find out what you can from the warders or anybody else who occurs to you. Use your own judgment. If you find out anything, communicate with the Yard. They'll know where I am."

He took down his overcoat and donned it slowly.

"Well, gentlemen," said General Mason, "that seems to be all for the moment. And I think we could all deal with a large brandy and soda. I can recommend my own, and I have some very passable cigars. If you'll do me the honor to come up to my rooms?"

Hadley hesitated; but he looked at his watch again, and shook his head.

"Thanks, General. It's good of you, but I'm afraid I can't. I have to get back to the Yard; I've the devil's own lot of routine business, you know, and I've taken far too much time as it is. I shouldn't be handling the affair at all." He frowned. "Besides, I think it's best that none of us go up. Sir William will be waiting for you, General. You know him best and you had better tell him everything. About Arbor, you see?"

"Hum! I'm bound to admit I don't like the job," the other said, uncomfortably. "But I suppose you're right."

"Tell him we shall probably pay him a visit in Berkeley Square tonight, and to be sure everybody is at home. Oh yes. And the newspapers. There will be reporters here soon, if they're not being held outside already. For the Lord's sake don't say anything yourself. Just say, 'I have no statement to make at the present time,' and refer them to Sergeant Hamper. He'll tell them what we want given out; he's an old hand. Let's see—I want a newspaper myself, at the moment."

He was already gathering up the objects which had been in Driscoll's pockets. Rampole handed him an old newspaper from the top of a bookcase; he wrapped the crossbow bolt inside it and stowed it away in the breast pocket of his overcoat.

"Right you are. But at least," said the general, "let me give you a stirrup cup before you go." He went to the door and spoke a few words. In a remarkably short time the impassive Parker appeared, bearing a tray with a bottle of whisky, a siphon, and four glasses.

"Well," he continued, watching the soda foam as Parker mixed the drinks, "this has been an afternoon. If it weren't for poor Bitton and the damnable closeness of this thing, I should even call it entertaining. But I'm bound to say I can't make head or tail of it."

"You wouldn't call it entertaining," Hadley asserted, moodily, "if you had my job. And yet—I don't know." There was a wry smile under his clipped mustache. He accepted a glass and stared into it. "I've been thirty years in this game, General. And yet I can't help getting something like a quickened pulse when I see 'Scotland Yard has been called in on the case.' What's the magic in the damned name? I don't know. I'm a part of it. Sometimes I am it. But I'm still as intrigued as a naive old dodderer like Dr. Fell."

"But I always thought you were dead against amateurs," said the general. "Thanks, Parker. Of course you can hardly call the doctor an amateur, but—"

Hadley shook his head. "I said once before today that I wasn't such a fool. Sir Basil Thomson, one of the greatest men the Yard ever had, used to say that a detective had to be a jack of all trades and a master of none. The only thing I regret about the doctor here is the deliberate way he patterns himself after the detectives in sensational fiction; of which, by the way, he's an omnivorous reader. His silences. His mysterious 'Aha's!' His—"

"Thank you," grumbled Dr. Fell, satirically. He had put on his cloak and his long shovel hat; he stood, a gigantic and bulky figure, leaning on two canes; and now his face was fiery with controversy. Stumping round near the door, he accepted a glass from Parker. "Hadley," he continued, "that's an old charge. An old charge, an outworn maxim, and a baseless slur on a noble branch of literature. Somebody ought to refute it. You say that the detective in fiction is mysterious and slyly secret. All right; but he only reflects real life. What about the genuine detective? He is the one who looks mysterious, says 'Aha!' and assures everybody that there will be an arrest within twenty-four hours. But, despite this pose, he doesn't go so far as the detective in fiction. He doesn't fix the taxpayer with a somber eye and say, 'The solution of this murder, sir, depends on a mandolin, a perambulator, and a pair of bed-socks,' and send the taxpayer away feeling he's really had the police in after all. He doesn't, because he can't. But he would like to be a master mind and say that, if he could. Who wouldn't? Wouldn't *you*? In other words, he has all the pose, whether he has the knowledge or not. But, like the fictional detective, very sensibly he doesn't tell what he thinks, for the excellent and commonplace reason that he may be wrong."

"All right," said Hadley, resignedly. "If you like. Well, good health, gentlemen!" He drained his glass and put it down. "I suppose, Doctor, this is a preamble to some mysterious predictions of yours?"

Dr. Fell was lifting his glass; but he paused and scowled heavily.

"I hadn't thought of doing so," he replied. "But as a matter of fact, I *will* give you three hints about what I think. I won't elaborate them"—his scowl became ferocious as he saw Hadley's grin—"because I may be wrong. Ha!"

"I thought so. Well, number one?"

"Number one is this. There was some dispute about the time Driscoll died. The only period in which we seem absolutely to be able to fix it lies between one-thirty when he was seen by Parker fighting a cigarette at the rail in front of Traitors' Gate, and ten minutes to two, which is the time Doctor Watson said he died. Mr. Arbor, coming into Water Lane at twenty-five minutes to two, was positive there was nobody near that rail."

"I don't see any implication there," General Mason said, after a pause; "unless it's the implication that Arbor was lying. What's your second hint?"

Dr. Fell was becoming more amiable. He juggled his glass.

"The second hint," he answered, "concerns that crossbow bolt. It was, as you saw, filed sharp into a deadly weapon. Now you are assuming, quite naturally, that this filing was done by the murderer. We have also noticed that the same hand had started to file off those words, 'Souvenir de Carcassonne,' but had stopped with three letters neatly effaced, and gone no farther. *Why weren't those other letters effaced?* When we found the body, we were of course bound to learn of the bolt Mrs. Bitton purchased at Carcassonne, and, since the victim was Driscoll, it would be too monstrous to assume a mere coincidence. I repeat: why weren't those other letters effaced?"

"Yes," said Hadley. "I'd thought of that point, too. I hope you're sure of the answer. I'm not. And the third hint?"

By this time Dr. Fell, and the black ribbon of his eyeglasses, quivered to his chuckle.

"And the third hint," he said, "is very short. It is a simple query. *Why did Sir William's hat fit him?*"

With a capacious tilt of his head he swallowed off his drink, glanced blandly about the group, pushed open the door, and shouldered out into the mist.

X

Eyes in a Mirror

THE GREAT clock in Westminster tower struck eight-thirty.

Dorothy had not been at the hotel when Rampole and the doctor arrived there on their return from the Tower. A note left for Rampole at the desk informed him that Sylvia Somebody, who had been at school with her, was taking her home for a gathering of some of the other old girls. Owing, she said, to previous knowledge of her husband's passionate aversion to jolly little evenings of this kind, she had informed them that he was in the hospital with a violent attack of delirium tremens. *They'll condole with me so,* she explained. *D'you mind if I tell them how you throw plates at the cat and come home every night by way of the coal chute?* She said he was to give her love to Dr. Fell; and not to forget to pin the name of his hotel to his coat lapel so that the cabman would know where to put him at the end of the evening. Even after more than six months of matrimony, too, she concluded with certain declarations which made Rampole throw out his chest. There, he reflected, was a *wife.*

He and the doctor dined at a little French restaurant in Wardour Street. Hadley, who had gone to Scotland Yard immediately after leaving the Tower, had promised to meet them there for a visit to the Bitton home that night. Dr. Fell was fond of dining in French restaurants; or, in fact, anywhere else. He dug himself in behind a steaming parapet of dishes and a formidable array of wine bottles; but throughout the meal he steadily refused to discuss crime.

Those various adventures he had mentioned that afternoon were a surprise even to the young man who knew him so well. He remembered the cottage in the drowsy Lincolnshire countryside. He remembered Dr. Fell smoking his pipe in a little study where three walls were built of books, or pottering about his garden in a broad-brimmed white hat. The sundial, the bird houses, the lawns starred with white flowers and asleep in afternoon sunlight: this had seemed to be Dr. Fell's domain. It was incongruous that those words he had used so casually that afternoon, "Cripps, the Notting Hill poisoner," or "that chap with the mirror in his watch," or the tales from the far-off days of the heavy guns. But, none the less, Rampole remembered how once a telegram of five words had brought several quiet armed men from Scotland Yard to do his bidding.

And this evening the doctor would not speak of crime. On any other subject, however, it was practically impossible to stop him. He discussed in turn the third Crusade, the origin of the Christmas cracker, Sir Richard Steele, merry-go-rounds—on which he particularly enjoyed riding—Beowulf, Buddhism, Thomas Henry Huxley, and Miss Greta Garbo. It was eight-thirty before they finished dinner. Rampole, comfortably lazy and warmed with wine, had just sat back for the lighting of the cigars when Hadley arrived.

The chief inspector was restless, and he seemed worried. He put his briefcase down on the table and drew up a chair without removing his overcoat.

"I'll have a sandwich and a whisky with you," he said, in reply to Dr. Fell's invitation. "Come to think of it, I forgot to get any dinner. But we mustn't waste time."

The doctor peered at him over the flame of the match for his cigar.

"Developments?"

"Serious ones, I'm afraid. At least two unforeseen things have occurred. One of them I can't make head or tail of." He began to rummage in his briefcase and draw out papers. "To begin with, somebody broke into Driscoll's flat about a quarter to five o'clock this afternoon."

"Broke into—"

"Yes. Here are the facts, briefly. You remember, when we questioned that Larkin woman I left orders to have her shadowed. Fortunately, Hamper had an excellent man there; a plainclothes constable, new man, whose only talent seems to be along that line. He took up Larkin's trail as soon as she left the gates. She walked straight up Tower Hill, without hesitating or looking back. Probably she knew she would be followed; anyhow, she made no attempt to give this man—what's his name—Somers, yes—to give him the slip.

"At the top of Tower Hill she cut across and went into the Mark Lane Underground Station. There was a queue in front of the booking office, and Somers couldn't get close enough to hear the station to which she booked. But Somers had a hunch. He took a ticket to Russell Square, which is the tube station nearest to where she lives. She changed at King's Cross, and then he knew he was right. He got out after her at the Russell Square station in Bernard Street, and followed her down Woburn Place to Tavistock Square.

"She went into the third entry of Tavistock Chambers, still

without looking round. Somers walked straight in after her, like a fool. But it's fortunate he did.

"He describes it as a rather narrow entry, badly lighted by a door with a glass panel at the rear, and with an automatic lift in the center. The doors to the two flats on that floor are on either side. He had seen her closing the door of Number One after her. And, at the same time she was going in, a woman slid out of the door of Number Two, darted past the lift, down a couple of steps, and out of the glass door at the back."

"The woman again, eh?" said Dr. Fell, blowing out smoke placidly. "Did he catch a glimpse of her?"

"Wait. Nothing at all definite, you see. There were no lights on, and what with the mist, the darkness of the hall, and the sudden run she made, he could just be sure it was a woman. Of course, he wasn't sure that anything was wrong. But as a matter of caution he went close and looked at the door, and then he was sure.

"The lock of the door had been splintered out from the jamb with some sharp instrument like a chisel or a heavy screwdriver. Somers ran down the way she had gone. The glass door opened on a large paved court, with a driveway going out to the street. Of course, the woman was gone. And Somers came back.

"Now, at the time he didn't know Driscoll lived there; he only knew the Larkin woman did, from what instructions he'd been given. But he struck a match and saw the card on the door, and then he was inside in a hurry.

"The place was in a wild state of disorder; somebody had been searching for something. But I'll come to that in a moment. Somers went out after the porter, and had the devil's own time finding him. The porter is an old man, rather deaf, and he was in a bad state when Somers made him understand what had happened. He said he had been in his room for several hours, and had heard nothing. The only person he had seen there that afternoon was a young man who had been there many times before, and had a key. He knew *he* hadn't burgled the place, because he had met the young man coming out of the door of the flat, and walked out to his car with him, and he knew everything had been in order then. Somers explained he meant a woman, who had been there just a moment ago; and the porter refused to believe him."

Dr. Fell was drawing designs on the tablecloth with a fork.

"Had anything been stolen from the flat?" he inquired.

"We can't tell yet. I haven't seen the place, but one of my best men is up there now. According to Somers's report, the desk had been broken open, every drawer in the flat ransacked, and most of Driscoll's papers were scattered over the floor."

"In search for some sort of letter or document?"

"Apparently. And I think we have an explanation of 'Mary.'"

"I rather thought we should," said the doctor. "Well?"

"One thing in the study struck Somers's eye because it seemed so out of place. It was your typical bachelor digs—hunting prints, leather chairs, a silver cup or two, sport groups, things like that. But on the mantelpiece were two plaster figures on bases, painted in bright colors—a man and a woman. They wore what Somers called 'old-time clothes, like the ones in Madame Tussaud's,' and they were labeled—"

Dr. Fell raised his eyebrows and grunted. "I see. Philip II and Mary Tudor. Rather an unfortunate instance of a romance, though. H'm. They probably got them at some outing together, and kept them for the sentimental remembrance. Well—who was the woman?"

The waiter brought Hadley a ham sandwich and a stiff whisky and soda. He took a pull at the latter before he answered.

"It looks fairly clear, doesn't it, after what we decided this afternoon?" he demanded. "It had to be somebody who already knew about the murder. She would realize that, with Driscoll dead, his papers would be examined immediately. And if there were any letters that incriminate *her*—?"

"In short, Mrs. Bitton," said Dr. Fell. "No, I don't have any doubt you're right. Let's see. We questioned her before we questioned Larkin, didn't we? And then let her go."

"Yes. And think back, now! Do you remember just before she was about to leave? Ah, Rampole, you remember it, I can see. You noticed?"

The American nodded. "Just for a moment; an expression of real and close terror. She seemed to remember something."

"And do you recall what General Mason had just said? I saw that expression on her face, and I tried to account for it; but I understand now. General Mason had been urging Sir William to go up to his rooms and rest, and he said, 'The Devereux record is in the portfolio on my desk.' And that instantly suggested to her the damning evidence that might be lying in Driscoll's desk for the police to discover. Evidently she has called herself 'Mary' only since he had reason to believe she was being watched."

"But would she have had time to get up to Driscoll's flat and do all this?" Rampole asked. "We didn't talk very long with Mrs. Larkin. And Sir William went out to put Mrs. Bitton into a cab—"

"Which she dismissed at the top of Tower Hill for the underground. She could have gone from Mark Lane to King's Cross in less than fifteen minutes; she could have even saved the risk of time lost in changing trains by getting out at King's Cross and walking to Tavistock Square. Oh yes. The taxi would have been much too slow. And as for getting into the flat, you've only got to take one look at her to realize that she could have broken open a much less flimsy door with no particular trouble. The deaf porter wouldn't be apt to hear any noise, and the only other person who could have discovered her was Mrs. Larkin—whom she knew to be detained at the Tower."

"That tears it," said Dr. Fell. "That undoubtedly tears it. *Hah!*" He put his big head in his hands. "This is bad, Hadley. And what I don't like is the symbolism."

"Symbolism?"

"I mean those two plaster figures you've described. God knows, they may have won them throwing balls at bottles at a country fair. But it's a curious and disturbing fact that the woman signed at least one of her letters 'Mary.' Suppose you and your lady-love have two china dolls in which you like to fancy an analogy to yourselves. One of them is labeled 'Abélard' and the other 'Héloïse.' You're very apt to look up Héloïse and Abélard, aren't you, and see who they were? If you don't already know. And I tell you, Hadley, I didn't like that Bitton woman's much too palpably idiotic prattle about Queen Elizabeth being executed. It wasn't like her."

"What are you driving at?"

"If there *is* a symbolism about those two figures," said the doctor, "we have got to remember two things about Queen Mary Tudor of England and her husband, King Philip II of Spain. One is that all her life Mary was violently in love with Philip, a passion almost as strong as her religious faith; while Philip was never in the least interested in her. And the second thing we must remember—"

"Well?"

"That they called her 'Bloody Mary,'" said Dr. Fell.

There was a long silence. The little restaurant, almost empty of diners, whispered to that suggestion as with the ticking of a clock. There was a little *fine* left at the bottom of Rampole's liqueur glass, and he drained it hastily.

"Whatever *that* amounts to," Hadley said, at length, with grim doggedness, "I'll go on to the second thing that's happened since I've seen you. And it's the really disturbing one. It's about Julius Arbor."

Dr. Fell struck the table. "Go on!" he said. "Good God! I might have known— That chases the cobwebs. Go on, Hadley."

"He's at Golder's Green. Listen.

"They didn't tell us this when we left the Tower, but Sergeant Hamper found it out and phoned to me, and I've just finished tracing down the rest. When Arbor left us, it couldn't have been much more than twenty past six o'clock. You remember, we all looked at our watches to be sure Arbor was right about the time? It was six-fifteen then, and he left shortly afterwards.

"Well, the word had already been carried up to the first tower you enter as you go in—it always confuses me, because it's called the Middle Tower—word had been carried up to let him go through. He told us, you remember, that he'd brought a taxi down there; told the driver to wait, and then couldn't reappear. After some length of time, the driver wondered what was wrong and came down to the Middle Tower to investigate. The Spur Guard barred his way, and the warder on duty said something about an accident. Apparently the driver had happy visions of his meter clicking into pounds; he planted himself there and waited. He waited, mind you, for over three hours. Such is the London cabby."

Hadley finished his sandwich, called for another whisky, and lit a cigarette.

"Then Arbor came out from the Byward Tower, where we were, and started to walk along the causeway between there and the Middle Tower. It was dark then, and still rather misty. But there's a gas lamp on the parapet of the bridge. The taxi driver and the warder on duty at the Middle Tower happened to glance along the causeway, and they saw Arbor leaning against the lamp standard as though he were about to collapse. Then he straightened up and stumbled ahead.

"They thought he was drunk. But when he reached them his face was white and sweaty, and he could hardly talk. Another of those attacks we witnessed, undoubtedly, but a worse attack because, somehow, he'd got a worse fright. The taxi driver took him over to the refreshment room, and he drank about half a tumbler of brandy neat. He seemed a bit better, and ordered the driver to take him to Sir William's house in Berkeley Square.

"When he arrived there he again told the driver to wait. He said he wanted to pack a bag and then to go to an address at Golder's Green. At this the driver protested volubly. He'd been waiting over three hours, there was a big bill on the meter, and he hadn't seen the color of his fare's money; besides, Golder's Green was a long distance out. Then Arbor shoved a five-pound note into his hand, and said he could have another if he would do as he was told.

"Naturally, the taxi driver began to suspect something fishy. During all the time he spent hanging about the Middle Tower, the warder had let slip a few hints about the real state of affairs. Arbor wasn't in the house long before he came out carrying a valise and a couple of coats over his arm. On the drive to Golder's Green the driver grew decidedly uneasy."

Hadley paused, and turned over a sheet of paper from his briefcase as though to refresh his memory. He spoke while his eye was still running down the typewritten lines.

"Did you ever notice how even the most reticent people will

speak freely to taxi drivers? They'll not only speak, but they'll be quite garrulous. I don't know why it is, unless it's because a taxi driver is never surprised at anything. If I were going to establish a system of police spies in England, I shouldn't make them concierges, as they do in France; I'd make them taxi drivers. Never mind that. Here we are."

He frowned, and then tapped the sheets on his palm.

"Now, but for what this driver knew of the murder, and Arbor's rather remarkable mumblings in the cab, I shouldn't have heard this at all. But the taxi driver was afraid he'd be mixed up in a murder. So after he drove Arbor to Golder's Green, he came straight back and went to Scotland Yard. Fortunately, he fell into the proper hands, and they sent him to me. He was one of the famous type—stout, patient, rather morose, with a red face and a large grayish mustache and a gruff voice. But, like most Cockneys, he had a flair for description and vivid pantomime. He perched on the edge of a chair in my office, turning his cap round in his hands and imitating Arbor to the life. You could see Arbor, nervous and ultra-dignified, holding to his glasses as the cab bumped, and every two minutes leaning up to ask a question.

"First Arbor asked him whether he carried a revolver. The taxi driver said 'Ho!' and laughed. Then Arbor suggested he must be a pretty ugly customer in a row. The driver said he could hold his own. Next Arbor wondered whether they were being followed; he began talking about how he wasn't in the directory at all, and he had a cottage at Golder's Green which nobody knew about except some friends near by. He kept hinting that London wasn't as full of criminals as New York; was it? But what the driver especially remembered was his constant reference to 'a voice.'"

"A voice?" Doctor Fell repeated. "Whose voice?"

"Arbor didn't say. But he asked whether telephone calls could be traced; that was the only point he definitely mentioned in connection with it. Well, they reached the cottage, in an outlying district. But Arbor said he wouldn't go in just at the moment—the place hadn't been opened for months. He had the driver drop him at a villa not far away, which was well lighted. The driver noted the name. It was called 'Briarbrae.'"

"The friends of his, I suppose. H'm."

"Yes. We looked it up later. It belongs to a Mr. Daniel Spengler. Now, that's about all. What do you make of it?"

"It looks bad, Hadley. This man may be in very grave danger. I don't think he is, personally, but there's just a chance—"

"I don't need you to tell me *that*," the chief inspector said, irritably. "If the damned fools would only come to us when they get into trouble! That's what we're for. But they won't. And if he is in any danger, he took the worst possible course. Instead of going to a hotel, as he said he intended, he thought he was choosing a spot where nobody could find him. And instead he picked a place ideally suited for—well, murder."

"What have you done?"

"I sent a good man immediately to watch the house, and to phone the Yard every half-hour. But what danger is he in? Do you think he knows something about the murder, and the murderer knows he knows?"

For a moment Dr. Fell puffed furiously at his cigar. Then he said, "This is getting much too serious, Hadley. Much. You see, I've been basing everything on a belief that I knew how all this came about. I told you this afternoon that everybody liked playing the master-mind. And I could afford to chuckle, because so much of it is really funny."

"*Funny?*"

"Yes. Ironically, impossibly funny. It's like a farce comedy suddenly gone mad. It's as though they introduced a throat-cutting into the second act of *Charley's Aunt*. Do you remember Mark Twain's description of his experiences in learning to ride a bicycle?"

"I'll be damned," said Hadley, stuffing papers back into his briefcase, "if I listen to any lecture when—"

"This isn't a lecture. Listen," urged Dr. Fell, with unwonted seriousness. "He said he was always doing exactly what he didn't want to do. He tried to keep from running over rocks and being thrown. But if he rode down a street two hundred yards wide, and there happened to be one small piece of brick lying anywhere in the road, inevitably he would run over it. Well, that has a very deadly application to this case.

"And I can't keep my pose any longer," the doctor said, with sudden energy. "I've got to separate the nonsense and the happenings of pure chance from the really ugly angle of the business. Chance started it, and murder only finished it; that's what I think. I must show you the absurd part of it, and then you can judge whether I'm right. But first there are two things to be done."

"What?"

"Can you communicate with that man you have on guard at Arbor's cottage?" the doctor asked, abruptly.

"Yes. Through the local police station."

"All right. Get in touch with him. Tell him, far from keeping in the background, to make himself as conspicuous as possible. Let him walk about the lawn, if he likes. But under no circumstances—even if he is hailed—to go near Arbor or make himself known to Arbor."

"What's the purpose of that?" the chief inspector demanded.

"I don't believe Arbor's in any danger. But obviously he thinks he is. He also thinks the police haven't any idea where he is. You see, there's something that man knows, which for one reason or another he wouldn't tell us. If he notices your man lurking about his cottage, he'll jump to the conclusion that it's his enemy. If he tries calling the local police, they will find nobody—naturally. It's rather rough on him, but we've got to terrify him into telling what he knows. As you said, the man has no courage at all. Sooner or later he'll seek *your* protection, and by that time we shall be able to get the truth."

"That," said the chief inspector, grimly, "is the only good suggestion you've made so far. I'm glad to see you're waking up. I'll do it."

"It can't do any harm. If he is in danger, the obvious presence of a guard will have a salutary effect on the enemy. If he does call the local police and there's a real enemy about, the police can have a look for the real enemy while they pass up your own man. The next thing, we've got to pay a very brief visit to Driscoll's flat."

"If you're thinking something is hidden there, I can tell you that my men will find it more easily than we can ever—"

"No. Your men will attach no importance to what I want to find. I don't suppose they bothered to look at his typewriter, did they?"

"His *what?*"

"Typewriter. You know what a typewriter is," said the doctor, testily. "And also, I want a brief look about the kitchen. If he has one, as I'm sure he has, we shall probably find it stowed away in the kitchen. Where's that waiter? I want the bill."

The mist was clearing as they emerged from the restaurant. Narrow Wardour Street was crowded; restaurant signs glowed with dull lights, a barrel-organ tinkled at the corner among a group of small boys, and there was a sound of jollification from several pubs. The theatre traffic had just begun to thin in the glare

of Shaftesbury Avenue, and Hadley had some difficulty in ma-
neuvering his car. But, once out of the center of Town and across
Oxford Street, he accelerated the big Daimler to a fast pace.
Bloomsbury lay deserted under high and mournful gas lamps;
silent, with the muffled rumble of traffic beyond. They cut across
into Great Russell Street, and turned left past the long and pris-
on-like shadows of the British Museum.

"Get that report out of my briefcase, will you?" Hadley requested. "I think Somers said it was on the west side of the square."

Rampole, craning his neck out of the tonneau, watched the
street signs. Montague Street; the bare trees and sedate house-
fronts of Russell Square; Upper Bedford Place, where Hadley
slowed down.

Tavistock Square was large and oblong in shape, not too well
supplied with street lights. Along the west side the buildings were
higher than on the others, and rather more imposing in a heavy
Georgian style. Tavistock Chambers proved to be a red-brick
block of flats with four entry halls, two on either side of an arch
beneath which a driveway led into the court. Into this court Hadley drove the car.

"So this," he said, "is the way the woman escaped. I don't wonder she wasn't noticed."

He slid from under the wheel and peered about. There was
only one lamp in the court, but the mist was rapidly lifting into a
clear, cold night. A few windows were alight in the plaster-faced
walls which hedged in the court.

"Lower parts of the windows frosted glass," the chief inspector
grunted. "I left instructions to question the tenants about her, but
it's useless. A red Indian in his war bonnet could have walked out
of here without being seen, even on a clear day. Let's see. Those
are the glass doors giving on the rear of the entry halls. We want

the third entry. There it is. That'll be Driscoll's flat, with the light in the rear window. Hum! Evidently my man hasn't left the place yet; I should have thought he'd be finished by this time."

He crossed to the glass door, stumbled over a rubbish can, and disturbed a hysterical cat. The others followed him up some steps into a red-tiled hall with brown distempered walls. Its only illumination was a sickly electric bulb in the cage of the automatic lift. But a thin line of light slanted out from the door on their left, which was not quite closed, and they saw the splintered wood about the lock.

Flat 2. Rampole's eyes moved to the door facing it across the hall, where the watchful and whaleboned Mrs. Larkin might be peering out from the flap of the letter slot. It was damp and cold in the hallway, and still except for somebody's radio talking hoarsely on an upper floor.

There was a crash, sudden and violent. The line of light in the doorway of Flat 2 seemed to shake, and the noise echoed hollowly up the lift-well. It had come from that door.

While the echoes were still trembling, Hadley moved swiftly across to the door and pushed it open. Rampole, peering over his shoulder, saw the disorder of Philip Driscoll's sitting room as it had been described a short time ago. But there was another piece of disorder now.

In the wall directly opposite was a mantelpiece with an ornate mirror behind the shelf. And in front of this mantelpiece, his back to the newcomers, a tall and heavy man stood with his head bowed. They saw past his shoulder a foolish plaster figurine standing on the mantelshelf—a woman painted in bright colors, with a tight-waisted dress and a silver hairnet. But there was no companion figure beside it. The hearthstone was littered with a thousand white fragments to show where the other figure had been flung down a moment before.

Just for a moment the tableau held—weird and somehow terrible in its power. The echo of that crash seemed to linger; its passion still quivered in the bent back of the man standing there. He had not heard the newcomers. He seemed weighed down, and lonely, and damned.

Then his hand moved out slowly and seized the other figure. And as he raised it his head lifted and they saw his face in the mirror.

"Good evening," said Dr. Fell. "You're Mr. Lester Bitton, aren't you?"

XI

The Little Plaster Dolls

NEVER BEFORE that time, Rampole afterwards thought, had he ever seen a man's naked face. Never had he seen it as for a brief instant he saw Lester Bitton's face in the mirror. At all times in life there are masks and guards, and in the brain a tiny bell gives warning. But here was a man caught blind in his anguish, as nerveless as the hand which held poised that little painted figurine.

And, oddly enough, Rampole's first thought was how he might have looked at this man had he seen him in his everyday existence: going in a bus to the City, say, or reading his newspaper at a club. Where you saw your staunch and practical British business man, you saw Lester Bitton. Well tailored, inclined to corpulence. Clean-shaven face, beginning to draw and go dry at the eyes and mouth, hard but pleasant; thick black hair frizzed with gray, and fresh from the clean hair-tonicy smell of the barber's.

He looked a little like his brother, though his face was inclined to be reddish and have heavy folds. But you could not tell now—

The lost, damned eyes stared back at them from the mirror. His wrist wobbled, and the figure almost slid through his fingers.

He took it with his other hand and put it back up on the mantel-piece. They could hear him breathing as he turned about. Instinctively his hand went to his tie, to straighten it; instinctively he felt down the sides of his dark overcoat.

"Who the hell," said Lester Bitton, "are *you?*"

His deep voice was hoarse, and it cracked. That almost finished him, but he fought his nerves. "What Goddamned right have you got to walk in—"

Rampole couldn't stand this. It wasn't right to look at him, in the way that man felt; it wasn't decent. The American felt mean and petty. He moved his eyes away, and wished he hadn't come inside the door.

"Steady," said Hadley, quietly. "I'm afraid it's you who have to make an explanation. This flat has been taken over by the police, you know. And I'm afraid we can't respect private feelings in a murder case. You *are* Lester Bitton, aren't you?"

The man's heavy breathing quieted somewhat, and the wrath died out of his eyes. But he looked heavy and hollow, and unutterably tired.

"I am," he said in a lower voice. "Who are you?"

"My name is Hadley."

"Ah," said the other, "I see." He was groping backwards, and he found the edge of a heavy leather chair. Slowly he lowered himself until he was sitting on the arm. Then he made a gesture. "Well, here I am," he added, as though that explained everything.

"What are you doing here, Mr. Bitton?"

"I suppose you don't *know?*" Bitton asked, bitterly. He glanced back over his shoulder, at the smashed figure on the hearthstone, and looked up again at Hadley.

The chief inspector played his advantage. He studied Bitton without threat and almost without interest. Slowly he opened his briefcase, drew out a typewritten sheet—which was only Constable Somers's report, as Rampole saw—and glanced at it.

"We know, of course, that you have employed a firm of private detectives to watch your wife. And"—he glanced at the sheet again—"that one of their operatives, a Mrs. Larkin, lives directly across the hall from here."

"Rather smart, you Scotland Yard men," the other observed in an impersonal voice. "Well, that's right. Nothing illegal in that, I suppose. You also know, then, that I don't need to waste my money any longer."

"We know that Mr. Driscoll is dead."

Bitton nodded. His heavy, reddish, rather thickly-lined face was assuming normal appearance; the eyes had ceased to have that dull and terrible glitter; but a nerve seemed to jump in his arm.

"Yes," he said, reflectively. His eyes wandered about the room without curiosity. "The swine's dead. I heard it when I went home to dinner. But I'm afraid it hasn't cut my detective agency off from much money. I was intending to pay them off and get rid of them tomorrow. Business conditions being what they are, I couldn't afford an unnecessary expense."

"That, Mr. Bitton, is open to two meanings. Which of them do you imply?"

Lester Bitton was himself again—hard, shrewd, very clear-eyed; a fleshy and utterly stolid version of his brother. He spread out his hands.

"Let's be frank, Mr.—er—Hadley. I have played the fool. You know I was having my wife followed. I owe her a profound apology. What I have discovered only does credit to her name."

Hadley's face wore a faint smile, as one who says, "Well done!"

"Mr. Bitton," he said, "I had intended having a conversation with you tonight, and this is as good a place as any. I shall have to ask you a number of questions."

"As you wish."

Hadley looked round at his companions. Dr. Fell was paying not the slightest attention to the questioning. He was running his eyes over the small, pleasant room, with its dull, brown-papered walls, sporting prints, and leather chairs. One of the chairs had been knocked over. The drawer of a side table had been thrown upside down on the floor, its contents scattered. Dr. Fell stumped across and peered down.

"Theater programs," he said, "magazines, old invitations, bills. H'm. Nothing I want here. The desk and the typewriter will be in the other rooms somewhere. Excuse me. Carry on with the questioning, Hadley. Don't mind me."

He disappeared through a door at the rear.

Hadley removed his bowler, gestured Rampole to a chair, and sat down himself.

"Mr. Bitton," he said, harshly, "I suggest that you be frank. I am not concerned with your wife's morals, or with yours, except in so far as they concern a particularly brutal murder. You have admitted you had her followed. Why do you trouble to deny that there was an affair between your wife and Philip Driscoll?"

"That's a damned lie. If you insinuate—"

"I don't insinuate. I tell you. You can hardly be very excited by an insinuation which you made yourself when you put a private detective on her movements—can you? Let's not waste time. We have the 'Mary' notes, Mr. Bitton."

"Mary? Who the devil is Mary?"

"You should know, Mr. Bitton. You were about to smash her on the hearth when we walked into this room."

Hadley bent forward; he spoke sharply and coldly.

"I warn you again, I can't afford to waste time. You are not in the habit of walking into people's houses and smashing ornaments off their mantelshelves because you don't approve of the decoration. If you have any idea that we don't know the meaning of those two figures, get rid of it. We do. You had broken the man, and you were about to break the woman. No sane person who saw your face at that moment could have any doubt of your state of mind. Do I make myself clear?"

Bitton shaded his eyes with a big hand, but a crooked vein stood out at his temple. "Is it any of your business," he said at length, in a repressed voice, "whether—"

"How much do you know about Driscoll's murder?"

"Eh?"

"Have you heard the facts of Driscoll's murder?"

"A few. I—well, I spoke to my brother when he returned from the Tower. Laura—Laura had come home and locked herself in her room. When I—when I came back from the City, I knocked at her door and she wouldn't let me in. I thought everybody had gone mad. Especially as I knew nothing of this—this murder. And Sheila said that Laura had run into the house as white as death and rushed upstairs without a word." The hand before his eyes clenched spasmodically. "Then Will came in about seven-thirty and told me a little."

"Are you aware, then, that an excellent case could be made out against your wife for the murder of Philip Driscoll?"

Hadley was in action now. Rampole stared at him; a placid merchant ship suddenly running out the masked batteries. Hitherto, the American knew, he had lacked proof of his most vital point, and Bitton had supplied it. There was about him now nothing of the urbanity with which he had treated witnesses that afternoon. He sat gray and inexorable, his fingers interlocked, his eyes burning with a glow behind the eyeballs, and heavy lines tightening round his mouth.

"Just a moment, Mr. Bitton. Don't say anything. I'll give you no theories. I simply intend to tell you facts.

"Your wife was having an affair with Philip Driscoll. She wrote a note telling him to meet her today at one-thirty at the Tower of London. We know that he received this note, because it was found in his pocket. The note informed him that they were being watched. Driscoll, I need not tell you, lived off the bounty of a quick-tempered and far from indulgent uncle. I will not say that if the uncle ever discovered any such scandal he would disinherit his nephew—because even that obvious point is a theory. I will not say that Driscoll saw the vital necessity for breaking off his liaison—because that obvious point is a theory, too.

"But he did telephone Robert Dalrye to get him out of a mess, just after he received that letter. And, later, someone did speak to Dalrye on the telephone, *in a high voice,* and lure him away on a wild-goose chase to this flat. You need not consider the following inferences, because they are theories. One. That Driscoll always ran to Dalrye when he was in trouble. Two. That all Driscoll's family knew this. Three. That Dalrye's level-headedness would have caused the impressionable Driscoll to break off such a dangerous entanglement. Four. That Driscoll was in a mood to break it off, because he had not seen his paramour for several weeks and he was a youth of roving fancy. Five. That his paramour felt convinced she could keep him in line if she saw him once again alone, without the interference of a cool-headed third party. Six. That Driscoll's paramour knew of this morning telephone call through Sheila Bitton, who had also spoken with Dalrye on the phone that morning. Seven. That the voice of Driscoll's paramour is, for a woman, fairly deep. And, finally, eight. That a voice on the telephone speaking quickly, chaotically, and almost unintelligibly, can pass without detection for the tones of almost anyone the speaker may choose."

Hadley was quite unemotional. He spaced his words as though he were reading a document, and his interlocked fingers seemed to beat time to them. Lester Bitton had taken his hand away from his face, and he was holding the chair-arms.

"I have told you these were inferences. Now for more facts," the chief inspector continued. "The appointment in the note had been for one-thirty. One-thirty is the last time Driscoll was seen alive. He was standing near the Traitors' Gate, and some person approached out of the shadows and touched his arm. At precisely twenty-five minutes to two, a woman answering to the description of your wife was seen hurrying away from the vicinity of the Traitors' Gate. She was hurrying so blindly, in fact, that she bumped squarely into the witness who saw her in a roadway no wider than this room. Finally, when Driscoll's body was found on the steps of the Traitors' Gate, he was discovered to have been stabbed with a weapon which your wife purchased last year in southern France, and which was ready to her hand in her own home."

He paused, looked steadily at Bitton, and added in a low voice, "Can't you imagine what a clever lawyer could to with all those points, Mr. Bitton? And I am only a policeman."

Bitton hoisted up his big body. His hands were shaking and the rims of his eyes were red.

"Damn you," he said, "that's what you think, is it? Well, I'm glad you saw me so soon. I'm glad you didn't make an unutterable ass of yourself before you told me how good your case was and arrested her. I'll tell you what I'm going to do, I'm going to blow your whole case higher than hell without stepping any further than that flat across the hall. Because *I* have a witness who saw her the whole time she was at the Tower of London, and can swear Driscoll was alive after she left him."

Hadley was on his feet in an instant. It was like the lunge of a swordsman.

"Yes," he said, in a louder voice, "I rather thought you had. I rather thought that was why you came to Tavistock Chambers tonight. When you heard about the murder, you couldn't wait for the usual report of your private detective over there. You had to go to *her.* If she knows anything, bring her over here and let her swear to it. Otherwise, so help me God! I'll swear out a warrant for Mrs. Bitton's arrest inside an hour."

Bitton shouldered out of the chair. He was fighting mad, and his usual good sense had deserted him. He flung open the door with the broken lock, and closed it with a slam. They could hear his footsteps ring grittily on the tiles of the hall; a pause, and the insistent clamor of a door-buzzer.

Rampole drew a hand across his forehead. His throat was dry and his heart hammering.

"I didn't know—" he said—"I didn't know you were so certain Mrs. Bitton had—"

There was a placid smile under Hadley's clipped mustache. He sat down again and folded his hands.

"Sh-h!" he warned. "Not so loud, please; he'll hear you. How did I do it? I'm not much of an actor, but I'm used to little demonstrations like that. Did I do it well?"

He caught the expression on the American's face.

"Go ahead, my boy. Swear. I don't mind. It's a tribute to my performance."

"Then you don't believe—"

"I never believed it for an instant," the chief inspector admitted, cheerfully. "There were too many holes in it. If Mrs. Bitton killed Driscoll, what about the hat on Driscoll's head? That becomes nonsense. If she killed him by Traitors' Gate with a blow straight through the heart at one-thirty, how did he contrive to keep alive until ten minutes to two? Why didn't she leave the Tower after she had killed him, instead of hanging about unnecessarily for nearly an hour and getting herself drawn into the mess without reason? Besides, my explanation of the faked telephone call to Dalrye was very thin. If Bitton hadn't been so upset he would have seen it. Dalrye, of course, never talked to Sheila Bitton this morning and told her Driscoll had made an appointment. But I had to hit Bitton hard and frequently while his guard was down. A little drama also did no harm; it never does."

"But, by God!" said Rampole, "I don't mind telling you it was good." He stared across at the smashed plaster on the hearthstone. "You had to do that. Otherwise you'd never have got Mrs. Larkin's testimony. If she followed Mrs. Bitton, she knows all Mrs. Bitton's movements, but—"

Hadley glanced over his shoulder to make sure the door was closed.

"Exactly. But she would never tell them to the police. This afternoon she swore to us she had seen nothing. That was a part of her job; she took the risk. She couldn't tell us she was following Mrs. Bitton without exposing the whole thing and losing her position. More than that—and a much sounder reason—I think she has tidy blackmail schemes in her mind. Now we've knocked *that* on the head. She's already told Bitton, of course. So if she won't tell, he will—to clear his wife. But I'll promise to forget what she said this afternoon if she gives us a signed statement. Bitton does all the work of persuading her to talk. Let him apply the third degree; *we* couldn't."

Rampole pushed back his hat.

"Neat!" he said. "Very neat, sir. Now, if your plan to persuade Arbor to talk works as well—"

"Arbor!" The chief inspector sprang up. "I'd forgotten it. I've been sitting here explaining my own cleverness, and I clean forgot that. I've got to telephone Golder's Green, and do it quickly. Where the devil is the phone? And, incidentally, where's the man who was supposed to be guarding this flat; how did Bitton get in here, anyhow? And where, by the way, is Fell?"

He was answered without delay. From beyond the closed door, somewhere in the interior of the flat, there was a scrape, a thud, and a terrific metallic crash.

"It's all right!" a muffled voice boomed out to them from some distance away. "No more plaster figures broken. I've just dropped a basket of tools off the shelf in the kitchen."

Hadley and Rampole hurried in the direction of the voice. Beyond the door through which the doctor had gone, a narrow passage ran straight back. There were two doors in either wall; those on the left leading to a study and a bedroom, and those on the right a bath—and a dining room. The kitchen was at the extreme rear of the passage.

To add to the confusion of the room, Driscoll had never been especially neat in his habits. The study had been cluttered up long before the woman's frantic search that afternoon. The floor was a drift of papers; rows of shelves gaped where whole sections of books had been tossed out; and the drawers of the desk hung out empty and drunken. A portable typewriter, its cover off, had become entangled with the telephone, and the contents of several brass ashtrays were sprayed across carbon paper, pencils, and an overturned bottle of ink. Even the green shade of the hanging lamp, which burned dully above the typewriter, had been knocked awry, and the iron fender pulled away from the fireplace. Apparently the intruder had concentrated her attention on the study.

Hadley glanced quickly into the other rooms as Dr. Fell opened the door of the kitchen. The bed was still unmade in the bedroom. The disarranged bureau was a gallery of large cabinet photographs of women, most of them with rather lurid inscriptions. This Driscoll, Rampole considered, had been a young man to be envied, even though his conquests seemed mostly of the housemaid type. The search here had been more perfunctory, confined to the bureau. And the dining room had not been touched at all. It had seldom or never been used for eating purposes, but there had palpably been a use for it. Two gigantic rows of empty soda-siphons had been lined up on the sideboard. Under a mosaic dome of lights over the table there mingled in confusion empty bottles, unwashed glasses, a cocktail shaker, ash trays, and several sportive pieces of orange peel. The whole had a dry, sticky appearance. Hadley grunted and switched off the light.

"The kitchen also," Dr. Fell observed at his elbow, "seems to have been used chiefly for mixing drinks. My estimation of the late Mr. Driscoll would have been considerably improved if I had not spotted a tin of that unmentionable substance known as cocoa." He swept his arm about. "You see? That sitting room he kept tidy for casual visitors like his uncle. This is where he really lived. H'mf."

He was wheezing in the kitchen doorway. Over his arm he carried a large market-basket which jingled with iron.

"You said tools?" inquired Hadley, sharply. "Was that what you were looking for? You mean a chisel or a screwdriver used to force open the outer door of this flat?"

"Good Lord, no!" snorted the doctor, with a grunt that rattled the basket. "My dear Hadley, you don't seriously suppose the woman got into the flat, came back here, found a chisel, and went out again so that she could break open the door for sheer amusement, do you?"

"She might have done just that," said the chief inspector, quietly, "to give the impression it was some outsider who had burgled the flat."

"It's entirely possible, I grant you. But, as a matter of fact, I wasn't interested in the breaking or entering. It was an entirely different sort of tool I was looking for."

"It may further interest you to know," the chief inspector pursued, rather irritably, "that while you have been poking about in the kitchen we've learned a great deal from Bitton."

The doctor nodded several times, and the black ribbon on his glasses swung jumpily. His shovel hat shaded the top of his face, so that he looked more and more like a fat bandit.

"Yes," he agreed, "I thought you would. He was here to get information from his private detective, and you've scared him into forcing her to tell what she knows by making out a thundering case against his wife. I imagined I could safely leave that to you. I wasn't needed. H'mf." He blinked curiously round the passage. "I know you have to get it down for the records, and keep everything in order. But from my point of view it wasn't necessary. I'm rather sure I can tell you what the Larkin woman knows. Come over here to the study for a moment, and have a look at Driscoll's character."

"You infernal old stuffed-shirt bluffer!" said Hadley, like one who commences an oration. "You—"

"Oh, come," protested the doctor, with a mildly injured air. "Tut, tut! No. I may be a childish old fool. I admit that. But

I'm not a bluffer, old man. Really, I'm not. Let's see, what was I talking about? Oh yes; Driscoll's character. There are some rather interesting photographs of him in the study. In one of them he—"

Sharply and stridently through the silent passage the telephone in the study rang.

XII

Concerning XNineteen

"THAT," SAID Hadley, whirling about, "may be a lead. Wait a moment. I'll answer it."

They followed him into the study. Dr. Fell seemed about to launch some sort of protest, whose nature Rampole could not imagine, but the chief inspector picked up the telephone.

He said, "Hello! . . . Yes, this is Chief Inspector Hadley speaking. . . . *Who?* . . . Oh, yes. . . . It's Sheila Bitton," he said to the others over his shoulder, and there was a tinge of disappointment in his voice. "Yes. . . . Yes, certainly, Miss Bitton." A long pause. "Why, I suppose you may, but I shall have to have a look at everything first, you know. . . . No trouble at all! When will you come over?"

"Wait!" said Dr. Fell, eagerly. He stumped across. "Tell her to hold on a second."

"What is it?" the chief inspector asked in some irritation, with his hand over the mouthpiece.

"She's coming over here tonight?"

"Yes. She says there are some belongings of Philip's that her uncle wants her to bring to the house."

"H'm. Ask her if she's got anybody to bring her over here."

165

"What the devil? Oh, all right," Hadley agreed, wearily, as he saw on the doctor's face that almost fiendish expression which people wear when they want a message transmitted by phone and have to keep silent themselves. Hadley spoke again. "She says she's got Dalrye," he transmitted after a moment.

"That won't do. There's somebody in that house I've got to talk to, and I've got to talk to him *out* of the house or it may be no good. And this," grunted the doctor, excitedly, "is the chance of a lifetime to do it. Let me talk to her, will you?"

Hadley shrugged and got up from the desk.

"Hello!" said the doctor, in what he evidently meant for a gentle tone suitable to women. It actually sounded as though he were gulping. "Miss Bitton? This is Dr. Fell, Mr. Hadley's—um—colleague. . . . You do? Oh yes; from your fiancé, of course. . . . *HEY?*"

"You needn't blow the mouthpiece out," Hadley observed, sourly. "What tact! What tact! Ha!"

"Excuse me, Miss Bitton. Excuse me. I may be, of course, the fattest walrus Mr. Dalrye has ever seen, but . . . No, no, my dear; of course I don't mind. . . ."

They could hear the phone tinkling in an animated fashion; Rampole remembered Mrs. Larkin's description of Sheila Bitton as a "little blonde," and grinned to himself. Dr. Fell contemplated the phone with an expression of one trying to smile in order to have his picture taken; presently he broke in.

"What I was trying to say, Miss Bitton, was this. You'll undoubtedly have a number of things to take away, and they'll be quite bulky. . . . Oh! Mr. Dalrye has to be back at the Tower by ten o'clock? . . . Then you will certainly want somebody to handle them. Haven't you somebody there who could? . . . The chauffeur's not there? Well, what about your father's valet? What's his name?—Marks. He spoke highly of Marks, and . . . But please don't bring your father, Miss Bitton; it would only make him feel worse. (She's weeping now!" the doctor added, desperately, over his shoulder.) "Oh, he's lying down? Very well, Miss Bitton. We shall expect you. Good-bye."

He turned about, glowering, and shook the tool-basket until it jangled. "She burbles. She prattles. And she called me a walrus. A most naive young lady. And if any humorist on these premises makes the obvious remark about the Walrus and the Carpenter—"

He set down the tool-basket with a clank.

"Dr. Watson—" Hadley muttered. "Thanks for reminding me. I've got to put a call through to the police station at Golder's Green. Get up from there."

He began a series of relay-calls through Scotland Yard, and finally left his orders. He had just finished informing some mystified desk sergeant on the other wire to phone him here after he had made sure the message was delivered to the guard at Arbor's cottage, when they heard footsteps in the sitting room.

Evidently it had taken some time for Lester Bitton to persuade Mrs. Larkin that it would be advisable to talk. Bitton was pacing the front room, looking flushed and dangerous. Mrs. Larkin, a straight figure with a face more square than ever, was holding back the curtain of the front window and peering out with extreme nonchalance. When she saw Hadley she examined him coldly.

"You tecs," she said, her upper lip wrinkling; "pretty damn smart, ain't you? I told his nibs here you'd got nothing on his wife. He should have sat tight and let you go ahead, and then we could both have got a sweet piece of change out of you for false arrest.

But no. He had to get scared and spill the beans. But I've been promised *my* pay for speaking out loud in meeting. So," concluded Mrs. Larkin, lifting her shoulders, "what the hell?"

Hadley opened his briefcase again. This time he was not bluffing; the printed form he opened carried two decidedly unflattering snapshots, one of which was a side view.

"'Amanda Georgette Larkin,'" he read. "'Alias Amanda Leeds, Alias Georgie Simpson. Known as "Emmy." Shoplifting. Specialty, jewelry, large department stores. Last heard of in New York—'"

"You needn't go through all that," interrupted Emmy. "There's nothing on me now. I told you that this afternoon. But go on and get his nibs to tell you what agency I work for. Then you'll tell them, and, *bingo!* I'm through."

Hadley folded up the paper and replaced it. "You may be trying to make an honest living," he said, "if I can be so polite about your profession. We'll certainly keep an eye on you, Mrs. Larkin. But if you give us a clear statement, I don't think I need warn your employers about Georgie Simpson."

She put her hands on her hips and studied him.

"That's fair enough. Not that I've got a lot of choice in the matter. All right. Here she goes."

Mrs. Larkin's manner underwent a subtle change. That afternoon she had seemed all tight corsets and severe tailoring, like an especially forbidding schoolmistress. Now the stiffness disappeared into an easier slouch. She dropped into a chair, saw some cigarettes in a box on the taboret beside her, selected one, and struck the match by whisking it across the sole of her shoe.

"Those two," she said, with a spurt of something like admiration, "were havin' one hell of a time! They—"

"That's enough of that!" Lester Bitton cut in, in a heavy voice. "These—these men aren't interested."

"I bet they're not," said Mrs. Larkin, with cool skepticism. "How about it, Hadley?"

"What we want to know is everything you did today, Mrs. Larkin."

"Right. Well, in my profession a man we always look out for is the postman. I was up bright and early, ready for him. He always puts the letters in the box of Number One, my place, first, and then goes across the way. I can time it so that I'm picking up the milk bottle outside my door when he gets out the mail for Number Two. And *that* was easy. Because XNineteen—that's the way we have to describe people in the confidential reports—XNineteen always wrote her letters on a sort of pink-purplish kind of paper you could see a mile off."

"How did you know," inquired Hadley, "that the letters were from XNineteen?"

She looked at him. "Don't be funny," said Mrs. Larkin, coldly. "It's not healthy for a respectable widow to get into people's flats with a duplicate key. And it's a damn sight less healthy to be found steaming open people's letters. Let's say I overheard them talking about the first letter she wrote him."

"All right. I'd been warned XNineteen was coming back to London Sunday night, and so I had my eyes open this morning. Well, I admit that I was kind of surprised when I went out to pick up my milk bottle and found Driscoll picking up his milk bottle just over the way. He never gets up before noon. But there he was, all dressed, and lookin' as though he'd had a bad night. He had his door open, and I could see the inside of the letter box."

She twisted round, and pointed with her cigarette at the wire cage just below the slot in the door.

"He didn't pay any attention to *me*. Then, while he had the milk bottle under one arm, and still holding the door open with his foot, he stuck his hand in the letter box. He pulled out the pink letter, and sort of grunted, and put it in his pocket without opening it. Then he saw me, and let the door slam.

"So I thought, 'What ho!' And I knew there was going to be a meeting somewhere. But I wasn't to watch *him*. I'd only been planted opposite so I could catch XNineteen with the goods."

"You seem to have been a long time in doing it," said Hadley.

She made a comfortable gesture. "Well, we detectives have to take our time, don't we, and be pretty sure before we act? No use finishin' off a good assignment too quick. But all the times she's been there I never saw anything. The best chance I had was the night before she went away, about two weeks ago. They come in from the theatre or some place, and they was both pretty tight. I watched the door, and everything was all quiet for about two hours, so I knew what was up. Then the door opened, and they both come out again for him to take her home. I couldn't see anything; it was black as pitch out in the hall, but I could hear. By this time she was tighter yet, but he was as drunk as a hoot-owl. And they stood there swearing eternal love to each other; and he was saying how he was going to do a piece of work that would get him a good newspaper job, and then they could get married—and, oh, they had a hell of a time.

"But I wasn't certain," explained the practical Mrs. Larkin, "because that's what they all say when they're drank. And besides, I heard him telling the same thing to a little red-head he had here while XNineteen was away, so I didn't believe he was as gone on XNineteen as she was on him. But that night, of course, I wasn't on duty. I was just getting home myself, and he came staggering down the steps with his arm around the red-head, and she was trying to hold him up, and he slipped and fell and said 'Jesus Christ.'"

"*Stop it!*" Lester Bitton suddenly shouted. The cry was wrung from him. He had been standing at the window, staring out, with the window curtain over his shoulder and hiding him. Now he whipped round, started to speak, and sagged. "You didn't," he said heavily, "you didn't put into your report—you didn't say this—"

"Time enough. But I am off the subject, ain't I?" said Mrs. Larkin. She studied him. Her hard, square face, which was neither young nor middle-aged, relaxed a trifle. She straightened the puffs of hair over her ears. "Don't take it so hard, mister. They're all like that, mostly. I didn't mean to give you the works. You seem like a pretty decent guy, if you'd come off your dignity and be human.

"I'll go on about today. Oh yes; I know where I was. I've got to tell the slops, ain't I?" she said, petulantly, as he turned away again. "Well, I got dressed and went up to Berkeley Square. It's a good thing I did, because she come out of the house fairly early. And believe it or not," said Mrs. Larkin in an awed voice, crashing out her cigarette, "that woman walked all the way from her place to the Tower of London! I damn near died. But I didn't dare take a cab, for fear I'd get too close and she'd see me or I'd lose her in the fog.

"I knew the Tower. My old man took me there once. He said it would be educational. Well, I seen her buying tickets for all them towers, and I had to buy 'em all, too, because I didn't know where she'd go. But I thought, 'This is a hell of a place to pick for rendyvoo,' and then I tumbled to it. She was wise to being watched. I thought probably that trip to the country tipped her off, and her husband had maybe said something to let her guess—"

"They had never gone there together before?" interrupted Hadley.

"Not while *I* was watching them. But wait! You'll understand that in a minute."

She was more subdued now when she spoke, and she told her story without comment. It was ten minutes past one when Laura Bitton arrived. After buying her tickets and a little guide, she had gone into the refreshment-room and ordered a sandwich and a glass of milk. All the time she ate she watched the clock with every sign of nervousness and impatience. "And, what's more," Mrs. Larkin explained, "she wasn't carrying that arrow thing you had on your desk this afternoon. The only place she could have had it was inside her coat; and when she got through eating she opened her coat and shook it to get rid of the crumbs. I'll take my oath there wasn't nothing there."

At twenty minutes past one Laura Bitton left the refreshment room and hurried away. At the Middle Tower she hesitated, looked about, and presently moved along the causeway, and hesitated again at the Byward Tower. There she consulted the map in her guidebook and looked carefully about her.

"I could see what was in her mind," Mrs. Larkin told them. "She didn't want to hang around the door, like a tart or something; but she wanted to be sure she saw him when he got there. But it was dead easy. Anybody who came in would've had to walk straight along that road—up towards the Traitors' Gate place and the Bloody Tower. So she walked along the road, slow, looking all around. She'd been walking in the center of the road, and I was just far behind enough to keep her in sight in that fog. Then when she got near the Traitors' Gate place she turned to the right and stopped again."

So that, Rampole reflected, was what Philip Driscoll saw when he "kept looking out of the window" in the general's quarters, as Parker had described. He saw the woman waiting for him down in Water Lane. And soon afterwards he said he would take a stroll in the grounds, and hurried out. In the American's brain the weird and misty scene was taking form. Laura Bitton with her free stride and healthy face; the brown eyes tortured; tapping the pamphlet guide against her hand and hesitating at the rail as she waited for the man who was already there. Driscoll hurrying downstairs, brushing past Arbor outside the King's House—

"She'd moved back," Mrs. Larkin went on, "in a doorway on the right-hand side of the Traitors' Gate. I'd flattened myself against the same wall a little distance back. Then I saw a little guy in plus-fours come out from under the arch of the Bloody Tower. He looked up and down, quick; and he didn't see—er—XNineteen because she was back in that door. I thought it was Driscoll, but I wasn't sure. Neither was she, I guess, for a minute, because she'd expected him to come the other way. Then he starts to walk back and forth, and next he goes over to the rail. I heard him use a cuss word, and there was a sound like a match striking.

"Now, here's the joker in the deck. I don't know whether you noticed. But that archway thing, where all them spikes in the gate are, sticks out about seven or eight feet on either side of the rail. If you're in that roadway, and looking down it in a straight line, you can't see the rail in front of the steps at all. For the time being it was fine for me, because I could get within a couple of feet of them without being seen.

"So XNineteen knew it was Driscoll all right. She slipped out of the door and turned the corner towards the rail. I couldn't see her and she couldn't see me, so I came up close. The fog was pretty thick, anyway."

Mrs. Larkin took another cigarette from the box. She bent forward.

"Now, I'm not making anything up. I can tell you every word

they said, because there wasn't much of it, and it's my business to remember. The first thing he said was, 'Laura, for God's sake what did you want to bring me down here for? I've got friends here. Is it true that he's found out?' What she said at first I couldn't hear, because it was so low. It was something about that was the reason why she had said to come here, because if either of 'em was seen they could be calling on people they knew. Then he said that was a crazy idea, and was it true that *he'd* found out; he asked that again. She said yes. And she said, 'Do you love me?' And he said, 'Yes, yes, but I'm in a frightful mess.' They was both pretty upset and got to talking louder. He said something about his uncle, and all of a sudden he stopped and said, 'Oh, my God!' It was frightful to hear him say it like that, I'm telling you, as though he'd just thought of something.

"She asked him what was the matter. Here's what he said. 'Laura, there's something I've got to do here, and I forgot all about it. It won't take two seconds, but I've got to do it or I'm ruined.' His voice was shaking. It sounded bad. He said, 'Don't stay with me. We might be seen. Go in and look at the Crown Jewels, and then walk up to the parade-ground. I'll join you there inside five minutes. Don't ask me any questions, but please go.'

"There was a kind of shuffling, and I was afraid of being seen, so I backed away. Then I heard him walking and he called out, 'It'll be all right; don't worry.' I heard her walk up and down for a second or two. Then she walked out in the roadway, and I thought for a minute she'd seen me. But she whirled around and started toward the Bloody Tower, and I followed. I didn't see *him*; I suppose he'd gone on ahead. That was about twenty-five minutes to two."

Hadley leaned forward. "You say you followed?" he demanded. "Did you see her bump into anybody?"

"Bump into anybody?" she repeated, blinking. "No. But then I mightn't have. I slipped inside that big arch of the Bloody Tower and up against the wall, in case she turned back. I have a kind of idea that some man passed me; but it was foggy, and under that arch darker than hell. I waited a second and followed again.

"I heard her speak to one of them birds in the funny hats and say, 'Which way to the Crown Jewels?' and he directed her to a door not very far on the other side of the arch, and I was still there."

Mrs. Larkin paused to light the cigarette she had been holding for some time.

"That's all," she said in a matter-of-fact voice. "He didn't come near her, because somebody killed him just after he'd left her. But I know *she* didn't, because I took a look in that place where the steps go down—I looked there, mind you, before I followed her up in the Bloody Tower. I was sort of craning my neck around to see up under the arch to the Bloody Tower, and I put out my hand to touch the rail so's I wouldn't fall over backwards, and naturally I looked over my shoulder. He wasn't there then. And I had her in sight the rest of the time. As I said, she went to see the Crown Jewels. So did I. But she didn't look at 'em much. She was kind of white and restless, and she kept looking out the windows. I left before she did. I didn't want to attract notice. And I'd seen that if you went *in* the Bloody Tower and up to a kind of little balcony—"

"Raleigh's Walk," the chief inspector said, glancing at Dr. Fell.

"—then you could see anybody who came back from looking at them jewels. Unless you went back the way you come, there was no other way out. So I waited. And before long she come back, and stood there a while in the road that goes up the hill from the Bloody Tower to that big open space."

"Tower Green."

"Yeah. Well, she started to walk up, kind of listless, and I walked up afterwards. But she didn't do anything. I could see her, because it was high ground and the fog was thin. She sat on a bench, and talked to one of them guards, and kept looking at her watch. But she was patient, all right. *I* wouldn't have waited that long for any man in God's world. She waited over half an hour just sitting on one of them benches in the wet, without moving, and finally she started to leave. You know the rest."

Mrs. Larkin's hard little eyes moved about the group and she drew in a gust of cigarette smoke. "Well. Feenee. There's the words and music. I promised to say 'em, and I did. I don't know who killed Driscoll, but I'm damn sure *she* didn't."

XIII

Wherein Miss Bitton Burbles

WHEN SHE had ceased speaking, nobody cared to break the silence. It was so quiet in the little sitting room that the hoarse mumble of the radio could be heard again from some flat upstairs. They heard footsteps on the tiles of the hall, the clang of an iron gate, and then the long, humming whir of the automatic lift. Distantly, motor horns honked and hooted from the other side of the Square.

For the first time Rampole felt how chill it was here, and drew his coat about him. A deeper stamp of death had come on the room, as of fingers slowly pressed into sand. Philip Driscoll was no more than the white fragments of the plaster image scattered on the hearth. The dancing tinkle of a barrel-organ began to make itself heard in Tavistock Square. Faintly, from upstairs, a creak and another clang; and the hum of the descending lift.

Lester Bitton moved the dusty window curtain off his shoulder, and turned about. There was about him now a curious, quiet dignity. "Gentlemen," he said, "I have done what had to be done. Is there anything more?"

They knew what it had cost him to listen to that recital in the presence of strangers, or alone. He stood quiet, conventional, almost polite, with the pouches showing under his eyes, and his bowler hat in his hand. And nobody knew what to say.

At length it was Dr. Fell who spoke. He was sitting spread out in a leather chair, the tool-basket in his lap like a dog, and his eyes old and tired.

"Man," he said somberly, "go home. You've done some sneaking things in your time, like all the rest of us. But you smashed only one figure when you might have smashed two. You spoke up like a man when you might have denounced her. Go home. We can't keep your name out of this altogether, but we'll save you all the publicity we can."

The doctor's dull eyes moved over to Hadley. Hadley nodded.

Lester Bitton stood for a time motionless. He seemed weary and a trifle puzzled. Then his big hands moved up, adjusted his scarf and buttoned up his coat. He walked rather blindly when he went to the door, but until he reached it he did not put on his hat.

"I—I thank you, gentlemen," he said in a low voice. He made a little bow. "I—I am very fond of her, you see. Good night."

The door with the broken lock closed behind him. They heard the vestibule of the outer hall open and shut wheezily. The tinkle of the barrel-organ grew louder and died.

"That's the 'Maine Stein Song,'" observed the doctor, who had been cocking an ear to the music. "Why do people say they don't like street organs? I'm very fond of street organs myself. I always feel like a Grenadier Guard, and throw out my chest, when I pass one. It's like going on errands to band music, as though there were some triumphal fête about buying two lamb chops and a bottle of beer. By the way, Mrs. Larkin—"

The woman had risen. She turned sharply.

"It's not going to be brought out at the inquest, you know, that there was really anything serious between Mrs. Bitton and

Driscoll. I imagine you've already been paid to keep quiet." Dr. Fell raised his stick sleepily. "It's money well earned. But don't try to earn any more. That's blackmail, you know. They put you in jail for it. Good night."

"Oh, that's all right," Mrs. Larkin agreed, patting the puffs of hair over her ears. "If you birds are on the level with me, I'm on the level with you—y'know what I mean? Men are crazy, anyway," she added, reflectively. The harsh, young-old face was cut into whimsical lines. "If I'd been that dame's old man, I'd have gone home and blacked both 'er eyes. But men are crazy. My Cuthbert was. Still, I loved that old buzzard till he got knocked off in a gunfight under the Third Avenue El in New York. Every so often he would walk out with some other skirt; and that kept me so upset I never thought of walking out on *him*. That's the way to treat skirts. Keeps 'em in line. Well, I'm off to the pub. G'night. See you at the inquest."

When she had gone the rest of them sat silent. Dr. Fell was wheezing sleepily. And again Hadley began to pace about the room.

"So that's settled," he said. "I think we can take Mrs. Bitton off the list of suspects. I doubt if Larkin's lying. Her information is too exactly in line with all the other facts she couldn't possibly have known. Now what?"

"What do *you* suggest?"

"Not much, for the moment. It all rests on what it was Driscoll remembered he'd forgotten to do when he spoke to Mrs. Bitton in front of the Traitors' Gate. He started for somewhere, but he didn't get very far away, and then he ran into somebody—the murderer."

"Fair enough," grunted the doctor.

"Now, first, there's the *direction* he might have gone. Larkin didn't see him go. But we know he didn't go along Water Lane towards the Byward or Middle Tower; towards the gate, in other words. Because Larkin was standing there, and she would have seen him pass.

"There are only two other directions he could have gone." From his invaluable briefcase Hadley took a small map of the Tower, which he had evidently been studying ever since his visit. "He could have gone straight along Water Lane in the other direction. The only place he could have gone in that direction is towards another arch, similar to the Bloody Tower and a hundred feet or so away in the same wall, the inner ballium wall. From that arch a path leads up to the White Tower, which is almost in the center of the whole enclosure. Now, unless *all* our calculations are wrong, and there's some piece of evidence we haven't heard, why on earth should he be going to the White Tower? Or, for that matter, to the main guard, the store, the hospital, the officers' quarters, the barracks, or any place he could have reached by going through that arch?

"Besides, he hadn't got very far away from the Traitors' Gate before he met the murderer. Traitors' Gate is an ideal place for murder on a foggy day. It would have occurred to anybody. But if Driscoll had been starting for the White Tower and met the murderer quite some distance from Traitors' Gate, it wouldn't have been very practical for the murderer to drive that steel bolt through him, pick him up, carry him back, and pitch him over the rail. Physically, it could have been easy; Driscoll's a featherweight. But the risk of being seen carrying that burden any distance, even in the fog, would have been too great."

Hadley paused in his pacing before the mantelpiece. He stared a moment at the idiotic painted face of the doll; and some idea seemed to pinch down the wrinkles round his mouth. But he dismissed it and went on.

"On the other hand, the murderer couldn't say, 'Look here, old man, let's stroll back to the Traitors' Gate; I want to talk to you.' And naturally Driscoll would have said, 'Why? What's the matter with telling me here?' Also he was in a fearful bother and stew to get somewhere and do something. He would more likely have said, 'Sorry. I can't talk to you at all,' and gone on. No, it won't do. Driscoll had no business in that direction, anyway. So there's only one alternative."

Dr. Fell took out a cigar.

"Namely," he inquired, "that Driscoll went the same direction as Mrs. Bitton did—through the arch of the Bloody Tower?"

"Yes. All indications show that."

"For instance?"

"For instance," Hadley answered, slowly, "what Larkin said. She heard Driscoll walk away, and then Mrs. Bitton walked up and down in front of the rail a minute or so—*to give Driscoll time to go on up there ahead of her.* Driscoll said they mustn't be seen together. And once you get inside the inner ballium wall, as Larkin said, you're in view of pretty well everybody; especially as it's high ground, and the fog is thin. Larkin had a positive impression that he'd gone on ahead of Mrs. Bitton. And, above all, that's the reasonable direction for him to have gone, because—"

"Because it's the way to the King's House," supplied Dr. Fell.

Hadley nodded. "Whatever he had forgotten, and went to do, was in the general's quarters at the King's House. That's the only part of the Tower he ever had any business in. He was going back. There was somebody he had to speak with on the phone, or some message he had to give Parker. *But he never got there.*"

"Good work," said the doctor, approvingly. "I seem to act as a stimulant. Gradually that subconscious imagination of yours, Hadley, is working to the surface. And by degrees everything seems to center round the arch under the Bloody Tower. Hence we perceive the following points: The arch under this tower is a broad tunnel about twenty feet long, and the road runs on a steep uphill slant. At the best of times it is rather dark, but on a foggy day it is what Mrs. Larkin, who has evidently read Dante, describes as black as hell."

Hadley broke off his fierce musing. He said, petulantly, "Look here. It seems to me that *I* do all the reconstructing. And when I find the right answer, you wave your hand calmly and say you knew it all the time. Now either you do or you don't, but if you *don't*—"

"I am pursuing," Dr. Fell said, with dignity, "the Socratic method. Don't say, 'Bah,' as I perceive you are about to do. I want to lead you along and see where this hypothesis gets us. Hence—"

"H'm," the chief inspector observed, struck with an idea.

"Now that I come to think of it, by George! I know where all this fictional-detective stuff started in the first place. With that Greek philosopher chap in Plato's *Dialogues*. He always annoyed me. A couple of Greeks would be walking along, not bothering anybody, and up would come this damned philosopher and say, 'Bon jour'—or whatever they said in Athens—'Bon jour, gents; have you got anything on hand this afternoon?' Of course the other chaps didn't. They never had. There never seemed to be any business to attend to in Greece. All they did was walk about hunting for philosophers. Then Socrates would say, 'Right you are. Now let's sit down here and talk.' Whereupon he would propound some question for them to solve. He knew the answer, of course. It was never anything sensible, like 'What do you think of the Irish question?' or 'Who will win the Test Match this year, Athens or Sparta?' It was always some God-awful question about the soul. Socrates asked the question. Then one of the other chaps spoke up, and talked for about nine pages; and Socrates shook his head sadly and said, 'No.' Then another chap took a shot at it, and talked for sixteen pages. And Socrates said, 'Ah!' The next victim must have talked till it got dark, and Socrates said, 'Possibly.' They never up and hit him over the head with an obelisk, either. That's what I wanted to do just from reading the thing, because he never would come out and say what he meant. That's the origin of your detectives in fiction, Fell. And I wish you'd stop it."

Dr. Fell, who had got his cigar lighted, looked reproving.

"I perceive in you, Hadley," he remarked, "a certain vein of unexpected satire. As well as the germ of an idea most biblio-philes seem to have overlooked. H'mf. I never had much patience with those fellows myself. However, stick to your subject. Continue with the murder."

"Er—where was I?" demanded Hadley. "This confounded case is beginning to—"

"You'd got Driscoll into the tunnel, where he is murdered. So. Now, it was dark in there. Why didn't the murderer dump him against the wall and leave him there?"

"Because the body would be discovered too soon. There's too much traffic in that place. Somebody might stumble over the body before the murderer could make a getaway. So he picked Driscoll up like a ventriloquist's dummy, took a quick look to each side in Water Lane, walked across, and chucked him over the rail on the steps."

The doctor nodded. He held up one hand and indicated points on his fingers.

"Driscoll walks into the tunnel, then, and meets the murderer. Mrs. Bitton waits a short time, and follows, because she doesn't know Driscoll is still *in* the tunnel. Now do you see what we've got, Hadley? We've got Mrs. Bitton at one end of the tunnel, Driscoll and the murderer in the middle—and our good friend Mr. Arbor at the other end. Haven't we?"

"Every time *you* begin to elucidate," said the chief inspector, "the thing gets more tangled up. But that seems clear. Larkin said Mrs. Bitton went into the arch twenty-five minutes to two. Arbor bumped into her on the other side of it at a coinciding time. Where's the catch?"

"I didn't say there was a catch. Now, following Mrs. Bitton at a little distance is the eagle-eyed Larkin, who enters the tunnel next. All this time you must assume the murderer was still in the tunnel with his victim; otherwise she would have seen him carry the body out. In the tunnel it's very dark and foggy. Mrs. Larkin *hears* somebody moving. That is probably Arbor on his way out from the other side. Thus the tunnel is cleared of traffic. The murderer, who has been crouching there with his victim in a deadly sweat of fear he'll be discovered, carries out the body, throws it over the rail, and escapes. That, I take it, is the summary of events?"

"Yes. That's about it."

Dr. Fell squinted down his cigar. "Then," he said, "where does the enigmatic Mr. Arbor fit in? What terrified him? He's out at his cottage now, in a complete funk. Why?"

Hadley slapped the arm of a chair with his briefcase. "He was passing through that dark tunnel, Fell, and when he was in such a bad state after he left us, the taxi driver said he kept repeating over and over something about a *voice*."

"Tut, tut," said the doctor. "Do you think the murderer leaned out and said 'Boo!' to him as he passed?"

"I don't expect much from you. But," the chief inspector said, bitterly, "a trifle less heavy humor. What are you trying to prove?"

But he was not paying a great deal of attention to what Dr. Fell said, Rampole noticed. His eye kept straying to the mantelpiece, to the smashed figure on the hearthstone, and up again to the other image on the shelf. There was a wrinkle between his brows. The doctor followed his glance.

"Let me tell you what you're thinking, Hadley," he observed. "You're thinking: Murderer. Big man; strength. Powerful motive. Man capable of murder, from the emotional depths we saw ourselves. Man with access to crossbow bolt. Man who certainly knew about crossbow bolt. Man so far not even questioned about whereabouts at time of murder—Lester Bitton."

"Yes," said Hadley, without turning. "I was thinking just that."

At the door of the flat the bell-buzzer rang. Somebody kept poking it in short bursts. But before Rampole had time to reach the door, it was pushed open.

"I'm *so* sorry we're fearfully late!" a girl's voice said, promptly, before the owner saw anybody. "But it was the chauffeur's night off, and we didn't want to take the big car, and we tried to use the other car, and it got halfway out into the street and stopped. Fancy. And then a crowd gathered, and Bob lifted the bonnet and started muttering to himself and pulling wires and things, and all of a sudden something exploded, and Bob used the most horrible language, and the crowd cheered. Fancy. And so we had to use the big car, after all."

Rampole found himself looking down at a small face which was poked round the edge of the door. Then by degrees the newcomer got into the room. She was a plump, very pretty little blonde, with two of the most beaming and expressive blue eyes the American had ever seen; she looked like a breathless doll. No shadow of any tragedy, you felt, could ever settle on her. When somebody reminded her of it, she would weep; in the meantime, she would forget all about it.

"Er—Miss Bitton?" inquired Rampole.

"*I'm* Miss Bitton," she explained, as though she were singling herself out of a group. "But my Bob is *never* any good at things like that, you see. Because Daddy bought me a cottage at the beach two years ago where all of us could go down, with Laura chaperoning, and I wanted the walls papered, and I had the paper, and Bob and his cousin George said, Ha! They would paper it themselves, and mix the paste, too. But after they spilled paste all over the floor getting it on the paper, then they got all tangled up in the paper with the paste on it. And then they were having the most terrible argument, and swearing and making so much noise the house shook, and a policeman looked in, and they got paper on him, too; and then George got so furious he walked straight out of the house all pasted up in a whole roll of my best paper with blue forget-me-nots on it. Fancy. What the neighbors thought, I mean. But the worst of it was when Bob got the paper on—only it was a wee bit crooked, and all sort of run together, and not very clean, you know. Because we lighted a fire, and it got warm, and all sorts of ghastly things began happening to the paper, and then they discovered that when they mixed die paste they'd used self-rising flour. Fancy. And that's why I've always said that—"

"My dear, please!" protested a mild and harassed voice behind her. Dalrye, thin and blinking, towered over her in the doorway. His sandy hair was disarranged under a hat stuck on the side of his head, and there was a smear of grease under one eye. As he put out his neck to peer into the room, he reminded Rampole irresistibly of one of those reconstructions of prehistoric dinosaurs he saw once in a motion picture. "Er—" he added, apologetically, "excuse my hurdy-gurdy, won't you? My dear, after all, you know why we did come here."

Sheila Bitton stopped in mid-flight. Her large eyes grew troubled; and then they wandered about the room. A shocked look came into them when she saw the broken plaster image; of all things, Rampole knew, these figures would appeal to her irresistibly.

She said, "I'm sorry. I—I didn't think, of course, and then all that horrible crowd offering suggestions—" She looked at Rampole. "You're not—oooh no! I know you. You're the one who looks like a football player. Bob described all of you to me. And you're much better-looking than I thought you'd be from what he said," she decided, subjecting him to a peculiarly open and embarrassing scrutiny.

"And I, ma'am," said Dr. Fell, "am the walrus, you see. Mr. Dalrye seems to have a flair for vivid description. In what delicate terms, may I ask, did he paint a word-picture of my friend Hadley, here?"

"H'm?" inquired Miss Bitton, arching her brows. She glanced at the doctor, and an expression of delight again animated her sparkling eyes. "Oh, I say! You *are* a dear!" she cried.

Dr. Fell jumped violently. There were no inhibitions whatever about Sheila Bitton. After one question to her, a psychoanalyst would have pulled out a handful of his whiskers and slunk back to Vienna in baffled humiliation. It would have embittered his life.

"About Mr. Hadley?" she inquired, candidly. "Oh, Bob said he didn't look like anything in particular, you know."

"Gurk!" said Dalrye. He spread out his hands behind her back in helpless pantomime to the others.

"And I've always wanted to meet the police, but the only kind I ever meet are the kind who ask me why I am driving down streets where the arrows point the other way; and why *not?* Because there's no traffic coming and I can go ever so much faster. And, No, miss, you can*not* park your car in front of the entrance to the fire station. Nasty people. Fancy. But I mean the real kind of police, who find bodies cut up and put in trunks, you know. And—" Then she remembered again why she was here, and stopped with a jerk; the rest of them were afraid there would be sudden tears.

"Of course, Miss Bitton," the chief inspector said, hastily. "Now if you'll just sit down a moment and—er—get your breath, you know, then I'm sure—"

"Excuse me," said Dalrye. "I'm going to wash my hands." He shivered a little as he glanced round the room, and almost seemed to change his decision. But he shut his jaws hard and left the room. Miss Bitton said, "Poor Phil," suddenly, and sat down.

There was a silence.

"You—somebody," she remarked in a small voice, "somebody's tipped over that pretty little figure on the mantel. I'm sorry. It was one of the things I wanted to take back with me."

"Had you seen it before, Miss Bitton?" asked Hadley. His discomfort had disappeared as he saw a possible lead.

"Why, of course I had! I was there when they got them."

"When who got them?"

"At the fair. Phil and Laura and Uncle Lester and I all went to it. Uncle Lester said it was all silly, and didn't want to go, but Laura used that sort of pitying way she has and he said all right, he'd go. He wouldn't ride on any of the swings or giddy-go-rounds or things, though, and then— But you don't want to hear that, do you? I know Bob says I talk too much, and now with poor Phil dead—"

"Please go on, Miss Bitton; I should like to hear it."

"You would? Truly? Oooh! Well, then. 'M. Oh yes. Phil started ragging Uncle Lester, and it was mean of him because Uncle Lester can't help being old, can he? And Uncle Lester got sort of red in the face, but he didn't say anything and then we got to a shooting gallery where they have the rifles and things, and Uncle Lester spoke up sort of sharp, but not very loud, and said this was a man's game and not for children, and did Phil want to try? And Phil did, but he wasn't very good. And then Uncle Lester just picked up a pistol instead of a rifle and shot off a whole row of pipes clear across the gallery so fast you couldn't count them; and then he put down the pistol and walked away without saying anything. So Phil didn't like that. I could see he didn't. And every booth we passed he began challenging Uncle Lester to all kinds of games, and Laura joined in, too. I tried some of them, but after we came to the booth where you throw wooden balls and try to knock over stuffed cats, they wouldn't let me do it any more; because the first ball I threw I hit the electric light in the roof, and the second one I threw hit the man who ran the booth behind the ear; and Uncle Lester had to pay for it."

"But about the dolls, Miss Bitton?" Hadley asked, patiently.

"Oh yes. It was Laura who won them; they're a pair. It was at throwing darts, and she was ever so good—much better than the men. And you got prizes for it, and Laura got the highest prize for her score, and she said, 'Look, Philip and Mary,' and laughed. Because that's what the dolls have written on them, and, you see, Laura's middle name is Mary. Then Uncle Lester said he wouldn't have her keeping that trash; it was disgraceful-looking, and of course *I* wanted them ever so badly. But Laura said no, she'd give them to Philip if Mary couldn't have them. And Phil did the meanest thing I ever knew, because he made the absurdest bow and said he *would* keep them—and, *oh*, I was furious! Because I thought he'd surely give them to *me*, you see. And what did *he* want with them, anyway? And Uncle Lester didn't say anything, but he said all at once we ought to go home; and all the way back I kept teasing Phil to give them to me; and he made all sorts of ridiculous speeches that didn't mean anything and looked at Laura, but he wouldn't give them to me. And that's how I remember them, because they remind me of Phil. You see, I even asked Bob to see if he could get Phil to give them to me; I asked him the next day—that was ages ago—when I called Bob on the telephone, because I always make him ring me up every day, or else I ring *him* up, and General Mason doesn't like that—"

She paused, her thin eyebrows raised again as she saw Hadley's face.

"You say," the chief inspector observed, in a voice he tried to make casual, "that you talk every day to Mr. Dalrye on the telephone?"

Rampole started. He remembered now. Earlier in the evening Hadley had made a wild shot when he was building up a fake case against Laura Bitton in front of her husband. He had said that Dalrye had informed Sheila of Driscoll's proposed visit to the Tower at one o'clock, because Dalrye talked to her on the telephone that morning; and that, therefore, anybody in the Bitton house could have known of the one-o'clock engagement. Hadley thought it was a wild shot, and nothing more. But, Rampole remembered, *Lester Bitton had shown no disposition to doubt it.* Which was, to say the least, suggestive.

Sheila Bitton's blue eyes were fixed on Hadley.

"Oh, please!" she said, "don't *you* preach! You sound like Daddy. He tells me what a fool I am, calling up every day, and I don't think he likes Bob, anyway, because Bob hasn't any money and likes poker, and Daddy says gambling's absurd, and I know he's looking for an excuse to break off our engagement and keep us from getting married, and—"

"My dear Miss Bitton," Hadley interposed, with a sort of desperate joviality, "I certainly am not preaching. I think it's a splendid idea. Splendid, ha! Ha, ha! But I only wanted to ask you—"

"You're a dear! You're a dear!" cooed Miss Bitton, as though she were saying, "You're another."

"And they rag me so about it, and even Phil used to phone me and pretend he was Bob and ask me to go to the police station because Bob had been arrested for flirting with women in Hyde Park, and was in jail, and would I bail him out, and—"

"Ha, ha," said Hadley again. "Ha, ha, ha. I mean, er, how—er—bad. Shocking. Preposterous. Ha, ha. But what I wanted to ask you, did you speak to Mr. Dalrye today?"

"In jail," the girl said, darkly, brooding. "My Bob. Fancy. Yes, I did talk to him today."

"When, Miss Bitton? In the morning?"

"Yes. That's when I usually call, you know, or make him call me; because then General Mason isn't there. Nasty old thing with whiskers. He doesn't like it. And I always know when it's Parker who answers the phone, because, before you can say anything, he says, 'General Mason's orderly on the wire!' sort of big and sharp. But when I don't hear it I naturally think it's Bob, and I'm so *jolly* glad to talk to him I say, *'Darling, diddums!'* You know how you'd say that, Mr. Hadley—and once I did that, and there was a sound sort of like frying eggs, and then a nasty voice said, 'Madam, this is the Tower of London, not a nursery. To whom did you wish to speak?' Fancy. And it was General Mason. And I've always been scared of him, ever since I was a child, and I couldn't think of anything to say, and I sort of wept and said, 'This is your deserted wife,' and rang off while he was still saying things. But after that he made Bob call me up from a public box, and—"

"Ho, ho!" chortled Hadley, with ghastly mirth. "Ho, ho! No sentiment to him, is there? No romance, poor fellow. But, Miss Bitton, when you spoke to Mr. Dalrye this morning did he tell you that Philip Driscoll—your cousin, you know—was coming to see him at the Tower?"

She remembered the shadow again, and her eyes clouded.

"Yes," she said, after a pause. "I know, because Bob wanted to know what sort of mess Phil had got into now, and did I know anything about it? He told me not to say anything about it to the others."

"And you didn't?"

"Why, of course not!" she cried. "I sort of hinted, that's all, at the breakfast table. Because we didn't have breakfast till ten o'clock that morning, we were so upset the night before. I asked them at the table if they knew why Phil was going to the Tower of London at one o'clock, and they didn't know, and of course I obeyed Bob and didn't say anything more."

"I fancy that should be sufficient," said Hadley. "Was any comment made?"

"Comment?" the girl repeated, doubtfully. "N-no; they just talked a bit, and joked."

"Who was at the table?"

"Just Daddy, and Uncle Lester and that horrible man who's been stopping with us; the one who rushed out this afternoon without saying a word to anybody, and scared me, and nobody knows where he is or why he went; and everything is so upset, anyway—"

"Was Mrs. Bitton at the table?"

"Laura? Oh! Oh no. She didn't come down. She wasn't feeling well, and, anyway, I don't blame her, because she and Uncle Lester must have been up all last night, talking; I heard them, and—"

"But surely, Miss Bitton, *something* must have been said at the breakfast table?"

"No, Mr. Hadley. Truly. Of course I don't like being at the table when just Daddy and that horrible Mr. Arbor are there, because mostly I can't understand what they're talking about, books and things like that, and jokes I don't think funny. Or else the talk gets horrid, like the night when Phil told Uncle Lester he wanted to die in a top hat. But there wasn't anything important that I heard. Of course, Uncle Lester did say he was going to see Phil today. But there wasn't anything important. Really."

XIV

"To Die in a Top Hat—"

HADLEY MADE a convulsive movement in his seat. Then he got out a handkerchief and mopped his forehead.

"Ha, ha," he said, automatically. He seemed to be getting quite used to it by this time; but the laugh sounded a trifle hollow. "Ha, ha, ha. You never hear anything important, Miss Bitton. It's most unfortunate. Now, Miss Bitton, please try to grasp the fact that some of the meaningless, unimportant conversations you overheard may be of the utmost importance. Miss Bitton, just how much do you know about your cousin's death?"

"Nothing much, Mr. Hadley," she said, fretfully. "They won't *tell* me. I couldn't get a word out of Laura or Daddy, and Bob just said there was a sort of accident and he was killed by this man who steals all the hats; but that's the only—"

She broke off short, rather guiltily, as Dalrye came back into the room again. He looked more presentable now.

"Sheila," he said, "whatever the things you want happen to be, you'd better go and pick 'em out. That place gives me the horrors. Everywhere I look Phil seems to be sitting there. The place is full of him. I wish I hadn't got any imagination."

He shivered. Automatically he reached for a cigarette in the

194

box on the taboret; then he seemed to remember, and closed the box without touching one. Rampole extended his case, and Dalrye nodded thanks.

"*I'm* not afraid," the girl announced, sticking out her underlip. "*I* don't believe in ghosts. You've been so long in that musty old Tower of London that you—"

"Tower!" Dalrye exclaimed, suddenly rumpling his sandy hair. "Lord! I forgot." He dragged out his watch. "Whoof! A quarter to eleven. I've been locked out three-quarters of an hour. My dear, your father will have to put up with me in the house for tonight. I'm dashed if I stay *here*."

His eye wandered over to a leather couch against one wall, and he shuddered again. Hadley said, "Now, if you please, Miss Bitton, let's go on. First tell us about this extraordinary business of your cousin wanting to die in a top hat?"

"Eh?" said Dalrye. "Good God! What's *this!*"

"Why, Robert Dalrye," Sheila Bitton said, warmly, "you know perfectly well— Oh no, you don't. I remember now, when you spoke about getting back to that hateful Tower. You had to leave the table early to get there. It was the first night that Mr. Arbor— no, it wasn't, because Uncle Lester wasn't there then. Anyway, it was *some* night."

"Undoubtedly, Miss Bitton," agreed the chief inspector. "Never mind the precise date. How did it happen?"

"Yes, I remember now. Just Daddy and Uncle Lester and Laura and I were at the table; and Philip, of course. It was a sort of spooky night, if you know what I mean; and I know just when it was, too, now, because it wasn't a Sunday night at all, and Philip was there. That's how I remember. It was the night before Laura and Uncle Lester went to Cornwall. And Philip was taking Laura to the theatre, because at the last minute Uncle Lester had business and couldn't go, you see; but they were taking the trip to Cornwall because Uncle Lester had lost a lot of money or something, and he was all run down and had things under his eyes, and the doctor advised it.

"Oh yes. I couldn't think for a minute. It was a sort of spooky night, you see, with rain and hail coming down, and Daddy never likes any lights in the dining room but candles, because he says that's like Old England, and a big fire, too, and the house is old and it creaks and maybe that's why we all felt the way we did. But, anyway, we started talking about death. And Uncle Lester talked about death, which was funny of him, and he'd got his white tie crooked and I wanted to straighten it, but he wouldn't let me, and he looked as though he hadn't been sleeping much, what with losing all that money. And he asked Daddy how he'd choose to die if he had to die. Daddy was in a good humor that night, which he isn't usually, and first he laughed and said he supposed he'd choose to die like some duke or other who said he wanted to be drowned in a barrel of wine—fancy! But then they got serious about it, the way people do, and I was getting scared because they didn't talk very loud, and it was storming outside.

"And finally Daddy said he thought he'd choose some kind of poison he talked about that kills you in one whiff when you breathe it, and Uncle Lester said *he* thought a bullet through the head would be best, and Laura kept saying, 'What rot, what rot,' and 'Come on, Phil, or we'll be late for the first-act curtain.' And when Phil got up from the table Uncle Lester asked him how *he'd* like to die. And Phil just laughed, and, I say, he *was* jolly good-looking with the candles and his white shirt and the way he had his hair combed and everything! And he said something in French and Daddy told me afterwards it meant, 'Always the gentleman,' and he said a lot of absurd things and said— Well, anyway, he didn't care so much how he died, if he could die with a top hat on and at least one woman to weep at his grave. Fancy! How absurd of anybody to get that idea, I mean. And then he took Laura to the theater."

Out in the square, the tireless barrel-organ was still tinkling out the "Maine Stein Song."

Four pairs of eyes fixed upon her had roused even Sheila Bitton to something like nervousness. As she came towards the end of her recital she was fidgeting and talking faster and faster. Now she cried, "Please, I *won't*—I won't have you looking at me like that! And I won't be put upon, and nobody ever tells me anything, and I know I've said something I shouldn't. What *is* the matter?"

She sprang up. Dalrye put a clumsy hand on her shoulder.

He said, "My dear—er—" and stopped, because he had nothing to say. He was looking pale. His voice had a sort of rasp and whir like a Gramophone running down.

A long silence.

"My dear Miss Bitton," the chief inspector said, briskly, "you've said nothing wrong at all. Mr. Dalrye will explain presently. But now about this morning, at the breakfast table. What was it your uncle said about seeing Philip today?"

"I say, Mr. Hadley," Dalrye struck in, clearing his throat. "After all, I mean to say, they treat her like a kid; and when the news came Sir William ordered her to go up to her room and stay there. He made me tell her it was a sort of accident. Do you think it's quite fair?"

"Yes," Hadley returned, sharply. "Yes, I do. Now, Miss Bitton?"

She hesitated, looked at Dalrye, and wet her lips.

"Why, there wasn't anything, much. Only Uncle Lester said he was going to have a talk with Phil today. And when I said that, about Phil meaning to go to the Tower at one o'clock, he said he thought he'd better run over to Phil's flat in the morning, then, before he got out."

"And did he?"

"Uncle Lester? Yes, he did. I saw him when he came back about noon. And I remember, Uncle Lester said to Daddy, 'Oh, I say, you'd better let me have your key, in case he isn't in this morning; I'll sit down and wait for him.'"

Hadley stared. "Your father," he asked, "has a key to this flat?"

"I told you," Sheila answered with some bitterness, "he treats us all like kids. That was one of the things that used to make Phil furious with him. He said he wouldn't pay for Phil's flat unless he could have a key, so that he could see what was going on when-ever he wanted to. Fancy! As though Phil were a kid. You don't know Daddy. But it was just—well, I mean, he didn't really *mean* it, because he never visited Phil except once a month. So Daddy gave Uncle Lester the key."

Hadley bent forward. "Did he see Phil this morning?"

"No, he didn't, truly. Because, as I say, I saw him when he came back. And Phil was out, and Uncle Lester waited half an hour and left. He seemed to be—"

"Angry?" prompted Hadley, as she hesitated.

"N-o. Sort of tired and shaky. I know he'd overexerted himself. And—funny. He seemed queer, too, and excited; and he laughed."

"*Laughed?*"

"Hold on!" Dr. Fell suddenly boomed. He was having trouble keeping his glasses on his nose, and he held them to look at the girl. "Tell me, my dear. Was he carrying anything when he came back?"

"This," she cried again—"this is something horrible to do with Uncle Lester, and I won't *have* it! He's the only one who's really frightfully nice to me, and he *is*, and I won't have it. Even when I was a little girl, he was always the one who brought me bunny rabbits, and chocolates, and dolls; Daddy said they were absurd. And—"

She was stamping on the floor, bewildered, turning suddenly to Dalrye.

"I'll be damned," the other flared, "if she answers you another question. Listen, Sheila. Go into the other rooms and see if there's anything you want to take along."

Hadley was about to interpose when Dr. Fell silenced him with a fierce gesture. Then the doctor spoke amiably.

"It's quite all right, my dear. I hadn't meant to upset you, and it wasn't important, anyway. Do as Mr. Dalrye suggests, please. But there is one thing— No, no," as she was about to speak, "no more questions about what you're thinking. You know, I asked you on the telephone whether you would bring somebody along to help you with your things? And I suggested your father's valet?"

"Marks?" she exclaimed, puzzled. "Why, yes. I forgot. He's out in the car."

"Thank you, my dear. There isn't anything else."

"You go in there and look about, Sheila," Dalrye suggested. "I'll join you in a moment. I should like to talk to these gentlemen."

He waited until the door had closed. Then he turned slowly. There was dull color under his cheek-bones; he was still visibly shaken, and his mouth worked.

"Listen," he said. His voice was thick. He cleared it with an effort. "I understand all your implications, of course. And you know how much I thought of Phil. But so far as Mr. Bitton's concerned—Mr. Lester Bitton—Major Bitton—I feel the way she does. And I'll tell you you're a lot of damned fools. I know him pretty well. Sheila didn't tell you he was the one who stood up for our marriage when the old man was against it. But *I'll* tell you.

"He's not likeable on the surface, as General Mason is. I know the general dislikes him, because the general's the old, roaring, damn-your-eyes type of army man. Bitton's cold and efficient when you just look at him. He's not clever, or a good talker. But he's—you're—a—lot—of—fools," Dalrye said, suddenly miserable. He struck the back of a chair.

Hadley drummed his fingers on his briefcase.

"Tell us the truth, Mr. Dalrye," he said, after a time. "We've pretty well found out that there was an affair between Mrs. Bitton and Driscoll. Well, *I'll* be frank: we know it for a positive fact. Did *you* know about it?"

"I give you my word," said Dalrye, simply, "I didn't. Believe me or not. I only got wind of it—well, afterwards." He looked from face to face, and they all knew he was telling the truth. "Phil wouldn't have been such a fool as to tell me. I'd have covered him, I suppose because—oh, well, you can see. But I'd have stopped it, somehow."

"And do you suppose Sir William knew of it?"

"Oh Lord, no! He's the last person who would. He's too tied up with his books and his lectures about how the government is running on senile decay. But, for God's sake, find out who killed Phil, and what all this nonsense is about, before we all go mad. Find out!"

"We are going to begin," Dr. Fell said, quietly, "in precisely two minutes."

There was a silence as sudden as the stroke of a gong.

"I mean," rumbled the doctor, lifting himself in his chair and raising one cane, "we are going to dispose of the nonsense, and then see our way straight to the sense. Mr. Dalrye, will you step outside and ask that valet chap, Marks, to step in here?"

Dalrye hesitated, running a hand through his hair; but at the doctor's imperious gesture he hurried out.

"Now!" urged Dr. Fell, hammering his stick on the floor. "Set that table over in front of me. That's it, my boy; hurry!" He struggled up as Rampole lifted the heavy table and set it down with a thump before him. "Now, Hadley, give me your briefcase."

"Here!" protested the chief inspector; "stop scattering those papers all over the table! What the hell are you doing?"

Rampole stared in astonishment as the doctor waddled over and picked up a bridge-lamp with a powerful electric bulb. Reeling out its cord from the baseboard, he set the lamp at some short distance from the table. Then he rolled a low chair under it, and switched on the light. Rampole found the chief inspector's black notebook thrust into his hands.

"That, my boy, is for you," said the doctor. "Sit down here beside me, on my left. Have you a pencil? Good! When I give you the word, you are to pretend to be making shorthand notes. Scrawl down anything you like, but keep your pencil working fast. Understand?"

Hadley made motions like one who sees a priceless vase tottering on the edge of a shelf. "*Don't!* Look here, those are all my notes; and if you muck them up! You fat lunatic, what is all this—"

"Don't argue," said the doctor, testily. "Have you got a revolver and a pair of handcuffs on you, by any chance?"

Hadley looked at him. He said, "You're mad. Fell, you're stark, staring mad! They only carry those things in the stories and on the films. I haven't had a revolver or a pair of handcuffs in my hands for ten years"

"Then I have," the doctor said, composedly. "I knew you'd forget them." With the air of a conjuror he produced from his hip pockets both the articles he had mentioned and held them up, beaming. He pointed the revolver at Rampole and added, "Bing!"

"Look out!" shouted the chief inspector, seizing at his arm. "You blithering idiot, be careful with that thing!"

"You needn't worry. Word of honor, you needn't. It's a dummy pistol; even a Scotland Yard man couldn't hurt himself with it. It's just painted tin, you see? The handcuffs are dummies, too, but they both look realistic. I got them at one of those curio-shop places in Glasshouse Street, where you buy all the trick things. Here are some more of them; I couldn't resist buying several. There's a mouse that runs across the table on some sort of roller when you press him down"—he was fumbling in his pockets—"but we don't need 'em now. Ah, here was what I wanted."

With manifest pride on his large red face he produced an enormous and impressive-looking gold badge, which he hung on his lapel conspicuously.

"To the man we're going to question," he observed, "we have got to look like a *real* crowd of detectives. That we do not look like the same to the chief of the C.I.D. is of no consequence. But we have got to look the part for Mr. Marks's benefit, or we shall get nothing out of him. Now, draw up closely to this table, and look as solemn as possible. We have it all arranged now; the light in his face as he sits in that chair I've pushed out; the handcuffs will lie before me, and you, Hadley, will be suggestively fingering the revolver. My young friend here will take down his testimony. Turn out those center lights, will you?" he added to Rampole. "Just the brilliant spotlight on his face, and ourselves in shadow. I think I shall keep on my hat. We now look sufficiently like the classic group, I think, to have our pictures taken. Ha!" added the doctor, very pleased. "I feel in my element now. Real detectives don't do this, but I wish to heaven they did."

Rampole inspected them as he went to turn out the center lights. There *was* a slight suggestion of people having their pictures taken at one of those beach-resort places where you put your head over the top of a cardboard airship and look foolish. Dr. Fell was sitting back sternly, and Hadley looked with a weird expression at the tin revolver hanging by the trigger-guard from one finger. Then there were footfalls in the vestibule. Dr. Fell said, "Hist!" and Rampole hastily extinguished the center lights.

Dalrye saw the tableau a moment later, and jumped violently.

"Bring in the accused!" Dr. Fell intoned, with a voice strongly suggestive of Hamlet's father's Ghost.

"Bring in *who?*" said Dalrye.

"Bring in Marks," said the Ghost, "and lock the door."

"You can't do it," said Dalrye, after a moment's inspection. "The lock's broken."

"Well, shoot him in," the Ghost suggested, in a more matter-of-fact tone, slightly bordering on irritation, "and stand against it, then."

"Right-ho," said Dalrye. He was not sure what was going on, but he caught the cue, and frowned sternly as he ushered in Marks.

The man who appeared was mild, and correct, and very nervous. Not a wrinkle in his neat clothes was out of place, and there was no guile in him. He had a long, lean head, with thin black hair parted sharply in the middle and brushed behind each large ear. His features were blunt and still more nervous. He advanced with a slight stoop, holding a good but obviously not new bowler hat against his breast.

At the sight of the tableau he froze. Nobody spoke.

"You—you wished to speak to me, sir?" he said, in a curious voice, with a slight jump at the end of it.

"Sit down," said Dr. Fell.

Another silence, while Marks's eyes took in the properties. He lowered himself gingerly into the chair and blinked at the bright light in his face.

"Sergeant Rampole," said the doctor, with a massive gesture, "take down this man's testimony. Your name?"

"Theophilus Marks, sir."

Rampole made two crosses and a squiggle.

"Occupation?"

"I am employed by Sir William Bitton, of Berkeley Square, sir. I—I hope, sir," said Marks, swallowing, "that this is not in connection with that dreadful business, sir, of Mr. Philip—"

"Do I take that down, too?" inquired Rampole.

"Certainly," said the doctor. Obediently, Rampole made a furious row of loops, and ended with a severe flourish. Dr. Fell had for the moment forgotten the voice of Hamlet's father's Ghost. He resumed it with a jerk that made Hadley jump.

"Your last position?"

"For fifteen years, sir, I had the honor to serve Lord Sandival," Marks said, eagerly, "and I'm sure, sir—"

"*Aha!*" rumbled the doctor, closing one eye. He looked rather as the Ghost would have looked had he caught Hamlet playing pinochle when he should have been attending to business. "Why did you leave your last place? Sacked?"

"No, sir! It was the death of His Lordship, sir."

"H'm. Murdered, I suppose?" inquired the Ghost.

"Good Heavens, no, sir!"

Marks was visibly wilting. The Ghost became practical. "Now, look here, Marks, I don't mind telling you you're in a very bad corner. You've got a good position, haven't you?"

"Yes, sir. And I'm sure Sir William will give me the highest—"

"He won't, Marks, if he knows what we know. Would you like to lose your position, and go to jail besides? Think of it, Marks!" rumbled Dr. Fell, picking up the handcuffs.

Marks moved backwards, his forehead damp. He tried to keep the light out of his eyes with a nervous hand. "Marks," said the Ghost, "give me your hat!"

"My *what*, sir?"

"Your hat. The one you've got there. Quickly!" As the valet held out his bowler, they could see under the light the large gold letters *Bitton* on the inside of the white lining in the crown. "Aha!" said the Ghost. "Pinching Sir William's hats, eh? That'll be another five years. Write it down, Sergeant Rampole."

"No, sir!" Marks cried, through a gulp. "I swear it, sir. I can prove it, Sir William *gave* me that hat. I wear the same size as he does. And he gave me that because he bought two new hats only recently, and if you'll only let me prove it, sir—"

"I'll give you your chance," said the Ghost, ominously. He thrust his hand across the table. It held something round and flat and black; there was a click, and it leaped full-grown into an opera hat. "Put this hat on, Marks!"

By this time Rampole was so bewildered that he almost expected to see Dr. Fell take from the hat several yards of colored ribbon and a brace of rabbits. Marks stared.

"*This* is Sir William's hat!" shouted the Ghost. "Put it on. If it fits you, I'll believe what you say."

Without further ado he began to stab with the hat in the direction of Marks's forehead. The valet was compelled to put it on. It was too large; not so large as it had been on the body of Driscoll, but still too large.

"So-ho!" rumbled the Ghost, standing up behind the table. Absently he had been fumbling in his pockets; the Ghost was excited, and making gestures with anything he could lay hold of. Dr. Fell lifted his hand and shook it in the air. "Confess, Marks!" he thundered. "Miserable wretch, your guilt has found you out!"

He crashed his hand down on the table. To Marks's stupefaction, and Dr. Fell's own irritation at the anticlimax, a large rubber mouse with white whiskers popped out of his hand and ambled slowly across the table towards Hadley. Dr. Fell snatched it up hastily and put it into his pocket.

"Hem!" observed the Ghost. Then he paused, and added something which really brought Hadley out of his chair.

"Marks," said Dr. Fell, "*you stole Sir William's manuscript.*"

For a moment it looked as though the other were going to faint.

"I—I didn't! I swear I didn't! But I didn't know, and I was afraid to tell when he explained it to me!"

"I'll tell you what you did, Marks," said Dr. Fell, forgetting all about the Ghost and threatening in a natural voice. "Sir William gave me all the facts. You're a good valet, Marks, but you're one of the stupidest creatures in God's world. Sir William bought two new hats on Saturday. One of the opera hats he tried on at the shop was too large for him. But a mistake was made, and they sent the large one to him along with the Homburg, which was of the right size. Ha? You saw it. You would, immediately. You wear the same size. But Sir William was going out to the theatre that night. You know what sort of temper he has. If he found a hat that slid down over his forehead, he'd make it hot for the first person he could lay hands on.

"Naturally you wanted his hat to be the right size, didn't you, Marks? Otherwise your soul would have been shocked. But there wasn't time to get another hat; it was Saturday evening. So you did the natural thing. You used the same quick makeshift people have been using since hats were invented. You neatly stuffed the band on the inside with paper, the first harmless-looking paper you could find—"

Hadley flung the tin revolver on the table. "Good God!" he said, "do you seriously mean to tell us that Marks tightened up the fit of that hat with Sir William's manuscript?"

"Sir William," the doctor said, amiably, "gave us two clues himself which were absolutely revealing. Do you remember what he said? He said that the manuscript consisted of thin sheets of paper folded several times *lengthwise*, and rather long. Try folding over any piece of paper that way, and you'll get a long, narrow, compact set, admirably suited for stuffing the lining of a hat. And do you remember what he said besides? The manuscript was wrapped in *tissue paper*. Taken all together, it was the obvious thing for Marks to use. Like the two laborers in the house where Bitton found it, and the owner of the house himself, Marks couldn't see any importance in a piece of tissue paper lying idly about—"

"But Bitton said it was in the drawer."

"I doubt that," said Dr. Fell. "Was it, Marks?"

Marks brushed a handkerchief over his damp forehead. "N-no, sir," he faltered. "It was lying there on the desk. I—I didn't think it was important. It was tissue paper with some crackly stuff inside, the sort of thing they use to pack objects in cardboard boxes. I thought it was something he'd discarded, sir. I swear I did! If it had been correspondence, or *any* other piece of paper, I take my oath I wouldn't have thought of going near it. But—"

"And then," said Dr. Fell, rattling the handcuffs, "you learned next day what you'd done. You learned it was worth thousands of pounds. And so you were afraid to tell Sir William what you'd done, because in the meantime the hat had been stolen." He turned to Hadley. "I rather thought this was the case, from Sir William's description of Marks's behavior when he interviewed him afterwards. Sir William made us an invaluable suggestion, which he thought was satiric. He said, 'Do you think I go about carrying valuable manuscripts in my hat?' And that's precisely what he did."

"And that," Hadley said in a queer voice, "*that* was why Sir William's hat fitted him. It's what you meant by your 'hint.'"

"It's what I meant by telling you we had got to clear away all the nonsense from this case before we could see the truth. That one little accident precipitated a whole series of ghastly events, like the loss of the horseshoe nail. It was the only point I wasn't sure of. I was staking everything on my belief that that's what had happened. Now I know the whole truth. But you can see for yourself why I couldn't have Sir William with me when I was questioning Marks."

The valet removed the opera hat and was holding it like a bomb. His face was dull and helpless.

"All right," he said in a normal, human, almost even tone. "All right, gents. You've got me. That means my job. What are you going to *do* with me? I've got a sister and three cousins I'm supporting; and respectable, too. But it's all up now."

"Eh?" said Dr. Fell. "Oh! No, Marks. You're safe enough. Now you walk out to the car again, and sit there till you're called. You did a stupid thing, but there's no reason why you should lose your place. *I* won't tell Sir William."

The mild little man thrust himself out violently.

"Honest to God?" he demanded. "Do you mean it?"

"I mean it, Marks."

There was a pause. Marks drew himself up and adjusted his impeccable coat. "Very good, sir," he said in a precise tone. "I'm sure I'm very grateful, sir."

"Turn on the center lights," Dr. Fell suggested to Rampole, "and give Hadley's notebook back before he gets apoplexy." Beaming, the doctor sat down behind the table and produced the rubber mouse. He pushed his shovel hat to the back of his head, and set the mouse to running in circles over the table. "This almost marred my effect. I say, Hadley, I'm devilish sorry I didn't think to buy a pair of false whiskers."

As the lights went on, Hadley, Rampole, and a very excited Dalrye almost literally seized him.

"Let me get all this straight," the chief inspector said, heavily. "On Saturday night Bitton walked out of his house with that manuscript in his hat. And this Mad Hatter chap stole the hat."

"Ah," said the doctor, somberly. He stopped the mouse and scowled at it. "And there you have the inception of the crazy comedy, Hadley. There's where *everything* started to go wrong. If there's one thing in the world young Philip Driscoll wouldn't have done, it was offend his uncle. Over and over, with tears in my eyes, I've implored you to believe that the last thing in the world Driscoll wanted to do was even touch Bitton's beloved manuscript. And so what must have been his horror when he discovered he'd done the one thing in the world he didn't want to do!"

During a frozen silence Dr. Fell picked up the mouse, put it down, and glanced thoughtfully at his companions. "Oh yes," he said. "*Driscoll was the hat thief, you see.*"

XV

The Affair of the Rubber Mouse

"Wait a minute!" protested Rampole. "Wait a minute. They're coming over the plate too fast for me. You mean—"

"Just what I say," the doctor answered, testily. "If you didn't see that, I'm surprised you didn't. Nobody could have doubted it from the first. I had proof of it here tonight; but I had to come here and get the proof before you would have believed me. Got a cigar, Hadley?"

He sat back comfortably when the cigar was lighted, the large gold badge still stuck on his lapel and the rubber mouse within reach.

"Consider. Here's a crazy young fellow with a sense of humor and lots of intelligence. I think myself that he was a good deal of a sneak and skunk; but we've got to allow him the nerve, the humor, and the intelligence. He wants to make a name for himself as a newspaperman. He can turn out a good, vivid news story when he has the facts; but he has so little news-sense that one managing editor swears he wouldn't scent a wedding if he walked through an inch of rice in front of a church.

"That's not only understandable, Hadley, but it's a further clue to his character. His long suit was imagination. The very imaginative people never make good straight reporters; they're looking for the picturesque, the bizarre, the ironic incident; and very often they completely neglect to bother about essential facts. Doing the routine work of covering regular news isn't in their line. Driscoll would have made a thundering good columnist, but as a reporter he was a failure. So he resolved to do what many a reporter has done before him—to create news, and the sort of news that would appeal to him. If you'll just think back over everything we know of his character, you'll see what he was up to.

"In every one of these important hat thefts there was a sort of ironic symbolism, as though the stage had been arranged by an actor. Driscoll loved gestures, and he loved symbolism. A policeman's helmet is propped on a lamp-standard outside Scotland Yard; 'Behold the power of the police!' says the Byronic Mr. Driscoll, with the usual cynicism of very young people. A barrister's wig is put on a cab horse, which was the nearest approach Driscoll could get towards underlining Mr. Bumble's opinion that the law is an ass. And next the hat of a well-known Jewish war profiteer is stolen and placed on one of the lions in Trafalgar Square. Now, Driscoll is really in his most Byronic vein. 'Behold!' he cries—and it's genuinely comical, as I tried to point out to you—'behold, in these degenerate days, the British lion's crown!'"

Dr. Fell paused to settle more comfortably. Hadley stared at him, and then the chief inspector nodded.

"Now I shouldn't go into this so thoroughly," the doctor went on, "except that it's a clue to the murder, as you'll see. He was preparing for another coup, a real and final coup, which couldn't help making—in his eyes—the whole of England sit up." The doctor wheezed and chuckled. Putting down his cigar, he pawed among the papers he had taken from Hadley's briefcase. "Here's his notebook, with those notes which puzzled you so much. Before I read them to you again, let me remind you that Driscoll himself gave the whole show away. You recall that drunken evening with Mrs. Bitton, which Mrs. Larkin described for us, when Driscoll prophesied what was going to happen a week before it did begin to happen? He mentioned events which were shortly to occur, and which would make his name as a newspaperman. An artist, when comfortably filled with beer, can talk at length about the great picture he intends to paint, without exciting the least surprise. A writer is practically bound to mention the great novel he will one day write. But when a newspaperman casually mentions what corking stories he is going to turn out about the murder which is to take place next week, there is likely to be considerable curiosity about his powers of foresight.

"But let's return to this big stroke Driscoll was planning, after having built up to it by degrees with lesser hats. First, you see, he carefully stole the crossbow bolt out of Bitton's house—"

"He did *what?*" shouted the chief inspector. Dalrye sat down suddenly in a chair by the table, and Rampole found another.

"Oh yes; I must tell you about that," Dr. Fell said, frowning as though he were a trifle annoyed with himself. "But I tried to give you a hint, you know, this afternoon. It was Driscoll who stole it. By the way—" he rummaged on the floor at the side of his chair, and brought up the tool-basket. After fumbling inside it, he produced what he wanted. "By the way, here's the file he used to sharpen it. It's rather an old file, so you can see the oblique lines in the dirt-coating where he sawed at the barbs of the head. And here are the straighter marks to show where he had started effacing the *Souvenir de Carcassonne*, before somebody stole the bolt from him to use for another purpose."

Hadley took the file and turned it over. "Then—" he said.

"I asked you, you know, why that engraving hadn't been entirely obliterated, provided the person who had sharpened the bolt was really the murderer. Let's suppose it *had* been the murderer. He started in to do it, so why in the name of madness didn't he go on? It was obvious that he didn't want the bolt traced, as it would have been and as it was. But he stopped after a neat, thorough job on just three letters. It was only when I realized what was up—an explanation provided by those abstruse notes in Driscoll's notebook—that I realized it wasn't the murderer's doing at all. It was Driscoll's. He hadn't finished his job of effacing when along came the murderer: who didn't care where the bolt came from, or whose it was. But actually this bolt was planned as a part of Driscoll's most daring venture."

"But, good God! *What* venture?" demanded Hadley. "There's no way to associate it with the hats."

"Oh yes, there is," said Dr. Fell.

After he had puffed thoughtfully for a moment he went on. "Hadley, who is the man, above all you can think of, who ranks in the popular eye as England's leading jingo? Who is the man who still makes speeches in private life, as he used to do in public life, about the might of the sword, the longbow, the crossbow, and the stout hearts of old? Who is always agitating for bigger armaments? Who is forever attacking the Prime Minister as a dangerous pacifist? Who, at any rate, is inevitably the person *Driscoll* would think of in that rôle?"

"You mean—Sir William Bitton?"

"I mean just that," nodded the doctor. A grin creased up his chins. "And that insane nephew of his had conceived a design which satisfied all the demands of his sensation-loving soul. He was going to steal Sir William Bitton's hat and nail it with a crossbow bolt to the door of Number 10, Downing Street."

Hadley was more than shocked. He was genuinely outraged.

For a moment he could only splutter; and Dr. Fell contemplated him with amiable mockery.

"Tut, tut!" said the doctor. "I warned you, Hadley, when the general and I were outlining fantastic schoolboy pranks and you were not amused. I was sure you would never see the back of the design unless you could put yourself into the place of the schoolboy. You've got too much common sense. But, you see, Driscoll hadn't. You don't appreciate dummy pistols and rubber mice. That's your trouble. But I do appreciate them, and I can become even as Driscoll.

"Look here." He opened Driscoll's notebook. "See how he's musing about this scheme. He hasn't quite worked it out yet. All he has is the idea of fastening Sir William's hat with this warlike instrument in some public place. So he writes, inquiringly, 'Best place? Tower?' But, of course, that won't do; it's much too easy, and a crossbow bolt in the Tower would be as conspicuous as a small bit of coal at Newcastle. However, he's got to have his properties first, and he writes, 'Track down hat,' which is obvious. Then he thinks about Trafalgar Square again, as he inevitably must. But that won't do, because he certainly can't drive his bolt into the stone of the Nelson monument. So he writes, 'Unfortunate Trafalgar, can't transfix!' But it wasn't so unfortunate, for his burst of inspiration comes—and you note the exclamation points to denote it. He's got it now. He notes down Number Ten, home of the Prime Minister. The next words you can easily see. Is the door made of wood? If it's steel-bound, or something of the sort, the scheme won't work; he doesn't know. He must find out. Is there a hedge, or anything that will screen him from observation while he does it? Are there guards about, as there are likely to be? He doesn't know this, either. It's a long chance, and a risky one; but he's jubilant about the possibility, and he means to find out."

Dr. Fell put down the notebook.

"Thus," he said, "I outline to you what I, like Driscoll, intend to call symbolically the Affair of the Rubber Mouse. Let's see what came of it. You *do* see, don't you, Hadley?"

Again the chief inspector was pacing the room. He made a noise almost like a groan.

"I suppose I do," he snapped. "He waited for Sir William's car in Berkeley Street; let's see, that was Saturday night?"

"Saturday night," affirmed the doctor. "He was still youthful and hopeful and all the rest of it. He was up in the clouds—just before the tumble came. And, incidentally, here's another ingenious feature of the scheme. In most cases there wasn't an enormous amount of risk. He stole the hats of the dignified people who wouldn't make a row about it. They certainly wouldn't report the theft to the police, to begin with. And if he were in a tight spot, it's unlikely the victim would give serious chase. That's the cunning feature. A man like Sir William would run halfway across London in pursuit of a man who'd picked his pocket of half a crown. It would be outraged justice. But he wouldn't run a step, for fear of looking a fool, after a man who stole a two-guinea hat. Well, reconstruct, Hadley."

"H'm. He waited for Sir William's car in Berkeley Street. Any sort of telephone call to the house, which he could properly have made in his own character, would have got him the information he wanted—where Bitton was that night, and the rest of it. And let's see. Bitton said, I think, that the chauffeur slowed down to let a blind man with some pencils get across the street."

"Any sort of vender," agreed the doctor, "would have crossed the street for a shilling. And Driscoll got the hat. He bargained on it that Bitton wouldn't give chase. He was right. Still, everything was fine and fair, until—"

He peered up inquiringly at Hadley.

"Until Sunday night," Hadley said, slowly. "Then everything came down on him at once when he called at the house."

"We're on debatable ground now. But it's not a question of great importance. H'mf. It's unlikely he discovered until Sunday night that he'd unwittingly pinched the manuscript," said Dr. Fell. "Why should he? You don't pay much attention to paper inside a hat band.

"But here's the point. On Sunday evening they told him about the theft of the manuscript. Whether he suspected something then I don't know. Undoubtedly he knew all about the manuscript, from Bitton's hints beforehand. But the other affair crashed down on him. Laura Bitton and her husband were back; Laura must have conveyed some hint of the state of affairs; there was a whispered row; Driscoll went wildly out of the house before Laura could make an appointment with him. Otherwise she would have made her appointment then, and not bothered to write. But Driscoll gave her no chance; that was like him."

"Up again, down again," muttered Hadley. "He was afraid of the scandal that might come up; of being cut off by his uncle—"

Dr. Fell nodded somberly.

"And a million other fancies that would come into a head like his. Mr. Dalrye said this flat was full of his presence," the doctor said suddenly, in a louder voice. "What must he have been like when he came home here and discovered, with one of the sickest feelings of horror he ever had, that he'd unintentionally stolen his uncle's most cherished possession? Good God! What would he *think*? In his muddled state he couldn't think at all. What would you think yourself if a ten-thousand-pound manuscript had been stolen, and turned up as stuffing for a hat-band? His difficulties were all childish and all horrible. How could he explain it? Here was his uncle raving, and here *he* was with the manuscript—how had it got into the hat to begin with? Not by any stretch of madness could he have imagined his uncle deliberately putting that fragile thing into a hat of his own accord, and wearing it about the streets. And, worst of all, Driscoll wasn't supposed to know about the manuscript in the first place!

"Imagine that wild, red-headed kid running about here like a bat trying to get out! A moment before, he'd been the reckless adventurer; swaggering, exhilarated—as immortal as a shilling-shocker hero. Women loved him, and he could imagine that men feared him. Now he was threatened with a hellish scandal, with the price of swaggering, and worst of all with his ugly-tempered uncle. I wonder how many drinks he had?"

"If he had been sensible," the chief inspector growled, striking the table, "he'd have gone to his uncle, and—"

"Would he?" Dr. Fell frowned. "I wonder if even a sensible person would have done that, at least, with Sir William Bitton. What could Driscoll say? 'Oh, I say, uncle, I'm sorry. Here's your Poe manuscript. I pinched it by mistake at the same time I pinched your hat.' Can you imagine the result? Driscoll wasn't supposed to know about the manuscript; nobody was. Bitton imagined he was being very sly and clever, when he was advertising its presence all the time. To begin with, he wouldn't have believed Driscoll. What would *you* think of somebody who walked in and said, 'By the way, Hadley, you know that thousand-pound bank note you've been hiding away from everybody in your drawer upstairs? Well, when I was stealing your umbrella last night, I accidentally discovered the bank note hanging by a string from the handle of the umbrella. Odd, what?' No, my boy. You'd scarcely have been in a receptive mood. And if, to cap the business, your brother later came in and observed, 'Yes, Hadley, and the curious thing is that

I discovered in that chap's flat not only your umbrella and your thousand-pound note, but also my wife.' I venture to suggest, old man, that you would have thought your friend's conduct at least a trifle eccentric."

Dr. Fell snorted.

"Perhaps that's what the sensible man would have done. But Driscoll wasn't sensible. Call him anything else you like, but not a clear-thinker. He was wild. *We* can sit here and say how humorous it was, and that he was a half-baked youth who imagined the world tumbling down on him. But he couldn't."

Dr. Fell bent forward and prodded the rubber mouse with his forefinger. It ran round in a circle on the table and bounced off.

"For Lord's sake," cried the exasperated chief inspector, "let that mouse alone and get on with—it! So he wrestled with this thing all night, and in the morning he telephoned Mr. Dalrye here and determined to tell him everything?"

"Exactly."

Dalrye, who had been sitting quietly all through this, turned a puzzled face; he looked like a disheveled Puritan elder.

"Yes, but there's another thing," he observed. "I say, Doctor, why didn't he come to me straightaway? He phoned in the morning, you know. If he were as upset as all that, he would have come down to the Tower immediately, wouldn't he?"

"No," said the doctor. "And I shall now expound to you, children, why. It is the point which confirmed my suspicions of the whole affair. I mean the second attack on Sir William Bitton."

"Good Lord, yes!" Hadley stopped his pacing and wheeled suddenly. "If Driscoll did all this, why did he steal a second hat from Bitton? That wasn't precisely the way to get him out of the scrape, was it?"

"No. But it was a piece of remarkably quick thinking in an emergency, for which we shall have to give him credit."

"Maybe it was," the chief inspector admitted, gloomily. "But it would seem to me somewhat to complicate matters. He'd have another explanation to add to his uncle when he'd finished the ones you were outlining a minute ago. 'Sorry to trouble you again, sir. But I've not only pinched your hat, your manuscript, and your brother's wife, but your first hat wasn't satisfactory, so I just popped round and took another.'"

"Be quiet, will you? Be quiet, and let me talk. Ha. Harrumph. Well. He was going to get Mr. Dalrye's help, but, before he did, he intended to make one last effort to help himself. You see, I rather wondered why he had definitely made the appointment at the Tower for one o'clock, as Mr. Dalrye says, when he could easily have gone down there in the morning. And, having made the appointment, he didn't appear until nearly twenty minutes past one! What held him up? If anything, you would have expected him to be ahead of time. What he was going to do was make an attempt to return the manuscript, unknown to his uncle.

"That was rather more difficult an undertaking than it sounds. He knew positively, from what he had heard at the house, that his uncle didn't connect the theft of the manuscript with the theft of the hat. Sir William thought the manuscript was stolen by itself. Suppose, then, Driscoll simply put it into an envelope and sent it back to his uncle by post? Too dangerous! Driscoll knew Arbor was in the house. He had heard Arbor's broad talk at the dinner table. He knew that his uncle was bound to suspect Arbor. But he knew his uncle would never believe Arbor had first stolen the manuscript, and then posted it back again. And if Arbor were eliminated—you see?"

Hadley rubbed his chin.

"Yes. If Arbor were eliminated, the only person who could have stolen it was a member of his own household."

"Then what follows? Sir William would know it hadn't been one of the servants; he ridiculed that idea when he talked to us. There would remain Lester Bitton, Laura Bitton, Sheila, and Driscoll. Lester and Laura Bitton were definitely several hundred miles away when it was stolen. Only four people could have known about that manuscript, and two of them were in Cornwall! Of the other two, Sheila could hardly have been regarded as the culprit. Inevitably Driscoll must come to be suspected, and be thought to have sent it back in a fit of conscience—which would be precisely like Driscoll, anyway. Rest assured Driscoll knew all this, and he knew that his uncle would suspect it if he posted back that manuscript. But what was he to do? For the same reasons, he couldn't slip into the house and drop the manuscript somewhere so that it would be found. Sir William knew damned well it *hadn't* been mislaid; he'd been over that house with a vacuum cleaner; he knew it wasn't there. The same drawbacks would apply to its being suspiciously 'found' as to its being suspiciously returned in the mail."

"I'm hanged if I can see what he could do," the chief inspector confessed. "Unless he simply sat tight and let his uncle suspect Arbor. That would be the logical thing. But a nervous type like Driscoll would always have the horrible fear that his uncle *might*, somehow, find out. What he'd want most to do would be get the thing out of his hands—quickly. Out of sight, out of mind sort of business."

"Precisely! And that," said Dr. Fell, rapping his stick on the floor, "is where, for a second, he completely lost his head. He wanted to get it out of his hands. It was almost literally burning his fingers. You see what he did? He couldn't make up his mind. He went out, on that misty day, and paced the streets. And with every step he was gravitating towards his uncle's house, with possibilities multiplying and whirling and hammering in his brain, until he lost his head altogether.

"Hadley, do you remember what time Sir William arrived this afternoon at the bar where he met us? It was close on two o'clock. And when he described the theft of his second hat to us, he said, 'It happened an hour and a half ago, and I'm still boiling.' It happened, then, roughly, at about twenty minutes to one. Sir William was ready to make his monthly round of calls, as he told us; and, as he also told us, they rarely varied. It was the afternoon for his monthly call on Driscoll, by the way. I believe he pointed that out. His car was standing in the mist at the curb. His chauffeur had gone down to buy cigarettes, and Sir William had not yet stepped out of the house. And Driscoll was there at the corner, watching it."

"I'm beginning to remember a lot of things Bitton said," the chief inspector answered, grimly. "He told us he saw somebody with his arm through the window of the car fumbling with the side pocket. You mean—Driscoll couldn't stand it any longer; and he wanted to shove the manuscript into the pocket of the car, anywhere out of sight?"

"I do. And he was prevented by Sir William's instant arrival on the scene. Sir William thought he was a sneak-thief. He didn't mind chasing sneak-thieves. He yelled, 'Hi!' and charged—and Driscoll probably instinctively did the only piece of quick thinking I've known him do yet. He snatched Sir William's hat and darted away in the mist."

"You mean—"

"Instinctive experience, my boy. Because he knew the old man wouldn't chase him. He knew Bitton would simply stand on the pavement and swear."

"Good," said Hadley, in a low voice, after a pause. "Damned good. But you're forgetting one thing. He may really have put that manuscript into the pocket of the car, and it may still be there."

Dr. Fell blinked sadly at the mouse he had resurrected from the floor.

"Sorry. I'm afraid you're about eleven hours too late. You see, even in the rush of going to the Tower in Bitton's car, I didn't neglect to examine the pockets this afternoon. It wasn't there. Driscoll never put it in; he left in too much of a hurry."

There was a very faint smile on Hadley's face. Again, Rampole felt, all through this conversation he had been holding himself back; he had been asking Dr. Fell the right questions, and quietly sorting out the pieces of the puzzle he wanted.

"Now, then, let me reassemble my facts," he suggested. "You say Driscoll went out comparatively early this morning, and never came back?"

"Yes."

"He took the manuscript. But the stolen top hat was here?"

"Probably."

"Also—the crossbow bolt was here? The bolt he was filing; likely in a conspicuous place?"

"Yes."

"Then," said Hadley, with sudden grimness, "our case is complete. Lester Bitton came over here to see Driscoll this morning, when Driscoll was out. He let himself in with a key he borrowed from his brother, and returned to his home at noon, where Miss Bitton saw him come in—what did she say?—'shaken,' and 'laughing.'

"Anybody could have taken that crossbow bolt from the Bitton house. But only Lester Bitton could have stolen it from this flat. Anybody might have stolen Sir William's top hat. But only Lester Bitton could have taken that top hat from this flat to put on the head of the man he stabbed at the Tower of London, so that he could give Driscoll the fulfillment of his wish. And Driscoll did die in a top hat, with at least one woman to weep at his grave."

Dr. Fell let his glasses fall on their black ribbon, and massaged his eyes fiercely. "Yes," he said from between his hands, in a muffled voice, "I'd thought of that, too. I'm afraid it rather sews him up. That's why I asked Miss Bitton whether he was carrying anything when he returned."

They had not realized, in the slow passing of hours, how imperceptibly the night noises of London had faded. Even the muted roar, always in the background, had died until their voices sounded unnaturally loud. They had not been aware of the creaking of boards, or how sharply rose the singing of tires when a late car hummed in the square. But even through a closed door they could hear the telephone bell.

Sheila Bitton's voice could be heard, too, when she answered it. And in a moment she thrust a rather grimy face round the door. She had been crying at one time, too, when she went over the contents of those rooms.

"It's for you, Mr. Hadley," she said. "Something about a Mr. Arbor? Is that *our* Mr. Arbor? You'd better come to the phone, please."

Hadley almost broke into a run.

XVI

What Was Left in the Fireplace

SHEILA BITTON jumped in astonishment when she saw the expressions on the faces of those who crowded past her. Her own expression indicated that it was undignified. She had discarded hat and coat, to show fluffy yellow hair tousled about her head, and a dark frock with the sleeves now rolled up about the wrists. There was a streak of dirt across her nose where she had jammed her elbow across her eyes; and Rampole had an image of her picking up Driscoll's possessions—taking one, discarding one— reminded by another of some association, and suddenly sitting down with the tears in her eyes.

He reflected that he would never understand the mental processes of women in the presence of death. They were cool and unruffled. And then they became hysterical. Each in its own turn, and intermingling.

Hadley was at the telephone, and Dr. Fell bent over him in the little study. On the doctor's face was an expression Rampole had never seen before: he could not decide whether it was nervousness, or fear, or hope. But Dr. Fell was certainly nervous. Rampole never forgot the weird picture they presented in that time—Hadley listening intently to a buzz where words were almost distinguishable in the silent room; his elbow on the table, his back to the door, the dust which Sheila had disturbed settling now round the green-shaded lamp. Dr. Fell bent forward against the line of the bookshelves; the black ribbon on his glasses dangling, his shovel hat on the back of his head, pinching at his mustache with a hand which still held the small rubber mouse.

Silence, except for the faint, rapid voice in the telephone. A board creaked. Sheila Bitton started to speak, but was hushed by Dalrye. Hadley spoke only once or twice, in monosyllables. Then, without hanging up the receiver, he turned.

"Well?" demanded Dr. Fell.

"It worked. Arbor left his friends, the Spenglers, early in the evening, and Spengler walked with him to his cottage. Our plain-clothes man was watching from the garden; he'd got his instructions already, and he seems to have played up to them. Hold on a bit, Carroll," he added into the telephone, and squared himself in the chair. "First Arbor went through the cottage, switching on all the lights, but he immediately closed the shutters after he'd done it. There are diamond-shaped holes in the bottoms of the shutters, though, and the constable worked close enough so that he could look in through the holes in the windows on the ground floor.

"Arbor and his friend were in one of the front rooms, where the covers hadn't been taken off the furniture. They were sitting in front of the fire, playing chess, with a bottle of whisky between them, and Arbor looked nervous. This, I judge, was about two hours ago. Then the constable got busy. He walked up and down loudly on the gravel, and then dodged round the side of the house. In a moment Arbor's friend, Spengler, opened the shutters and looked out; then he closed them again. That sort of game went on for some time. They phoned for a policeman and the policeman flashed his bull's-eye all round the garden, but of course he didn't find our man. When it had all quieted down again, and our man was back at the window, he decided to rush matters. The whisky was about half gone and somebody had knocked the chessboard over. Arbor seemed to be trying to persuade Spengler of something, and Spengler wouldn't listen. Then our man went back and rattled the knob of the scullery door. The next minute he was around the side of the concrete garage, and it's a good thing he was. Somebody opened the scullery door and stuck out a revolver and began firing shots blindly all over the garden. That brought down all the policemen within half a mile; there was a devil of a row and Spengler had to show his pistol permit. When the row quieted down, Arbor was all in. He insisted on going to the station with them and getting in touch with me. And he insists on speaking to me personally."

Dr. Fell did not look as pleased as circumstances seemed to warrant.

"What are you going to do?"

Hadley glanced at his watch and scowled. "It's almost ten minutes past twelve. H'm. But I'm afraid to put it off until morning. He'll get a return of cheerfulness with daylight, and he may decide not to talk. We've got to catch him while he's in a funk. But I don't want him at Scotland Yard— People of his type are very, very reticent when you come the high official over them— And I'm hanged if I'm going out to Golder's Green myself."

"Why not bring him here?"

"I don't suppose there would be any objection." Hadley looked at Sheila Bitton. "That's best. Dalrye can take Miss Bitton home. Yes, that's it. I'll have him brought in a police car, so he'll know he's safe. This is as good a base of operations as any."

"Wouldn't he talk over the telephone?" the doctor demanded.

"No. For some reason, the man seems to have developed an unholy horror of telephones. Well." Hadley gave brief instructions to the other end of the wire, and hung up. "Fell, what do you think he knows?"

"I'm afraid to tell you what I think. I'm literally afraid. Remember, I asked you the same question when we decided Driscoll was stabbed in the tunnel of the Bloody Tower, with Mrs. Bitton at one end and Arbor at the other." He had been mumbling, and now he stopped short altogether as he remembered Sheila's presence. The girl was behind Dalrye in the passage, and apparently had not caught words which might have caused unnecessary questions. The doctor peered towards the passage, and chewed the end of his mustache. "Never mind. We shall know soon enough."

Hadley was examining the study. Sheila Bitton had added to its disorder, a thing which nobody would have believed possible a while ago. In the center of the floor she had been piling all sorts of mementoes: a couple of silver cups, framed photographs of sport groups, a cricket bat, a runner's jersey, a china mug inscribed *Birthday, from Sheila*, a stamp album, a broken fishing rod, and two warped tennis rackets. In this bleak room now, Rampole thought, memories were gathering and strengthening. It came to him horribly, with a new force: *This man is dead*.

"I wish you men would get *out!*" the girl's voice complained, fretfully. She pushed her way past Dalrye with doll-like aggressiveness, and stood contemplating them. "Everything is in such a *mess!* Phil would never keep tidy. And I'm sure I don't know what to do with his clothes; such a lot of them, all scattered about, and there's one brand-new nice gray hat I know belongs to Daddy, because it's got that gold lettering he uses on the inside, and how it came to be here I can't think."

"Eh?" demanded Hadley, roused out of his musing. His eyes narrowed and he looked at the doctor. "Do you think he came back here after he'd—I mean, just before he went to the Tower?"

"I'm fairly certain he did," Dr. Fell answered. "After he'd done what you're thinking about, he still had over twenty minutes to get to the Tower in time for his appointment, you remember. But he was twenty minutes late for it. It's all right, Miss Bitton. Just put the hat aside with the other things."

"Anyhow, I hope you'll get out," she said, practically. "Bob, you might call Marks and have him take an armload of those things out to the car. I'm filthy, absolutely filthy. And he's got oil spilled all over the desk where the typewriter is, and a piece of sharp stone I almost cut my finger on—"

Hadley turned round slowly to inspect the desk. Rampole had an image of Driscoll sitting under the green-shaded lamp in this cluttered room, patiently sharpening the crossbow bolt which was to be driven into his own heart.

"Whetstone," murmured the chief inspector. "And the typewriter. By the way, Doctor, you found the tool you wanted, right enough; but I remember you said you were looking for something in his typewriter. What was it?"

Dr. Fell juggled his mouse. "I was looking for the beginning of a certain news story which gave an account of something before it occurred; I mean that little business at Number Ten. I wasn't sure he'd started it, but I thought I'd better have a look in case you didn't believe me. It wasn't in his typewriter, but it was on the desk; I have it in my pocket. If he intended to scoop Fleet Street, you see, he wanted time to prepare a corking-good story before the other reporters even heard of it. But there was such a litter of manuscript I almost overlooked it. He's been doing a bit of dabbling with fiction, too, I see. I was about to call your attention to his character in that respect when we went out to interview Mrs. Larkin. The stories have lurid titles, and they seem all of the adventure-mystery school. *The Curse of the Doornaways*, things like that: feudal mansions with galleries and ghosts, and all that sort of thing. I fancy Driscoll always wanted a feudal mansion, and regretted that Sir William's title went no farther back than Sir William."

Sheila Bitton stamped her foot. "Oh, good *gracious*, will you get out? I think it's mean of you, when poor Phil's dead, to sit here in his room like this, just talking. And if you want any of that writing, or all those papers, or anything, you'd better tell me, because I'm just going to put it all in a suit box and take it home for Daddy; he'll want to keep it. Besides, some of it's burnt in the fireplace and you can't have it, and I looked in there because it was written in longhand and it might be a letter—" She paused and flushed suddenly. "Anyway, it was just an old story, and all burned, and—"

"*Oh my God!*" said Dr. Fell.

His great bulk lunged across the room to the toy fireplace with its bright-red bricks round the grate. He added, "Get your flashlight, Hadley," and bent to his knees, pushing away the iron fender. There was a startled expression on the chief inspector's own face as he yanked out his flashlight.

The fireplace was full of charred and feathered paper. As the bright beam played inside, they saw that the edging of some of the paper not wholly burned was of a dull mauve color, blackened by smoke.

"The 'Mary' letters," Hadley said, as Dr. Fell tried lightly to lift the mass. "All that's left of them."

Dr. Fell grunted wheezily. "Yes. And here underneath them—"

He tried to draw it out gently, but it was only a delicate black shell, and it crumbled to ash. All that remained were a few smoke-fouled inches at the top. It had been a very thin sheaf of damp-stained sheets, folded three times lengthwise, and now open. Holding it gently in his open palms, Dr. Fell put it close to Hadley's light. There had been a title, but the smoke had yellowed and obliterated it; likewise it had obliterated all the letters in the corner except an ornate *E*. But, in brown and curly script, they could faintly see a number of lines which the fire had not destroyed:

Of the singular gifts of my friend the Chevalier C. Auguste Dupin, I may one day speak. Upon my lips he has placed a seal of silence which, for fear of displeasing the eccentricities of his somewhat outre humour, I dare not at present violate. I can, therefore, only record that it was after dark one gusty evening in the year 18—that a knock sounded at the door of my chambers in a dim, decaying pile of buildings of the Faubourg St. Germain, and . . .

They all read it slowly. Dr. Fell did not move; it was as though he were kneeling and offering this piece of blackened paper to a god in the fire.

"There it is," the doctor growled in a low voice, after a pause. "All of him, in the start of one paragraph. The finger on the lip. The suavity, the hint of deadly secrets. The night, the night wind, the distant city, the date mysteriously left blank, the old and crumbling house in a remote quarter. H'm. Gentlemen, you are looking at all that is left of the first detective story ever written by Edgar Allan Poe."

Rampole's brain was full of weird pictures—a dark man with luminous, brooding eyes, thin shoulders in a military carriage, a weak chin, and an untidy mustache. He saw the candlelight, the mean room, the shabby tall hat hung behind the door, the pitifully thin rows of books. Never in his life would that dark man have anything but dreams, to exchange at last for the cold coin of an immortal name.

Hadley arose and switched off his light. "Well," he said, gloomily, "there goes ten thousand pounds. It's a good job Arbor doesn't have to pay the rest of his agreement to that fellow in Philadelphia."

"I hate having to tell this to Sir William," muttered Dalrye. "Good God! He'll be a maniac. It's a pity Phil couldn't at least have kept the thing."

"*No!*" said Dr. Fell, violently. "You don't see the point. You don't grasp it at all, and I'm ashamed of you. What happened?"

"He burned it, that's all," Hadley returned. "He was so terrified at nearly being caught when he tried to return it, that he came home and chucked it in the fire."

Dr. Fell pushed himself to his feet with the aid of one cane. He was fiery with earnestness.

"You still don't understand. What happened? Who knocked at the door of this man's house in the Faubourg St. Germain? What terrible adventure was on the way? That's what you *should* think of, Hadley. I say to you, to hell with whether this manuscript is preserved for some smug collector to prattle learnedly about and exhibit to his friends like a new gold tooth. To hell whether it costs ten thousand pounds or a halfpenny. To hell whether it makes fools write more books trying to psychoanalyze a dead man of the nineteenth century according to the standards of the twentieth. To hell with whether it's in manuscript, first edition, vellum and morocco, or sixpenny paper. What I'm interested in is what magnificent dream of blood and violence began with that knock at the door."

"All right, then—to hell with it," the chief inspector agreed, mildly. "You seem a bit rabid on the subject. *I* don't mind. If you're really so curious, you can ask Bitton about the next installment. He's read it."

Dr. Fell shook his head. "No," he said. "No, I'm never going to ask. That last line will be a deathless 'to be continued in our next' for me to weave answers about it all the rest of my life."

During this unenlightening discussion Sheila Bitton had gone into the bedroom, and they heard her moving things about with sundry suggestive knockings on the communicating wall.

"Well, let's get out," the chief inspector suggested. "Whatever you want to dream about, that fireplace has at least one thing to tell us. The manuscript was lying *under* those burnt 'Mary' letters. Driscoll burnt the manuscript before he left here on his way to the Tower. Mrs. Bitton broke in at five o'clock, and destroyed the evidence against her."

"That's right, I know," the doctor said, wearily. "But look here. I know it's bad taste, and we shouldn't do it, and all that. Still, it's warm work, and I've been several hours without a drink. If we could find one hereabouts—"

"Sound enough," said the chief inspector. "Then I'll outline my case to you."

He led the way out of the little room and down to the for-lorn dining room, where he snapped on the lights of the mosaic dome over the table. Undoubtedly, Rampole thought, that dome had come with the flat; it was of ornate ugliness, with golds and reds and blues jumbled together; and it threw a harsh, weird light on their faces. Curiously enough, the impalpable presence of the dead man was stronger here than anywhere else. It was growing on Rampole with a ghostly and horrible reality. On the mantel-piece of this dusty dining room, a marble clock with gilt facings had stopped; stopped many days ago, for the glass face was thick with dust. But it had stopped at a quarter of two. Rampole noted the coincidence with a vivid memory of Driscoll lying white-faced and sightless on the steps of Traitors' Gate. He suddenly felt that he could not drink liquor from this man's flat.

You might, any moment, hear Driscoll's step in the passage. It wasn't merely that a man died. It was the abrupt severance, like the fall of an axe, the pitching out into nowhere when the marks of his teeth were still visible in the half-eaten biscuit, and the lights still burning against his return. Rampole stared at the pieces of orange peel on the spotted cloth of the table, and shuddered.

"Sorry," he observed, with a sort of jerk and without conscious volition. "I can't drink his whisky. It doesn't seem right, somehow."

"Neither can I," said Dalrye, quietly. "I knew him, you see."

He sat down at the table and shaded his eyes with his hand.

Dr. Fell turned from rummaging at the back of the sideboard, where he had found some clean glasses. His small eyes were wrinkled up.

"So you feel it too, do you?" he demanded.

"Feel what?" asked the chief inspector. "Here's a bottle nearly full. Make mine strong, with very little soda. Feel what?"

"That's he's here," said Dr. Fell. "Driscoll."

Hadley set down the bottle. "Don't talk rot," he said, irritably. "What are you trying to do—throw a scare into us? You look as though you were beginning to tell a ghost story. Give me the glasses; I'll rinse 'em out in the kitchen."

Balancing himself heavily against the sideboard, the doctor wheezed a moment and ran his eyes slowly about the room.

"Listen, Hadley. I'm not talking about ghost stories. I won't even say premonitions. But I'm talking about a wild surmise I had earlier in the evening, when we were talking to Lester Bitton.

There was a tiny germ of reason in it, and it frightened me. Possibly it's strong now because the hour's so late and we're none of us at our brightest. By God! I'm going to take this drink, and several others, because I genuinely need 'em. And I should advise the rest of you to do the same."

Rampole felt uneasy. He thought he might look a fool or a coward; the strain of the day had made his thoughts more than a little muddled.

"All right," he said, "all right. Pour a big one." He glanced across at Dalrye, who nodded wearily.

"I think I know what you're talking about, Doctor," Dalrye said, in a low voice. "I know I wasn't here, and I'm not sure, but I still think I know what you mean."

"The person *I'm* interested in talking about," Hadley interposes, "is Lester Bitton, as a matter of fact. You're pretty well aware, aren't you, Fell, that he's the murderer?"

The doctor was setting out glasses. He took the bottle from Hadley, waved away the other's suggestion of washing the glasses, and filled them. He said, "Suppose Bitton has an alibi? You've got almost a case to go to the jury on—unless he has an alibi. That's what's worrying me. But it's late, and the old man's wits are none of the best. Tell me, Mr. Dalrye, when did you last see Sir William Bitton?"

"Sir?" Dalrye raised his head and regarded the other with puzzled eyes. "Sir William?" he repeated. "Why, at the house to-night. General Mason suggested that I go back with him when he returned from the Tower of London."

"Did the general tell him about who really owned the manuscript? Arbor, I mean? Or did you know about it?"

"I knew about it. Sir William goes about telling everybody,"

Dalrye answered, grimly, "that nobody knows of the manuscript, and then proceeds to share his secret with everybody. Did he tell you that *you* were the first to hear of it?"

"Yes."

"He's told both the general and myself the same thing. We heard of it weeks ago. But nobody has ever seen it—until tonight. Oh yes, I knew about the blasted thing."

"What did he say when Mason told him it belonged to Arbor?"

"That's the funny part. Nothing much. He just said, 'I see,' and got very quiet. It's pretty clear that he suspected as much all along. Then he said—"

Dalrye looked towards the door with dull eyes. It had become like a warning, repeated over and over until it grows horrible. The telephone bell was ringing again.

There was nothing in that ring which should have sent a chill through anybody. But Rampole went cold. And in the silence beneath the clamor of that insistent bell Dr. Fell said, "I shouldn't let Miss Bitton answer that, Hadley."

Hadley was out of the door in a moment into the study, and the door closed behind him.

While nobody moved, the rest of them could hear Sheila moving about in the kitchen down the passage. Hadley did not speak for a long time on the phone. He opened the study door presently—they could hear the sharp squeak of its hinge. Then he came with slow steps down the passage, entered, and closed the dining room door behind him.

"It's all up," he said. "Get your coats on."

"What is it?" the doctor asked, in as low a tone as Hadley.

The chief inspector put a hand over his eyes.

"I know what you mean now. I should have seen what sort of mood he was in when he left us. At least, I should have been warned by what Miss Bitton said. That was the way he said he wanted to die."

Dr. Fell brought his hand slowly down on the table. "Is it—"

"Yes," Hadley answered, nodding. "That's it. Lester Bitton has shot himself."

XVII

Death at Bitton House

DURING THE ride in Hadley's car to Berkeley Square, the only words spoken were brief questions and answers on the little Hadley had been told about the tragedy.

"It happened about ten minutes before they phoned," he explained. "That was the butler talking. The household had been up late, and the butler was still sitting up; he'd been ordered to wait for Sheila Bitton's return. He was in his pantry when he heard the shot, and he ran upstairs. The door of Lester Bitton's room was open; he smelled the smoke. Bitton was lying across the bed in his room, with the gun in his hand."

"What happened then?" Dr. Fell demanded.

"Hobbes—that's the butler—tried to wake up Sir William. But he'd taken a sleeping-draught and the door of his room was locked; Hobbes couldn't rouse him. Then Hobbes remembered Miss Bitton's talking to us, and where we were, so he phoned on the chance of getting me. He didn't know what else to do."

"What about Mrs. Bitton?"

"I didn't ask."

"H'm," muttered the other. "H'm, yes. I suppose it really was suicide."

Rampole, wedged between them in the front seat, scarcely heard them. Inanely, all he could think of in connection with Lester Bitton was that foolish remark of Sheila's, "He brought me chocolates."

The moist, chill air whipped through the open windscreen; the tires of the car sang, and above the roofs there were stars. It had been very quiet, Hadley's handling of the situation. Sheila Bitton had not been told of her uncle's death. They had left her there, with Dalrye to break the news when they were gone.

"I'd better not take her back to the house," Dalrye had said. "She'd only be in the way and she'd get hysterical. He was her favorite. I know a great friend of hers, a girl who lives in Park Lane. I'll drive her over there and get Margaret to put her up for the night. Then I'll join you."

The only thing that had surprised Rampole was the doctor's insistence that Hadley should see Arbor.

"Or, on second thought," the doctor had added, with a curious expression, "you'd better let *me* see *him*. He still thinks I'm Chief Inspector Hadley, you know. And if we try to explain matters at this stage, when he's in terror of his life, he may suspect all kinds of a put-up job."

"I don't care *who* sees him, so long as he talks," the chief inspector replied, testily. "You can stay here and wait for him, if you like. But I'd much prefer that you came along with me. We can leave Mr. Rampole to talk to him until we get back."

"I have a better idea. Tell them to bring him to Bitton's."

"To Bitton's? But, good God, man! You don't want—"

"I have rather a fancy," said the doctor, "to see how he acts there. The idea has been in my mind for some time. Let poor Marks stay in the flat and direct them over when they get here."

It had been arranged that way. Hadley's Daimler flashed

through the quiet streets, and the hands of the illuminated clock on the dashboard pointed to nearly one o'clock when they reached Berkeley Square.

The old houses were heavy and somber against the stars. A thin piping of night traffic drifted up from Piccadilly, and the footfalls of a late passer-by were uncannily loud. A taxi honked its way out of Charles Street. What faint mist was left from the day seemed to have gathered round the high street-lamps and in the thin branches of the trees. When they went up the shallow steps of the Bitton house, Hadley paused with his hand on the bell.

"I know only two quotations," he said, quietly, "but I'm going to tell you one of them now. Do you know what it is?"

Dr. Fell dropped the ferrule of his cane on the step with a hollow *thock* which had its echo. He stared out at the glow along the roofs towards the south.

"'It must be confessed,'" he repeated, "'it will be confessed; there is no refuge from confession but suicide, and suicide is confession.'"

Hadley rang the bell.

There was no sign of confusion in the house when the heavy door was opened. All the blinds had been drawn and the curtains closed, but every light was on. It was the absolute hush which was sinister. An old, grave-faced man ushered them into a massive blue entrance hall with a crystal chandelier. He closed the door again and fastened a chain across it.

"Chief Inspector Hadley, sir?" the old man asked. "I am Hobbes, sir; I telephoned you. Shall I take you upstairs?" He hesitated as Hadley nodded. "Under such circumstances, sir, I have always heard that it is customary to summon a doctor. But Mr. Bitton was obviously dead, and unless you wish it—"

"It will not be necessary for the moment. Is Sir William up yet?"

"I have not been able to rouse him, sir."

"Where is Mrs. Bitton?"

"In her room, sir. This way, if you please."

Rampole thought he heard a whispering at the back of the hall, near a staircase going down; but still there was that massive calmness and order. The butler took them up a heavily carpeted stair, with bronze figures in the niches, and along a passage at the top. It was stuffy up here, and Rampole could distinctly smell the stale reek of cordite.

A bright light streamed out against the gloom of this upper hall. At the door Hobbes stood aside for them to enter.

Here the odor of burnt powder was stronger, but nothing seemed disturbed. It was a high room, with cornices and another long chandelier, severely furnished against a background of dull brown and yellow-threaded walls. A reading desk, the shade taken off its bright lamp, stood against the foot of the bed, and the drawer was slightly open. But that was all the disturbance. The electric heater was on in the fireplace.

Lester Bitton lay sideways across the bed; they could see his feet from the door. Closer, they could see that he was fully dressed. The bullet had gone through the right temple and emerged about an inch above the left ear; following Hadley's glance, Rampole could discern the splintered place where it had lodged in the ceiling. The dead man's face was curiously peaceful, and there was very little blood. His outflung right hand, turned under at the wrist, held a Webley-Scott service automatic of the standard forty-five caliber army pattern. The only really horrible thing, Rampole thought, was the smell of singed hair.

Hadley did not immediately examine him. He spoke in a low voice to Hobbes.

"I think you told me you were in your pantry and heard the shot. You ran up here immediately, and found him just as he is. Did anybody else hear it?"

"Mrs. Bitton, sir, I believe. She came in a moment later."

"Where is Mrs. Bitton's room?"

Hobbes indicated a door near the fireplace. "A dressing room, sir, which communicates with her own room."

"What did Mrs. Bitton do?"

The butler was very guarded, at the same time as he conveyed an impression of disinterest. "Nothing, sir. She stood looking at him for a long time, and then suggested that I wake Sir William."

"And then?"

"Then, sir, she returned to her room."

Hadley went over to the writing table, looked at the chair beside it, and turned. "Mr. Bitton was out this evening. He must have returned here before eleven o'clock. Did you see him?"

"Yes, sir. He returned just before eleven, and went directly to the library. He asked me to bring him a cup of cocoa, and when I brought it he was sitting in front of the library fire. When I passed by the door of the library, about an hour later, I went in and asked him if he wished anything more. He was still sitting in the same chair. When I spoke he said, 'No, nothing more.' Then he rose and walked past me and up the stairs—" For the first time Hobbes faltered a trifle; the man's self-control was amazing. "That was the last I saw of him, sir, before—before this."

"How long afterwards did you hear the shot?"

"I am not positive, sir. Not more than five minutes, I should say, and probably less."

"Did his manner seem strange?"

A slight pause before the answer. "I am afraid so, sir. Mr. Bitton has not been exactly himself for the past month. But there was nothing—well, sir, *excited* about him. He seemed unlike himself; that's all."

Hadley glanced down at the floor. The carpet was of so thick and smooth a nap that it was almost possible to trace the path a man had taken, as though by footprints. They were standing near the door, and as Rampole followed the chief inspector's glance he could see with terrible clarity what Lester Bitton must have done. For Lester Bitton was a heavy and gigantic man; his footfalls were there where a lighter person's might not have been visible. First he had gone to the fireplace. Then he had walked to the reading table facing the fireplace, the open drawer telling where the gun had come from. From there he had gone to the bureau, whose mirror was now tilted so that a tall man could look at himself clearly. The impress of his feet, together, was heavy there; he must have stood for some time. Lastly he had walked straight to the bed, stood with his back to it so that he should fall there, and raised the automatic.

"The gun is his own?" Hadley asked.

"Yes, sir. I have seen it before. He kept it in that table drawer."

Softly Hadley punched his fist into his palm, softly and steadily as he looked about.

"There will be little more, Hobbes. I want you to give me a complete account of everything Mr. Bitton did today, so far as you know."

Hobbes's hands plucked at the sides of his trousers. His old, square, bony face was still impassive.

"Yes, sir. I observed him, sir, because I was a trifle concerned about his welfare. I feared he had been overworking. You see, sir"—his eyes shifted slightly—"I have been with Major Bitton for a long time. He left the house this morning at about half-past ten, sir, and returned at noon. I believe he had been to Mr. Philip's flat."

"Was he carrying anything when he returned?"

"Carrying anything, sir? I believe"—a hesitation —"I believe he had a package of some sort, wrapped in brown paper. He left the house again early in the afternoon. I know that he ate no lunch, sir, because on this Monday of the month luncheon is at noon instead of one o'clock, so that Sir William can go out early; I reminded him of this when he returned, and he said he merely wanted a cup of cocoa sent to his room. He left before the—unfortunate occurrence at Sir William's car; the thief, sir."

"He left for the City?"

"N-no, sir, I believe not. As he was leaving, Sir William, who intended to go to the City himself later, offered him a lift in the car. Major Bitton said he did not intend to go to his office. He—he mentioned that he was going for a walk."

"What was his manner then, nervous, upset?"

"Well, sir, say restless; as though he wanted fresh air."

"When did he return?"

"I'm afraid I don't remember, sir. Mrs. Bitton had brought back the horrible news about Mr. Philip, and—" Hobbes shook his head. He was biting at his lips now, trying to keep calm; trying to stop his voice from shaking and his eyes from wandering to the bed.

"That's all, thank you. Please wait downstairs. I suggest that you make another effort to wake Sir William before you go."

Hobbes bowed and closed the door behind him as he went out.

"I think," Hadley said, toning to his companions, "you two

had better go downstairs also. I've got to make an examination—
just in case—and I warn you it won't be pretty. There's no good
you can do. I want you to be there for Arbor when he arrives. I
wish to God we hadn't got *him* on our hands. So?"

Dr. Fell grunted. He went over, bent across the body, and held
his eyeglasses on while he had a brief look at it. Then he signaled
to Rampole and waddled towards the door without a word.

In silence they descended the stairs. Rampole thought he
heard behind them somewhere the click of a closing latch. He
thought he saw a figure somewhere in the upper hall; but his
thoughts were so warped with stealth and murder, and the ghost-
liness of this ancient house, that he paid scant attention. Of all
the districts in London, he had thought, this Mayfair was the
place of echoes and of shadows. He liked walking in a strange
city by night; and once, he remembered, he had prowled through
Mayfair in gray twilight, with a scent of rain in the air, and he
had not believed that anybody really lived there. There were gaps
in these little streets; unexpected houses, a sudden curve that
showed a chimney stack against the sky, and, in the midst of
great shuttered houses, lanes full of lighted shops like a country
town. All around was the weird realm where people had lived,
once, when Becky Sharp rode in her coach and news of Waterloo
was fresh, but did not live now. A plane tree rustled. A delivery
boy on a bicycle careened past, whistling. Through an opening
off Mount Street you could see the rails of the Park, and a few
stolid taxicabs burnt patient lamps in the square. Then, presently,
the rain began to fall.

You could imagine red buses plunging down past the grenadier pillars of Regent Street; and Ares aiming an arrow at a wall of
electric signs; and the crowds spilling out from every byway into
the roulette wheel of Piccadilly Circus. But you could not think

of this Mayfair as real. It was something out of Thackeray, which Thackeray had got in turn from Addison and Steele.

Rampole, catching up images like cards drawn from a pack, found himself following Dr. Fell down the lower hallway. The doctor had found the library, apparently by instinct. It was another high room at the rear, done in white. Three walls, even around the window spaces, were built entirely of books; the white-painted lines of the shelves showed up startlingly against the dark old volumes. The fourth wall was cream-paneled, with a white marble fireplace above which hung a full-length portrait of Sir William Bitton in a massive gilt frame. Flanking the fireplace, two long windows looked out on a garden.

Dr. Fell stood in the middle of the dusky room, peering about curiously. A low fire flickered on the brass and irons; a pink-shaded lamp burned on a table amid the heavy upholstered furniture round the fireplace. Otherwise the library was so dark that they could see stars through the blue windows, and the dead shrubbery of the garden.

"There's only one thing now," the doctor said in a low voice, "that I've got to be profoundly thankful for. Arbor still thinks I'm Hadley. I may be able to keep him away from Hadley altogether."

"Thankful? Why?"

"Look behind you," the other said, nodding.

Rampole switched round. He had not heard Laura Bitton come in over the thick carpet. And for a moment he scarcely recognized her.

She seemed much older and much quieter. Nor was she the vigorous young woman with the firm step and the level brown eyes who had walked so confidently into the Warders' Hall that afternoon. The eyes were a trifle red; the face fixed and dull, so that freckles showed against its muddy pallor.

"I followed you down," she said, evenly. "I heard you in the other room." The voice was queer, as though she could not quite understand yet that her husband was dead. Then she added, abruptly, "You know all about it, don't you?"

"All about what, Mrs. Bitton?"

Her gesture recalled some of the determination, the imperiousness; some of the poise and light cynicism.

"Oh, don't quibble. About Phil and me. I knew you would find out."

Dr. Fell inclined his head. "You should not have broken into his flat this afternoon, Mrs. Bitton. You were seen."

She was not interested. "I suppose so. I had a key, but I broke the lock of the door with a chisel I found there to pretend it was a burglar; but it didn't go down. Never mind. I just want to tell you one thing—" But she could not go on with it. She looked from one to the other of them, and shut her lips.

There was a silence.

"Ma'am," said the doctor, leaning on his cane, "I know what you were going to say. You only realized just then how it would sound if you said it. You were going to say you never loved Driscoll. Ma'am, isn't it rather late for that?"

His rumbling voice was colorless; it did not lift or vary, but he studied her curiously.

"Did you see what he had in his hand?"

"Yes," he replied, as she closed her eyes. "Yes ma'am, I did."

"Not the gun! The other hand, I mean. He got it out of the drawer. It was a snapshot of me."

She spoke steadily, the brown eyes level and glazed, the jaw firm. "I looked at it, and went back to my room. I have been sitting at the window in the dark, looking out. If you think I'm trying to excuse myself, you're a fool. But since I saw him lying on that bed, I think I've seen a thousand, million, God knows how many images; and they're all his. I've seen all my life with him. I can't cry now. I cried today, about Phil's death, but I can't cry now. I know I loved Lester. It was only because his ideas were so different from mine that I had to hurt him. I'm not the first woman who's made a fool of herself. But I loved Lester. I don't care whether you believe me or not, but I wanted to tell you that. Now I'll go. And maybe I can cry."

She paused in the doorway, a hand unsteadily on her rumpled brown hair.

"There was only one other thing," she said, in a quiet voice. "Did Lester kill Phil?"

For a long space the doctor remained motionless, a big silhouette against the lamp, bulked over his cane. Then he nodded his head.

"Keep *that* thought with you, ma'am," he said.

The door closed behind her.

"You see?" Dr. Fell asked. "Or don't you? There's been enough tragedy in this house. I won't add another. Lester Bitton is dead and the Driscoll case is closed. If Hadley is satisfied, there needn't be any publicity. It can go down as 'unsolved'; and Lester Bitton shot himself over money troubles, real or imaginary. And yet—"

He was still standing there brooding, under the vast walls of books, when Hobbes knocked at the door.

"Excuse me, sir," said Hobbes. "I have succeeded in waking Sir William. The key was on the inside of his door; I took the liberty of getting a pair of pliers and turning it from the outside. He is upset, sir, and not very well. He has not been well since Mr. Philip's death. But he will be down presently, sir. And there is something else."

"Eh?"

"Two policemen are at the door, sir. A recent guest of ours"—Hobbes spoke slowly, but with a certain inflection—"is with them. A Mr. Arbor. He says Mr. Hadley told him to come here."

"H'm. Got a little confidential work for you, Hobbes. Do you follow me?"

"Well, sir?"

"Put those policemen somewhere out of sight. Tell Mr. Arbor Mr. Hadley is here in the library, and send him back to me. You needn't inform Mr. Hadley yet. Got it?"

"Yes, sir."

There was a brief interval while Dr. Fell stumped back and forth on the padded floor, muttering to himself. He turned sharply as the door opened again, and Hobbes ushered in Julius Arbor.

XVIII

Mr. Arbor Hears a Voice

RAMPOLE HAD withdrawn to the fireside. It was all very neat, the hearth rug not even disarranged. An upholstered chair had been drawn up close, and on a taboret beside it stood an empty cup with the brown dregs of cocoa inside. Here Lester Bitton had sat quietly, staring at the fire and drinking his cocoa, before he went upstairs to his room. From that blue china cup the American's eyes moved up to the man who was just entering at the end of the room.

Mr. Arbor was now imbued with a certain degree of calmness. But he was not at his ease. His glance had gone to the portrait of Sir William, a white eagle in the dusky room, and his discomfort seemed to grow. He had not let Hobbes take his hat or coat; he was much on his dignity. Two lines were drawn about the mouth in the swarthy face; he kept touching his eyeglasses with a light finger, and smoothing the thin black hair that was brushed straight across his large skull.

"Good evening, Inspector," he said. He shifted his hat to his left hand and extended the other in a fishy gesture. Dr. Fell did not notice this. "Tritely, I suppose I ought to say good morning.

I—er—I confess, Inspector, that your request to come here some-what startled me. I—was about to refuse. You must understand that the unpleasant circumstances—"

"Sit down there," interrupted the doctor, leading him to the fire. "You remember my colleague here, don't you?"

"Yes. Er—yes, of course. How do you do?" Arbor said, vaguely. He added, "Is Sir William about?"

"No. That's it, sit down."

"I presume he has been informed of my purchase of the man-uscript?" inquired Arbor, his nervous eye straying to the portrait.

"He has. But it doesn't matter now, you know. Neither of you will ever have it. It's burned."

The man's finger darted to his eyeglasses to keep them on. He said, "You mean—he—somebody—that is," Arbor made an un-certain gesture. "How was it destroyed? This is terrible, Inspector! I could take the law to prove—"

The doctor drew out his pocket book. Carefully he took from it the only part of the manuscript which remained, and stood weighing it thoughtfully.

"May I—may I see that, Inspector?"

He took the flimsy strip of paper in unsteady hands and held it close under the pink-shaded lamp. For some time he studied it, back and front. Then he looked up. "Undoubtedly—ah—un-doubtedly. Inspector, this is an outrage, you know! I own this. I—

"Is it worth anything now?"

"Well—"

"I see that there's some hope for you, then. Now, I'll tell you how it is, Arbor," said Dr. Fell, in an argumentative voice sugges-tive of the elder Weller. "If I were in your shoes, I should take that bit of paper, and put it in my pocket, and forget all about it for the present. You're in enough trouble as it is, and you don't want more."

"Trouble?" demanded Arbor, in rather too challenging a voice. The way he held the paper reminded Rampole of a man with stage-fright holding his notes on a lecture platform; calm in every way except that betraying flutter of the paper

"Do you know," continued the doctor, pleasantly, "that all evening I've been of half a mind to let you cool off in jail for a day or two? You might be able to prove your innocence, but the newspaper publicity would be sad, my friend. Sad. Why did you run away?"

"Run away? My dear man!"

"Don't try to deceive *me*," said the doctor, in a sinister voice. It was a rather less blatant resurrection of Hamlet's father's Ghost. "Scotland Yard sees all. Shall I tell you what you did?"

He then proceeded to give a graphic account of Arbor's behavior after leaving the Tower. It was accurate enough in its details, but so neatly distorted that it sounded like the flight of a guilty man from the law.

"You said," he concluded, "that you had important information to give me personally. I am willing to listen. But I warn you, man, that your position is very bad. And if you don't tell me the whole truth, or I have any reason to doubt what you say, then—"

Arbor leaned back in the chair, breathing noisily. The strain of the day, the late hour, all his experiences since the murder, held him limp and nerveless. He kept adjusting his glasses, staring at Sir William's portrait, until he had recovered himself.

"Ah yes," he murmured. "Yes. I perceive, Inspector, that circumstances have put me in a false light. I will tell you everything. I had intended to do so, but now I see I have no choice. You see,

I felt that I was in a doubly unfortunate and precarious position. I feared that I might not be threatened only by the police, but by some criminal as well."

He got out his ornate cigarette case and hurriedly solaced himself with a breath of smoke before he went on.

"I am—a man of books, Inspector. My life is leisured; I may say sheltered. I do not mingle with the more—ah—tempestuous portions of the world. You, who are a man of rough existence, and—ah—accustomed to hand-to-hand encounters with desperate ruffians, will not understand what I felt when I was faced with a bewildering problem of criminal nature.

"It began with that cursed manuscript. I needn't go into details; I gave you enough of them this afternoon. I came here for the purpose of getting the manuscript from Bitton. Not unnaturally"—a querulous note raised his voice —"I wanted my own property. But I hesitated. Due to the unpredictable eccentricities of Bitton's nature, I was placed in a distressing dilemma."

"I see," said Dr. Fell. "What you mean is that you were afraid of Bitton, and so you had to hire somebody to pinch it for you."

"*No!*" Arbor insisted, gripping the arms of the chair in his earnestness. "That is precisely what I do not mean. I feared you would think so, as your colleague indicated this afternoon. And I was careful to point out to all of you there could have been no legal steps taken against me had I done so. But, Inspector, I did not do it. I will take my oath on it. I confess that the procedure had occurred to me; but I dismissed it. It was absurd and mad, and if I were discovered— No! I would hire no burglar." He spread out his hands. "When the manuscript was stolen it was as much of a surprise to me as it was to Bitton. The first I heard of the theft, you see, was when he telephoned to my friends, the Spenglers, on Sunday night to—ah—to see where I was. But *then*—"

He caught Dr. Fell's cold eye, and there was a new vehemence in his tone. They knew he was telling the truth.

"Then, considerably later the same night, I received another phone call at the Spenglers.'"

"Ah!" grunted the doctor. "From whom?"

"The person refused to give his name. But I was almost positive I knew whose voice it was. I have rather a good ear, and I was sure I knew it, though I had heard it only once before. I thought it was the voice of young Mr. Driscoll."

Dr. Fell jumped. He glared at Arbor, who returned his gaze with a dogged steadiness. Arbor went on.

"I reviewed everything in my mind, and I was sure. I had met this young man at dinner the week before, when I had made almost reckless remarks and exceedingly broad hints about the Poe manuscript. The only other persons who could have heard them were Miss Bitton and Sir William; they were the only others at the table. Hence I was sure when this voice spoke. He asked me whether I was interested in a Poe manuscript belonging to Sir William Bitton, and gave such details of what I remembered having said, that I had no doubt. He asked me what price I should be willing to pay, no questions asked, if the manuscript were handed over to me.

"I am—ah—accustomed to rapid decisions and prompt action, Inspector. I was sure I was dealing with a member of the family. The voice, it is true, was somewhat gruff; but I had little difficulty, in seeing through the disguise. Dealing with a member of the family was very different from dealing with a hired burglar. In case of trouble, there would be no scandal. In any case, there could be no prosecution against me. This person naturally did not know I was the owner of the manuscript; nobody did. If, therefore, he had any ideas of blackmail in his mind after the theft, I could afford to smile. *He* would be the only one to take the risk.

"I reviewed my position in a moment, Inspector, and I perceived that this was—ah—the easiest solution of my difficulties. After the manuscript came to my hands, I could always drop a note to Sir William explaining my ownership, and referring him to my solicitors in case he did not believe me and wished to prosecute. I knew he would not do so. Besides, it was—ah—obvious," said Arbor, hesitantly, "that the amount of the commission—ah—"

"You could promise him whatever he asked," said the doctor, bluntly. "And when you got the manuscript you could give him fifty pounds and tell him to whistle for the rest because you owned it and *he* was the only thief. And the fifty pounds would be much less than you'd have to pay Bitton."

"Considerably less. You—ah—state matters very succinctly, Inspector," Arbor nodded. He took a few short puffs at his cigarette. "I agreed to what the unknown person said, and asked him whether he had the manuscript. He replied that he had, and again demanded how much I should pay for it. I mentioned rather a large sum; he hesitated, and I named a sum considerably larger. I had nothing to lose. He agreed, and stated that he would name a rendezvous in the course of the next day. I was to be communicated with through the Spenglers. His stipulation was that I must never inquire into his identity; he said he would find a means of concealing it altogether. Again I smiled."

"Well?" prompted the doctor.

"I—er—naturally I attempted to trace the call, when he had hung up. It was impossible. In fiction it is—ah—very simple, I have noticed. But my utmost efforts were unavailing; I was told curtly that it was impossible."

"Go on."

Arbor glanced over his shoulder. The nervousness had come back again; he peered into the shadows of the room, and spilled some ash on himself without noticing it.

"I looked forward to it with—ah—a light heart. The following day, today, I went about my affairs as usual. I paid a long-delayed visit to the Tower of London; and I proceeded exactly as I have told you. When I was detained on my attempt to leave by the news of a murder, I was not unduly upset. I thought, indeed, that it would be fascinating to watch the—ah—famous Scotland Yard at work, and I assumed that it was some member of the underworld who had been killed; I was, if anything, pleased, and I resolved to be a good witness if the police spoke to me."

Again Arbor adjusted his glasses. "You will own, Inspector, that it came as a shock when you began your questioning of me by inquiring about Poe manuscripts. Even so, I flatter myself that I was cool and—you will pardon me—triumphant over you. I was nervous, yes; I fancied all sorts of possibilities, but I effectively deceived you. It was not until you mentioned the name of the dead man that—" He drew out the silk handkerchief and mopped his forehead. "My heart, Inspector; I could not see it would make me betray weakness. The possibilities had suddenly become menacing and horrible. Driscoll, at my order, had promised to deliver me that manuscript; and now he was murdered. I must assume even now that he was killed because of it. It occurred to me that in some heinous fashion *I* might come into the case as accessory of some sort. A *murder* case." He shuddered. "I told you, Inspector, that I am—a man of books. This ghastly thing—I could not see how it might concern me directly, but there were any number of dangers. And where was the manuscript? You had not found it on Driscoll's body; I knew you had not found it at all. I wanted to forget it. As you saw, I wanted no search for it, above all things, because a search might uncover evidence to lead to *me*."

"So far," said the doctor, "very well. What then?"

Rampole was puzzled. If the doctor had insisted on anything in the case so far, he had insisted Driscoll would never attempt to dispose of the manuscript to Arbor. But here he was, nodding ponderously and firing his sharp little eyes on the collector as though he believed every word. And Rampole, too, was compelled to believe Arbor. There was only the possible explanation that Driscoll, in a moment of panic, had made to Arbor an offer whose dangers he saw in a calmer moment the next day, and decided to drop the whole affair.

"Now," said Arbor, clearing his throat—"now, Inspector, I come to the amazing, the incredible part of my whole story. It is only fortunate, with my weak heart, that I am not now a dead man. If you could have imagined—"

"Just after you left us in the Warders' Hall," the doctor interposed, slowly, "you got the fright of your life, and it sent you out to Golder's Green in a blind panic. What was it?"

Arbor replaced his handkerchief inside his coat. He seemed to have come to a jumping-off place in his narrative; he hesitated on the brink of the leap, tapping his glasses and peering over.

"Inspector," he said, "before I tell you what you must regard as completely incredible, let me ask you a question or two. I assure you"—he held up his hand as the doctor shifted—"I am not trying to divert you. In that room where you were questioning me, who was present?"

Dr. Fell regarded him narrowly. "While we were speaking to you, you mean?"

"Yes!"

"H'm. There was Hadley, my—my colleague; and Mr. Rampole here; and General Mason, and Sir Wil— Hold on, no! I'm
wrong. Bitton wasn't there. He had gone up to Mason's rooms so
that we could question you more fr— He had gone up to Mason's
rooms. Yes. There were just the four of us."

Arbor stared. "Bitton was at the Tower?"

"Yes, yes. But he wasn't in the room with us. Proceed."

"The next thing," Arbor said, carefully, "is—ah, what shall
I say?—an impression, rather than a question. Speaking with
someone on the telephone is, in a certain sense, and aside from
the mechanical interventions, somewhat like speaking to a person in the dark. You follow me, Inspector? You hear the voice
alone. There is no personality or physical appearance to distract
you from your impressions of the voice itself. If you heard a voice
on the telephone, without having seen the speaker, and later you
meet the speaker in real life, you might not recognize him, because his appearance or his personality might destroy the impressions of the voice. But if you heard him in the dark—"

"I think I understand."

"Ah! I was afraid, Inspector, that the subtlety of the point I
was endeavoring to make would—ah—not be fully apprehend-
ed by—by the police," Arbor said, with evident relief. "I feared
ridicule or even suspicion." He swallowed hard. "Very well. You
dismissed me after the questioning, you will recall, and I went
outside.

"The door of the room in which you had been talking to me
was not quite closed. It was very dark and quite misty under the
arch of the tower there. I stood outside the door to accustom my
eyes to the gloom, and to draw my scarf more tightly about my
neck. As it was, I was terrified; I admit it. I could with difficulty
make a good exit from the room. There was a warder on duty, but

he stood at some distance from me. I could hear you talking in the room I had left; a mumble of voices.

"Then, Inspector," said Arbor, bending forward with his fist clenched, "I think I received the most horrible shock of my life. In the room I had not noticed it, I suppose, because the influence of personalities had overborne the impressions of my hearing; if I may put it that way. But—

"As I stood there in the dark, I heard a voice speak from the room. It sounded little louder than a whisper or a mumble. But I knew that the voice I heard from that room was the same voice which has spoken to me on the telephone the day before, and offered to sell me the Poe manuscript."

XIX

Under the Bloody Tower?

THIS ASTOUNDING intelligence did not seem to affect Dr. Fell in the least. He did not move or even blink. His wonderfully sharp dark eyes remained fixed on Arbor; he was still bent slightly forward, balanced on the cane.

"I suppose," he said at length, "the voice really came from that room?"

"Why, yes. Yes, I assume so. There was nobody else about who could have spoken, and the words were not addressed to me; they were a part of a conversation, it seemed to me."

"What did the voice say?"

Again Arbor became tense. "Now I know, Inspector, that you won't believe me. But I cannot tell you. I have tried until I am ill, but I cannot remember. You must understand the shock of hearing that voice—" He moved his arm, and the fist clenched spasmodically. "To begin with, it was like hearing a dead man's voice. I had been willing to swear that the voice over the telephone belonged to Bitton's nephew. Then Bitton's nephew was dead. And suddenly this hideous whisper. Listen, Inspector. I told you that the telephone voice seemed disguised; gruffer, as it were; and I had attributed it to Driscoll. But *this was the telephone voice*. Of that I am absolutely certain now. I don't know what it said. I only know that I put my hand against the wall of the tower and wondered whether I were going mad. I tried to visualize with whom I had spoken in the room, and I discovered that I could scarcely remember who had been there. I could not remember who had talked, or who had remained silent; it was impossible to think which one of you had uttered what I heard.

"Try to consider what my position was. Everything had gone upside down. I thought I had spoken to Driscoll; yet here was the voice. I had been speaking in that room to somebody—certainly a criminal and in all probability a killer. I had outlined completely my position as owner of the manuscript. And somebody—I had forgotten which one—made it clear that if I had employed a thief to take my own property, he could expect only pay for his thievery and not the immense sum I had mentioned I would pay. I—well, to tell you the truth, I was not thinking at all. I was only feeling. I felt certain, without knowing why, that the 'voice' had killed Driscoll. Everything had gone mad, and, to make it worse, if I could believe my ears this 'voice' *was one of the police.*

"Otherwise I should have gone back immediately and confessed the whole business. But I was afraid both of having the police on my side, and of having them against me. I suppose I acted insanely. But I could think of nothing else to do. It was only late this evening, when I was certain I heard somebody trying to get into my cottage, that I determined to end the suspense, one way or the other. That's all, Inspector. I can make nothing of it, and I hope you have better luck."

He sat back, bewildered, dejected, with his handkerchief again at his forehead.

"Still," said Dr. Fell, musingly, "you could not swear the voice came from that room?"

"No. But—"

"And there is not one word you can definitely remember its having said?"

"I'm afraid not. You don't believe me, I dare say—"

Dr. Fell drew back his chins and pushed out his chest in a meditative fashion, as though he were about to begin a lecture.

"Now, I've heard you out, Arbor, and I've got a few words to say. We're all alone here. Nobody has heard your story but Sergeant Rampole and myself. We can forget it; that's our business when no crime has been done; but I shouldn't advise you to repeat it to anybody else. You would be in grave danger of being confined either in jail or in a lunatic asylum. Do you realize what you've said?" he inquired, slowly, lifting his cane to point. "There were four people in that room. You must, therefore, accuse the voice of being either the chief inspector of the C.I.D., one of his highest and most trusted officers, or the deputy governor of the Tower of London. If you retract *that* statement, and decide that the 'voice' actually was Driscoll, you lay yourself open to grave trouble in connection with a murder case. Your status is that of madman or suspected criminal. Do you want to take your choice?"

"But I'm telling you the truth, I swear before—"

"Man," said Dr. Fell, with a real ring and thunder of earnestness in his voice, "I have no doubt you think you're telling the truth. I have no doubt that in your obsession you might have heard anything. You heard a voice. The question is, what voice, and where did it come from?"

"All right," Arbor said, despondently. "But what am I going to do? I'm in an impossible position whichever way I turn. My God! I wish I'd never heard of Poe or manuscripts or any— Besides, I'm in potential danger of my life. What the devil are you laughing at, Inspector?"

"I was merely smiling," said Dr. Fell, "at your fears for your own skin. If that's all you're worrying about, you can stop. We have the murderer, safely. The 'voice' can't hurt you, I guarantee that. And you don't want to be tangled up in this affair any farther, do you?"

"Good God, no! You mean you have caught—"

"Arbor, the murder had no concern with your manuscript. You can forget it. You'll feel like forgetting your fears, too, in the morning. You're a secretive beggar and you can hold your tongue when it's to your own advantage; I strongly advise you to hold your tongue now. The murderer is dead. Any inquest on Driscoll will be a private and perfunctory thing; it'll be kept out of the press because it can't serve any useful purpose. So you needn't worry. Go to a hotel and get some sleep. Forget you ever heard the 'voice' on the telephone or anywhere else; and, if you hold your tongue, I'll promise to hold mine."

"But the man trying to get at me tonight—"

"He was one of my own constables, to scare you into telling what you know. Run along, man! You never were in any danger in the world."

"But—"

"Run along, man! Do you want Sir William to walk in here on you and make trouble?"

It was the most effective argument he could have used. Arbor did not even inquire too closely into the identity of the murderer. So long as the murderer had no designs on him, his aura conveyed that he was averse to the gruesome details of a vulgar murder. When Dr. Fell and Rampole walked with him to the front door, they found Hadley, who had shortly dismissed the two constables, in the front hall.

"I don't think," the doctor said, "that we need detain Mr. Arbor any longer. I have his story, and I'm sorry to say it doesn't help us. Good night, Mr. Arbor."

"I shall walk," said Arbor with cool dignity, "to a hotel. The walk will do me good. Good night, gentlemen."

"He was not long in letting himself out."

"You dismissed him damned quickly," growled the chief inspector, but without much interest, "after all the trouble he gave us. But I was afraid it might turn out to be a mare's nest. What did he say?"

Dr. Fell chuckled. "Driscoll phoned him and offered him the manuscript. He thought he might get mixed up as some sort of accessory."

"But, good God! I thought you said—"

"Blind panic, my boy. Driscoll would never have done it, you can rest assured. And, as you pointed out, it was in blind panic that he burnt the manuscript. Then Arbor had some sort of wild idea that he heard the dead man's voice talking to him. You know, Hadley, if I were you I should never bring that man before a coroner's jury. He'd make us all sound mad. But you don't need him, do you?"

"Oh no. He wouldn't have been called unless he turned up some evidence bearing on the murder." The chief inspector rubbed a hand wearily over his eyes. "Voices! Bah! The man's as neurotic as an old woman. I wasted people's time for nothing, and made myself look a fool into the bargain. 'Voices'! And all the time that confounded manuscript's been only a red herring. Well, I'm glad he didn't complicate matters by trying to identify the murderer's voice."

"So am I," said Dr. Fell.

264 · JOHN DICKSON CARR

Stealthily the night noises of the house creaked against the stillness; a ghostly tingle from the crystal pendants of the chandelier, a footfall somewhere which echoed and passed.

"It's all over, Fell," Hadley remarked, in a tired voice. "All over in a day, thank God. The poor devil took the best way out. A few routine questions to go over, and we close the book. I've had a talk with the wife—"

"What do you do with the case, then?"

Hadley frowned. His dull eyes wandered about the hall. "I think," he said, "it will go down officially as 'unsolved.' We'll let it die down, and issue a bulletin to the Press Association to handle it lightly. There's no good in the stink of a public inquest, anyway. Don't you think there's been enough tragedy in this house?"

"You needn't justify yourself, my boy. I think there has. By the way, where is Sir William?"

"In his room. Hobbes got his door open and waked him up. Did he tell you?"

"Have you told him about—"

Hadley took a nervous turn about the hall. "I'm not so young as I used to be," he observed, suddenly. "It's only two o'clock in the morning and I'm dog-tired. I've told him a little. But he can't seem to grasp it; the opiate hasn't worn off. He's sitting by a fire in his room, with a dressing-gown over his shoulders, as stupid as an image. All he kept saying was, 'See that my guests have refreshment; see that my guests have refreshment.' I think he had a vague idea he was a feudal lord, or a dream had got mixed into his thoughts. He's seventy years old, Fell. You don't think of his age when you talk to him."

"What are you going to do, then?"

"I've had to send for Dr. Watson, the police surgeon. When he gets here I'll have him fix something to wake the old man up; and then"—Hadley nodded grimly—"we'll share the pleasant duty of telling him everything."

They could hear a night wind muttering in the chimneys. Rampole thought of that portrait, the white eagle face, standing with shoulders back, in the library. And he thought again of a lonely man in a lonely house; the old war-eagle now, huddled in a dressing-gown before a low fire in his room, and counting armies in the blaze. He saw the long sharp nose, the tufted eyebrows, the orator's mouth. *He* belonged to this ancient Mayfair which had never existed since it bloomed with flags for Wellington and nodded its head to the tap of ghostly drums.

Hobbes emerged from the rear of the hallway.

"At Sir William's suggestion, gentlemen," he said, "I have prepared some sandwiches and coffee in the library, and there is a decanter of whisky, if you should care for it."

They moved slowly along the hall, back to the library, where a bright blaze was licking up round the coal in the grate, and a covered tray stood on a side table.

"Stay with Sir William, Hobbes," Hadley directed. "If he— wakens, come down after me. Admit the police surgeon when he arrives, and show him upstairs."

They sat down wearily in the firelight.

"I got the final proof," Hadley declared, as the doctor did things with a tantalus, "when I talked to Mrs. Bitton a few minutes ago. She said she'd been down here and spoken to you. She said you were convinced her husband had killed Driscoll."

"Did she? What did *she* think about it?"

"She wasn't so sure, until I told her the full story; that's what took me so long upstairs. I couldn't get much out of her. She seemed almost as drugged as the old man. Her idea was that Bitton was quite capable of it, but that he'd be more likely to walk into Driscoll's rooms and strangle him rather than waylay him in a dark corner with a crossbow bolt. And she couldn't reconcile his putting the hat on Driscoll's head. She was willing to swear he didn't think along those lines; he wasn't an imaginative type."

Hadley frowned at the fire, tapping his fingers on the arms of the chair. "It bothers me, Fell. She's quite right about that, unless Bitton had unsuspected depths."

The doctor, who was mixing drinks with his back to Hadley, stopped with his hand on the siphon. There was a pause, and then he spoke without turning.

"I thought you were satisfied?"

"I am, I suppose. There's absolutely no other person who can fit the evidence. And what makes it certain— Did you know Bitton had a gift for mimicry? I didn't, until she told me."

"Eh?"

"Yes. His one talent, and he never employed it nowadays; he didn't think it was—well, fitting. But Mrs. Bitton said he used to burlesque his brother making a speech, and hit him off to the life. He could easily have put in that fake telephone call."

There was a curious, sardonic expression on the doctor's face as he stood up. His eye wandered to Sir William's picture, and he chuckled.

"Hadley," he said, "that's an omen. It's coincidence carried to the nth degree. I couldn't have believed it, and I'm glad we didn't hear it at the beginning of the investigation; it would only have confused us. It's too late now."

"What are you talking about?"

"Let's hear the full outline of what Bitton did, as you read it."

Hadley settled back with a chicken sandwich and a cup of coffee.

"Well it's fairly plain. Bitton had made up his mind to kill

Driscoll when he returned from the trip. He was a little mad, anyhow, if his behavior tells everything; and it explains what happened afterwards.

"I don't think he intended at first to make any secret of it. His plan was simply to go to Driscoll's flat and choke the life out of him; and he made up his mind to do it that morning. He was determined to see Driscoll, you know. He borrowed Sir William's key to be sure he could get into the apartment—which isn't the course of a person paying a casual visit.

"He arrived there, and Driscoll was out. So he prowled through the apartment. In all likelihood he was looking for incriminating evidence against his wife and her lover. You remember the oil and the whetstone on Driscoll's desk? The oil was fresh; Driscoll had probably been working on that crossbow bolt, and it was lying there conspicuously. Remember that the bolt had a significance to Bitton; *it was one which he and his wife had bought together.*"

Dr. Fell rubbed his forehead. "I hadn't thought of that," he muttered; "the omens are still at work. Carry on, Hadley."

"And he found the top hat. He must have surmised that Driscoll was the Mad Hatter, but that didn't interest him so much as a recollection of Driscoll's wish to die in a top hat. You see the psychology, Fell? If he'd merely run across a top hat of Driscoll's, the suggestion mightn't have been so strong. But a hat belonging to his brother—a perfect piece of stage-setting.

"Suddenly his plan came to him. There was no reason why he should suffer for killing Driscoll. If he stabbed Driscoll at some place which wouldn't be associated with Lester Bitton, and put the stolen hat on the body, he would have done two things: First, he would have put suspicion on the Mad Hatter as the murderer. But the hat thief was the man he was going to kill! And consequently, the police could never hang an innocent person for murder. Bitton was a sportsman, and I'll give him credit for thinking of that first. Secondly, he would have fulfilled Driscoll's bombastic wish.

"Further, from his point of view the choice of that bolt as a weapon was an ideal one. It had its significance, to begin with. And, though Driscoll had stolen the bolt secretly from his house, *he didn't know that.* Seeing the bolt on Driscoll's desk, he naturally imagined that Driscoll had got it openly—asked for it—and that anybody in his own house would know it was in Driscoll's possession. Hence suspicion would be turned away from his own house! That was what he imagined. He couldn't have been expected to think that Driscoll had carefully concealed a theft of that trumpery souvenir, when it could have been had for the asking. Can you imagine what must have been his horror, then, when he found us suspecting his wife?"

The doctor took a long drink of whisky.

"You've got a better case than I thought, my boy," he said. "The Gentleman who pulls the cords must have been amused by this one. I am listening."

"So, in his half-crazy brain, he evolves a new plan. He knew Driscoll was going to the Tower at one o'clock, to meet Dalrye, because he had heard it at breakfast. He didn't know his wife was going there, of course. His one idea was to get Driscoll alone. If Driscoll went to the Tower, he would be certain to be with Dalrye; and a murder might be devilish awkward.

"You can see what he did. He took the hat and the bolt home with him, and left the house early; before one o'clock. He phoned Dalrye from a public box, imitated Driscoll's voice, and got Dalrye away. At one o'clock he was at the Tower. But Driscoll didn't appear; Driscoll was twenty minutes late."

Hadley drank a mouthful of scalding coffee and set down the cup. He struck his fist into his palm. "Do you realize, man, that, if we look back over our *times* in this case, Driscoll must have walked into the Tower of London no more than a few minutes, or more likely a few *seconds*, before Laura Bitton did? Driscoll was late; she was early. And as soon as Driscoll got up to General Mason's rooms he looked out of the window and saw Laura Bitton by Traitors' Gate. In other words, Lester Bitton, lurking about for a suitable opportunity to kill Driscoll as soon as he could, saw both of them come in. He hadn't bargained on *her*. There was to be a meeting, clearly. For fear of detection, he couldn't strike until it was over.

"He waited. As he had thought, a person of Driscoll's wild and restless nature wouldn't sit cooped up in General Mason's rooms. He would wander about, in any event. And he would certainly come down now, for his rendezvous with Laura. Fell, when Driscoll came downstairs and met Laura at the rail, Bitton must have been concealed under the arch of the Bloody Tower, watching them."

The doctor was sitting back, one hand shading his eyes. The fire had grown to a fierce heat now. Rampole was growing drowsy.

"He saw the interview, with what rage we can imagine. It must have grown on him until he was tempted to go out and strike them both down. He heard Laura Bitton say she loved him—and then, a thing which must have crazed him by its perverse irony, he saw Driscoll leave her, hurriedly and almost contemptuously, and walk towards him under the arch of the Bloody Tower. Driscoll had done more than loved his wife; he had scorned his wife. And now Driscoll was walking towards him in the dark and fog, and the crossbow bolt was ready in Bitton's hand."

Dr. Fell did not take his hand away from his eyes; he parted two fingers, and the bright eye gleamed suddenly behind his glasses.

"I say, Hadley, when you talked to Mrs. Bitton, did she say Driscoll really *did* go under the arch of the Bloody Tower?"

"She didn't notice. She said that she was so upset she didn't watch him. She turned away and walked in the roadway—where, you remember, Mrs. Larkin saw her, walking with her back to the Bloody Tower."

"Ah!"

"She didn't conceal anything," Hadley said, dully. "I thought, when I spoke to her, that I was talking to an automaton—a dead person, or something of the sort. Driscoll went under the arch. It was all over in a moment: Bitton's hand over his mouth, a wrench and a blow, and Driscoll died without a sound. And when Mrs. Bitton walked through the arch a few seconds later, her husband was holding against the wall the dead body of her lover. When they had gone, he took off Driscoll's cap, opened the top hat—it was an opera hat, you know, and collapsible, so that it was easily concealed under a coat—and put it down over Driscoll's eyes. He went out quickly and flung the body over the rail, where it got that smash on the back of the head. Then he went out one of the side gates, unobserved, threw Driscoll's cap into the river—and, I dare say, went to the lunch room and refreshed himself with a cup of cocoa after his work."

When Hadley had finished, he did not immediately go on eating his sandwich. He stared at the sandwich queerly, put it down; and they were all very quiet. A fierce blaze was roaring and snapping in the fireplace, but it only intensified the stillness of that drugged hour. Over their heads, now, somebody was pacing with slow steps. Back and forth, back and forth.

A cold wind seethed in the dead shrubs of the garden beyond the windows. They heard a clock strike a musical note; then, very faintly, voices in the front hall, and the boom of the big door closing.

It echoed hollowly through the house. The steps upstairs hesitated, and then resumed their slow pacing.

"'That'll be the police surgeon," said Hadley. He rubbed his eyes drowsily and stretched stiff muscles. "A bit more routine work, and I'm going home to bed. It's been years since I've taken hold of a regular investigation of this sort. I let the others work. I'm tired—"

"Excuse me," interrupted a voice at the door. "May I see you a moment?"

The tone was such that Hadley spun round. It began levelly, and then gave a sort of horrible jerk. It was a dead voice. Coming out of the shadows they saw Dalrye. His tie was loosened and there was sweat on his face. His eyes, as he moved them from one to the other of these men, were glazed.

"Don't say anything!" Dr. Fell suddenly boomed. He lurched out of his chair and seized the young man's arm. "For God's sake keep your mouth shut! You'll think better of it—you'll—"

Dalrye put out his hand. "It's no good," he said. His eyes fixed on Hadley.

"I wish to give myself up, sir," he said, in a clear voice. "I killed Philip Driscoll."

XX

The Murderer Speaks

In the utter and appalled silence of that library, even the footsteps upstairs seemed to have stopped as though they had heard him. The fire drew clearly and quietly; it drew yellow light on the long, pale, dull face. Dalrye mechanically yanked open his collar. His eyes were on the fire as he went on.

"I didn't mean to kill him, you know. It was an accident. I shouldn't have attempted to conceal it afterwards; that was the mistake. So now I don't suppose you'll believe me. I don't care, much. I shouldn't have told you at all if it hadn't been for your suspecting Major Bitton—and then his killing himself, and your being sure he'd done it. I couldn't stand that. He was—a real— friend. Phil never thought about anybody but himself. But Major Bitton—" He fumbled at his eyes. "I've lost my glasses, and I can't see very well without them. May I sit down, sir? I'm all in."

Nobody moved. He stumbled over to the fire, sat down, and as he spread out his hands before it they saw he was shivering.

"You young fool," Dr. Fell said, slowly. "You've ruined everything. I've been trying to cover you all evening, ever since I saw that girl of yours. And now you've wrecked it. There wasn't any sense in your telling. You've only brought more tragedy on this house."

Hadley straightened himself up, almost as though he were trying to recover from a blow in the face. He remained staring at Dalrye.

Then Hadley cleared his throat.

"This isn't real," he said. "It can't be. Are you telling me, as a police officer, without any joking—"

"I've been walking the streets for an hour," the young man answered. His shoulders were still quivering with cold. "When I kissed Sheila good night over at her friend's place, I knew it was the last time I'd ever see her outside the dock. And so I thought I couldn't tell you. But I realized I couldn't go on this way, either. I'm rotten, but I'm not so very rotten. I tried to look at myself while I was walking. I don't know. It's all mixed up." He put his head in his hands. Then an idea seemed to strike him and he peered round. "I heard somebody say—*did* somebody say he knew it already?"

"Yes," snapped Dr. Fell, grimly. "And if you'd had the sense to keep your mouth shut—"

Hadley had taken out his notebook. His fingers were shaking and his voice was not clear. "Mr. Dalrye," he said, "it is my duty to warn you that anything you say may be taken down—"

"All right," said Dalrye. "I'll talk in a minute. I'm cold; Oh, my God, but I'm cold! Let me sit here. Is that—?" He peered blindly at the drink Rampole was holding out, and clutched it. "Thanks. Thanks. I can use that. I suppose there's no good telling you it was an accident, is there? He really killed himself, you know; that is, he jumped at me, and in the fight—Christ knows, *I* didn't want to hurt him. I liked him. I only—I only tried to steal that damned manuscript."

He breathed noisily for a moment.

"This may be true," the chief inspector said, studying him

queerly. "But I hope it's not. I hope you can tell me how you answered the telephone in Driscoll's flat at a quarter to two and killed Driscoll at the Tower of London a few minutes later."

Dr. Fell rapped his stick against the edge of the mantelpiece. "It's out now, Hadley. The damage is done. And I may as well tell you that you've put your finger on the essential point. It's where your whole case went wrong. You see, Driscoll was not killed at the Tower of London. He was killed in his own flat."

"He was— Great God!" Hadley said, despairingly. "All this is nonsense!"

"No, it isn't" said Dalrye. He took another swallow of the whiskey, and it seemed to warm him. "It's true enough. Why Phil came back to his flat I don't know; I can't imagine. I'd taken good care he should be at the Tower. That was why I faked the telephone call to myself. But I—I only wanted to keep him out of the way so that I could steal the manuscript and—and pretend it was some burglar."

His trembling had almost ceased now; he was only dull and drowsily tired. He spoke in a queer, absent-minded voice, like a sick man.

"I feel better," he said, suddenly. "I feel better, now I've told you. I couldn't have kept it up long. I'm not built that way."

"Suppose we get this thing from the beginning," said the chief inspector. "You say you wanted to steal the Poe manuscript."

"I had to," the other said, as though that explained everything. "I *had* to, you see."

"You had to?"

"Oh!" muttered Dalrye. His hand went to his eyes automatically, and found no glasses. "Oh yes. I didn't tell you. It was all on the spur of the moment. Bing. Like that. I don't think I should ever have thought of stealing it out of the house here. That wouldn't have been—oh, I don't know! I can't explain it. But when he telephoned me early Sunday evening at the Tower and told me that when he'd pinched his uncle's hat he'd stolen the manuscript with it—"

"You knew Driscoll was the hat thief?"

"Oh, Lord!" said Dalrye, with a sort of feeble irritation. "Of course I did. Of course he'd come to me. I helped him. He—he always had to have help. And of course, you see, he'd have told me, anyway. Because one of his choicest ideas was to get a Yeoman Warder's cap from the Tower of London."

"By God and Bacchus!" muttered Dr. Fell. "I overlooked that. Yes, certainly. Any respectable hat thief would have tried to—"

"Be quiet, will you?" snapped Hadley. "Listen, Mr. Dalrye. He told you about it?"

"And that's when I got the idea," Dalrye nodded absently. "I was pretty desperate, you see. They were after me, and it would have come out within a week. So I told Phil over the telephone to hang on to that manuscript; not to stir until I found him a plan; and to go round to the house Sunday night and find out what he could before he acted. And in the meantime—" He sat back in his chair. "I knew where Arbor was, over the week-end. I'd been out with Sheila Saturday night, and so of course I knew. I wouldn't have dared phone him if he'd been in this house."

"*You phoned Arbor?*"

"Uh. Didn't he tell you? I was afraid he had recognized the voice, and I was panicky tonight when I heard he was coming in."

Hadley stared sharply at Dr. Fell. "What did Arbor mean, then? I thought you told me he said he was sure it was Driscoll?"

"He did," said the doctor. "But I'm afraid you didn't pay close enough attention to what Miss Bitton said tonight, Hadley. Don't you remember her telling us about how Driscoll had played jokes on her, by telephoning and telling her he was Dalrye here; and she believed it? You've got a voice very much like Driscoll's haven't you, my boy?"

"If I hadn't had," muttered the other, "I couldn't have put this thing over. I'm no actor, you know. But if he could imitate me, then I could imitate him, and talk to Parker on the telephone to change the appointment and send myself up to his flat—"

"Hold on!" snapped Hadley. "This is getting ahead of me. You say that first you phoned Arbor and offered him the manuscript, when you didn't have it yet, and then— But why! Why did you want to steal it?"

Dalrye drained his glass. "I had to have twelve hundred pounds," he said, evenly.

Leaning back in his chair, he stared at the fire. His eyes were wrinkled up and his heavy breathing slowed down.

"Let me tell you a little about it," he went on. "Twelve hundred pounds wouldn't be much to most of the people I know. But to me it might as well have been twelve thousand.

"I don't know whether you know anything about me. My father is a clergyman in the north of England, and I'm the youngest of five sons. I never got much, to speak of. I don't suppose I ever wanted much. I got an education, but I had to work for my scholarships, because I wasn't one of these tremendously bright chaps. If I had anything, it was imagination, and I wanted—someday— and this is funny—no, I won't tell you what I wanted. It was something I wanted to write. But imagination doesn't help you in passing examinations, and it wasn't easy going to keep at the top. Still, nothing ever bothered me much. I'd been doing some research work on the Tower of London, and I happened to meet General Mason. He liked me, and I liked him, and he asked me to become his secretary.

"That was how I met the Bittons. It's odd but, you know, I admired Driscoll. He was everything I wasn't. I'm tall, and awkward, and near-sighted, and ugly as a mud fence. I was never good at games, either, and women thought I was—oh, nice and pleasant, and they'd tell me all about how they fell in love with other chaps.

"Driscoll—well, you know him. He had the air. And it was the case of the brilliant meteor and the good old plodding cab horse who helped him out of difficulties. And I told you I was flattered to have my advice taken. But then I met Sheila.

"It's damned funny why she looked at me. Other women never did. I'm telling you everything, so I—I—well, I can't tell you how much I worship her. I mean to say, it sounds ridiculous or something."

He glared round him; but every face was expressionless.

"And they thought it was funny, too. I mean Phil's friends. And by funny, I mean comical, this time. One nice young dandy made a remark about 'Old parson-face and that moron daughter of Bitton's.' I didn't mind being called parson-face; they all did it. But the other— I couldn't do anything then. I had to find another occasion, so I ran into him one night, and said I didn't like *his* face, and knocked it off. He didn't get out of the house for a week. But then they began laughing again, and said, 'Good old Bob; he's a sly one,' and they said I was after Sheila's money. That was awful. And it was worse when Sheila and I knew we loved each other, and told each other so, and the old man learned about it.

"He took me over for an interview and as much as said the same thing. Then I made an ass of myself. I was sick of the whole performance. I don't remember what I said, but I know I told him he could take his dirty money— Well, you know. That surprised him. Sheila and I were going to be married, anyhow. Then he thought it over, and thought it over, and Major Bitton intervened.

Somehow, I don't think the old man was so upset about what I said as I thought he'd be. He came down to see me, and scratched his chin, and all that, and said, 'Well, let's not have a break-up in the family.' He said Sheila wasn't capable of looking after herself, and that if we'd promise to wait a year, and still felt the same way—there it was. I said that was all right, provided I did all the supporting of the new family without any help.

"I'll skip over the next part. Phil said he could tell me a way to make some easy money, and everything would be fine. And I was pretty desperate; Bitton's 'year' only meant—and we both knew it—that at the end of the time he'd say my prospects were no better, were they? And I couldn't expect Sheila to wait for me when she had so many chances for a good match, could I? That was the point of it.

"I got into a jam with my 'money-making.' Never mind that. It was my own fault. Phil—"

Dalrye hesitated. "*That's* neither here nor there. We were both in it, but I was the one who did the— Anyhow, if it ever got to the old man's ears, I was through. And I had to raise twelve hundred pounds in a week."

He leaned back in the chair and closed his eyes.

"Queer. I can't think of anything except 'old parson-face.' They even used to laugh to see me make cocktails. But then was when I got this wild idea of stealing the manuscript from Phil and selling it to Arbor. It was insane. So was I. I don't excuse it; I was as childish as Phil, when it came to a real difficulty.

"You know the scheme. I'd told him on Sunday night to phone me in the morning. He did—wild-eyed. He was in some fresh difficulty. It was the—the wife matter, you know, but I didn't know it then. I had already impressed it on his mind that he had to *conceal* the manuscript; keep it in his room. Over and over I impressed that on him. It was so that I could get it out of the flat.

"And he did. He tried putting it back in the old man's car—you know about that—before he came to the Tower to see me. But my instructions had so impressed him that, before he came to the Tower, he returned to his flat and hid the manuscript at the back of the grate in his study.

"Arranging the fake telephone call had been easy. The first one was genuine. When the second came through, I was in the record room; I'd simply rung up Parker and spoken as Driscoll. I knew he would call me on the speaking-tube. Then I would go to the phone again, say 'Hallo, Phil!' to myself, and answer myself in his voice, and Parker would hang up. I thought everything was arranged."

Dalrye brooded a moment, his head in his hands. The fire crackled. Hadley had not moved.

"But I had to work fast. The plan was simple. I was going to leave the general's car at a garage in Holborn, hurry to Driscoll's flat, and pinch the manuscript. Then I was going to open a window, ransack the flat a bit, and steal a few odd things so that it would look like the work of a burglar. I didn't have any hesitation about stealing it. I knew Phil would never be blamed for stealing it from the old man; the old man would never know. The only danger Phil ran was in trying to return it. And, by God! If you think I hesitated to steal from the old man—I'd pinch his shirt off his back; that's what I think of *him*. The damned— Never mind."

He took the bottle of whisky from the table and poured out almost half a tumbler. He was growing defiant, with a dull stain of color in his cheeks, and the edge of the bottle clicked nervously against the glass. Dalrye swallowed most of the drink neat.

"It sounded good enough. I didn't think Phil would ever suspect *me*. When I got to the flat and found he wasn't there, I had time enough to search. A phone call came from Parker at the Tower while I was searching. I made a mistake by answering it; but I was rattled. Still—later," he choked a little, "later it gave an alibi. It was just before a quarter to two.

"Listen! I'd tumbled the study about some, because at first I didn't think of looking in the grate. But I did look there, and found it. I wasn't hurrying, because I thought Phil was safely at the Tower. I found the manuscript, and examined it carefully, and put it in my pocket. I was just going on to rumple up the room some more—

"I turned round; heard a noise or something—I don't know. And there was Phil in the doorway, looking at me. I knew he'd been standing there, and he'd seen everything."

The rest of the whisky was tossed off. Dalrye's fixed, absent look had turned horrible. He put one hand a little way out, as though he were groping.

"You never saw Phil in one of his rages, did you? When he had them, he was a crazy man. He was standing there, breathing hard, with his mouth pulled back. I'd seen him that way before. He tried to kill a man once, with a penknife, because the man had made fun of something he was wearing. He would go what they call—berserk, and he was as dangerous as hell. It was cold and quiet in the room, and I could hear him breathe, and my watch ticking—and—

"Well, he started to scream. Literally screamed at me. I don't think I've ever heard anybody curse in my life the way he did then. It was so violent it sounded—I don't know how to describe it—obscene. He had a brown cap, all pulled over one ear. I always knew when he would jump. We'd had boxing bouts with soft gloves several times; but I stopped sparring with him because I was a better boxer, and when I got inside his guard too smartly he'd fly off the handle and tell me he wanted to fight with knives. And he was dangerous, a sort of wildcat; he'd just as soon kick you below the belt as anything else. I saw him crouch down. I said, 'Phil, for God's sake don't be a fool—' and he was looking round for something and he saw it. It was that crossbow bolt, lying on a low bookcase beside the door.

"Then he jumped.

"You couldn't avoid him in that little room. I tried to dodge aside and get him by the collar, the way you might a charging dog; I knew if I could get him in a wrestling grip I could keep him quiet. But he landed full. We whirled around. I—I don't exactly know what happened. I heard a chair hit the floor. And the next thing I knew we smashed over together, with me on top of him, and I heard a sort of dull crunch. And just after that—

"F-funny," Dalrye said wildly. "When I was a kid I had a rubber toy once, a sort of doll-like thing that wheezed and squeaked when you punched it. I thought of that. Because the noise he made was just like that toy, only a hundred times louder and more horrible. Unearthly; can you see. Then there was a kind of hiss and gurgle of the toy getting the air in it again. And he didn't move any more.

"I got up. He'd driven that bolt into himself, or my falling on him had done it, until the point hit the floor. The back of his head had hit the iron fender when we went over. There wasn't much blood, except a little stream not much thicker than a lead pencil, that came out the side of his mouth."

Dalrye sat back with his hands over his eyes.

XXI

Unsolved

FOR A moment he could not go on. He reached blindly after the whiskey again. Rampole hesitated; and then helped him pour some more. Hadley had sat down now, and he was staring blankly at the fire.

"I don't understand," Dalrye muttered in a dull voice; "I don't know why he came back."

"Perhaps," said Dr. Fell, "I can tell you. Sit quietly for a moment, boy, and rest yourself. Hadley, do you see now?"

"You mean—"

"I mean this. It should be plain to you; you gave me the clue yourself. When Driscoll stood there at the Traitors' Gate, at the Tower of London, talking to Mrs. Bitton at one-thirty, he remembered something. The recollection of it startled him nearly out of his wits. He said he had to go and attend to it. What did he remember?"

"Well?"

"Think back! He was talking to her, and he mentioned something about his uncle. *That* was what made him remember, for his outburst followed it. Think! You've heard it a dozen times today."

Hadley sat up suddenly. "My God! It was the afternoon of his uncle's monthly visit to him!"

"Exactly. Bitton didn't intend making the call, but Driscoll didn't know that. He'd forgotten that visit, Driscoll had, in all the excitement of the last two days. *And Bitton had a key to his flat.* He would walk in there—and there, in the flat with no attempt to hide them, were the two hats he had stolen. That was bad enough. But if Bitton grew suspicious, and searched, and found his manuscript—"

Hadley nodded. "He had to get back to his flat faster than he ever made it before, to head off Sir William."

"He couldn't explain to Laura Bitton, you see. And, if he could, he couldn't take the time. She would want explanations, or to complicate things; and he *couldn't delay.* So he did what many another man has done with a woman. He shooed her away and said he would join her in five minutes. Of course, without any idea of doing it.

"And do you see what he did? Remember your plan of the Tower, Hadley. Remember what General Mason told us. He couldn't walk back along Water Lane towards the main gate. The way led *only* to the way out; he couldn't have pretended an errand, and it would have roused the woman's suspicions. So he went the other way along Water Lane, and out one of the other gates to Thames Wharf—unnoticed in the fog. That was at half-past one."

The doctor looked down at Dalrye and shook his head.

"You yourself told me, Hadley, that by underground a person could go to Russell Square in fifteen minutes or even less. And it seemed to me, if Mrs. Bitton could do it at five o'clock, why couldn't Driscoll have done it at one-thirty? He would arrive at the flat, in short, about ten minutes to two or a trifle later—the time the police surgeon said he died. But, you see, where all your calculations went wrong was in assuming Driscoll had never left the Tower. The possibility never entered your head. I don't think we should have found a warder who saw him go out, even if we had tried, at that side gate. But the thing simply didn't occur to anybody. If it had, it would have been a much more reasonable solution than his remembering an urgent phone call."

"But he was found on the Traitors' Gate! I— Never mind," said Hadley. "Do you feel like going on, Dalrye?"

"So that was it," the other said, dully. "I see. I see now. I only thought he might have suspected me.

"Let me tell you what I did. He was dead. I saw that. And for a second I went into a sheer panic. I couldn't think straight; my legs wouldn't move, and I thought I must be going blind.

"I saw that I'd committed a murder. I had already prepared the way for a theft, and I was in deeply enough, but here was a murder. Nobody would believe it had been an accident. And where I made my mistake was this: I thought Driscoll had told them at the Tower he was coming back there! I could only imagine that they knew! And I had already definitely proved that I was at the flat, because I'd spoken to Parker on the telephone. I thought Driscoll had just changed his mind, and returned—and there I was with the body, when everybody knew we were both there."

He shuddered.

"Then my common sense came back all in a rush. I was cold, and empty inside, but I don't think my brain ever worked so fast. I had only one chance. That was to get his body away from this flat, somehow, and dump it somewhere out in the open. Somewhere, say, on the way to the Tower—so that they would think he'd been caught on the way back.

"And it came to me all in a flash—*the car*. The car was in that garage, not far away. The day was very foggy. I could get the car and drive it into the courtyard with the side-curtains on. Phil's body was as light as a kitten. There were only two flats on the floor, and the windows overlooking the court were blank ones; with the fog to help me, there wasn't great danger of being seen."

Dr. Fell looked at Hadley. "Quite right. The chief inspector was positive on that point, too, when he was considering how Mrs. Bitton could have got out of the flat. I think he remarked that a red Indian in a war bonnet could have walked out of that court without being observed. It was suggestive."

"Well—" Again Dalrye rubbed his eyes unsteadily. "I hadn't much time. The thing to do was to save time by shooting over to the garage by the underground—I could do it, with luck, in two minutes, where it would have taken me ten to walk—to get the car, and come back for the body.

"I don't know how I did it. I don't know what sort of face I put up in front of those garage people. I told them I was going home, rolled out, and shot back to the flat. If I'd been arrested then—" He swallowed hard. "I took up Phil's body and carried it out. That was a ghastly time; carrying that thing. My God! I nearly fell down those little steps, and I nearly ran his head through the glass door. When I'd got him stowed in the back of the car, under a rug, I was so weak I thought I hadn't any arms. But I had to go back to the flat to be sure I hadn't overlooked anything. And when I looked round, I got an idea. That top hat. If I took that along, and put it on Phil—why, you see, they would think the Mad Hatter had killed him! Nobody knew who the hat thief was. I didn't want to get anybody else in trouble, and that way it was perfectly safe."

"The chief inspector," said Dr. Fell, "will have no difficulty in understanding you. You needn't elaborate. He had just finished outlining the same idea himself, as being the murderer's line of thought, before you came in. What about the crossbow bolt?"

"I—I left the bolt—you know where. You see, I'd never seen the damn thing before. I didn't know it came from Bitton's house. I simply assumed it was one of Phil's possessions and couldn't do anybody harm. I didn't see the 'Souvenir de Carcassonne,' be-cause—you know why. It was hidden."

Dalrye's nostrils grew taut. His hands clenched on his knees and his voice went high. "But one thing I remembered before I left that flat. I remembered that manuscript in my pocket. I might have killed Phil. I might have been the lowest swine on earth, and I was pretty sure I was. But, by God! I wasn't going to put dirty dollars in my pocket by selling that manuscript to Arbor now. It was in my pocket. But it had blood on it. I think I was thinking more about that than even about Phil. I wasn't going to use *that* if I needed it to save me from being hanged. I remember, I took it out. I was so wild that I was going to tear it up and take a hand-ful of the pieces along to throw in Bitton's face. But if I tore it up here— Oh, well. They'd find the pieces, and there wasn't any use doing Phil dirt, even if I had killed him. Sounds funny, eh, from a murderer? I can't help that. It's the way I felt. I knew I was wast-ing time, but I touched a match to it and threw it in the grate. I had the top hat, squashed flat, under my coat, and I thought I'd attended to everything. Funny, too. I kept looking around that study, the way you do when you're leaving a hotel room, and you wonder if you've left your toothbrush on the washstand, or some-thing."

"You should have put back the fender in its place," said Dr. Fell. "Nobody merely searching that flat would or could have shoved a solid iron fender round the way you did when you had your fight with Driscoll. Well?"

"Then," said Dalrye, reaching automatically after the whisky, "then I had the first of my two really horrible shocks. When I was just getting outside the door of the flat, I ran into the porter. If I had met him earlier, when I was carrying out Phil! I don't know what I said. I said, 'Ha, ha,' or something of the sort, and told him what a good fellow he was, and for no reason at all I handed him half a crown. He walked out to the car with me."

"Son," said Dr. Fell, with a sudden grunt, "you told an unnecessary lie today, and that car gave you away. When you were telling your story to us at the Tower this afternoon, you said you had never taken the car to the flat at all. You said when you left the flat you had to go to the garage and get it, and then start home. Still, I suppose you couldn't say anything else. But when Mr. Hadley here explained this evening about your having the car there, as the porter told him— No matter. Then?"

"I drove away. I was thinking until I thought my head would burst. But I believed I was safe now. I'd put the top hat on Phil, and stuffed his cap into my pocket. All I had to do was find a side lane somewhere down near the Tower, and pitch him out in the fog. I didn't bother about fingerprints, for, as God is my judge, I'd never touched that crossbow bolt. And then, just as I'd laid my plans, and I was getting away from Bloomsbury, do you know what happened?"

"Yes," said Hadley. "You met General Mason."

"Met him? Met him? Do you think I'd have stopped if I'd *seen* him? The first thing I knew he'd hopped on the running-board, and there he was grinning at me, and saying what a godsend this was, and telling me to get over in the front seat, so that he had room to shove in beside me.

"I stopped the car dead. I've read in books about how they feel when they think their hearts have stopped. I didn't think that exactly; I felt as though the whole car started to collapse under me. I couldn't move. I tried to move, and my foot jumped so much on the accelerator that I stalled the car. Then I turned my head away and glared out the side as though I were looking at a tire, and I tried to swear at it, but I couldn't seem to get my tongue up out of my throat.

"Then the car got started somehow. I could hear the general talking, but I don't remember anything he said. He was in a very good humor, I know, and that seemed to make it worse. All I thought of, just as though I saw words written on a board, was, 'Come on, parson-face; steady, parson-face; keep your nerve, parson-face,' and I thought that Phil's friends would stare if they saw old parson-face now. I wanted to yell, and slap him on the back and say, 'Glance under that rug in the rear seat, and see what a surprise old parson-face has for you, General.'

"But I didn't. I covered myself by cursing every car that passed so violently that even the general thought something must be wrong. I was headed for destruction now, I could see that. We should go straight back to the Tower, and no power this side of hell could change it. Straight back. Excuse me a second—a drink. Funny this stuff doesn't seem to have any effect. A few drinks will get me tight, usually.

"I had, during that time, about twenty minutes to think and think hard. I'd thought it must be hours since I'd seen Phil lying dead there. But when I looked at my watch I couldn't understand; it was only eight minutes past two. And all the time my brain was going like a machine-shop I was talking to the general—I don't know what we talked about. It began to dawn on me that I had one chance. And that if I worked that chance I might have a real alibi.

"You see? If I could get inside the Tower grounds, and dump

the body somewhere without detection, no sane person would ever believe I had ridden from Town beside General Mason with a corpse in the rear of the car. It began to seem as though my worst danger might be my—well, my salvation. They would believe, it suddenly dawned on me, that Driscoll had never left the Tower.

"I had to nerve myself for one last effort. And I was thankful I'd put on a bad humor and taken to cursing other cars, because now I told the general about the 'fake' telephone call that had lured me away; and I wondered what it was all about.

"Then we were inside the Tower grounds as two-thirty struck. I had calculated it neatly, and I knew the place. If there were nobody else about as we went along Water Lane, I knew what I should do. You were quite right, Doctor, in saying that anybody would think of Traitors' Gate as the place to hide a corpse on a foggy day. And this was the place, because *I could stop there without suspicion.*

"You see?" Dalrye demanded, leaning forward eagerly. "I had to let the general out opposite the gate to the Bloody Tower. I waited until he was well up under the archway on his way to the King's House, and then I acted. I opened the rear door, tossed the body over the rail, and was back in the car in a second, driving on.

"But, my God! I cut it fine! The general, on his way up, remembered an errand or something in St. Thomas's Tower, and he discovered the body. That—that's about all, sir. There's—there's only one other thing. With this terrible thing over me, I'd forgotten about the money Phil had—the money I owed to— Well, I'd forgotten it, anyway. When the general sent me after the doctor, and the rest of it, I had to go up to my room to get something to steady my nerves. The reaction was too much. There was a letter on my table. I don't remember opening it; I don't even know *why* I opened it. I found myself standing with a brandy and soda in my hand, and the letter in front of my face. The letter said," suddenly Dalrye gagged, as though he were swallowing medicine, "the letter said, 'Don't worry any more about it. It's paid. Don't mention this to my brother, and don't be such a quixotic young fool again.' It was signed 'Lester Bitton.'"

Dalrye got up out of his chair and faced them. He was flushed and his eyes burned brightly. There was a pause, and he had a curious expression of puzzled uncertainty.

"I'm drunk!" he said, wonderingly. "I'm drunk. I hadn't noticed it, not till this minute. Old parson-face is drunk. Never mind.

"Lester Bitton got rid of what I owed, and never said a word.

"And when you accused him tonight—and he shot himself—you see why I had to tell you."

He stood straight, a little wrinkle between his brows.

"I told you I was a swine," he went on in an even voice, "but I'm not so bad as that. I know what it means. It means the rope. They won't believe me, of course, after what I did to cover myself; and I can't blame them. They shoot you out of a door, and it's all over in a few seconds. Don't mind old parson-face. I can't think how I came to be so drunk. I don't drink much, as a rule. What was I saying? Oh, yes. If you hadn't blamed it on Major Bitton, if you gave out that you hadn't been able to find out *who* the murderer was, I'd have kept quiet. Why not? I love Sheila. Some day I might have— Never mind. I'm not going to let you think I'm pitying myself. It's only that I appreciate people who are kind to me. I never had much kindness. People all thought I was too much of a joke. But, by God! Old joke parson-face had the police guessing, didn't he?" Momentarily there was a blaze in his face. "Old—joke—parson-face!" said Robert Dalrye.

The fire was sinking now. Dalrye, his hand clenched, stared across the dusky room. He had spoken for a long time. There was a faint hint of dawn in the windows towards the garden; Mayfair lay quiet and dead.

Hadley rose quietly from his chair.

"Young man," he said, "I have an order for you. Go out into one of the other rooms and sit down. I'll call you back in a moment. I want to speak to my friends. There is one other thing. On no account speak a word to anybody until you are called back. Do you hear?"

"Oh, well," said Dalrye. "Oh, well. Go ahead and phone for your Black Maria, or whatever you use. I'll wait. By the way, there was something I didn't tell you. I'm afraid I nearly scared that poor devil Arbor into a fit. I didn't mean to. I was in the Warders' Hall on the other side of the Byward Tower, where the visitors were detained, when he was coming out from your conference. And I was talking to your sergeant, only about ten feet away from Arbor. He hadn't recognized my voice before, but I was afraid he did then. It nearly killed him. I say! I feel as though I had no legs. I hope I'm not staggering. That would be a devil of a way to go to jail. Excuse me."

With his shoulders back, he moved with careful steps towards the door.

"Well?" asked Dr. Fell, when he had gone.

Hadley stood before the dying fire, a stiff military figure against the white marble mantelpiece, and in his hand were the notes he had taken of Dalrye's recital. Hadley hesitated. There were lines drawn slantwise under his eyes; he shut his eyes now.

"I told you," he said, quietly, "I was getting old. I am sworn to uphold the law. But—I don't know. I don't know. The older I get, the more I don't know. Ten years ago I should have said, 'Too bad,' and— You know what I'm thinking, Fell. No jury would ever believe that boy's testimony. But I do."

"And without speaking of Lester Bitton," said the doctor, "the case can remain unsolved. Good man, Hadley! You know what I think. If this is a tribunal, will you put it up to a vote?"

"Lord help me," said Hadley, "I will. Well, Fell?" He assumed a stem air, but a curious, wise, ancient smile crept about his mouth. "Dr. Fell, your vote?"

"'Unsolved,'" said the doctor.

"Mr. Rampole?"

"'Unsolved,'" said Rampole, instantly.

The dying firelight lit Hadley's face as he half-turned. He up-turned his hand; the white note-sheets fluttered from it and drift-ed down into the blaze. They caught fire and leaped in a puff. Hadley's hand remained motionless, the ancient, wise smile still on his face.

"'Unsolved,'" he said.

AMERICAN MYSTERY CLASSICS

from

PENZLER PUBLISHERS

*Available now
in hardcover and paperback:*

Charlotte Armstrong . . . . *The Unsuspected*

Erle Stanley Gardner. . . . . . *The Case of the Careless Kitten*

H.F. Heard . . . . *A Taste for Honey*

Dorothy B. Hughes. . . . . *The So Blue Marble*

Frances & Richard Lockridge . . . . *Death on the Aisle*

Stuart Palmer . . . . *The Puzzle of the Happy Hooligan*

Ellery Queen . . . . *The Dutch Shoe Mystery*

Ellery Queen . . . . *The Chinese Orange Mystery*

Patrick Quentin . . . . *A Puzzle for Fools*

Clayton Rawson . . . . *Death From a Top Hat*

Craig Rice . . . . *Home Sweet Homicide*

Mary Roberts Rinehart . . . . *The Red Lamp*